AF244491

THE POPPY AND THE ROSE

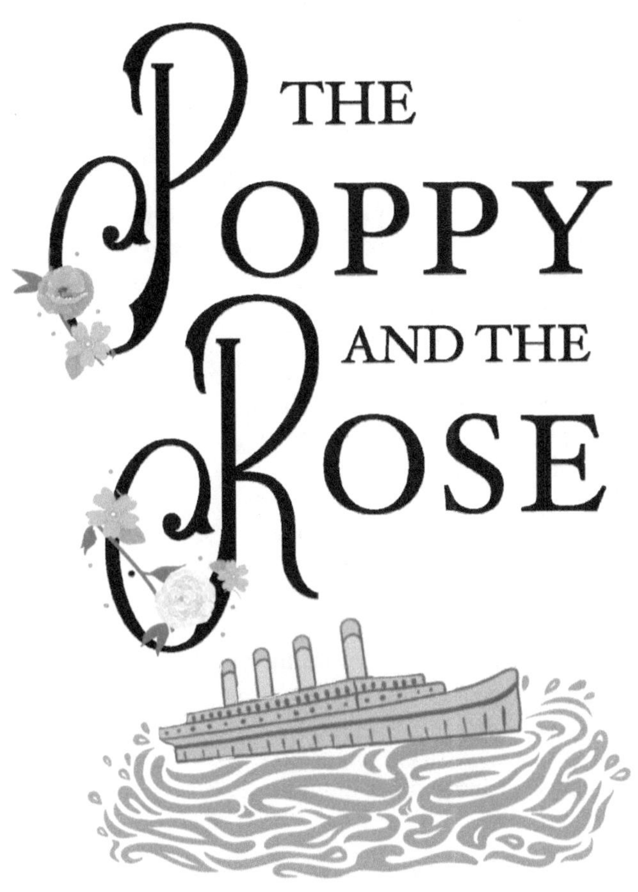

ASHLEE COWLES

OWL HOLLOW PRESS

Owl Hollow Press, Springville, UT 84663

The Poppy and the Rose

Library of Congress Cataloging-in-Publication Data
The Poppy and the Rose / A. Cowles. — First edition.

Summary:
When Taylor Romano arrives in Oxford for a summer journalism program, she learns secrets about her family's past and must use some historical sleuthing to uncover her link to a *Titanic* survivor named Ava Knight, a young English aristocrat, who boarded the *Titanic* and met three people who changed her life forever.

ISBN 978-1-945654-64-0 (paperback)
ISBN 978-1-945654-65-7 (e-book)
LCCN 2020943971

OWL HOLLOW PRESS

For Isla and Jack

Time present and time past
Are both perhaps present in time future,
And time future contained in time past.
If all time is eternally present
All time is unredeemable.
What might have been is an abstraction
Remaining a perpetual possibility
Only in a world of speculation.
What might have been and what has been
Point to one end, which is always present.
Footfalls echo in the memory
Down the passage which we did not take
Towards the door we never opened
Into the rose-garden. My words echo
Thus, in your mind.

For us, there is only the trying. The rest is not our business.

~T.S. Eliot, *Four Quartets*

TAYLOR

A few months before the anti-aircraft missile took his life and forever changed mine, Dad and I played our favorite game. We called it Treasure Hunt. We hadn't played since I was eleven or twelve, but there's nothing like an old ritual to resurrect the person you used to be. Not to mention the people you used to be together.

Death can take a lot of things, but it can't take your memories. Some moments stretch beyond time and smell as fresh as the day we lived them. They're what we keep coming back to, even when the person who made the moment what it was is long gone. Stronger than nostalgia, these eternal glimpses never wither, never seem less real. That's because they're the Most Real Thing there is. Usually they have something to do with love, and if you're lucky, you get to experience a handful in a lifetime.

A September twilight two years ago is one of mine.

The last time Dad was Dad, and I was me.

I'm alone in the forest. Everything is soft and damp—the liquid gold of late afternoon, the scent of recent rain, the carpet of pine needles cushioning my bare feet. A blanket of humidity wraps my body with its muggy embrace. Beneath my tank top, sweat trickles down my back. I pull my frizzy hair away from my face, securing it with a rubber band. There's no telling where this hunt will take me. When I was younger, this game made me feel like I was a princess in search of a lost artifact—one that would restore my people if found or destroy them if lost. A silly kid thing, but I can't stifle the time-honored tickle in my stomach as I unfold Dad's first clue.

What goes round the house and inside the house but never touches the house?

I smile. This is just like Dad. Whenever he returns from a deployment, military training exercise, or really any long trip, he brings me back a little gift. Only instead of handing it over right away, I have to find the gift by solving clues. I have to go on a Treasure Hunt. The only things Dad gives away for free are advice and goodnight kisses. Anything else worth having requires effort.

"Because that's life," Dad says.

Too bad our carefree life in the Blue Ridge Mountains is coming to an end. Late September is always an in-between season, a time when the dawn and dusk chatter like siblings about the coming frost. The trees cling to the remnants of summer's glow, but their leaves are turning traitor already. Thankfully, the canopy manages to trap in some of the afternoon warmth until nightfall. That's when the hills fade to the periwinkle blue of a fresh bruise and the lightning bugs come out for one last dance.

Despite the heat, it doesn't feel like summer anymore. My parents haven't told me much, but I know Dad is going away again. Just because the news channels rarely cover these wars doesn't mean there aren't still people fighting them.

No. Not yet.

Dad doesn't have to go away now. *Right now, he's here, and he's giving me something to search for, which is the same thing as giving me something to hope for.*

I follow the large shadow that stretches like a lazy cat across the bleached shingles of our cabin, clutching the clue in my hand.

What goes around the house…

Too easy. Sunlight goes around and inside the house but never touches it.

I jog to the western side of the property, locating the sundial Dad made from lake stones when I was nine. A long shadow paints the sixth stone at the bottom of the circle. I lift the rock and uncover my second clue, scrawled on brown paper torn from a grocery bag, edges burnt so it looks ancient. I grin at Dad's efforts to make my quest real, just like he used to.

"Magic," he says, "is for the detail oriented."

What goes round and round the wood, but never into the wood?

"Seriously?" Dad needs to up his game.

I sprint to my favorite tree—a sturdy oak with gnarled octopus arms perfect for sitting in. My reading tree. My thinking tree. A tree that was here before we bought the lake house and will be here after we're gone—which should be a long time from now, seeing how Dad wants this cabin to stay in our family forever.

"That way you'll always have a home, Tay. A place to come back to no matter what."

My eyes scan the tree's trunk for the riddle's answer and the right spot.

Bark.

There it is. I stick my hand down a hole in the trunk just big enough to house a single squirrel. It's where I used to hide my trinkets, but it looks like I'm not the only one who noticed the secret stash potential.

My treasure sits inside the hollow space, resting on a bed of moss.

A key.

One of those old-fashioned skeleton keys, the kind some stoic housekeeper in a classic film wears in a cluster on her belt. The key's only distinguishable feature is its handle—two rings that link together. My fingers tingle as I trace the circular pattern. Even though it's plain, I know this key has a story, that I'm holding something special.

And Dad gave it to me.

Most of the treasures Dad picks up for our game are just like this—objects from the past that other people don't want anymore. The kind of stuff that sits around collecting dust in antique shops. Old coins. Gaudy turquoise jewelry. Rare first-edition books.

Down the hill, my father sits at the edge of the dock with his fishing pole. Key in hand, I join him, slipping my feet into the cool water next to his. When I was younger, I used to sit here while he fished and compare our legs—his tan and muscular from twelve-mile ruck marches, mine skinny and scattered with mosquito bites. Now his thighs have less flesh and mine more. Also, my tan is way better.

Dad fastens a worm to his hook. We rarely catch anything, but fishing isn't why we come here. In a world that never stops spinning, Dad says everyone needs a still point.

A place to just sit and be.

"I see you found your treasure." Dad sips his beer, a gradual smile forming in the corner of his mouth. Ever so slowly, the dimple in his cheek deepens.

My own emerges in the same spot. "Don't you think I'm getting a little old for this?"

"I'd rather not see the day you're too old for an adventure."

I wait in silence for the key's backstory—all his hidden objects have one—just like I'd wait for a fish to bite. With Dad, the best things unfold in his own time and on his terms.

Recasting the line, Dad inhales a long pause. "The past is made by one of two things, Tay. By what we remember, or by what we forget. At some point, we all go looking for something that can tell us who we are and where we came from."

Cryptic messages. Another of Dad's specialties. I reach for the plastic container of worms, uprooting one from its shifting soil so I can watch it squirm in my hand. "Too bad I'm not from anywhere."

Dad nods. "Moving around so much can make it feel like you've got no roots, but everyone is from somewhere. And it's our memories of that somewhere that get us through the tough times."

Tough times. Which, in our household, translates to "most of the time." I push out the question before it gets stuck in my throat. "Why do you have to go again? You've deployed twice already. Haven't you done enough?"

It sounds way whinier than I want it to.

Dad pats my leg, his large hand covering most of the kneecap. "Things happen, Tay. Tragedies no one planned on. Wars start and ships sink and all you can do is figure out how to respond."

Then it's radio silence. The hush that fills the space is thicker than the twilight mist rising from the lake. We breathe it in as the bullfrogs surface with the dusk, the moment stretching beyond both of us.

Like all beautiful things, it ends too soon.

"Listen, Tay, I won't lie to you. The next few months aren't going to be easy. The life I chose for us has never been easy, but I think it's been good."

I don't really understand what he means. All I know is when Dad reels in his line this final time, the rumors the dusk has been spreading come true. Summer is over.

"Promise me you'll take care of your mother while I'm gone. She wasn't born into a whirlwind of change like you were. She needs you to be her rock."

Only I'm not her rock. He is.

The solid ground of his presence didn't last, though. It never did. Soon after our visit to the lake house, Dad left for a land I could hardly spell, taking every promise of home with him. Not long after his funeral, Mom put our cabin in the Blue Ridge Mountains up for sale. It was gone before I could even whisper a goodbye.

"Too many memories," she whispered, shuddering like a ghost slid its icy finger down her neck. When her shoulders tensed, it felt like the raising of a wall. I've seen that wall go up many times since.

Only Mom was wrong. Memories are the one thing you can never have too much of. Through them, the dead linger and speak.

All we have to do is listen.

TAYLOR

There was no possibility of taking a walk that day.

Last night I dreamt I went to Manderley again.

No one who had ever seen Catherine Morland in her infancy would have supposed her born to be a heroine.

Ever since Susan, my mom's best friend, handed me a worn copy of *Jane Eyre* at Dad's funeral luncheon and said, "You need to read this," I'd committed to memory the opening lines of all my favorite Gothic novels. It couldn't be a coincidence that many of their main characters felt the cold kiss of death at an early age. Maybe this loss was what gave each heroine the inner resolve to face the horrors that awaited her in life.

"It is not those who can inflict the most, but those who can suffer the most who will conquer in the end," Susan, who's Irish, often quoted in her Belfast brogue.

That, at least, is what I'm counting on. Unlike the secret-keeping estates of Manderley and Thornfield Hall, the medieval building and courtyard in front of me is all well-cut grass and smirking gargoyles.

"Stay off the grass, please."

I turn toward the frowning man who stands near the small security station just inside the open gates of Magdalen College. He gestures to the obtrusive sign sticking out of the damp lawn, which gives the exact same command in a voice that is also supremely polite but makes you feel like a moron—something British signage, I'm learning, excels at.

I'd received a similar response when I asked a local woman where the college was located after lugging my giant suitcase through Oxford's cobblestone streets.

"Why, it's right over there, dear." The woman—an aging bottle blond who wore head-to-toe spandex while speed-walking the largest Yorkshire terrier I'd ever seen—had pointed to the wrought-iron gate. Twisted among its filigree vines are decorative, though not obvious, letters that spell out Magdalen College. I guess I'm used to getting my directions American-style: supersized, on a billboard, and covered in flashing neon lights.

Oxford isn't like Boston College or Middlebury. There isn't really a campus, per se, just a bunch of independent colleges sprinkled throughout the city. What irks me is I shouldn't have had to go on a scavenger hunt in the first place. A representative from the university was supposed to pick me up at the bus station, but I waited for over an hour and no one showed or answered my phone calls. Once I found a map of the city, I figured I could locate the college where I'd be staying on my own, but it turns out the Magdalen *Grove* on the map was literally a big field full of deer, not dormitories.

"Do ye mind?"

I glance down to where my big toe is still resting on the gate guard's turf. The man wears an amphibian scowl that reminds me of Mr. Toad from *The Wind and the Willows*.

"Sorry." I take a few steps back until 100% of me is safely on the sidewalk by the road. I already saw the guard tell a guy he couldn't come onto campus unless he had either a visitor's pass or paid the tourist fee. I don't have a pass, but I might have enough change for the fee after breaking a twenty-pound note at the airport coffee shop.

"You wouldn't happen to be Taylor Romano?" asks an out-of-breath voice behind me as I dig through my wallet.

The perceptive gaze I meet belongs to an equally perceptive face dusted with Irishman freckles that are striking when paired with his dark, almond eyes.

"Yes. I'm Taylor."

The kid exhales his relief. I get the sense he wants to hug me, but instead he straightens his posture with cool British composure. "My sincere apologies, Miss Romano. I intended to meet you at the station right when your bus arrived, but my car got a flat on the way, so I'm afraid I'm a bit late."

"And you are?"

"Nathaniel Price." He points to the sleek Rolls Royce parked alongside the curb. "The late and rather useless driver."

Driver as in chauffeur? He can't be older than eighteen or nineteen, but his tweed driving cap *and* vest are straight out of the closet of a middle-aged Oxford don. The formal air he exudes is as English as cricket, Earl Grey tea, and Prince William. Plus, I'm pretty sure the only people who drive Rolls Royces are crotchety old men like Mr. Toad here.

"No problem." I shrug. "Looks like I ended up in the right place regardless."

"Again, I'm truly sorry about that. Here, let me carry your bag inside." Nathaniel eagerly reaches for my suitcase's busted handle.

"No, wait—"

One good pull and the worthless piece of trash detaches. Mouths hanging open, we watch as the handle sails through the air, landing in the middle of the street.

Where it's promptly run over by a double-decker bus.

"Bloody hel—I am *so* sorry, Miss Romano."

If embarrassment were an illness, Nathaniel Price might just die from it. Seeing how this poster child of propriety has already messed up twice in one morning, I should probably cut him some slack before he throws himself in front of the next bus.

"Don't worry about it," I say. "The cobblestones did a number on my suitcase long before you showed up."

"Still, I assure you, this is *not* the hospitable welcome Lady Knight intended." Nathaniel studies the sidewalk as his face turns the full spectrum of red.

"Lady *who*?"

"Lady Maebeline Knight, the last living descendant of one of England's most illustrious families. She sits on the board of the Oxford Summer Exchange Program and is one of the benefactresses of your scholarship. You'll meet her soon enough."

Heat rushes to my cheeks. I break Nathaniel's gaze and focus on the remains of my cheap suitcase handle. Checking the little box next to the question *Would you like to be considered for financial assistance?* is the only reason I can afford this summer abroad, but I didn't realize that status would be broadcasted to everyone, including the shuttle service.

I brush off my shame with a nod to the Royce. "So, your boss is a legit aristocrat? That explains the sweet old-man ride."

"Lady Knight wanted you to be as comfortable as possible." Nathaniel gestures toward the sandstone statues staring down on us from the college entrance. "I'll show you to your dorm. You can catch a bit of shut-eye before afternoon tea."

"Afternoon tea, a private chauffer… is this a study abroad program, or a stint on PBS Masterpiece?"

"I suspect Lady Knight will have more to say on the matter." The driver doesn't even crack a smile at my lame attempt at humor; he just hoists what's left of my suitcase onto his shoulder and flashes the gatekeeper an ID as we pass through the entrance. "Not to worry, Clive. She's with me."

Mr. Toad gives Nathaniel a disapproving scowl, but when another unsuspecting tourist walks onto his precious lawn, we're quickly forgotten. The guard speeds across the courtyard like an enraged Doberman, barking orders in a Cockney accent I can hardly understand.

"That poor French tourist won't know what hit him." This gets a grin out of Nathaniel, at least. He walks with a slight spring in his step as he leads me through a monastic-looking courtyard lined with rosebushes. It's as if a weight lifts from the driver's shoulders once he's within the college walls.

"Are you a student here?"

Nathaniel nods. "Just finished my first year in Modern History. The chauffer thing is part-time. You're not the only one who needs funding to attend Oxford."

He doesn't look at me when he says this, but the assurance lowers my anxiety by a few degrees. I assumed I'd be spending the summer with diplomats' kids and academic geniuses driving their *own* luxury cars, so it's a relief that the first Oxford student I've met is, well, average.

"Breakfast in the hall just finished, but I imagine you're feeling peckish after your long flight. We can duck into the Medieval Hall and grab a few biscuits if you'd like. The head cook adores me, so I bet I can even convince her to fetch the chocolate-covered ones."

"Chocolate… biscuits?" My repulsion must show. That's bad international manners, but I can't help it. I spent much of my childhood in the Deep South, so the only way I know biscuits is smothered in sausage gravy.

Nathaniel grins full-on this time. "A common error in translation, I'm afraid. What you Americans call cookies, we call biscuits."

"Oh. That makes more sense." The mere thought of baked goods makes my stomach rumble. "You seem to know the staff around here. Is Magdalen your hall?"

"For now. I'm taking a few summer courses here to get ahead."

He ushers me into an oak-paneled hall with vaulted ceilings and exposed wooden beams. Stained-glass windows featuring an array of family crests fill the space with colorful light, which shines down on the rows of dining tables lined with silverware and little green lamps.

I walk to the middle of the open space, my face turned upward as I spin in circles, humming the theme song from *Harry Potter*. I realize I look like a wizard-loving fool, but I don't care. Not when the Sorting Hat will appear at any moment to give my directionless life meaning, though I'm pretty sure I know where I belong.

A small smirk rests on Nathaniel's lips when I return. "The movies were actually filmed over at Christ Church College. Many of our visiting students from North America have a similarly verbose reaction, though I assure you this old hall loses its Hogwarts charm once the winter draft sets in."

Good, I'm not the only Gryffindor who's geeked out over this pilgrimage. Though I'm getting a strong sense that Nathaniel might be in House Slytherin. Or maybe Ravenclaw.

As soon as Nathaniel retrieves the chocolate-biscuit things (which are delicious), we head toward the historic rooms of the First Court—my home for the next few weeks.

"Here we are." Nathaniel unlocks the dormitory door as I prepare for the worst an ancient building has to offer. Scenes of decaying tenements in a Charles Dickens's novel flash through my mind.

In reality, it's not bad. The room is sparse, but from the central window I can see the courtyard roses and a few of Oxford's spires in the distance. Two twin beds, two desks, two dressers, a small sink in the corner for teeth-brushing—what I imagine to be your typical dorm room. The wooden beams in the ceiling and a slightly musty smell are the only signs this place is several hundred years older than it looks.

"I'll have the car waiting in front of the main gate at 4 p.m. sharp. Lady Knight is looking forward to meeting you. Until then, rest well, Miss Romano."

Nathaniel closes the door, leaving me in a silent room, off an empty hallway, in what appears to be a vacant building. My journalism workshop is one of several high school programs hosted in Oxford each summer, but it doesn't seem like anyone else is even staying in Magdalen College. As soon as he's gone, the quiet makes the dull ache I first felt when boarding the plane return.

I'd call it homesickness…if I had a home worth missing.

I stretch across the bed closest to the window. In the quad below, a few tourists armed with umbrellas brave the drizzle that's steadily picked up since I arrived. I should really call Mom to let her know I made it, but that conversation is going to take a lot of energy, and my jet-lagged brain could use a nap first.

Eye closed, I try to relax—but my mind won't stop spinning with all the questions that drove me to England in the first place. On the surface, I'd come to Oxford for a summer journalism workshop, but Dad and his secrets are the deeper reason I'm here.

Journalism is all about exposing the truth, but now that I'm here, I'm not sure I can bear its iron weight. The folded photograph I carry around in my back pocket is begging for attention, so I dig it out. Even though I come up with a thousand stories to explain its faded image, none of them are satisfying.

It's freaky to think Dad will never age. Even when I'm going gray, his hair will remain the unbroken black of an eternal thirty-seven-year-old, thanks to the magic of photography. Below dark eyes sagging with fatigue, he wears a serious five o'clock shadow, but he's still a good-looking guy. At Dad's back, a bleak ocean blends into a gloomier sky. The most telling detail in the photo is the crumbling castle to his right, perched on the edge of a cliff that's as green as the lawn Mr. Toad guards with his life.

North America doesn't really do castles.

Which means this photo must have been taken here in the UK. Possibly Ireland, but definitely this part of the world. I found the photo in Mom's closet a few months ago, shoved in a cardboard box with the rest of Dad's belongings. Mom never wants to talk about my father, but when I finally worked up the courage to ask her if Dad ever visited the British Isles, her answer was succinct… and not at all helpful.

"No, Taylor. He never traveled anywhere the military didn't send him."

In other words, she lied.

Dad *did* visit England. Mom just doesn't want me to know about it. But why?

Because of her.

The siren song has me unfolding the photo. I've been avoiding the face on the other side of the crease because it raises too many questions. She's pretty, no doubt about that, but something in the woman's gem-like gaze, something *behind* it, chills me to the core.

It's the look of someone planting her flag, staking her claim.

And it doesn't help that her arms are wrapped around my father's waist.

The bells of Oxford's spires unravel my spider web of dreams. My eyelids flutter. Resting in that space between alertness and deep sleep, I feel like I'm lying in a boat on open water, rocking back and forth, back and forth.

"Oops. Sorry to wake you."

I shoot up at the unfamiliar voice in an unfamiliar accent. The girl standing in my doorway doesn't seem quite real. She's dressed in a fuchsia sari decorated with elaborate gold embroidery. Her waterfall of luscious locks has me smoothing the straw-like strands that have escaped my messy bun.

"Uh, hey. You must be my roommate. I'm Taylor."

"Dalia Usman." The girl drags in two large designer suitcases that put my shabby luggage to shame.

"Nice to meet you. A relief, actually. I was starting to think I was the only journalism student staying here."

The gorgeous Indian girl wrinkles her nose. "Journalism? No, I'm here for the Shakespeare workshop." At that, Dalia clears her throat as her expressive face turns comically serious, like she's staring out over a large audience from high on stage.

"Two households, both alike in dignity, in fair Verona, where we lay our scene. From ancient grudge break to new mutiny, where civil blood makes civil hands unclean. From forth the fatal loins of these two foes, a pair of star-crossed lovers take their life…"

On and on she goes, beaming like she's performing at the Globe Theater itself, complete with a small bow at the end. "My flight from Mumbai was torture, so I passed some of the time by memorizing the prologue to *Romeo & Juliet*. My goal this summer is to read Shakespeare's Collected Works from cover to cover."

"Then you're way more ambitious than I am." I glance around the room for a clock. "Do you know what time it is?"

Dalia whips out her bejeweled cell phone. "4:05. Just in time for tea."

"Are you serious?" I must have dozed deeper than I thought.

"I'm *always* serious about tea. Especially after a long flight."

"No, I mean… Nathaniel…" I don't even know where to begin. "Sorry to rush off, but I've got to be somewhere." I jump off the bed and throw on my sneakers. "Make yourself at home."

When I fling open the door, I bump into a young woman with thick-rimmed glasses who stares at me over her clipboard. "Taylor Romano?"

I nod.

"Thank goodness! Where have you been? Why didn't you wait for us at the bus station with the other students like your participant packet instructed?"

"I, uh… Nathaniel…"

The woman, who must be one of the postgrad supervisors for the summer program, scans her paperwork. "There's no person by that name authorized to pick up students. Who's Nathaniel?"

I frown. Good question.

TAYLOR

Nathaniel's car idles by the curb near Magdalen's main gate. He opens the rear door of the Rolls Royce in such a fluid, *I-saw-this-on-Downton-Abbey-once* motion that I almost expect a celebrity to emerge.

"Don't bother. I'm not getting in the car with you."

"What's wrong?" Nathaniel's eyes widen, but I don't buy his feigned innocence.

"I've only been here a few hours and I'm already in trouble with the staff, that's what's wrong. You weren't authorized to pick me up at the bus station. Now who are you?"

Frowning, Nathaniel nods at the open door. "I'd better let her explain."

I bend down to peer inside the car, where I meet the stare of a Queen Elizabeth II doppelganger so dead-on, it's scary.

"Ah, Taylor, my dear. A pleasure to finally meet you."

The elderly lady leans back against the red leather interior, the smile on her face as warm as the outdated fur stole in her lap. It's like she's from a different era entirely, stuck in the fashion of her youth. Which—based on her liver spots and miniscule bone structure—was around the turn of the *last* century. Beneath all the layers of fur, the woman wears a beaded black gown with so much lace, it looks like old lady lingerie. I breathe in the sharp scent of moth balls mixed with rose perfume and a wave of nausea hits me.

"We had quite the time intercepting you, didn't we, Nathaniel?" The woman speaks with an aristocratic accent as light and airy as the cloud of white hair piled on top of her head.

"*Intercepting* me?" Nope. Not getting in the car.

The woman smiles like there's nothing sketchy about her revelation. "The coordinators of these summer programs always make you poor students wait at the station for hours until everyone arrives, so we were merely doing you a favor. Besides, I wanted to make sure we spoke before the summer staff whisked you away. They keep you young people so busy, never giving you a moment of unsupervised freedom. Really, it's a shame the summer holiday is no longer a true *holiday*—"

"Listen, Lady Knight..." I don't want to appear ungrateful, but all my internal alarm bells are going off. I mean, what kind of scholarship requires the benefactress to stalk its recipient upon her arrival?

Always trust your gut, Dad often said in his extra-military moments.

And right now, my gut is telling me not to buy a word this lady is selling.

"I appreciate the financial assistance, but I don't understand why you need to meet with me alone. How do you know my flight arrival details or anything else about me?"

"Oh, we'll get to all that." The woman scoots over and pats the empty seat.

"No, thanks. I'm fine right here."

"Ah, well, suit yourself." She shrugs, then clasps her hands together, as if struck by a brilliant idea. "How about some tea, Nathaniel?"

I bend my head to get a good look at the driver through the rolled-down window. His thumbs dance across the steering wheel on beat with the classical music playing on the radio. He sets two dainty cups, complete with bone china saucers, on the dash. The floral scent of bergamot floats out the window as Nathaniel pours the steaming Earl Grey from a large thermos. It's the only tea scent I recognize since Mom started drinking the stuff nonstop once we moved from North Carolina to bitter cold Maine.

"Do you take milk and sugar, Miss Romano?"

"Uh, no. Straight up." I'm a coffee person, so I have no idea how to use proper tea lingo. Honestly, after almost twenty hours of travel, an IV of pure caffeine would be preferable.

A cell phone in the car's center console starts ringing to the tune of "God Save the Queen," delaying Nathaniel's tea service.

"Hello?" He frowns as he answers it, as if the driver expects it to be bad news. Apparently, his instincts are right. "I don't know how you got this number too, but how many bloody times do we have to explain it? She isn't interested."

With that, Nathaniel hangs up the phone and passes my cup out the window with a grip as steady as his gaze.

The old lady seems flustered by the call, but she gives me a forced smile. "Telemarketers. They're as plentiful as rabbits on both sides of the Atlantic, I'm afraid."

The china cup rattles in my hands, but I don't drink from it. "So, why'd you want to speak with me?"

Lady Knight sips her tea as if it puts her in a state of pure tranquility. But then her smile becomes a thin line, almost like the Earl Grey leaves a bitter aftertaste. "Because, my dear. I possess something you desire, even if you don't realize it yet."

"You have something *I* want?" My voice cracks as my mouth goes so dry, I almost risk drinking the tea.

"You know of what I speak. Of *whom* I speak. Answers, my dear. You want answers, and I have a story that needs telling. Sounds like the beginnings of an ideal partnership, does it not?"

I don't know what to say, so I poke the lemon slice bobbing in my teacup. This heiress may look like a harmless old lady, but every time she casts me a leveling glance, it feels like she sees *everything*. All my questions. All my fears.

Lady Knight releases a dramatic sigh. "Besides, God knows how much longer I'll even be around to tell the tale! There are those who would profit from my silence, but I won't tolerate their threats. The past must be shared because we never truly get *past* it, now do we? No, some memories linger like radiation. They remain eternally present. The journalistic aspirations you described so well in your scholarship application assured me this is a sentiment you understand."

I have no idea what she's talking about, but she has my attention. "What kind of answers?"

Lady Knight flashes another hair-raising smile. "It's much too complicated to get into now, and I wouldn't want to burden you after such a long day of travel. Come to my estate for tea tomorrow morning and we shall talk at length, though I do have something to… whet your reporter's appetite, shall we say. Nathaniel, if you please."

Without a word, Nathaniel thrusts a roll of cream-colored pages out the car window. Hanging from the red ribbon securing the scroll is a small business card stamped with the image of a grand estate.

Meadowbrook Manor, the fancy font below it reads.

"Meadowbrook, as you'll soon discover, is a strange old house where the spirited personalities who once lived there continue to speak. Naturally, a house with such a legacy has as many secrets as it does rooms, and some of those doors have remained locked for years, even to me. My hope is you, Taylor dear, might be the key we've been waiting for. What do you say? Care to join me on a journey through the past?"

Insane. This old woman is clearly nuts. No way am I visiting her creepy estate so she can have me buried beneath the floorboards.

Luckily, I have a good excuse.

"My summer classes start tomorrow. If I skip, I could get sent home."

Lady Knight nods. "Yes, that's something to consider, isn't it? Though I do hope you'll indulge me one thing, at least. Read this initial chapter, and then you can decide if my story is worth the risk." The old woman's eyes shimmer with a century of secrets. "Besides, you know what they say, my dear. Well-behaved women rarely make history."

Dalia is gone when I return to the dorm room. I really don't want to be alone right now, and I should probably call Mom to let her know I've made it safe and sound. Well, things aren't exactly *sound*—I'm being stalked by an unhinged aristocrat who's trying to lure me into her upper-class gingerbread house—but at least I can assure Mom that the flying metal tube I boarded yesterday made it across the Atlantic in one piece.

I text Mom to meet me online so we can video chat. She appears on the webcam in her ratty bathrobe, a sign she hasn't left the house today. Her mousy brown hair looks like a bird nest that survived a hurricane… but just barely.

"Taylor, I've been worried sick. I thought you'd call hours ago!"

"Sorry, Mom. It's been a little hectic around here."

"Well, there's a lot of rain in the forecast. Have you been dressing warm enough? Did you take those Vitamin C tablets I gave you? You wouldn't believe how many people get the flu from airplanes, especially on international flights..."

I nod repeatedly at each friendly reminder and warning about all the things that can kill me, which we've gone over a million times. By the time we finish discussing every aspect of my health, safety, and general well-being, I am reaching my overprotective-parent boiling point.

It wasn't always like this. We used to be a lot closer—back when I was younger, and the leash Mom kept me on didn't feel so tight. I understand that after what happened to my dad, Mom is afraid of losing me and has transferred that anxiety to tracking my daily consumption of sugar, gluten, and soy. But a reporter *deals* with the truth by uncovering it, and I resent that my mother's coping mechanism is to ignore it entirely—or maybe even try to keep the truth buried.

Lady Knight was right about one thing: I *do* want answers, so I hold the photo of Dad up to the laptop screen, watching Mom's eyes widen as she takes in the woman with curly red hair. The woman who clings to my dad like he's a life-preserver she'll drown without.

A sign they knew each other well... or were on their way.

Mom presses a hand to her mouth, as if she's receiving the news of Dad's death all over again. "Where did you get that?"

"Doesn't matter. You said Dad never visited the UK. Why did you lie?"

"Because I never knew he made the trip." Mom's voice sours along with her expression. "At least not until after his death."

"What's that mean?"

"It means your father loved you... but he also had secrets. That's why I—"

"Buried any trace of him? Forgot all about him?" Now that the cork's unplugged, two years of bottled frustration comes pouring out. I don't know if I'll ever forgive Mom for packing up everything that reminded us of Dad almost as soon as he was gone. Instead of grieving like a normal person, she smothered and replaced—finding herself a new husband only a year later and dragging me to the dull-as-dirt town of Evergreen, Maine.

Mom's eyes refuse to focus on the webcam. "It's difficult to explain, but after I learned about *her*, I had two people to mourn. The man I thought your father was, and the man he really was. What would be the point in ruining your memories of him? You've gone through enough, Taylor."

"What are you saying? You think Dad had an affair? All because of one photograph?" I admit I've wondered the same thing since I found the photo, but voicing it aloud makes me feel like the one promise I've been clinging to these past few years—the belief that my father was a loyal man who died a hero—is crumbling beneath my fingertips.

Mom's mouth quivers, like she doesn't want to confirm the accusation and cause me more pain but can't deny it outright either.

"*Well*. Who is she then?"

Mom shakes her head. "I never wanted to find out. After the funeral, I discovered records of your dad's flight to London when I thought he was away at a military training exercise. Then that photo turned up in his sock drawer."

His *sock drawer?* Really? What was Dad thinking? That's the most obvious place to hide a secret—which gives me a glimmer of hope. If Dad was trying to conceal something, he'd have chosen a better hiding place.

A place like our cubby hole by the lake.

"And you assumed the worst? This photo doesn't *prove* anything." I won't let Mom get away with playing judge and jury to my dad's memory. Not without a fair trial first.

"You're jumping to bold conclusions. That's bad journalism, not to mention bad faith."

I don't need to wonder why Mom hasn't investigated any further. She's afraid. Despite my anger, my heart still aches for this shell of a woman, sitting there in her bathrobe in the middle of a weekday afternoon because she's worried something horrible will happen whenever I'm out of her sight. She used to be so adventurous, so fun, but ever since Dad left us, the dead weight of fear has hung from her wrists in heavy chains.

She meets my eyes now, fear replaced by irritation. "No evidence? Taylor, your father took a trip to England without telling me, *his wife,* anything about it. And he visited another woman! What am I supposed to think?"

"That he would have explained himself if he had the chance!" Now I'm on the verge of slamming the laptop shut. "Why are you doing this, Mom? Why do you have to take away everything?"

"I'm not trying to take away anything, Taylor. I'm trying to protect the few good memories you *do* have." Mom's face crumbles, but I can't tell if it's from guilt or from my harsh tone.

Great, and now I feel like the jerk.

"I thought you'd at least try to understand why I handled your father's death the way I did. It's not that I wanted to forget him… I just didn't know *who* to remember. Of all people, I'd expect you to understand and take my side."

"See, that's the thing about family," I say as a familiar shadow settles over Mom's face. A shadow that means a lot more days before her hair sees a comb. "There aren't supposed to *be* sides."

I make an excuse and log off before I'm tempted to throw my computer against a four-hundred-year-old wall. I'm staring at the photo when Dalia walks into the room wrapped in a towel and wearing shower flip flops. She halts, as if she can feel the electricity sparked by my argument with Mom. After a few tense seconds of towel-drying her hair in front of the room's only mirror, Dalia breaks the ice. "Hey, want to grab a bite to eat? I'm famished."

"Sure. I guess." But I can't tear my eyes from the pretty ginger in the photograph. My mind is heading down a familiar spiral of endless possibilities, so with a groan, I shove the incriminating photo in my pocket and reach for my sneakers.

"Is something wrong?" Dalia asks once we've started down Oxford's dusky streets. The rain patters lightly on our umbrellas. "I know we only just met, but you seem a bit… preoccupied. Let me guess. A bloke? Some guy back in the States giving you trouble?"

"Not a guy." Though a possible betrayal by the person I admire most is its own kind of heartache. "I don't get it. Why is love, *all* love, such a pain?"

Dalia grins. "*If love be rough with you, be rough with love; Prick love for pricking, and you beat love down.*"

I can't help but smile. My roommate is a Shakespeare fangirl freak, and it's kind of adorable. "Thanks for that, Mercutio. Speaking of love, when did you first fall for the old Bard?"

"Oh, years ago. My father introduced me to Shakespeare's plays when I was quite young." A sadness that wasn't there before settles in Dalia's eyes, but she shakes it off with a sigh. "Oh, how I wish there was a good chippy in Oxford."

"A chippy?"

"Fish and chips. With extra vinegar and salt. I crave it constantly back in India, but you've got to head into London to find a decent take-away. If we want to avoid a sit-down restaurant, we'll have to settle for a kebab."

I'm glad someone knows what she's doing. My program packet said we were responsible for our own meals on the day of our arrival, and since I'm pretty broke, I'd planned on grabbing a semi-edible, pre-packaged sandwich from a gas station or grocery store. But a kebab sounds much better.

We cross the street, where Dalia marches to the take-away window of a small Turkish shop and orders for both of us like a seasoned pro. I can't pull my eyes away from the giant spit of rotating meat behind the counter.

"I hope you like garlic," she says as she hands me the stuffed pita delicacy, streaked with an array of unidentifiable sauces.

"Love it," I mumble, my mouth half-full of amazing flavors we just don't have in my part of Maine. "You must visit England often."

Dalia nods. "I've done an Oxford program for the past three summers. I'll be attending university here next term, as long as I do well on the English Literature Admissions Test."

"No wonder you take Shakespeare so seriously."

The rain has stopped, so we keep walking, the scent of damp lilacs lingering in the late spring air. Once we reach the large dome of the Radcliff Camera—Oxford's most recognizable landmark—we grab a park bench and enjoy our greasy dinner beneath the soft lavender sky.

Dalia, talkative at first, goes silent. I follow her eyes as she surveys the charming scenery: a tangled snare of tethered bicycles, groups of international students, the final rays of golden sunlight streaming through the lush, damp trees. It's like she's left our bench behind to travel to some distant memory.

"Okay, now *you* look like the one with a boy on the brain."

Dalia smiles slightly, but her eyes don't leave the postcard before us. "Not a boy… at least not like that. It's my father. We used to visit this spot often."

I recognize that ache in her voice. Though I barely know this girl, those of us marked by an unexpected death share a bond that bypasses small talk. "What happened?"

"Cancer." Dalia keeps staring off. "How about yours?"

"War," I reply. "Though I guess cancer is a kind of battle, too."

My roommate nods. "And in my father's case, a very long one."

I hand Dalia the wrinkled photo of my dad. By nature, I'm a private person, but I sense she'll understand. "Do you think you really *knew* your father?"

"Of course." Dalia studies the photograph, her eyes flitting between Dad and the red-haired woman. "What's this about?"

"The backdrop has to be England, right? Only I've never seen this woman before. My mom seems to think…"

Dalia's eyes snap up to meet mine. "I can guess what she thinks, but I don't think you need to worry."

"What makes you say that?"

"Only honest men make decent fathers." Dalia touches the photograph, her glittery purple fingernail tracing the edge of the rocky cliff. "And this man doesn't have the eyes of a liar."

British electrical outlets are weird. There isn't a free one near my bed, so my phone is plugged in by the sink on the other side of the room. Dalia is fast asleep, so I forego the lamp protruding from the wall by my bed in favor of a tiny flashlight stashed in my backpack.

Maybe it's the fancy ribbon that screams "Privacy!", but something told me I should dive into Lady Knight's letter alone, so it's been waiting for me in the empty drawer of my desk. I'm grateful to have such a stellar roommate, but the whole thing with Nathaniel and the old lady feels so weird, I'd rather not be guilty by association until I have a better sense of what the heck is going on.

I untie the red ribbon of Lady Knight's parting gift. The blue LED glow catches a note written in an elegant, loopy cursive no one younger than eighty-five can write with anymore.

Dearest Taylor,

I intend to tell you this story in person when you come to Meadowbrook for tea, but I suspect you'd like to know if the ramblings of an old woman are worth your time. A writer friend of mine once told me it's vital to hook your reader from the first chapter, and I trust this initial sample will not disappoint. It was recorded by someone very dear to me, a young woman who survived a great calamity when she was about your age.

The Titanic *sinking may have been the first disaster of the 20th century, but she was not the last. Over the past hundred years, we've seen multiple shipwrecks of humanity along the banks of the Somme, the beaches of Normandy, and the gas chambers of Auschwitz. Some say violence is the result of clinging to the past, but I believe it is more often the consequence of forgetting it—of forgetting who we are, a core nature not even time can change. Humankind will never avoid tragedy by keeping our eyes fixed to the horizon's rosy glow, for only those brave enough to peer into the past can hope to see the lighthouses meant to warn us of jagged rocks. If we are to weather the storms of the future, we must first defeat the neglect of memory.*

From these pages you will learn that the past is never simplistic and never dead. I have always regarded history as a realm painted in shades of grey, capable of turning on the actions of a single individual. Our choices reverberate in the memories of all who come after us, creating paths where there was once only forest. As poets more eloquent than I have claimed, the journey is as important as the destination, the beginning as crucial as the end.

Your father was not the man you thought he was, my dear.

My hope is you'll soon discover our stories are really one and the same—different threads woven into a single tapestry. Be patient towards the questions that come your way, for the Truth must be discovered; it can never be told. Even when others try to drown it, trust that the Truth will always surface in time.

Keep searching, my dear. And keep listening. For the dead continue to speak.

Eternally Yours,

Lady Maebeline Knight

I read the letter a few more times. I can follow the enigmatic words well enough, but my mind can't grasp their full meaning. One thing is for certain—they don't sound like the incoherent ramblings of a crazy person. They sound more like the most cherished notions of a woman who has seen a lot and knows exactly what she believes.

Still, what does all this talk of war and sinking ships have to do with my dad? And how could Lady Knight have known him like she seems to suggest? My trout-fishing, craft beer-drinking, soldier father would have been the *last* person on earth to hang out with an elderly English aristocrat.

The next page in the bundle is a photocopy. It's typed rather than written by hand. The first line reads:

In many ways, my story begins on April 15, 1912. But as anyone who has lived through tragedy knows, the seeds of survival are often planted much earlier.

My eyes catch on the date. I recognize it from a report I did back in middle school.

It's the day the *Titanic* sank.

4

$\mathcal{A}$VA

I never wanted to be a spy. All I wanted was my Brownie box camera and the blank film roll of my future, but Fate is not a piano player who accepts requests.

And Fate, it seemed, had sentenced us to a slow, agonizing death.

That's how the long night in the lifeboat felt at the time anyway. Looking back, it's clear we had all, collectively, chosen this end. At least those of us who believed we had the power to bend Nature to our own designs.

The Ship of Dreams. What rubbish.

The only dream *Titanic* rode upon was a gilded illusion, a trick played on us by the moon. On the night of the sinking, its fickle glow cast a deadly mirage over a field of ice, yet like all deceptions, the brightness left us blind because we stood too close.

It was all my fault. I trusted him, but I was a fool—a target from the very beginning, the weakest link in the Knight chainmail. Worst of all, I trusted *myself.*

If *Titanic* taught me anything, it was that no one was who they seem. My father was not the man I thought he was, and I was not the dutiful daughter I always believed myself to be. If I could go back and do it all over again, when the soldier with the marble eye asked me what I wanted most in the world—and what I would do to get it—my answer would be *nothing*. I would do nothing to help him, for nothing was worth this lingering regret, an ache bitter enough to shatter bone.

Perhaps the only way to purge the guilt and receive the pardon of the dead was to first confess one's sins openly, which is why I decided to record my memories of that fateful voyage, both the good and the painful, in the pages that follow.

We said goodbye to England on April 10, 1912. The woman in front of me—waiting to board *Titanic* like the rest of us—was a bad omen. I sensed that as soon as I captured her essence with the click of my camera.

For one thing, she did not belong in first class. Oh, she wore a fancy feathered hat and had a maid attending her children, a toddler and a second babe asleep in an extra-large pram. But her white gloves, one holding an intricate jewelry box while the other clasped the platform handrail, were already sullied. I knew the frenzied look of a person who felt entirely out of place, for I'd felt that way a thousand times myself.

Lowering my camera, I met the woman's obsidian gaze. Her eyes shifted nervously from the black hull that cast a hundred passengers in shadow to the place where Father and I stood, ready to set sail on the ship that would take us from our common misfortune:

My mother.

Everyone said I took after her. *Black Irish* they called us, a rather vague description that referred to descendants of Spanish *Armada* survivors who'd supposedly washed up along the shores of western Ireland during the reign of Elizabeth I. While this romantic story might explain the origin of Mother's raven hair in a clan of Galway gingers, what remained a mystery was how the golden skin tone we'd both inherited first entered the bloodline. The most scandalous speculation was that our *Armada* ancestor wasn't a Spaniard after all, but a mercenary sailor from a more exotic land—Hispaniola, or even the Far East. An ivory complexion on par with Bram Stoker's *Dracula* may have been all the rage among girls my age, but the best way to achieve such a blank canvas was to remain indoors like a common house cat.

And I had no intention of doing that.

In any case, my resemblance to Mother ended with our shared coloring, for the woman was quite unwell. Her enduring sickness—both of body and mind—was the reason Father had rescued me from that dreadful boarding school and booked us this extended holiday. Mother's enduring stubbornness was what guaranteed our passage would be aboard the finest ship to ever set sail across the Atlantic.

After all, if we were going to abandon her, Mother insisted we do it in style.

"Really, Father, how long must we wait here like cattle in the stocks?" I lifted my gaze from the viewfinder of my Brownie No. 2. "You'd think with all this advanced machinery, they'd find a way to speed up the queue."

"Why complain, darling?" Father's blue eyes remained glued to *The Daily Telegraph* in his hands. He was naturally aloof, even for an Englishman, but you'd think he'd pick up on his own daughter's inner turmoil—especially given his chosen profession. But alas, no. "Every headline speaks of war brewing in the Balkans, and yet here we are, leaving Europe's troubles behind."

"If one even counts the Balkans as Europe." I sighed deeply. My father followed developments in the eastern region closely, some might say obsessively. Yet photographing reality for the sake of posterity felt far more productive than pouring over the

West's latest chess game for world domination, which we could do nothing about.

"Come now, Ava." Clearing his throat, Father tucked the newspaper beneath his arm before opening the pocket watch that never strayed far from his hand. "In a few minutes' time, you'll have nothing to do *but* wait. It's a five-day journey, you realize."

"Yes, but ideally I'll do most of my waiting in the ship's Turkish baths, not out here in the smog of Southampton." When my father reopened the newspaper and did not respond, I stifled a groan and turned away to document what was starting to feel like a death march.

Snap, snap.

Two rotund women with outrageous hats that made them look like peacocks.

Snap, snap.

A row of sailors beaming in their freshly starched uniforms.

It was all so unbearably dull. These were safe scenes of the pampered and the tedious, scenes I'd witnessed a hundred times before. No, I needed something original.

Scanning down the row of alternately excited, bored, and irritated passengers, I found it.

A well-dressed man—accompanied by his pregnant wife who held tightly to the small hands of two daughters—stood arguing with a White Star Line officer. The scene would have been as mundane as the rest, if not for one significant detail.

The husband was of African descent, and his wife was most certainly not.

I stepped out of line to get a clearer shot as I snapped a photo of the unconventional family. "Why are the officers pestering them so? They appear to have paid for the passage."

It took a moment for my statement to rouse Father from the fog of his internal thoughts, but finally he glanced at the old sailor scouring the family's tickets with his monocle, as if to verify they were valid. "I hope he's not giving them too much trouble.

Mr. Laroche is the man's name. I spoke with him and his lovely wife while you were running around with that silly black box. His is a most remarkable story. Laroche is an engineer, you see. Born in Haiti but educated in Paris. The man assured me *Titanic* is as sturdy as they come. I hope he's able to board with his family."

"So do I." My belly burned to think that anyone might try to separate a man from his wife and children. "I'm shocked, Father. You're becoming more democratic by the day. William Wilberforce would be proud."

That was sure to get my father's attention. Or at least his acknowledgement that I could carry on a conversation about matters more meaningful than my seasonal wardrobe allowance. When in doubt, long-dead members of Parliament always captured his interest.

"I should do well to remind you, my dear, that Wilberforce only managed to get the Slavery Abolition Act passed because he had the support of the Tories."

"That is debatable, but regardless, Mr. Wilberforce considered himself an independent thinker whose opinions were based on the evidence, not blind political loyalty. I tend to agree with that approach."

Father muttered something under his breath and returned to his paper.

So much for parliamentary politics. As usual, his apathy sank my spirits without a single word. It wasn't likely that my father would ever pay much attention to my ideas, but it was possible I could garner his respect through my art. I glanced at the small suitcase beside me, reassuring myself that it hadn't been carted off. The rest of our luggage would be loaded by bellboys, but I refused to let my camera equipment out of my sight. Not when my entire future depended on it.

Lifting my chin, I again met the dark, piercing gaze of the woman ahead of us. It was obvious she did not share the enthusiasm of the other passengers waiting to board. The poor creature looked positively dreadful, as if she saw something no one else could see. With an expressive face dominated by high cheekbones and a prominent nose, she was neither ugly nor pretty. Simply unusual.

The mere look of her made goosebumps break out across my arms. "My, what's the matter with her?"

No response from Father but the turning of another page, so I cleared my throat and repeated my query with increased annoyance. "*My*, what's the *matter* with her?"

"Really, Ava." Father sighed at my tone, closing his paper. He didn't even glance at the woman. "Why the sour mood?"

He knew why. My heart was torn. I desired this holiday like a miner longed for fresh air. For years I'd dreamed of seeing Manhattan's skyscrapers and the seventeen luxurious floors of the Waldorf Astoria. Yet more than anything, I hoped to study with the great Gertrude Käsebier, the most renowned female photographer in America, known for her strikingly intimate portraits of young mothers as well as the Sioux chiefs of the Great Plains.

Unfortunately, the cost of our transatlantic adventure was far more extravagant than the first-class fare. We'd left Mother in the hands of servants, and no matter how I tried to justify it, I couldn't escape the pangs of guilt. The unstable woman was impossible to live with, but she was still my mother and deserting her left a bitter taste in my mouth.

So, I spat out that taste in words.

"I'm not sour. I simply maintain that some people shouldn't sail."

Father responded with a twist of his moustache, a tick that arose when he was either amused or on the verge of losing patience. On this occasion, he certainly wasn't amused.

Shame skated across my skin, but I refused to let it sink in. I knew I still acted like a pampered child, despite my seventeen years. Worse, I relied on it. Milked it for all it was worth. After all, when a girl lived with a mentally ill mother and a father obsessed with his work, playing the spoiled brat was what it took to be noticed. Most of the time, I hated myself for it.

But not today.

"Tickets please," the crewman requested when we reached a large door in the side of the ship. The sailor seemed flustered when I included a resolute gaze with my boarding pass. I'd recently discovered that making young men nervous—especially lower-class men—was quite fun.

"Your accent, sailor. It's familiar." The crewman's name badge read *Donohue*, but he didn't sound like the Dubliners who worked on our estate. "Where are you from?"

"The north of Ireland, miss." Turning as red as the hand of Ulster itself, the sailor studied his stack of tickets like they were sterling notes. "Belfast these days, but I'm originally from a village not far from Derry—"

"Yes, I know Derry." I glanced at Father, feeling unnerved by the stark reminder of our abandonment. "That's where Mother was born."

This ship was built by Ulstermen, so it made sense that Ulstermen would man it. Yet the sailor's mere mention of my mother's birthplace felt like the promise of her willful presence on this journey, which meant worry and guilt would be close behind. How was it possible to love someone and resent her at the same time?

"You don't say? Well, it's a lovely place, so your mother must be a lovely lady." The crewman smiled shyly before tipping his sailor's hat, black with gold stitched lettering that spelled out White Star Line above the forehead. "Enjoy the voyage, miss."

"Thank you. I intend to." And with that, I stepped onto *Titanic*.

Right before a shriek left me frozen stiff.

The scene unraveled in slow motion. The woman ahead collapsed in the middle of the first-class entryway, taking the wooden chest she carried with her. From its small drawers poured a collection of colorful jewels across the black-and-white tile floor, like candy spilling from a broken jar.

"No! Please. This is a mistake!"

Ah, I was right. The woman's accent was from the East. Bohemia, perhaps. Her panic amplified with each syllable, despite the reassurances of her maid.

"You don't understand. You refuse to *see*!"

A form rushed by me, and I realized with surprise that Father had gone to assist the frantic creature. With a few soft words, he sent the maid to collect the scattered jewels. Crouched on the floor like a common physician, Father held the woman's shaking hand, speaking words that either soothed or enchanted, for she soon calmed.

As I approached, Father looked at me with the most gratified expression I'd never witnessed. Perhaps the intangible rewards of altruism were truly the reason he'd become a psychologist. It certainly hadn't been for the money.

To be honest, it was rather embarrassing—Lord Jonathan Knight, a middle-aged English gentleman, throwing himself into a relatively new field of study with such abandon. And a field attached to a *profession,* no less.

But, as the French say, *a chacun son gout.* To each his own.

Father seemed to find some fulfillment in helping people conquer their fears and failures, even if the one psychological demon he'd not been able to exorcise was trapped inside the mind of his own wife.

The look on his face made me feel as though I must *do* something, so I bent down to retrieve a large brooch that had skittered toward me. My two-piece travel suit—a fitted jacket and matching wool skirt made of navy-and-gray plaid—tensed around the bosom with the movement. It was tighter there than it had been last season, but there'd be plenty of shopping in New York.

Speaking of style, these jewels indicated the woman at least had *that* going for her. I followed the trail of glittering brooches, necklaces, and rings until I reached her jewelry box, made of dark, gleaming mahogany. The maid had set it upright on the floor but was still picking up the broken pieces of a necklace several meters away. I knelt and tried to open the top compartment, but it was locked. Only the little drawers would budge. As I struggled to return the gems to their proper place, a set of hands covered my own. Swarthy skin and patches of dark hair assured me they did not belong to the freckled maid.

I raised my eyes slowly, meeting the cool gaze of a mustached man with murky eyes the color of an overcast sky. Or should I say *eye*, seeing how the other was made of blue-gray glass. The man held firm to the small chest, using it as leverage to lift me up from the floor. "Allow me to assist you, young lady."

His accent was foreign. The rigid man wore the high-necked uniform of a soldier, and the row of medals across his chest declared to the world that he was successful at it. Perhaps he lost his eye in battle, a thought that sent a thrilled shiver through me. The glass marble in its place never abandoned my gaze, whereas his real eye wandered across me like a spider. It was a bit alarming but intriguing all the same.

For a moment we both gripped the mahogany box in a resolute stalemate. The solider, despite his deformity, was quite handsome. He nodded at my father and the distraught lady he tended to. "I see you know this woman."

My father's rather intimate aid and the fact that I had retrieved her jewelry box must have made this soldier assume we were acquaintances of the woman. "Not really, I—"

"Allow me to ask you a question," the man continued. "You will think it strange but humor me by responding with the first thing that comes to your mind. Don't think, just speak. Understand?"

I inhaled sharply. I was accustomed to *giving* commands, not taking them. His condescending tone was a minor annoyance, yet something about this soldier demanded respect, so I nodded. My skin tingled where our hands touched.

The soldier pulled the box toward his broad chest, dragging us behind a marble pillar out of Father's view. He lowered his voice, as if revealing a dreadful secret. "If you could have anything in the world, and I mean *anything*, what would it be?"

Something inside me resisted answering such a ridiculous question—as if speaking it could make it come to pass, as if this man had a right to even ask—but the stranger's glass eye must have cast a spell, for I did exactly as he commanded.

I gave him the answer that sealed my destiny.

"I would have my mother well again."

The response came as a shock, even to me. Naturally, I wanted my mother's mental state to improve, but I'd always thought my deepest desire was to study photography. After all, the prospect of working under Gertrude Käsebier in New York was why I'd agreed to board this ship in the first place. And yet, every artistic ambition I had was due to Mother's encouragement. If not for her, I never would have peered through a camera lens.

The soldier nodded, as though he'd expected this answer. His eyes scanned the crowds boarding the ship. "We can say no more here, but I promise you, Lady Ava—I will take your desires more seriously than any person here. However, you must trust me in return. Tonight, at eight o'clock, meet me on the roof of the first-class smoking room."

"Why, whatever for?" I did not know how people conducted their affairs in whatever backwoods nation this soldier hailed from, but in England a respectable man *never* asked a lady to meet him alone at night. His request broke every standard of good breeding.

Which was precisely why I entertained it.

"Rest assured, Lady Ava. If you want to see your mother well again, you'll come and find out." With a wink of his one good eye, the soldier released his grip on the box, the apparent lifeline that had linked us long enough to have this most unusual conversation.

It was only when the young man walked off that I realized I never caught his name. It was only after he disappeared into the crowd that I wondered how this soldier from a foreign land had known mine.

5

TAYLOR

The repetitive drumming of rain wakes me just before there's a tap on my dormitory door. I swing my legs over the edge of the bed, mind as cloudy as the sky.

Where am I?

England. The gray mist outside the window assures me of that. But for some reason, the clock on my nightstand has the audacity to claim it's 10 a.m.

Not possible. That would mean I slept for over twelve hours! And orientation starts in thirty minutes.

My eyes fall to the pile of papers on the floor beside the bed, and I understand what's happened. I managed to keep my eyes open through Lady Knight's *Titanic* teaser, and then I passed out, sleeping like only the jet-lagged can sleep.

I'm going to be late. As usual. That postgrad with the clipboard is going to hate me. In fact, that's probably her at the door, here to rouse us from our airplane-induced comas.

The light tapping becomes an annoyed knock.

Dalia is still asleep, but the poor girl won't be snoozing for long if this lady doesn't quit it with her tenacious rapping. Slipping out of bed, I tiptoe toward the door.

"Ready to go?" Nathaniel asks the second I open it. His eyebrow lifts at the sight of my nearly vertical bangs. "No. *Clearly* you're not."

"What are you doing here?"

"Uh, your tea with Lady Knight. Ringing any bells?"

I stifle a huge, awkward yawn. "Remind me when I gave you my RSVP."

"The look on your face yesterday said as much."

"You two are persistent, I'll give you that."

It almost impresses me that Nathaniel can read me so well. Too bad he's the henchman for some eccentric with way too much time on her hands. After a full night's sleep, I can see the situation with fresh eyes. I don't fear Lady Knight and her uncanny knowledge of me as much as I pity her. The poor old woman must be dying for someone to talk to if she's making this much effort to have me over for tea.

I glance at the loose pages by my bed again. Ava's story has its talons in deep, that's for sure. I have no idea what the girl becoming a spy on the *Titanic* has to do with me or my dad, and Lady Knight of Meadowbrook Manor is the only person who can clarify that.

The weight of this decision lands in the middle in my chest. Nathaniel's resigned expression assures me he's as sick of this song and dance as I am and doesn't much care what I decide to do. If I close the door on him now, he isn't coming back to offer me a ride later.

"Give me five minutes." I slip back into the room and dig through the pile of wrinkled clothes stuffed into my suitcase. "Now what does one wear for tea with an elderly benefactress?" I mutter to myself.

"Not those," Dalia murmurs sleepily as I reach for my go-to Chucks. "Really. Do American girls even *own* dresses, or does everyone prefer your gender-neutral style?"

"My dad always said if the shoes don't allow you to run from an attacker, then they're not worth wearing."

"How practical. Not to mention a tad paranoid. I doubt you'll have any reason to run during orientation, though. The first few sessions are incredibly dull. It's basically our postgrad supervisors going over a long list of rules, half a dozen of which are about not snogging in the halls."

"Good. The boring part, not the kissing part. But if orientation is that pointless, it shouldn't be a big deal if I miss the beginning."

Dalia raises a perfectly sculpted eyebrow. "I'm pretty sure *not* skipping sessions is going to be rule number one."

"And there's my loophole." I start stuffing pillows under the comforter to make it look like someone's still sleeping in my bed. "I can't break the rules if we haven't *officially* gone over them yet."

"You're serious?" Dalia says. "You're really leaving?"

"I've got a quick errand to run."

"Mmm," Dalia murmurs. "An errand involving that delightfully deep male voice out in the hall? Yes, I've heard that one before."

Good. Better that she thinks I'm skipping orientation to meet up with a boy. "If the clipboard Gestapo come looking for me…" I point to Pillow Taylor, who's looking a little bulky but should get the job done. "I'm in bed with a migraine after an awful flight."

"First of all, that pillow trick never works. But it's your life, I suppose. I'm not lying for you, though. Sorry. Oxford acceptance letters are much too hard to come by."

"And I wouldn't ask you to lie," I assure her. "Just let Pillow Taylor do the talking. You don't have to say a word."

There's a good chance the program staff will figure out my tired ruse, but I'm willing to take the gamble. Getting in trouble for skipping orientation seems a small price to pay if it allows me to hear the rest of the story Lady Knight is going to such great lengths to tell. And maybe she really does know something about my dad. Something about the photo.

After removing one of two semi-dressy outfits in my suitcase—a black, knee-length skirt splashed with crimson flowers—I throw on a cherry red cardigan, shove Dad's photograph into one of its pockets, and grab my raincoat.

"Much better." Dalia nods approvingly from her horizontal position, then points to the ballet flats sticking out of my suitcase. "With those."

I'll have to go with Dad's practical paranoia on this one, so I shove the flats into my purse and pull on my bright red wellies. "It's pouring. I'll change shoes in the car."

"You look ridiculous." Dalia laughs as I twirl around in my skirt and clunky rain boots while brushing my teeth. "Though I suppose it's better than sneakers and jeans."

Spitting into the sink, I flash her a smile. "Thanks. See you this afternoon."

Out in the hall, Nathaniel leans against the far wall, checking his watch like he's been waiting for ages. His eyes give off a little spark when they scan my outfit—which, I must admit, is a major improvement over yesterday's hooded sweatshirt and grass-stained sneakers ensemble. I guess my posh roommate knows a thing or two.

"All set," I say, glancing down the hall to see if any of the supervisors have started making their rounds. No sign so far.

"Then let's be off."

Once we're in the Rolls Royce, I expect Nathaniel to give me a little more background on this bizarre situation, but he's keeping up the stone-cold silent act. His gaze follows the headlight beams into the morning fog, the muscles in his neck tensing. If I didn't know better, I'd assume he doesn't like me much. He was nice enough yesterday, so the change is odd, but maybe he took my reaction to his unauthorized pick-up personally. Or he takes his tea-brewing skills *really* seriously and is offended that I wouldn't join him and Lady Knight in the car yesterday.

Not one for small talk anyway, I focus on the city scenery. When we're well outside of Oxford and headed down a country road, the fog thickens, making it hard to see much, and our quiet drive gets even more awkward.

I reach into my raincoat pocket for my phone—now would be a good time to post about my UK arrival on social media—but find only the travel-sized tissues Mom insisted I pack. I groan and slump down in the seat.

"What's wrong?" Nathaniel asks, though he doesn't seem too concerned.

"My phone. I left it charging in the dorm."

Nathaniel shrugs. "Is there anyone here who would call you besides the postgrads who are expecting you at orientation?"

I guess he's right, but the way he says it feels like a dig. Not to mention he doesn't even offer to drive back to the college. But at least I've got him talking. "So. Tea. Any idea what this meeting is all about?"

"Not a clue." Nathaniel's eyes stay fixed in front of him. Not even his thumbs are dancing to the classical tunes, and it's this exertion of control, this effort not to fidget, that makes me suspicious.

He's lying. He knows more than he's letting on.

Before I can press him, the car pulls up to an iron gate decorated with two filigree M's.

This is it.

Meadowbrook Manor.

Nathaniel presses a device that resembles a garage door opener attached to his sun visor and the gate parts. At first the road is bordered by thick hedges, but then the road takes a sharp turn, leading us over a wooden bridge just wide enough for a single car. A little dirt foot path darts into a fairy-like forest to the right of the river, but I'm too captivated by the mansion at the end of the long gravel drive. The sprawling structure practically exhales history. There are enough rooms in this house to lock up a hundred stories—tales of war and wealth, scandal and success.

A thick mist whips through the trees like icing. Based on the arches and detailed stonework, I'd say the manor's style is Victorian neo-Gothic. That's one thing my new stepdad is good for. Derek thinks his real estate background also makes him an expert in architecture, which means he loves to explain *ad nauseam* the purpose of each pillar and the function of every buttress. Whatever its style, Meadowbrook belongs on the cover of a Gothic romance.

The only blight on the historic scenery is the white vehicle sitting in front of the manor's entrance. At first, I wonder if Lady Knight is having our lunch/tea/whatever-this-is catered by professionals, but when we get closer, it becomes clear the vehicle is not a delivery van.

It's an ambulance.

My stomach churns like it did the day we learned about Dad. I can still see Mom collapsing on our front porch when the two men in military uniforms exited that black car with government plates.

"Wait here," Nathaniel orders in a voice that's higher than normal. He parks a safe distance behind the ambulance and bolts up the manor's steps, just as the EMTs exit the front door carrying a stretcher covered with a white sheet.

Nathaniel tugs his hair, eyes glued to the human form beneath the death tarp. After a brief exchange with the EMTs, he sprints into the mansion like he won't accept what he's heard.

What he's seen with his own eyes.

It's a surreal sensation, and I know it all too well. At Dad's viewing, I couldn't decide which was more ridiculous: the sight of my father's scarred face caked in makeup, or the fact that he didn't really look dead, though he didn't look alive either.

My heart pulsing, I climb out of the car and watch the EMTs load the body into the ambulance. Everything starts spinning, but the slam of the van's doors brings reality back into sharp focus. I make my way to the manor on wobbly legs, feet tingling in the cold rubber boots like they've fallen asleep.

"But that doesn't make any sense!" Nathaniel is standing in the foyer, arguing with a stout man with heavy jowls and slick-backed hair. The tuxedo makes the guy look like an angry bulldog dressed up as a penguin. "Come on, Giles. How can you just let them take her like that?"

"It's still *Mr.* Bosko to you." The older man shifts his beady eyes from the driver to me. "Good heavens. Is *this* the girl?"

Nathaniel nods without giving me a glance, and the stern little man scans me like I'm here for a modeling audition and likely won't make the cut.

"How did this happen?" demands Nathaniel, still focused on the older man.

Both the driver and the butler—if butlers still exist—eye me, and after a beat I realize their expressions are suspicious. Seriously?

"Let's discuss this in private, Mr. Price." The brusque Mr. Bosko ushers Nathaniel down the hall, leaving me alone in the foyer.

"No worries, I'll just wait here," I mutter.

With no phone to distract me, my eyes travel up the oak staircase, its railing engraved with grape leaves, monkey faces, and an array of mythical creatures—some playful and some downright creepy. Cherubs balance on top of each balustrade, their varnished smiles glistening in the colored light that drifts in from the stained-glass windows.

The full weight of what's happened begins to sink in. The person under that sheet has to be Lady Knight. Death is always sad because it doesn't feel natural even though everyone claims it is, but I'm not sure how to take the loss of an old lady with some strange stalker tendencies. Regardless, her mysterious answers are about to be buried with her.

And the manservants she left behind were glaring at me like *I'm* the one responsible.

A woman's sobbing cuts through my thoughts. My heart leaps into my throat when a redhead descends the staircase, but when she reaches the bottom, I see that she is way older than the woman in Dad's photograph.

She grabs my hands, her moist, teary eyes bulging like a fish's. "Oh dear. Oh dear. You must be Taylor."

I force myself to not pull away from her grasp. "That's right. And you are?"

"Mrs. Porter. The housekeeper." The woman releases one hand to blow into a handkerchief and begins bawling again. "I'm sorry, but you're too late. I should have been with her. Really, I should have. Lady Knight was a wonderful woman. She shouldn't have passed over all alone like that."

And there it is. Verbal confirmation that Lady Knight is dead. The woman was a stranger, but she was still a person. A person who was here one moment and gone the next.

Gone forever. Lights out. End scene.

Mrs. Porter drops my hands to race out the door as the ambulance pulls away, wailing, "I should have been there!" over and over.

The stillness of the foyer after her departure makes something unravel inside me. The way all the people in the paintings seem to be following me with their eyes certainly doesn't help. I stare at the portraits, their phantom voices filling my mind.

Poor dear, you were so close.

Yes, Lady Knight was going to tell her everything, wasn't she?

How sad. Now she'll never know the truth.

Then an actual voice, indistinct, drifts down from upstairs. Maybe it's a police officer or an emergency responder who can explain what exactly happened here.

My hand reaches for the bannister. The well-worn wood makes me flinch like I've grazed a hot dish. Climbing this staircase means breaking a hundred rules of etiquette.

"Hello? Anybody up there?"

No answer. These eerie portraits are sending my overactive imagination into overdrive, so maybe I should wait… but something is calling me up this staircase.

Ava.

If Lady Knight is gone forever, I may never get to read the rest of Ava's story, whoever she is.

Unless I uncover more details before Giles and Nathaniel usher me out of here.

So up the stairs I go. At the top, a long, dim hallway leads to half a dozen doors. I walk toward the rectangular patch of light coming from the only one that's open. My conscience pricks with each intrusive step, but my growing curiosity makes it impossible to turn back now.

The large bedroom beyond the open door radiates the soft light of a glass Tiffany lamp that must be worth a small fortune. An antique rocking chair sits between the room's towering double windows, covered by thick velvet curtains. A collection of porcelain dolls smiles at me with painted lips from their shelf above the king-sized canopy bed, where the sheets and blankets are resting all the way back.

I shiver at the empty shell the raised fabric creates. The air in the room feels charged, like when you rub your socks across a staticky carpet. Something *big* just happened here, and even the tiniest atom knows it.

Finally, I drag my eyes away from Lady Knight's final rest place. On the nightstand beside the bed, its drawer pulled all the way out, sit pictures frames of all shapes and sizes. Some showcase recent shots of Lady Knight posing with a fluffy white cat, but most feature black-and-white faces from earlier eras. Every single person wears the same sullen expression, one that must have been a requirement a long time ago.

I step forward to study the pictures more closely, wondering if Ava is in one, and something crunches beneath my feet. The edge of a saucer juts from beneath my boot, and I jump back with a gasp. Next to the now broken plate is a matching blue-and-white paisley teacup. Beside the cup split perfectly in half, a dark stain seeps into the carpet. It looks like blood.

Don't be ridiculous. It's spilled tea.

Kneeling beside the broken cup, I press my hand to the stain and bring my fingers to my nose. It isn't blood, but it doesn't smell like peppermint either. The scent is strong. Earthy. Putrid, even.

A throat clears behind me. "May I assist you with something?"

I shoot to my feet and struggle to meet Giles's eyes. "Sorry, I was just—"

"Having a good snoop," the butler finishes, looking more intrigued than angry.

"Will you request an autopsy?" I blurt.

The butler scoffs as if mortally offended. "And why would I . . ." He shakes his head, cutting himself off, then straightens and continues more formally. "Lady Knight recently celebrated her one-hundredth birthday. We're all saddened by the sudden loss, but it certainly doesn't come as a surprise. What would be the point of conducting an autopsy?" He narrows his eyes at me.

The question isn't rhetorical. The butler's glare suggests that if anyone has something to hide, I'm the most likely candidate. Which is ridiculous.

The first dubious thing I've done was wander to the scene of Lady Knight's death without permission . . .

I grimace. "I, well—"

"Listen, Giles. Mrs. Porter is a wreck." Nathaniel enters the room, saving me from having to mumble through another apology for my morbid curiosity. "I better drive her home before she has a nervous breakdown."

Giles's face turns red. "Mrs. Porter? I think you need to take *her* out of here immediately." He thumbs toward me without looking in my direction, but Nathaniel is already shaking his head.

With both men distracted, I turn my attention back to Lady Knight's bed. Something about this scene isn't right. It just doesn't *feel* like an old woman passed away peacefully in her sleep. The whole setup has a frantic vibe that makes me uneasy. All my reporter instincts are wide awake and on high alert.

Something is off with the nightstand. The drawer looks like someone ripped it open in a hurry. I peer inside. Instead of tissues or cough drops like you'd expect in an old lady's nightstand, there's a book bound in dark red leather.

I glance over my shoulder at the still arguing butler and chauffer. My eyes return to the open drawer. Things stored in nightstands tend to be personal, and Lady Knight promised me a personal story. What if this is it?

Before my left hand knows what the right is doing, I slip the book beneath my raincoat.

"Taylor?"

I whirl around, trying to look casual by stuffing my hand into my pocket. "Yeah! What's up?"

Nathaniel gives me a *what's wrong with you?* look that makes my face burn. "I'll run you back to the university when I return from dropping off our housekeeper. Mrs. Porter lives in the opposite direction of Oxford and she's in a rather bad state, so it'd be best if you waited here."

"Downstairs. In the parlor." Giles studies me like he feels the need to count the silverware.

"No problem." These Meadowbrook people aren't going to tell me anything helpful anyway. Giles and Nathaniel clearly consider me an outsider who can't be trusted, which means I'll have to figure out what Lady Knight wanted with me on my own.

If the book beneath my jacket proves a decent place to start, an hour without Nathaniel breathing down my neck sounds about perfect.

Even the way Giles escorts me downstairs makes me feel like a criminal caught in the act. "Now," he says as he ushers me into a parlor as ornate as the rest of the place. "You are to remain here until Mr. Price returns to deliver you back to Oxford. I have at least a dozen phone calls to make, and I'm afraid Meadowbrook Manor is not a museum open to exploration—no matter how much those pesky developers would like that to be the case."

The butler turns abruptly, leaving me staring after him. Developers? I shake my head. No idea.

The relentless tick of the antique clock on the mantel brings me back to the parlor. That noise is going to drive me insane. I take a seat in a brocade armchair that sits as far from the clock as possible, then look around the room one more time. I don't know if it's the big old house or the fact someone just died, but I feel like someone is watching me, like the walls have eyes.

After verifying that I'm alone, I remove the leather book from beneath my jacket. It seems wrong that I don't feel more upset about Lady Knight, but what am I supposed to feel? If I'm honest, any grief I've experienced isn't really for her—it's for the answers I might never receive now that the old woman is gone. Tracing the cracks along the volume's spine, I pray an explanation awaits me inside.

Out of Nowhere: A Memoir reads the simple title page.

Someone has scratched out the dedication with thick black ink, but there are two bold words below it, scrawled by a hurried hand.

FIND WILL

When I turn the next page, my lips curl into a slow smile.

AVA

The soldier with the marble eye came and went like a phantom no one else had seen. For a moment, I stood by the pillar staring into the crowd where he'd disappeared, trying to convince myself that what had just happened was real.

"I'll be taking Mrs. Lakovic's jewelry chest now, m'lady." The distraught woman's maid plucked the box from my hands. Opening the front drawer, she shoved a handful of jewelry inside and marched back to her mistress, her proud, freckled nose held high.

Mrs. Lakovic. Not a countess or lady. *That* was who Father had abandoned me for? Who, I plainly saw, he was still consumed with?

I needed some fresh air.

My camera in hand, I headed toward the edge of the first-class deck, where passengers stood waving their goodbyes to loved ones on the pier below. The lighting there was perfect, and I had to act quickly, for it would not last.

Nothing that dances on the edge of perfection ever lasts.

I rounded a corner and saw her. A little girl on the ground in front of me, basking in the glory of toddlerhood, as close to irreverent excellence as she'd ever be. With her red coat unbuttoned and her tights torn at the knees, she lay in the middle of the deck floor, skirt hiked up and legs lifted high, oblivious to the passengers walking by. Blind to any stares that declared this ardent display of her bloomers "unladylike."

That would certainly be Mother's critique. Only she would say it out loud, not merely with her eyes.

I had to capture it. I had to capture *her*. Preserve the girl's fearless soul in sepia before the world stripped her of wonder, replacing a child's God-given awe with a hundred petty rules on how to dress, what to say, who to be.

While changing out my film strip, another little girl with curly dark hair toddled onto the scene, joining the blonde in the red coat in what appeared to be an upside-down tandem bicycle ride.

"Strength in numbers," said a voice in a cheerful French accent.

I lifted my chin from my camera and met the smiling eyes of the Haitian engineer. *Mr. Laroche, was it?* "Yes, that is often the way of revolutionaries."

Mr. Laroche laughed, full and proud. "True. And my Simonne has been a rebel from birth." The man gave me a knowing glance. "Some girls simply *are*."

I nodded, smiling at his candor before searching for the toddlers in the camera's viewfinder. I held the box firm, keeping it perfectly still while the shutter opened and closed. My eyes never left the children—fast friends who did not see any of the barriers that boxed in most adults. I could always count on my camera to capture such connections, for it had this magical ability to see *through* my subjects to their very essence, harnessing all the power of light.

We become what we behold, as Mother would say.

Exhale. Inhale. Exhale.

Snap, snap, snap.

There—I'd done it. I'd preserved a moment in time.

"You know, I'd pay handsomely for a copy of that," said Mr. Laroche with a smile.

I tried to remain poised even as my heart threatened to burst from my rib cage. Not only was someone interested in my photograph, he was willing to *pay* for it. "Of course. I'd be delighted to make you a print."

Now if I could just figure out a way to develop the film during our voyage, I might even have a history-making image to share with Gertrude Käsebier upon our arrival in New York. Everyone said *Titanic*'s crossing was exactly that—historic—though the newspaper photographers snapping pictures as we boarded had focused only on the "important people." Like Captain Edward J. Smith, of course, not to mention Mr. John Jacob Astor, the wealthiest person on *Titanic* and a man the other passengers could not stop gossiping about. Yet the rich and powerful did not interest me, for I couldn't fathom that staged shots of frowning men in crisp uniforms were what future generations would care to remember. No, they'd want to glimpse the tiny blond in torn tights lying on the deck floor with a half-Haitian, half-French girl born to push down walls.

They'd want to glimpse the truth of things.

"What are you doing, child? Get up or you'll sully your dress!"

And there it was. The slow stifling of all wonder from the world.

The little sprite must belong to the panic-stricken woman my father was assisting, for her Irish maid had returned to drag the poor girl away.

Mr. Laroche took hold of his daughter's hand. "We'd better head to our part of the ship. Good day to you."

"And you." I placed my camera back in its case.

"Ava, dear. Let's be off," Father called, beckoning to me.

Mrs. Lakovic hung unsteadily on Father's arm, her eyes downcast in humiliation. Poor wretched thing. She must have suffered a panic attack. Thanks to Mother's frequent fits, I knew the spectacle all too well.

Father pulled back the canopy of the woman's buggy to make sure the infant was all right—a rather forward act, seeing how this woman and her children were strangers. The large pram contained not a newborn, but a *second* toddler, fast asleep despite his mother's very public meltdown. So the sprite had a twin. No wonder this poor woman was at her wit's end.

As we made our way through the enormous ship, my eyes narrowed on Father's back like it was a moving target. He walked ahead with Mrs. Lakovic, showering the woman with more attention than he'd paid me all day. Apparently, Father's ego—I'd picked up on this new term and theory proposed by Dr. Freud, one of my father's heroes—preferred playing the good doctor to unhinged women over those who could carry on a rational debate.

The pair were so lost in hushed conversation that they failed to notice the extravagance all around them. *Titanic* was exquisite in every possible way. It was not merely an ocean liner, but a palace on waves.

And I am not so easily impressed.

We strolled the tiled floors until we reached a large glass dome supported by iron bars so thin, they were nearly invisible. The elegant structure seemed to float as if by magic, suspended over a polished oak staircase that reflected my image back to me. I paused to photograph the illuminated bronze cherub lamp at the center of the banister. Electricity was a novelty for a ship this size. My gaze climbed to the gorgeous clock at the top of the staircase, surrounded by an oak panel with a carving of two angels. One fanned a palm leaf and the other inscribed a tablet.

Snap, snap.

"Come along, Ava." Father turned down a long corridor leading to the staterooms. When we reached the end of the hallway, Father handed me the key to our suite. "Go ahead and get settled. I'll see that Mrs. Lakovic finds her room. The porters will bring our trunks shortly."

I'd tried remaining mature about this situation, but Father was taking things a step too far. Escorting this strange woman to her room? Really? Hadn't he done enough?

With an exasperated sigh, I plucked the key from Father's hand and let myself in, not bothering to prevent the door from slamming behind me.

Tears stung my eyes. This was supposed to be *our* holiday. Why must Father insist on playing the knight in shining armor to every unstable woman who crossed his path? Perhaps *I* should fake a fainting. Maybe then he would finally notice me.

Removing my hat and gloves, I channeled my frustrations into exploration of our suite. It had two bedrooms joined by a small sitting area. The crimson bedding and wallpaper gave the space an air of luxury, and each bedroom was large enough to contain its own wardrobe and writing desk. Although the cabin was nowhere near the size of my bedroom back home, it would be fine for a few days.

I stepped into the miniature washroom to wipe the harbor's soot from my face. *Ah, this will be perfect.* The washroom's tub was the tiniest I'd ever seen, but the claustrophobic space would make an ideal darkroom. I returned to my suitcase for my processing supplies. To start, I lit the candle inside my safety lamp, which was covered in a red fabric that allowed the lamp to be folded down during travel but still enabled me to see in the darkroom without exposing the film to too much light. Absorbed in the familiar act of setting up the series of chemical baths, I forgot about my father, the woman, and the solider for three blissful minutes. Baths arranged, I removed the film from my camera and dipped it into the developing solution. The seconds ticked by as I waited for the murky blotches to form a coherent image.

Knock, knock, knock.

I poked my head outside the washroom. "One moment!"

Before I could answer the door, two porters and a crewman burst into the suite, dragging a large cart piled high with steamer trunks and leather suitcases.

"Hello again, Lady Ava," said the Irish sailor—the same who had checked my ticket, I realized with surprise. He met my gaze for a moment before dipping his head respectfully. "Where would you like us to stow your luggage?"

"Next to the sofa is fine. Thank you."

The porters unloaded the bags, stacking them neatly in the corner.

"Is there anything else I can do for you?" The sailor brushed the hair away from his forehead, revealing pale green eyes the color of sea foam. He fidgeted with his hat while awaiting my command. The pause allowed me to study his hands, a most important feature on a man.

Strong, yet elegant. Piano hands, Mother would say.

Not that a sailor could afford a piano.

Though shy at first, when the sailor lifted his chin, his gaze threatened to soften all my sharp edges with its polish. It was as if he *saw* me in a single glance. Unlike most people, he did not flinch.

"Yes, that will be all. Thank you…"

"Caleb Donohue, Able Seaman." The sailor smiled. Only this time, he did not try to hide it. "At your service, Lady Ava."

It was my turn to lower my eyes as heat crept into my cheeks. "Thank you, Mr. Donohue."

"Of course." The crewman tipped his hat and turned to depart, leaving me bewildered by the pounding in my chest. And for what? Was I truly so desperate for attention that I was swooning over the first sailor to cast me a *smile*? Mother's reputation certainly hadn't lengthened my list of suitors, but I cared little for suitors to begin with. A female photographer of the modern age could bind herself to no man.

My photograph.

"Bloody hell!"

Mother would chastise me for this crude slip of the tongue, but bad manners were the least of my worries. If I'd destroyed this priceless photo, I'd never forgive myself.

Grabbing hold of the metal tongs, I plucked the wet paper from the solution and threw it into the stop bath to prevent it from developing further. A second knock sounded from the main room, and with a sigh of relief, I left the saved photo to answer it.

"Did you forget something, Seaman Dono—"

The eyes on the other side of the door were not born of sea foam. These were much darker pools. Mrs. Lakovic. The woman Father had supposedly delivered to her room ten minutes ago.

I pushed past her, glancing down the clean white corridor. "Where is my father?

Mrs. Lakovic ignored my question, her accented words lucid in their urgency. "You must convince him to leave this ship in Cherbourg and find another. He will not listen to me, and we're nearly out of time."

"And why *would* he listen to you?" I cast a critical glance at her. "Who are you?"

"While we were boarding, I saw how our journey ends…" Her voice dropped to a whisper. "In disaster. In death."

My, this woman *was* dramatic. When we reached Cherbourg, Mrs. Lakovic should look up Miss Dorothy Gibson, the American actress rumored to be boarding the ship following her grand tour of France. I smiled the way one does when listening to a child repeat a tall tale. "I'm afraid I don't understand what you mean."

The woman grabbed my hand, taking her performance to the next level. A faraway look filled her eyes. I tried to release myself from her grip, but she was stronger than she appeared. The deeper the woman's nails dug into my skin, the more unraveled she became. Perhaps she was not putting on airs after all. Perhaps she truly feared for her life. Her outburst bordered on insanity, but her words sent a shiver through me nonetheless.

"Someone is trying to kill me," she hissed. "Kill us. All of us. But we *must* make it to New York. If not, the death count will reach the millions."

"Millions? There are only a few thousand passengers on *Titanic*." I ripped my hand from hers and took a step back into my stateroom. "Besides, that's what lifeboats are for."

"It does not matter. If we fail in our mission, there will be no stopping the coming bloodshed." The woman backed down the hall slowly, a claw-like hand to her head. "But there is still time to chart a different course. You must convince your father to take another ship before it is too late."

"All right, will do. Thank you for the visit." I slammed the door, making sure the lock was secure. "And I thought Mother's fits were bizarre."

It seemed boarding *Titanic* meant I'd traded one unstable woman for another.

Father hadn't said a word about where he'd gone after escorting Mrs. Lakovic to her room, and if he could have his secrets, then so could I. And so, in the middle of our first dinner onboard Titanic, I excused myself to the lady's room and slipped outside.

I would meet this soldier and hear his offer. I just hoped his price was not more than I was willing to pay—a thought that had me covering my silk dress with a wrap of bulky fur before entering the bitter night.

"May I escort you somewhere, Lady Ava?"

I nearly jumped out of my skin at the disembodied voice.

"Up here, miss." The Irish sailor looked down on me from a higher deck.

No, this wouldn't do. I couldn't have him following me, but I also couldn't bear to crush the hope that lit up his face in the darkness.

"Ah, Seaman Donohue. I appreciate the offer, but I'm hoping to clear my head with a bit of fresh air. As I'm no stranger to silence, there's no need to trouble yourself."

"All right, but it'd be no trouble. I'm headed that direction anyway."

"I'll be fine. But thank you for your concern. I trust this ship is quite safe. Thanks to vigilant sailors such as yourself, of course."

Even in the shadows, the seaman seemed to blush at my overt flattery. Or maybe it was just the bitter cold that left his cheeks so pink. "We're mainly watching for icebergs, but we do our best to keep all passengers safe."

I gave the sailor the most charming smile I could muster. "I feel more secure already. Goodnight, Seaman Donohue."

"Goodnight, Lady Ava."

When he was gone, I took in gulps of cold air, willing my pulse to slow. The last thing I wanted was for this sailor to know I was meeting a man out here alone. I knew how that would look, and it seemed I cared what Caleb Donohue might think.

A strange warmth spread through me as I walked away, but I shoved it down with another breath of icy Atlantic air. The seaman was thoughtful to care about my safety, but I had no room in my life for young men, no matter how courteous. I picked up my pace, praying I wasn't too late. The stranger had said eight o'clock, and the fact that he was a soldier implied "on the dot."

First a soldier and now a sailor.

What was it about this ship? From the moment I'd boarded, I'd become a homing beacon for men in uniform. *Men who have no chance with the daughter of an English lord,* Mother's voice reminded me.

As if I'd even consider a match so preposterous.

After climbing the stairs to the rooftop deck, I noticed a long shadow leaning against the railing, overlooking the black sea. The man's perfectly erect posture betrayed his identity. At the mere sight of the soldier, the risk I was taking struck me with the force of a tidal wave.

A man I didn't know from Adam wanted to speak with *me.* Alone.

And here I was, flying to him like a moth to an oil lamp.

The clouds over the moon parted, revealing the soldier's overcoat and black bowler hat. The absence of his uniform and its symbolic trappings of authority had me gripping the handrail with hesitation. What if I was walking into a trap? Surely Jack the Ripper had used similar tactics to lure his victims away from the crowd.

I started turning away, but it was too late. The soldier had whirled around at the click of my heels. There was only one thing left to do—show the man such confidence, he'd know without a doubt that Lady Ava Knight of Meadowbrook Manor was not some barmaid he could dally with in the dark.

I cleared my throat, calling out over the roar of *Titanic* plowing through the sea. "You were clever enough to unearth my family name, but you have yet to do me the courtesy of acknowledging yours. I suspect that in your homeland it is as impolite as it is in mine to request a meeting with a young lady without first revealing your identity."

The soldier returned my candor with a grin. "I would not presume to understand the incoherent customs of the English, but I am happy to introduce myself. My name is Vaso Plavsic. I am a lieutenant in the Serbian Army."

"I see. And why would a soldier from Serbia be interested in aiding my mother?"

"Ah, you assume I wish to help you. No, Lady Ava, what I desire is for *you* to help *me*. Yet I am not so naïve as to believe your assistance will come without cost. Tell me, what is your mother's ailment?"

"An addiction to laudanum."

My own forthrightness nearly floored me. For heaven's sake, why was I trusting this stranger with such a personal matter? Perhaps it was his one eye, a fastidious orb that sought to order the entire universe, assigning every person and thing to its proper place. No matter what wasteland he came from, this man exuded power.

The power to *do* something.

And action was exactly what I desired. I wouldn't let myself become trapped in the colorless life my mother had escaped to— through a daily opiate that promised to diminish her every pain. If only the peddler who'd sold her the drug after a series of miscarriages had mentioned that the opioid would also diminish everything else: her mind, her memory, even her ability to love.

An old ache squeezed my heart as I pictured the sad person my mother had become—a shell of the beautiful, lively woman she'd once been.

Stop it. This man is trained to sniff out weakness.

"Laudanum, you say." Lieutenant Plavsic seemed to roll the word around his tongue as he considered the devil substance. "Then you're in luck, for I know a man in Munich who is a colleague of Dr. Carl Jung. The Swiss psychiatrist's latest theories on the unconscious mind have had great success in helping patients overcome their addictions. If Dr. Jung is unable to restore your mother's mind, I doubt anyone can."

Carl Jung? I braced myself against the railing, staring down at an ocean that seemed bottomless. What this stranger proposed would not only give me back my mother, it would fulfill my father's greatest aspirations to boot. Though I rarely took Father's esoteric dinner conversations with his eccentric friends seriously, even I knew the name of Dr. Carl Jung, Sigmund Freud's protégé and a living celebrity among psychologists.

"I'm certain I can arrange a visit with Dr. Jung," Plavsic continued, seeming to sense I was hooked. "But you must assist me in return. Help me achieve what *I* desire, and I will see that your mother is cured."

I straightened my posture, for this man needed to know I would not be an easy conquest. "And how do I know you're telling the truth? That you will fulfill your promise once I give you what you want?"

The soldier frowned, as if I'd offended his honor. "You don't, Lady Ava. Just as I have no proof that you are anything but a silly, pampered girl who has never known the sting of suffering. So, it seems we shall both have to take a risk in trusting each other."

Well. Obviously, this man assumed that because I came from wealth, I knew nothing of heartache. The pompous judgement transformed any initial spark of attraction into a hardened resolve to prove him wrong.

"And what *is* it that you want?" I demanded.

Plavsic's good eye traveled along the fur wrap that had slipped from my shoulder, stopping at the skin of my throat. "What any modern man wants in an age of unlimited progress. Freedom from tyranny. A home of his own. In my case, that means a united kingdom for all Serbians."

Oh, thank heavens. He was a nationalist. *That* I could handle.

"That witch of a woman your father was assisting is Galena Lakovic." The young lieutenant shook his head in disgust. "She can help achieve a united Serbia, but she rejects her own people and refuses to follow reason. Even worse, she is attempting to thwart the plans of the Serbian military. What I need is for you to watch her closely. If I continue following her, I won't be able to conceal my identity for long. Yet Mrs. Lakovic will not be suspicious of an aristocratic young woman so charming… and so lovely. You must tell me what you learn, everything she says, no matter how insignificant it seems."

Was this soldier truly asking me to become his *spy*?

"But… why?" I couldn't comprehend this woman's significance.

"I need you to follow her because she's dangerous." The solider turned back to the sea, unwilling to elaborate.

That I believed. Her haunted eyes as she stood outside my stateroom… I nearly told Plavsic about her frenzied words, but something told me not to show all my cards at once.

"Lieutenant, I'm afraid I shall require more than that," I said, crossing my arms. "If you want me to do your bidding, then you must at least tell me *why*. We have no choice but to trust each other, remember?"

Plavsic sighed. "I'm trailing Galena because I believe she carries information that will… stack the deck, shall we say. Her secret is a document of some kind, and I believe that with your careful eyes and ears, one of us may be able to recover it. Believe me, when war comes—and it *will* come—you of all people will want to be on the right side. I can assure you Europe's aristocracy will be the first plank thrown onto the fire."

What was he talking about? The primeval skirmishes of this soldier's homeland meant little to England or the rest of the civilized world. His request was absurd, yet the appeal of his promise was strong. If Dr. Jung was able to cure Mother, then perhaps my father would fall in love with her again. I'd have both my parents back. Finally, they would smile at each other the way they had in the wedding photograph that had sat on my nightstand ever since I was a little girl. It was a glance frozen in time—one I'd never seen in real life.

Curiosity crushed any remaining doubts. "Let's suppose I do hear or discover something worth noting. Where should I plan on finding you in this floating city?"

"Not to worry, Lady Ava. I'll find you." A knowing smirk curved Lieutenant Plavsic's full lips. "After all, there aren't many places to hide onboard a ship."

TAYLOR

Even my toes tingle from the chill that passes through me as I lower the book. Why hadn't I ever heard of this memoir? Didn't Lady Knight realize she had a priceless piece of history? I study the opening pages again. There's none of the normal publishing info—no date, no publishing house. It seems this Ava self-published her story long before self-publishing was even a thing.

Still, my confusion about how this account of a girl in 1912 relates to Dad's photograph is only growing, especially since Lady Knight's letter mentioned my father so directly. And who *is* this Ava? Some relative of Lady Knight, given the shared last name, but how distant?

A floorboard creaks, providing enough warning for me to hide the book beneath the raincoat draped across my lap before Giles enters the parlor.

"I apologize, Miss Romano," the butler says in his all-too-brisk manner. "It's almost time for lunch, but I'm afraid that with Mrs. Porter away, I have nothing to offer you. However, there's a decent pub in the village and the walk is quite pleasant, so perhaps you'd prefer to take a meal there. Nathaniel should be back to deliver you to Oxford by the time you return."

"Sounds good." I suspect the pantry in this place is far from bare, but I'll oblige Giles and get out of his hair. Plus, I skipped breakfast, so the mere mention of food already has me salivating. "I could use some fresh air anyway."

"Yes, that would be best." He opens the door leading to the front foyer, waving me through while muttering, "I'll be preoccupied with making funeral arrangements, not to mention handling the blasted lawyers who've been calling nonstop."

He doesn't meet my eyes as I walk past him, and it's my turn to study him suspiciously. Something about this butler's shifty gaze suggests he knows more than he's letting on.

Maybe Mae Knight knew her staff couldn't be trusted. Maybe her outreach to me in Oxford was her final cry for help. But that still doesn't answer the question: Why *me*?

A suffocating feeling presses my chest. It's an unfortunately familiar sensation, and the recognition makes me sink even faster. Right after Dad died, I had lots of panic attacks. They always hit me out of nowhere, usually when I didn't even *know* I was feeling anxious.

But the body knows. It recognizes when it's in a bad situation and needs *out*.

Meaning I should probably leave this house. I grab an umbrella in the foyer, but when I open the front door, a flood of sunlight fills the tomb-like entryway.

"Miss Romano?" I turn back, expecting an accusation of some kind, but Giles's rigid features have softened. "Yesterday, when you spoke with Lady Knight, did she… well, did she say anything unusual?"

"Not really." It's almost the truth, seeing how Mae told me nothing I can make sense of. Besides, I don't know what's usual for the woman in the first place. I eye the door and try to calm my quickening breaths, willing my pulse to slow.

Giles looks puzzled, like he expected more. He resumes his bristled stance. "Enjoy your lunch then. Just follow the footpath by the bridge into town. The Abbotsville pub is quite good—for a pub, that is." The door closes behind me with a snap.

Out on the gravel path, a blue sky greets me for the first time since I set foot in England. The weight on my chest begins to lift, my lungs expanding more with each breath.

As I cross the bridge and take the path toward the village, I try to enjoy the peaceful scenery, but the loop of unanswered questions keeps replaying in my head. Giles obviously thought Lady Knight intended to tell me something important. Now she's gone, and I can't shake the sense her "something" was more than a self-published memoir written by a girl on the *Titanic* who has nothing to do with me. I'm wasting time in my search to figure out why my dad came to this country. To figure out if Dad was who I thought he was.

But where to begin? So far, Ava Knight is my only lead.

My walk ends at a whitewashed cottage with an old-fashioned thatched roof. The historic sign hanging above the pub's door uses symbols instead of words—a hatchet and one of those tools required for geometry class.

The Axe and... Compass?

An odd name for a pub, but the jingling bell in the doorway means the place is still up and running. I step inside, pausing to let my eyes adjust to the relative gloom. Except for the two old guys playing chess in the corner, the dining area is empty. The place is exactly what I would expect of a traditional English pub: low ceilings, thick beams, and a Premier League soccer game playing above a bar stocked with more types of gin than I knew existed.

"Fine day," says the bartender before cursing Manchester United's latest goal under his breath. A faded mermaid tattoo covers his meaty forearm, and his plump nose reminds me of a cherry tomato. "What can I do for ye? Don't even ask for a jigger. I can tell ye aren't old enough."

By jigger, I assume he means a shot.

"Uh, no. I'm just looking for a bite to eat."

The man glances at the clock above the bar, which reads 11:45 a.m. He grins, revealing a missing tooth. "Aye. It's a bit early for a proper drink anyhow."

His accent sounds more Scottish than English. Or maybe it's Welsh… I'm not really good with British dialects. I climb onto a stool and lean over the bar to study the handwritten menu on the blackboard behind it. "I'll take a coffee and the traditional English breakfast."

I'm not sure what I just ordered, but anything with "traditional" and "English" in the title can't be too crazy since the Brits aren't exactly known for their radicalism. All I really need anyway is a cup of strong coffee to clear my brain fog.

"American, are ye?" The bartender wipes down the bar with a resolve that suggests destroying germs is his sole mission in life. "What's a young American doin' in a place like Abbotsville?"

"I'm visiting Meadowbrook Manor."

"Meadowbrook," the man grumbles, as if the mere word is an offense to his working-class sensibilities. He studies me with wary eyes. "What do you want with them?"

"Well, I—"

"A strange place, that manor is. Mighty strange. People say Lady Knight hasn't been doing well, what with her family troubles and all. Yes, it's been a good long while since she's come in for a hot toddy. Always her favorite on a blustery afternoon."

I don't think *I* should be the one to tell the village bartender—and, by all appearances, the town gossip—that he won't be making Mae a hot toddy ever again. "What kind of family troubles?" I ask instead.

"Why, the curse, of course." At my wide eyes, he continues eagerly, happy to have an audience on such a quiet morning. "Odd folks, the Knights. Now I'm not one to talk, but they've never been the most sociable people. And they don't take kindly to unexpected callers, so you best be on your way. Trust me, you don't want to get involved with the likes of them, not if you can help it. Mae's a nice enough lady, but common courtesy has never stopped the family curse from wreaking havoc."

My ears start tingling. "A curse?"

The man gives me a knowing glance. "That's right. The Knights have lived in these parts since the 1540s, right around the time old Henry VIII seized England's monasteries after breaking with the Church so he could divorce his first wife and marry another. *Several* others, in fact. You've heard of the Tudor tyrant, haven't ye?"

Come on, everyone with access to Showtime has heard of the king who killed most of his wives. Instead, I nod and smile. "That's one history lesson that's hard to forget."

"Right ye are, lass." The bartender chuckles. "Old King Henry started going after any monk who refused to bow the knee. His nobles did the dirty work, of course, and Sir Edgar Knight was one of the king's most trusted men. In fact, King Henry gave Lord Knight the monastery of Meadowbrook as a reward for getting rid of a particularly troublesome abbot from Glastonbury, a right stubborn man who refused to hand over his abbey's keys."

"So, you're saying the Knights gained possession of Meadowbrook through *murder*?"

"How else, lass?" The man chuckles again, as if murder is an everyday occurrence in these parts.

And there's that pressure squeezing my heart again.

"Abbot Whiting was executed on top of the Glastonbury Tor in the most horrific way imaginable," the bartender explains. "Dismembered, he was—torn to bloody pieces. But not even a beheading could stop old Whiting from being *re*membered by those who regarded him a most holy man. Some say the descendants of Edgar Knight were forever cursed for their ancestor's crime, and I'd swear on my own mum's grave it's true. All the Knight sons died young and in some violent fashion, leaving their wives and daughters behind… most of them going mad with grief."

The bartender pauses to serve my breakfast—a smorgasbord of steaming pink meat. Under normal circumstances, I can eat bacon every day of the week, but this variety of animal products suddenly reminds me of dismembered body parts. The fried tomato and sautéed mushrooms piled on top of the neon orange egg yolk almost feels like a joke—the chef's last-ditched effort to make this plated heart attack *seem* like a semi-balanced breakfast.

"Lady Mae's the most normal of the Knights, but even she has her odd ways." The bartender peers out from between the cask ale handles, the rag in his hand motionless for once. He speaks in a low voice, as if letting me in on a secret. "If you ask me, Lady Knight should bulldoze the place and start fresh. Quite a few folks have seen some strange happenings over at Meadowbrook. Mighty strange, indeed. Some say that when a person dies within its walls, their spirit never leaves. It's stuck in the house, see? Trapped in a vortex, like."

The only response I can muster is an open-mouthed stare, which makes the man laugh heartily as he slaps the bar. "Easy there, lass. I'm only messin' with you. Part of the job, see? Bill's the name, by the way."

I give a weak chuckle. "Nice to meet you, Bill." I set Ava's memoir next to my plate and open it, hoping old Bill the yarn-spinning bartender will take the hint and give me some space. My eyes don't trace the words on the page—I'm too caught up with what I've just heard. Bill's told me more about the Knight family than both Nathaniel and Giles combined—and I'm grateful—but I need to settle my stomach if I'm going to force down this carnivore-lover's breakfast that's set me back ten British pounds.

Seriously, though—a *curse*?

If Ava Knight managed to survive the *Titanic,* how cursed can her family be?

8

$\mathcal{A}$VA

"Cursed, cursed, cursed!" the woman hissed as she scribbled on stationary in the far corner of the first-class writing room. "The entire family is cursed!"

Muscle by muscle, my body tensed as I watched her. Galena Lakovic hadn't made a public appearance since our Southampton departure a day ago, which made spying on her rather difficult. I didn't want to frighten her away now, so I sat motionless in the lemon-yellow armchair, my face hidden behind a novel even as my eyes peered over it to study the woman's erratic movements. The other passengers seated at desks throughout the room didn't bother to hide their staring. Most were writing leisurely letters to friends and family back home, but not Mrs. Lakovic. The woman wrote as if in a trance, as if the hand moving the pen was not her own.

Start. Stop. Start. Stop.

I shivered at the sight. Galena's jerky movements and vacant eyes gave her an air of demonic possession. She wrote as if her life depended on it. The time she had been at it could be seen in the pages stacked beneath the beams of sunlight turning the cream-colored walls of the writing room a warm gold.

In an effort to temporarily distract myself from the disturbing woman, I turned back to my novel. It was a story of forbidden love called *The Broken Wings*, written by a little-known Lebanese poet named Khalil Gibran.

Though I'd sworn off romantic attachments—my sights were set on grander aspirations—I couldn't help but fall in love vicariously through the poet's words. Any man who wrote lines like "solitude has soft, silky hands, but with strong fingers it grasps the heart and makes it ache with sorrow" seemed worthy of my time. Each hour of our voyage together, Gibran sharpened his words against the beating stone in my chest. The novel became a slim dagger I stored beneath my pillow each night, hidden from Father's watchful eye. If it were up to him, *The Secret Garden* would be the most passionate work I ever encountered.

Mother, however, would likely approve of this maturing in my literary tastes. Years ago, when I was young and she was well, she'd read to me every day in the rocking chair beside her bedroom window. I'd craved the escape into my imagination ever since, but on *Titanic* even books did little to soothe my restless soul.

At least Vaso Plavsic had given me something useful to do. I'd already penciled in several observations about Galena Lakovic's behavior in the margin of my book, including the woman's current stream of gibberish about some poor accursed family. Really, I couldn't understand why Lieutenant Plavsic considered this woman a threat to his political ambitions. She was clearly insane—a danger to nothing but decorum.

"Excuse me, miss. Would you mind if I included you in my photograph of the room?"

I lifted my eyes and met a Roman collar. What a relief! Perhaps this priest was here to perform the exorcism Mrs. Lakovic surely required.

"Not at all," I replied. "Though I'm more accustomed to staging photographs rather than posing for them."

"Then you know there's nothing to it, really." With a smile, the young priest lifted his Kodak. "Try to look natural."

I straightened my posture, removing any trace of a smile that would make me resemble some harlot from London's East End.

The priest raised his box camera and snapped a few photographs. So, this was what it felt like to be on the other end of the lens. My skin tingled at the thought of my fresh young face preserved for all eternity in the heart of *Titanic*.

"Thank you, miss—?"

"Knight." I rose from my seat, extending my hand. "Lady Ava Knight."

"Father Francis Browne. A pleasure. Do leave me your address and I'll forward a copy of your portrait."

"Forgive me, but I did not realize priests were trained to be photographers."

"Ah, we Jesuits are trained in many arts." The young man nodded at the book resting on my seat, a playful sparkle in his eyes. "And *I* was not aware the daughters of the English nobility were permitted to read esoteric romance novels that explore the plight of women."

Well. I found I rather liked this priest.

Covering the side of his mouth with one hand, Father Browne whispered in his smooth Irish accent, "Not to worry, Lady Knight. Your secret is safe with me. I'm a bit of a Gibran fan myself."

Yes, I most certainly liked this priest.

Too bad our budding camaraderie wilted when I returned my gaze to the writing desk I was supposed to be watching. It was empty.

"No. She's gone!"

Confused, the priest glanced around the room. "Is everything all right?"

"Tell me, Father. Did you see the woman sitting at that desk?"

"Why, yes. She left while I was taking your photograph, looking rather frantic, in fact. Come to think of it, I believe I've seen that woman before." Father Browne opened the folder he carried and shuffled through a stack of developed photographs. "My lodging's washroom is little more than a closet, but it serves as an excellent dark room."

I began to tell the priest I'd made the same discovery, but he pressed on excitedly, "Yes, here we are. It's a pity—this one must have been double exposed. See that shadow there? The effect is rather unsettling, isn't it?"

His photograph showcased *Titanic*'s second-class deck, bustling with activity as passengers strolled the promenade, enjoying the sunshine. Galena Lakovic was the only creature in the frame who stood entirely still, her gown and wild hair flowing around her in a jet-black swirl. She stood in the middle of the crowd, staring down the camera like it had a soul. As if the dark pools of her eyes weren't disturbing enough, a ghostly shadow hovered along the deck railing just above her head. It had no visible face, but the form almost seemed human. I held the photograph with a trembling hand, pulling my shawl around my shoulders.

"Father Browne, this will seem an odd request... but may I have this photograph?"

The priest frowned. "Well, I suppose—"

"You see, I'm an aspiring photographer myself," I explained. "I'd like to study what you've done here to achieve such an interesting effect."

With a hearty laugh, the Jesuit gave his box camera an affectionate pat. "It certainly wasn't due to any skill on my part. This old Brownie has been a faithful friend, but I'm eagerly awaiting the release of the new 35-millimeter cameras. Multiple exposures like this should be a thing of the past."

"Of course," I murmured, unable to tear my eyes from the image. This spectral shadow felt like a sign. A sign Mrs. Lakovic was not a person who should be crossed.

Yet…my mother. I had no choice but to continue watching the woman if I wanted the chance to see my mother well again. I tucked the photograph between the pages of Gibran to give to Lieutenant Plavsic at our next meeting. He had asked me to report on anything unusual, and this picture was as strange as it got.

"The image is of no use to me, so I don't see any reason why you shouldn't have it." With a friendly wink, Father Browne added, "Besides, we need more photographers who can tap into the feminine genius."

"Thank you. Really, I—"

"Forgive me for rushing off, but I'm due to disembark the ship in Queenstown."

"So soon? You're headed home to Ireland then?"

"Afraid so. I'd hoped to travel on to New York to photograph those marvelous skyscrapers, but when I asked my superiors in Cork for permission, their telegram response was rather unambiguous: GET. *Stop*. OFF. *Stop*. THAT. *Stop*. SHIP. *Stop*." Father Browne chuckled lightheartedly, which left me perplexed. "It seems our will is not always God's will."

A sentiment I could hardly understand. For why on earth would the Almighty wish to prevent this friendly priest from sailing to New York to fulfill his passion for photography?

Something told me this Jesuit could handle a bit of pushback without taking offense. "What about forging your own destiny?"

He chuckled again. "As if we'll ever have such power. No, Lady Ava, I believe the divine lives in the details of the present moment. It's the past and future we have to worry about, for that's where the devil aims to turn our attention and whisper his lies." Still smiling despite his odd words, Father Browne gathered up his camera supplies. "Oh, one more thing. You might try searching for your friend in the mail room. I photographed it the other day—marvelous spot, outfitted with all the latest technology. That seemed to be the direction she was heading. To mail her letter before *Titanic*'s final stop, I imagine."

I stared at him, then nodded slowly. "Thank you, Father. I shall go have a look right now."

With that, I bid farewell to the Jesuit photographer. As I made my way toward G Deck, the same sensation I'd experienced earlier returned—this vulnerable chill that made me feel as if I stood on *Titanic*'s deck in my sheerest nightgown.

If this woman was truly dangerous, was I a fool to be following her?

"Why, Seaman Donohue," I sputtered as I stepped into the mailroom's sorting area. "Good afternoon."

The sailor froze like an animal caught in the crosshairs, a stack of letters in one hand. "I, uh, good afternoon, Lady Ava. I, well, you see… I'm just helping out a friend."

"Yes, I can see that."

A second young crewman lay in a mail cart on wheels, partially buried by sacks of postcards and parcels. Caleb looked at the crewman, then back at me.

"And just what kind of trouble are you up to?" I asked, amused by the ridiculous sight. "Do we have a stowaway?"

The man half-buried by packages shot up from his hiding spot. "It was my idea, miss. Donohue here was simply kind enough to do a pal a favor, I swear it. The name's John Coffey. I was a coal stoker on the RMS *Olympic*."

That explained the man's filthy attire. I cleared my throat. "*Was?*"

"That's right, miss. The *Olympic* returned home to England a week ago, where I received word that my mother, who lives right here in Queenstown, had fallen ill. On death's doorstep, see? Now when I first signed up for service, the White Star Line promised me paid leave and a return trip home in between every voyage, but once we reached Southampton, the boss said I was being shipped out straight away on *Titanic* and there wasn't a thing I could do about it."

"So, you're jumping ship when we anchor in order to visit your dying mother."

"That's it, miss. That's it exactly."

Poor man. His situation was indeed criminal… on the part of the White Star Line. Yet something about the way Coffey's eyes flitted anxiously toward the mailroom entrance told me there was more to this story. "I don't mean to pry, Mr. Coffey, but you seem to be in a state of distress. Is there something else bothering you?"

"Well, you see, I've got this awful feeling. About the voyage, I mean. All thanks to *that* woman." The stoker pointed behind me, as if a ghost stood in the entryway. I turned to look, but there was no one there. "Said we were doomed. Kept repeating it over and over, as if the devil himself had her tongue."

"You speak of," I removed the photograph from my book, "this woman here?"

"That's her all right." The stoker shuddered. "Darkest eyes I ever saw."

"The woman interrupted Coffey's escape a few minutes before you arrived," Seaman Donohue explained. His calm manner suggested he was not nearly as disturbed by Mrs. Lakovic's ominous prediction as his superstitious friend here.

"And what did she want?" I asked.

"Said she needed to send an urgent message. When I told her the mail clerks were on break and would be back on the hour, she tossed her letter onto this stack and stormed off in a huff."

My pulse quickened. I'd only just missed her, but Galena Lakovic had left behind another piece of valuable evidence. Perhaps I was cut out for this spy business after all.

"Please don't report us to the captain, miss," Coffey begged. "I've got to see me ma and say my goodbyes before it's too late. You can understand that, can't you?"

Of course I understood. Coffey was abandoning his post, but only because his employers had broken their promise first. Reporting him was the furthest thing from my mind.

"I know what it is to be bound by the higher authority of one's mother." I smiled, putting an end to the stoker's misery. "Your secret is safe with me."

John Coffey beamed. "Oh, thank you, miss!"

"On one condition."

My eyes found Caleb Donohue, who studied me closely.

Despite the chill in the mailroom, warmth rushed to my face. I looked away, focusing on the envelope Mrs. Lakovic had left behind. As I picked it up, I read the intended recipient: a Dr. Frederick Bligh Bond in London. The name was familiar, but I couldn't place it.

The letter grew heavy in my hands. I'd vowed to keep Coffey's secret, but could I trust these young men to keep mine? Stealing someone's mail was a serious offense, yet I needed to assure Lieutenant Plavsic that I was holding up my end of the bargain.

I looked from one man to the other. "I must take this letter. And I'd appreciate your discretion—"

"Not a problem," both crewmen blurted. I could have asked for the keys to Captain James Smith's private cabin and these sailors would have likely obliged me.

With a nod, I tucked the document beneath my shawl and left them to the execution of their escape plan. Out on the deck upstairs, I opened the envelope, guilt creeping up my neck with every tear of the thick paper.

Dear Frederick,

I believe we've finally lost him. When we last saw you in Glastonbury, I worried the man had learned of our booked passage across the Atlantic, but now I suspect I was being overly anxious. And yet all is not well on Titanic.

It happened again, Frederick. Not nearly as vividly as our sessions at the abbey, but the premonition was unmistakable. This voyage will end in disaster. There is someone on this ship who seeks to do us harm—do me *harm—as I have experienced in the past, only this time the presence was unmistakably feminine.*

Yet what other choice do I have? Our evidence must make it to New York. I send you this final letter, so you'll know what to think if I do not make it off this ship alive.

G.L.

The wind fluttered the stationary paper as I folded it, though I was tempted to throw the letter over the guardrail and into the sea.

A feminine presence.

How did Galena know I followed her? What was the evidence she carried to New York? More importantly, how was I supposed to get close to a woman who was already expecting me?

9

TAYLOR

A "feminine presence" is the perfect way to describe what I feel on the walk from the pub back to Meadowbrook. It's as if someone is peering out from the tree line as soon as I cross onto the manor's grounds. Not in a threatening way, or even a creepy way—she's simply watching, the way a mother resting in a lawn chair might glance up at her small child at play in the yard every now and then.

It makes me wonder if there's some truth to the bartender's story about Meadowbrook being a place where a person's essence remains trapped. Some things, some people, are like that— they endure.

Meadowbrook has certainly stood the test of time. According to old Bill, the house has seen its share of turmoil, and yet it survives. Beyond the wooden bridge, the manor rises like a disciplined soldier, enclosed by an army of chaotic turrets and peaks. Its shadow is muted by the gathering blueberry storm clouds, and tangled vines crawl along the walls of speckled stone, giving the house a wild feel that doesn't go with the immaculately groomed grounds.

As I pick up my pace to cross the river bordering the estate, the roar beneath the bridge is unsettling. The river seems high, though that's probably not unusual for England in the spring. The extra rain also explains the overflowing rosebushes that line the gravel path—rosebushes with flowers as bright as splatters of pink and yellow paint. I'm nearly to the gravel drive when the sky sends down marble-sized raindrops that sting when they land. I sprint to Meadowbrook's front door, which greets me with a low creak.

"There you are." Nathaniel's voice is hoarse… but with grief or anger? His face is serious. "We need to talk. In private."

I don't think there's anyone one else in this house but Giles, so I don't get why Nathaniel's concerned about privacy. Unless it's Giles he wants to avoid.

"Lead the way." I pause to point out the dour couple staring down on us from the oil paintings above the staircase. "But first you've got to tell me more about these two rays of sunshine."

"That would be the first Lord and Lady Knight of Meadowbrook, the couple who built this manor on the site of an abandoned church following Henry VIII's Dissolution of the Monasteries." Nathaniel's tone has all the authority of a museum curator as he rattles off a few more historical tidbits. By the time we're halfway down the hall, my attention has drifted from the words to the person delivering them.

The guy has the complexion of a scholar who rarely leaves the library, but also, I notice as he gestures at several pictures, broad shoulders, which suggests he's an athlete. When Nathaniel catches me staring, I quickly turn to the photos, feigning interest.

It only takes a moment for my interest to become genuine. Old-fashioned portraits and framed photographs cover the wall's forest green paper in no apparent order. It's a random collection, one that reminds me of the rambling branches of a family tree.

My gaze falls to a photo of a dark-haired young woman. She sits in an ornate room filled with plush, antique furniture, an open book resting in her lap. The lighting is perfect, extra impressive since this photo was taken decades before Photoshop.

My stomach flips. I've seen this image before. Not *seen it* seen it—rather, I conjured it up through the spell of Ava's words and the power of my imagination.

"It's her."

Nathaniel turns around. "Who?"

I pull the red book from my purse, almost in a trance. "*Her*. Ava Knight." The memoir's voice perfectly matches the proud and fiercely pretty face staring back at me from *Titanic*'s writing room.

Nathaniel frowns. "How'd you get that?"

I guess it's confession time. Nathaniel is the only person who seems to know that Lady Knight invited me here with the intention of telling me a good story, so he's my only potential ally.

"I, uh… I found it in Lady Knight's bedroom," I mutter, quickly adding, "Do you think this is what she intended to share with me over tea? Her letter kept mentioning the past."

"Mae said she planned on giving you that book of family history, but I wasn't sure if she'd actually do it. Or why." A strange expression overtakes Nathaniel's face. "All right, we *really* need to talk."

The chaotic hallway of photographs leads to a large room with stone walls and a cathedral ceiling held up by thick wooden beams. An antique fainting couch with navy blue upholstery, along with a pair of oversized armchairs, sit before a fireplace so large, I'm certain I could stand inside it without slouching. Books make up for the stark lack of other furniture in the open, chapel-like room, their cracked spines lining the walls from floor to ceiling, filling the spaces between the Gothic windows. The room reminds me of an old church—ceremonially stiff, but serene all the same.

"We're now in the oldest part of the manor," Nathaniel explains. "This was the first Lady Knight's personal chapel back in the 1500s."

"How do you know so much about this house from a part-time driving gig?" I ask, genuinely curious.

Nathaniel grins. "I'm a History major. Why do you think I jumped at the driver job? To be honest, the Knight family and their unusual past has become a bit of an obsession."

Perfect. Maybe Nathaniel can help me figure out what exactly Lady Knight wanted me to learn about them and what it has to do with my dad.

"This old chapel makes for one incredible library." I flop down in an armchair, kicking up the scent of old leather and cigar smoke. A white bust of Shakespeare sits on the fireplace mantel, which makes me think of Dalia. The girl would freak out over a library like this. I'm guessing that's a bust of Chaucer hanging out beside The Bard, but I could be wrong. Dead English poets start to look alike after a while.

Nathaniel takes a seat across from me with a bit more finesse. The guy is formal to the point of being uptight, as if we're meeting to discuss legal documents or dental records. Part of me wants to shatter the ice by asking him how he's taking Lady Knight's death, but Nathaniel seems more like the stiff upper lip type.

His eyes scan the rows and rows of old tomes. "Mae was an avid reader, as you can see. I bet she made it through most of these books. She certainly had enough years to do it."

"I'm s-sorry you lost her so suddenly," I stammer, knowing from experience that forced platitudes are the worst. "In the car she seemed so… lively."

"That's Mae for you." Sadness fills Nathaniel's eyes, but a smile traces his lips. "She'd just celebrated her one-hundredth birthday, but her enthusiasm for life was as large as ever. Giles and I used to joke that we would both die long before she did."

"Really? I can't imagine that man joking about *anything*." Rumbling outside draws me to a nearby window. Now the sky is nearly black. The room's already heavy atmosphere intensifies as I pick up on the presence again. The presence from the gravel path. It's somehow followed me into the library.

The thunder seems to awaken Nathaniel to his task. "Let's cut to the chase. Why are you here?"

I spin to face him in surprise. "You and Lady Knight *invited* me here, remember?"

"Yes, and I get that she wanted to share her family history, but I still don't understand why *you*." Nathaniel's frown suggests he thinks that if Lady Knight was going to share that history with anyone, it should have been him, given his field of study. "But Mae always did keep her cards close to the chest. Are you sure she didn't tell you anything else?"

"I didn't even know who Mae Knight was before you tracked me down yesterday! Just what kind of information are you after?"

Nathaniel presses his lips together, takes a deep breath, then forces the words out. Almost like he's worried he'll regret what he's about to say. "A few days a week, I drove Mae into the village to pick up her mail at the post office, and if it was extra dreary, to the pub for an afternoon hot toddy. Most of the mail she received was junk, but lately she'd been getting letters sent on the same stationary. Lady Knight never told me who they were from but based on how she looked as she read them, they upset her. A lot. She seemed… well, honestly she seemed terrified."

Nathaniel stares at me. Hard. "Tell me the truth. Were the letters from you? Is that why she was looking for you in Oxford?"

I cross my arms and return his look. "For the last time, I didn't know Meadowbrook or any of you people even *existed* until you stopped me on the street. How am I supposed to know why she wanted to see me?"

"And yet she dies before we have the chance to find out," Nathaniel says, voice an octave lower.

"Do you think something sketchy is going on?" To be honest, it would be a huge relief if he does. Because that would mean I'm not crazy for having my own suspicions.

"Not necessarily. The woman lived an entire century, so there's no reason to assume she died of anything other than natural causes."

I pick up on his uncertainty. "But…"

"*But* it does seem a tad coincidental, doesn't it? You show up out of nowhere and Mae checks out. For good."

I nod slowly, processing his words— "Wait, you think *I* contributed to her death somehow?"

"I don't know what to think. I just know something doesn't feel right." Nathaniel walks over to the row of windows, where lightning streaks across the blue-black sky. He sighs deeply. "There go all of Mae's flowers."

We fall silent as the hard rain pounds the old woman's roses into a pulp. When Nathaniel finally looks up at me, his expression is as bleak as the view.

"Don't worry, Taylor. I don't suspect you of murder. But I do suspect you know more than you're letting on."

Funny, I feel the same way.

He stares out the window for a few tense seconds. "Right. It's getting late. We'd better get you back to Oxford."

"How fast are you willing to drive?" Orientation is probably over, and the thought of angry clipboard lady going berserk when she discovers I'm missing is all the motivation I need to get moving. I head for the exit.

Nathaniel follows me toward the foyer. "Taylor, wait a sec. There's something else I want to ask you—"

Before he can finish his thought, Giles cuts us off by the staircase. "Ah, Miss Romano. Afraid I have some bad news. A flash flood has taken out a large section of the bridge. We won't be able to take the car across the river until repairs can be made."

I hear the words, but I can't absorb their consequences. I just gape at him like a fish floundering on land.

Giles smiles thinly. "You'll have to stay here until the storm has passed and we can get repairmen to come. Based on the weather forecast, it may be overnight. In case of that, I've seen a guest room prepared for you. Nathaniel, it's the Primrose Suite. Would you kindly show our guest the way?" With his usual briskness, the butler turns on his heel and struts back down the hall.

My palms go slick as my pulse picks up. When we first arrived, Nathaniel and Giles kept looking at me like I was a criminal they needed to be rid of, and now, all of a sudden, they want me to stay overnight in this increasingly creepy house. I can't read them or this bizarre situation, and it's just the kind of thing that would ignite a major panic attack. It's time to get out of here.

"Sorry, there's no way I'm staying overnight." I grab my rain jacket from the coat rack. "I need to get across that river now."

"Relax, I'll go assess the damage." Nathaniel speaks slowly and calmly, as if to an upset child, which only increases my panicked feelings of being trapped. "Sometimes Giles can overreact, if you can imagine that. Sit tight and I'll let you know the status."

My eyes bore into Nathaniel's back as he heads into the storm, though his nonchalant stride is the last thing I'm studying. He seems like a nice enough guy on the surface, but how do I know he's trustworthy?

I guess I don't. There's no one here who seems consistent enough to trust, which is why I need to see Meadowbrook in a rearview mirror ASAP.

But you haven't finished our story yet.

The invisible woman's presence fills the foyer, making my skin tingle like someone just lit a crackling fire. Only instead of pushing my anxiety past its tipping point, my breathing slows, as if someone has wrapped a blanket of calm around my shoulders. Giving in to the surge of warm relief with a sigh, I take a seat on the stairs and open the book.

AVA

The following morning, I raced to the deck to fill an entire roll of film with the dawn. Yet my heart sank as I lowered the camera, for not even my faithful Brownie could do justice to the sky's swirling hues.

And this is why I prefer portraits over landscapes.

It was far easier to capture a person's soul in shades of grey, whereas nature demanded the full spectrum of color.

At least the ship was peaceful this early in the morning. *Titanic*'s deck felt strong as solid ground beneath my feet, a surface made to match my resolve. I'd awoken with the unwavering sense I was sailing toward my destiny. Once Gertrude Käsebier saw my photographs, she'd surely agree to mentor me. Based on the interview I'd read in *The New York Times*, Käsebier was an enthusiastic supporter of women pursuing photography. If she could not sympathize with my artistic ambitions, then no one could.

What I failed to understand was why *this* was not the dream I'd shared with the one-eyed soldier. Mother's mental health meant the world to me of course, but I never thought that when given one wish, my response would be so… altruistic. The thought of studying with Gertrude Käsebier had consumed my every waking moment, yet it seemed I wanted something else even more.

My mother back.

I returned my lens to the infinite ocean, its solitude hugging my body like a shawl that shielded me from the morning chill. My eyes focused on the sherbet horizon—a fiery line that remained as out of reach as it had always been, untouched by the tycoons who'd subdued both the earth and sea. At the thought of such power, the Serbian soldier's handsome face pushed its way into my mind.

Though I felt foolish for agreeing to his request, I was glad for the distraction. *Titanic* may have been the greatest ocean liner in the world, but I was bored already. The Turkish baths were agreeable enough. So were the strolls on deck with Father. Yet these pleasures grew dull, as pleasures always did. I needed to *do* something. To *create* something that mattered.

And I held the means in my hands.

My photographs *must* earn the admiration of Gertrude Käsebier. To study with serious artists, to be taken seriously myself— this was my only way out. If I failed, it was right back to England, where Father would marry me off to some tedious bore as soon as possible, lest I end up an old maid. And I was only seventeen for heaven's sake, not some withered flower of twenty-seven!

This camera was my passport to a far more interesting life. My world widened through its lens, whereas my existence back at Meadowbrook seemed to grow smaller with each passing year. Photography was my sole sanctuary, the only time I felt right in my own skin, the only place I was truly at home. Mother, a decent painter once upon a time, called such experiences *timeless moments*—flashes of imagination that gave all artists their insight. These intuitive bursts weren't *new* creations, but remembered truths brought forth from the realm of muses. The artist's job was to uncover the living fossil, molding it anew in the fresh plaster of one's own time and place.

Art is our foretaste of eternity, Ava dear.

This favorite saying of Mother's brought a smile to my lips. It was hard to believe how wise she'd been, how spirited, how unabashedly Irish. As I breathed in gulps of cold, salt-laced air, it felt as if her shadow lingered over me.

Keep searching, my darling. Do not let them turn you into me.

I obeyed her command. Through my camera's viewfinder, I searched for my timeless moment, steaming toward it with all the power of *Titanic* at my back.

With a few final adjustments, I steadied my hand for the shot, only to see a dark form glide into the tranquil scene.

The woman leaned against the ship's railing on the deck below. It was a bit annoying how she'd pushed into my photograph, but the more I studied her, the more intriguing she became. Likely in her late fifties, she possessed the handsome profile and slim figure of a woman half her age. Her youthful style of dress—a straight, high-waisted silhouette of pale blue satin and chiffon, with a champagne sash tied below the breast—added to the ageless illusion. From her hands, a wide-brimmed hat dangled over the railing, as if she were tempted to release it to the breeze and see how far it might fly.

I knew this woman. Mrs. Helen Crawford was an American author who'd caused quite a stir when she divorced her upper-crust husband, in spite of the rumors of his frequent abuse. To everyone's astonishment, Mrs. Crawford had gone on to earn a good income, supporting herself through her lucrative career as an ex-patriot and travel writer. Based on the attention she'd received at dinner last night, the bold lady had managed to earn the respect of the first-class passengers—the men especially, which I imagined had much to do with her enduring attractiveness and witty charm.

Yes, this was simply perfect. I could already envision Gertrude Käsebier admiring my portrait of such an independent woman planning her destiny as she peered out across a sea of possibility.

"Is Mrs. Crawford aware you're immortalizing her forever on the bow of *Titanic*?"

The unexpected voice made my finger press the shutter lever a second too soon. "Bollocks! And that was the end of the film strip!" Whirling around, I met the wide-eyed stare of Seaman Donohue.

I nearly cursed again—a bad habit he had a knack for igniting. Why did this sailor keep showing up at every turn, bringing the unsteadying effect he had on my hands with him?

"Sorry about that, Lady Ava. I didn't mean to disturb you."

"Well, you have, Mr. Donohue."

"Please, call me Caleb. My father is Mr. Donohue."

"Regardless of your name, you may have cost me an award-winning shot."

Helen Crawford glanced over her shoulder, aware she was not alone. After refitting the massive boater hat over her chestnut curls, she resumed her morning stroll.

"Splendid," I huffed. "Now she's leaving!"

"I've an idea. Why not take a picture of her strolling the deck with the hat *on*?" Caleb said, as if that would not result in the most pedestrian photograph imaginable. "I always figured those giant bonnets would come in handy for something, though my guess was they'd be used as floatation devices for the pint-sized dogs you first-class women seem to cart around like children."

I pressed a hand to my mouth to stifle my laughter. Father despised those poor little dogs with an unwarranted zeal. "It *is* rather pathetic, isn't it? Soon they'll be carting them around in specialty-made handbags."

"I don't doubt it." Caleb smiled in a manner that held nothing back. His grin deepened further when he noticed *The Broken Wings* on the lounge chair beside me.

"Would you look at that? I did not take you for a tragic romantic, Lady Ava."

He was mocking me, surely. "And I did not take *you* for a reader."

"No? Tell me then, what do you make of Gibran's definition of love as 'the only freedom in the world because it so elevates the spirit that the laws of humanity and the phenomena of nature do not alter its course'?"

My mouth nearly dropped to the deck floor. "*You* know Khalil Gibran?"

Caleb laughed. "Even us lowly Irish like to read books on occasion. We've actually got a few poets who aren't half bad. Let's see, there's this fellow named William Butler Yeats. And I keep hearing about some upstart called Joyce…"

I rolled my eyes. "Yes, yes, I understand. Your people practically invented storytelling."

What this sailor must have thought of me. Surely, he saw me as nothing but a pampered aristocrat, putting on the airs of an artist though I hadn't experienced the impoverished misery so often associated with such vision. There may have been some truth to that, but I resented him for making me aware of it.

"It's been a pleasure, but I should really be going—"

"Here, let me help you with that." Caleb reached for my suitcase of camera equipment. "I'm not on duty for another twenty minutes."

I cannot explain it, but I suddenly felt the need to put this sailor in his place, to remind him that even though I was not yet free to do as I liked, I possessed a degree of power as a first-class passenger—and he would yield to it.

"Splendid. I have a tea date with Mrs. Astor in a few minutes." Dangling the room key in front of him, I added a smug, "Do be sure to lock back up."

The gibe was minor, but if my study of art had taught me anything, it was that even the smallest symbolic act could have the impact of dynamite. And my curt reminder of Caleb's station was certainly that. After all, he'd offered to carry my bag as a gentleman escort, perhaps even as a friend.

And I'd treated him as a servant.

In the end, there was no triumph in it. As Caleb's face fell and assumed an indifferent expression, my stomach twisted into knots. I understood then—as I had never before—that no matter the ticket I carried or the designer gown I wore, I was no better than anyone else.

Perhaps I was even worse.

11

AVA

As I made my way to the Café Parisian, my legs felt like two iron anchors, reminders of the shameful way I'd treated Caleb. Only as I walked through rows of empty lounge chairs did a pair of creeping eyes uncurl my spine. I glanced around the vacant deck, doubtful the mild-mannered sailor could send me such a chill.

The prickly stare came from a lone figure resting in a lounge chair, his face hidden by a newspaper and the shadow of a bowler hat. I did not need to see the man's face to know this was my commissioner, for I could feel Plavsic's calculating eye studying my movements with more heat than a jealous lover. He wished for an update. I hadn't seen Galena Lakovic since I lost track of her in the writing room the day before, but her unsent letter was secure in the novel I clutched against my chest. I opened the book to draw it out, but something had me snapping it shut again. My loyalty was not to this soldier, and I wanted to discover what he knew of this woman before I handed over my one piece of intelligence.

"It appears your prey suffers from sea sickness. She refuses to leave her stateroom," I called out over the expanse of hard-wood slats. The excuse felt weak as soon as it left my lips.

"Then try harder."

The lieutenant's deadpan reply littered my arms with goose-bumps. What if this man had no intention of helping my family? What if we were merely pawns in his game of global chess, and he'd discard us as soon as he got what he wanted?

If Plavsic was the person Galena mentioned in her corre-spondence—the man who'd been following her in England—she was obviously as frightened of him as he was of her. I prayed I hadn't made a deal with the wrong person and that an innocent, if eccentric, woman would now pay the price.

Plavsic spoke with confidence from behind his paper. "Do not let her cast her spell over you, for you would not be the first to make such a grave error in judgment."

It seemed he had read my mind. Remarkable, really, given that it was a whirlwind of confusion. Even if this Serbian soldier was as dangerous as he seemed, taking the ravings of a mad-woman seriously did not make much sense either.

Meeting his eyes, one lifeless and one glittering, I felt cer-tain that Plavsic's loyalty to his nationalist cause would never waver, though his favor toward *me* could alter in a moment's no-tice. Even pawns were expected to be obedient, and if I failed to give him what he wanted, he'd not let go of me without inflicting harm.

Try harder. Plavsic's cold words echoed in my head. Two little words uttered in a tone that revealed so much. The unwa-vering command of a man who saw a world as black-and-white as my photographs, a man who'd do anything to achieve his pur-poses.

Perhaps even kill for them.

I should have recognized all this from the moment we first spoke, of course, but I had fallen prey to the heart's great weakness: We typically see in other people what we want to see, which is often what will most benefit *us*. My best option to protect both myself and anyone else Plavsic might make a victim was to pretend I was getting close to uncovering the secret information Galena Lakovic carried to New York.

"Not to worry, Lieutenant. I shall have more to report by this evening. I'm sure of it." The false cheerfulness cracked my voice like a dropped teacup. "Enjoy your morning."

As the stiff soldier rose from his chair, he tipped his hat and turned away—frigid movements that left me cold.

Yes, I had been sufficiently warned.

But what kind of devil had I bargained with?

"Ava, how wonderful to see you."

Madeleine Astor, the richest woman on *Titanic* at the ripe age of eighteen, gave me a sham of a smile as I approached her table in the Café Parisian. I wondered if her cream-puff skin was always this radiant, or if the pregnancy glow women often speak of was her true beauty secret. So far, Madeleine wasn't advertising this detail. No doubt the chatter surrounding her recent marriage to American millionaire John Jacob Astor—a divorced man thirty years her senior—was enough gossip for one season. No need to add a babe conceived before the wedding into the mix. Unfortunately for Mrs. Astor, no amount of fluffy taffeta or flowing silk could hide the little bump protruding from her willowy frame.

"Good morning, ladies." I took my seat as gracefully as possible, though I still felt chilled from the morning breeze and my encounter with Lieutenant Plavsic.

"Oh Ava, I adore that dress!" Madeleine cried, turning to her companion, Mrs. Margaret Tobin Brown. "Doesn't that jade green complement her coloring nicely?"

Mrs. Brown was an outspoken miner's wife from the heart of the Rocky Mountains. She was about my mother's age but a million times sturdier. All her friends called her Maggie, which suited her much better than Margaret. Her husband's engineering efforts in the silver mines of Leadville, Colorado, had earned the Browns tremendous wealth overnight. Yet Mrs. Brown never seemed to forget that her parents had been poor Irish immigrants, like so many of the steerage passengers on this ship. The blunt woman cared little for propriety—a trait that made me adore her from the moment we'd met. I couldn't say the same about Madeleine Astor.

"Indeed, though Ava looks ravishing in *any* color." Mrs. Brown smiled as she wiped a black smudge of film ink from my cheek with her gloved thumb.

Mrs. Brown was on her way home from a tour of Europe and Egypt with the newlywed Astors. She was "new money," but at least she *did* something with her wealth, using her influence to work for women's suffrage and the welfare of neglected children. I'd heard she had campaigned for the US Senate recently and hadn't done half bad in the polls. And women in America did not even have the right to vote!

In fact, the vote was precisely what I hoped to work into our conversation over tea. Running off to become a photographer in a land that deemed women unfit for democracy could be a risk to the freedom I assumed I'd find in New York, especially when things were finally changing in Britain as the suffrage movement picked up speed. I hoped Mrs. Brown would report that the tides were turning in America, too.

Sadly, Madeleine Astor had no stomach for politics, preferring the catty chitchat that made men long to bar us from the polling booths for good. Resting her lace-gloved hand over mine, she leaned forward, her eyes aglow with the intoxication of hearsay. "Oh Ava, you will never believe what we just heard."

Madeleine's rose perfume—an indication she must be past the morning sickness phase—nearly made me choke. That the young Mrs. Astor regarded me with a phony affection was obvious, but the fact that I was one of the few first-class girls close to her in age seemed enough of a reason for Madeleine to *act* like we were bosom friends. I'd rather drink my weight in sea water, thank you very much, but I'd promised Father I'd play nice. The Astors did rule the world, after all.

Madeleine released me to turn to her companion. "Oh, you tell her, Mags. You're so much better at explaining these kinds of things."

"I don't know what you're so excited about." Mrs. Brown set her teacup down with a clank. "Back in Denver, we have psychics on every street corner, not to mention tarot card readers, apothecaries, and enough prostitutes to repopulate the earth two times over. Why, I even visited one myself back in Cairo."

Madeline and I glanced at each other with open mouths.

"A *psychic*, that is!" the older woman exclaimed with a hoot.

"And just what did your soothsayer reveal?" I asked.

"Well, first he kept saying he saw a lot of water in my future." Mrs. Brown released a dismissive snort. "A sure bet for reading the palm of an American, seeing how we have no choice but to cross the entire ocean. I should have asked for my money back right then."

Madeleine tsked. "Maggie dear, you're not getting to the good part. Would you believe it, Ava? There's a psychic here on *Titanic*!" Madeline's doe eyes made her seem so much younger, not at all like a millionaire's wife and soon-to-be mother.

I frowned, thinking of a friend of Father's I had said hello to on my way to the café. "You can't possibly mean Mr. Stead. I admit the man's interest in Spiritualism is a bit over the top, but he's a kind and most reverent man. It would not please him to be lumped in with charlatans, I assure you."

"No, of course not. William Stead is a respected journalist. The medium I speak of is," Madeleine lowered her voice to a whisper, "a woman. *And* she's in first class. Have you ever heard of such a thing? Anyway, I visited her cabin last night and she promised that my first child would be a boy. Won't John be pleased? When the time for all that comes, of course. I'd like to enjoy newlywed life for a bit before we even *think* of children, but a boy with John's light eyes followed by a girl with my complexion would be divine."

Madeleine's suggestion that babies could be ordered off a menu made my stomach sour. Mother had prayed for another child, any child, for so long. "Yes, well, from what I hear, children often arrive before we have carved out a sufficient spot for them in our plans. And at other times, they refuse to make an appearance at all."

Madeline's nervous chuckle revealed she wasn't sure if my words were meant as an insult or a joke, when really, my only intention was to inject some truth into the conversation. I had to pity the young heiress, though. The girl was so accustomed to putting on airs, she'd managed to convince herself that no one else knew of her "condition."

"So, the woman predicted a boy, huh? Well, the odds are 50/50 she's right." Mrs. Brown snorted again. "Some fortune teller."

"Then listen to this." Madeleine draped a lazy hand across her belly. "She also told me she had a most powerful vision while boarding the ship—"

"Look, there goes your medium now," Mrs. Brown cut in. "With Lord Knight, by the looks of it."

We all turned as my father stood up from a table on the other side of the café. He was indeed leaving with Galena Lakovic—

Madeleine's psychic, it seemed. The woman *I* was supposed to be watching.

But what was she doing with Father?

The perplexed faces of my companions told me they wondered the same thing. Then Madeleine's eyes widened, and she glanced at Mrs. Brown. In a futile gesture of discretion, both women lowered their gazes to tea that suddenly required a good stirring. Their flushed cheeks made me suspect this was not the first time my father had been seen frolicking around *Titanic* with an odd woman who was most certainly *not* his wife. The wandering eyes and whispers around the café only seemed to confirm this libel.

Father's scandalous behavior was enough of a social blunder that I should have been humiliated, but instead, I was furious. But like all well-bred girls, I hid it well.

"Ah yes, Mrs. Lakovic," I said with a wave of my hand. "Father offered her some assistance after she experienced a most unfortunate panic attack. Poor woman. She must be terrified of the open water."

"Yes, of course." Mrs. Brown's generous smile proved she was the least pompous person on this ship. "Your father is a compassionate man."

Madeleine was not so gracious. "You should warn your father about spending too much time with such a strange creature, or people will start to talk. I honestly don't know how she ended up in first class. And *where* is her husband, hmm? When I met with her the other night, in secret of course, the woman's English was absolutely dreadful." She sipped her tea to hide her slow smirk. "But if Lord Knight was aiding her mental health, perhaps Mrs. Lakovic is simply in need of *additional* treatments."

Well. Apparently when a person was the center of high society gossip for as long as Madeline Astor, it was a relief to find other victims of merciless slander. But I was not one to sit by and let this snob turn my father into her convenient scapegoat.

"You'll have to excuse me, ladies." Rising from my chair, I tossed my napkin onto the table. "It's growing a bit stale in here, so I think I'll take in some fresh air. Do be sure to get some rest, Maddie dear… that baby boy needs it."

Madeleine dropped her teaspoon with a loud clank. Under different circumstances, I'd never expose her secret—even if everyone knew it already—but I was sick of the show, weary of the pretense. Especially since my recent encounter with Mr. Donohue had revealed I was part of the problem.

Well, no more.

From now on, the one trait I'd demand of any person I associated with was honesty.

And this café was filled with gossiping liars.

My father had his quirks, yes, but he was not the man their denouncing eyes accused him of being, and I would prove it. Storming out of the café, I trailed Father and Mrs. Lakovic at a distance, ducking into doorways whenever they glanced back. Father was leading the woman to the staterooms below deck, which meant he'd once again offered Mrs. Lakovic the gentlemanly courtesy of escorting her back to her cabin. Yet that didn't explain what had reunited them over tea in the first place. He must know how such a thing *looked*—a married man dining with a young mother whose husband, if she even had one, was nowhere to be found. And not only that, but a woman who was apparently a fortune teller—a scandal in itself to the respectable people in first class.

When Father and Mrs. Lakovic reached her stateroom, I crouched behind a laundry cart parked in the hallway and waited for him to say his goodbyes. My silent stalking had turned out even better than I'd hoped—now that I knew the location of her room, I could return later to siphon more information out of the woman. I did not trust the Serbian soldier, but it couldn't hurt to have options.

Not to mention leverage.

"Do be sure to get some rest, my dear. I'm sure your maid won't mind looking after the children a while longer if you need to lie down." Father scanned the hallway behind him before leaning forward to peck Mrs. Lakovic on the cheek—a kiss *much* too close to the corner of her mouth.

My sweaty palms clenched the stack of starched sheets I was hiding behind. What in the world was he doing? Father had had cordial relationships with his patients before, but that was no excuse for such a level of intimacy with a woman who was not his wife!

Worst of all, Mrs. Lakovic did not seem shocked by Father's behavior. In fact, she returned this inappropriate gesture with an affectionate stroke of his cheek. "Why don't you come inside and lie down, Jonathan? Annabelle can take the children outside for a stroll in the buggy."

Oh no Anabelle won't!

It took all my resolve to resist pulling a broom from the cleaning cart to show this jezebel what a deranged woman truly looked like! Biting down until I tasted copper, I fought the urge to heave the watercress sandwich from tea all over the stack of white towels.

Father glanced down the corridor once more, his eyes glistening like a naughty schoolboy about to steal licorice from the candy shop. With a resigned sigh, he slipped inside the wanton woman's room.

I ducked out of sight seconds before Mrs. Lakovic's black eyes grazed the laundry cart. She closed the stateroom door. The woman hadn't seen me, but I'd seen her. Mrs. Lakovic was not insane. She knew *exactly* what she was doing. And she would pay.

I would see to that.

TAYLOR

I slam the book shut in surprise as a floorboard creaks down the hall.

"Nathaniel?"

No answer.

"Giles?"

Nothing but the echo of my own voice.

I shiver, then trace the worn spine of the red volume. I'm not in the mood to read anymore. Apparently when Ava wrote *my father was not the man I thought,* what she really meant was *my father was unfaithful pond scum.* Is that the "shared story" Lady Knight meant to tell me by leaving behind this book? If it is, I'm not sure I want to hear it.

I return to the wall of photographs, stopping in front of a large filigree frame. The brass sconce above it flickers, casting a warm glow over the faces in the family portrait. A tall, stoic man stands on Meadowbrook's front lawn, dressed in a solid military uniform. Beside him, a slender young woman rests her hand on his arm. The straw hat covering the girl's dark hair casts a shadow that obscures her face, but the protective way she grips the shoulders of the child in front of her makes me think she's a mother. A young mother. Her little girl reminds me of Shirley Temple in the old movies I watched with my babysitter. The child has curls so fair, they almost look white because of the photograph's sepia toning. I peer into the younger girl's face.

I knew it. I've seen that playful glint before.

"Mae," I whisper.

"Unmistakable little imp, isn't she?"

I whirl around, swinging arms almost socking Nathaniel in the face. "Don't sneak up on me like that!"

Nathaniel doesn't even flinch. Beads of water stick to his dark lashes and drip down his freckled cheeks. His drenched button-down shirt sticks to the lean muscle beneath.

Yep, he's definitely a rower.

"Sorry I scared you." Nathaniel's half grin translates the sentiment to *sorry-not sorry*. "I figured you'd hear me coming, what with the squishy sneakers and all."

I look down at the puddle of water at his feet. How hadn't I heard him? I swear, every time I stop to look at old photographs, it's like they suck me into another dimension.

Nathaniel nods at the portrait. "Kind of eerie, huh? This was taken right at the start of World War I. That's Jonathan Knight on the left—poor man was killed in France not long after. I'm not sure what happened to the girls' mother… Mae never talked about her much."

"That isn't Mae's mom?" I point to the dark-haired girl, her identity hitting me all at once. "You mean Mae and Ava were *sisters*?"

Nathaniel looks at me like this is obvious. "Mae often said Ava felt more like a mother than a sister, seeing how she practically raised her after Lord Knight was killed in France."

I study the man's stern face. It's hard to imagine that someone so uptight could be such a playboy, but that's what Ava's memoir implies. "He doesn't look like the most involved father to begin with."

"Yes, based on the stories Mae shared, Jonathan Knight was a rather odd duck. All the Knights were eccentric, but her father more than most."

"How so?" I jump at the flash of lightning followed immediately by a crack of thunder. The storm is right on top of us.

"He was a member of the Society for Psychical Research, or SPR, this bizarre group of scientists who blended psychology with paranormal investigation. The man was obsessed with the idea that the living could communicate with the dead."

Sadly, I'm familiar with the temptation. During Dad's deployments, my mom visited her fair share of tarot card-loving swindlers. I can't count how many knick-knack cluttered waiting rooms I sat in after school while Mom got her palm read by some quack. Every single one told us the same thing:

Dad would be safe. Dad would come home.

Exactly what we wanted to hear.

"So, Lord Knight liked hanging out with psychic weirdos on a regular basis, not just on *Titanic*," I mutter to myself.

"Wait, what? Lord Knight was *on* the *Titanic*?"

I look at Nathaniel in surprise. "So was Ava." I hold up the book. "You didn't know? That's pretty much what this entire thing is about."

Nathaniel runs a hand through his wet hair. "I don't understand. Why wouldn't Mae mention something so historically significant?"

Once again, Nathaniel seems to take it as a personal slight that Lady Knight didn't share this information with him, the budding historian. Despite his disappointment that he hadn't been privy to this major part of Mae's past, I'm tired of dancing around the issue that brought me here.

"Her reasons for keeping it a secret don't matter. I'm done playing games. If Lady Knight had something important to tell me, she should have done so in Oxford when she had the chance." I nod at the door. "What's the status of the bridge? I really need to get back to campus."

When Nathaniel doesn't answer fast enough, I walk past him toward the exit, but he grabs my arm. "I hate to tell you this, Taylor, but you can't leave."

"Watch me." I pull back, but Nathaniel tightens his grip. Looks like I won't be counting on him to help me out after all. "I'm leaving. *Let. Go.*"

The feeling of being trapped descends again and I give one more hard pull at my arm, breath coming faster. Nathaniel relaxes his grip, and I stumble forward. "I'm sorry, Taylor, but it's dangerous out there."

"I get the feeling it's more dangerous in here." The seriousness of this situation is hitting me—I've got no phone, and no one knows I'm trapped in a haunted mansion where a woman just died, not even Dalia, who thinks I skipped orientation to take a joy ride with a cute British boy. On top of all that, the bedroom scene suggests Lady Knight's death may not have been as natural as everyone is claiming. Do Giles and Nathaniel really think I'll just happily spend the night here?

I speed-walk to the foyer, where I open my purse and remove the plastic bag that had been filled with homemade trail mix for my long flight. After popping the last few M&Ms into my mouth, I seal Ava's book inside. Mae's final letter made it clear I was meant to read it, and I intend to, stolen property or not.

"Giles was right." Nathaniel's voice calls after me. "The bridge is completely flooded. There's no way we'll be able get a car over it tonight."

"Then I'll find another way."

I can always wade across the river in my wellies and pick up the footpath on the other side. There's got to be a bus stop somewhere in the village. If not, Bill the bartender can call me a cab.

When I fling open the door, I meet a torrential downpour that suggests the end is near, and I may need an ark instead of a cab. Every tree on the property is reeling in a frantic dance to the primal rhythm of thunder. The white gravel path gleams an eerie blue-green whenever a bolt of lightning streaks across the sky. Which is often.

"You're bloody nuts, you know that?" Nathaniel shouts behind me.

Yes, why leave now? We want you to stay a while longer.

I glare at the portrait in the foyer. I'll admit I have an active imagination, but even I don't normally hear whispers inside my head. All the warnings and stories I heard in the pub swirl in the torrent of wind and rain in front of me. The logical thing to do would be to wait a few hours to see if the storm passes, but every intuitive cell in my gut is shouting, *Don't wait! Get out now while you still can.*

I sprint into the storm.

The wind pushes my body back toward the manor, nearly knocking me off my feet. I fight against it with all my weight, digging my toes into the gravel, building momentum with each step. The pounding rain stings my cheeks as I trudge down a path littered with rose petals—like the aisle of some bride's nightmare wedding.

Splashing behind me indicates Nathaniel is hot on my tail, but there's no going back. My need to know the truth about my father is strong, but I'm not convinced this place has any answers, and my survival instincts are on red alert.

Breath coming in rapid gasps, I'm soaked and exhausted when I reach the edge of the property. The river has turned into rapids, foaming white where it eats at the banks. Giles and Nathaniel were right—the bridge is useless. As I watch, the current snaps a board from the structure, whirling it downstream.

It doesn't look that deep.
I'm a strong swimmer.
I can make it.

The things you tell yourself when a preternatural fear has dug its fangs into the back of your neck. All I know is I'll take the *natural* danger offered by a rushing river over a mansion that traps the souls of the dead within its walls.

"Don't do it, Taylor. It's worse than it looks!"

I ignore his warning. Staying here is unthinkable. Every stiff muscle in my body is telling me to get away from this house… *and* the people who care for it.

You've got this. You were a lifeguard, remember?
Yeah, a lifeguard about to do something stupid.

I silence my two minds by running further upstream, away from the bridge, where the river seems a little calmer. The distance to the other bank is only a few steps. I take a decisive step into the water. Frigid waves pour over the top of my wellies as a thousand tiny needles stab my calves. I bite the inside of my cheek, holding my purse high above my head as I press on, battling both wind and water to stay upright. Soon the river is up to my knees, then my hips. My teeth won't stop chattering.

"Watch the current," Nathaniel calls in a resigned tone from the shore.

As if summoned by his comment, the water slams against me with even more force than the wind. I've got to keep my footing—no easy task since my waterlogged wellies now weigh a ton. I fix my eyes on the pair of willow trees across the river, their droopy leaves flailing like a wild banshee's hair. Beyond the trees, I see a low iron fence surrounding a row of moss-covered stones.

Headstones. Silent witnesses waiting to welcome me. The spectral presence I felt earlier when walking to the pub returns in full force. I wouldn't be surprised if a woman in a white nightgown was to walk out from the willow trees, the culmination of this Gothic nightmare, but as the water surges above my waist, my attention is brought forcefully back to the task at hand. Each step is heavier than the last.

Almost there. Almost there.

I lurch forward... but my foot falls past where the ground should be and I stumble. The slate-gray sky disappears as water fills my ears, pushing its way into my mouth. Icy pins slash at my throat. My legs flail, trying to regain my footing, but the current lifts my body and I'm carried downstream by a force much stronger than my will. Nathaniel's muffled shouts flow in and out, lost in the fury of the waves. I cling to his voice. With all my remaining strength, I kick until my head breaks through the water's surface.

"Nathan—"

More water.

So much water.

So, so cold.

Each time I come up for air, the bridge is closer, jagged wooden edges waiting like skewers. I sputter out a scream, but Nathaniel's voice sounds impossibly far away. My legs, numb and exhausted, are deadweights as I give in to the current, bracing myself for the inevitable collision of bridge and bone.

Bam. With the force of a cavalry charge, I ram into the partially submerged structure. Shards of pain shoot through me as splintered wood scrapes my side raw as the water continues to pull me against the barrier. I release one final scream before the river sucks me under the bridge.

The entire world sinks into an icy darkness.

13

TAYLOR

A bright light is the first thing I register, but I doubt crackling and the smells of burning wood exist in heaven, which has me worried. The darkness of my peripheral vision is cozy, and I don't want to leave it behind. A loud *pop* forces me wide awake, though my vision is still hazy. A violent shiver rushes through me, even as my face feels hot. Soon the hovering shadows merge into normal shapes.

"How do you feel?" asks a hoarse voice I hardly recognize.

A moan escapes my lips. "Like I just went through the spin cycle."

I try to focus on the blurred face above me, but the room won't stop swirling. Ever so slowly, Nathaniel comes into focus. His wet hair lies flat against his forehead, which is weirdly attractive in my disoriented state. He's changed into a sweatshirt—one with two crossed oars on the front.

I knew it. He *is* a rower.

A few more moans and I manage to push myself upright despite the pile of heavy blankets on top of me. Sprawled across a most appropriately named fainting couch, I come face to face with a large fire spitting and crackling in the library's huge fireplace. As I shift, my clothing sticks to me, still wet.

No wonder I'm freezing.

"Wh-why am I s-still in all my wet c-clothes?" I can barely speak around my chattering teeth.

Nathaniel, doing an impression of a ripe tomato, looks away. "You were out cold, and I didn't want to undress… it didn't seem right. Giles said he would play no part in it."

Why am I not surprised? The butler would rather let a girl die of hypothermia than subject himself to the terrifying sight of a bra. I almost laugh, but it turns into a wince. Even the slightest movement hurts, but Nathaniel's embarrassment is still kind of cute. Then I remember I wasn't the only one who went for an afternoon swim. "The m-memoir!"

"Don't worry, your plastic bag protected it. For the most part. I took care of the rest." Nathaniel retrieves the red book from where it's laid out in front of the fireplace.

"Did you really dive in after me?" Now it's my turn to look away as my face gets even hotter.

"Well, I couldn't just let you drown, now could I? Even if you are by far the most mental girl I've ever met." Nathaniel's mouth curls into a half smile.

I groan and lie back down, drained. "Why does it feel like someone took a bat to my ribs?"

"Ah, that would be the large beam of splintered wood you hit head on. We should probably take a look at that now that you're awake." Nathaniel rises to his feet, then hesitates, like he's worried I might try to make another break for it. "Sit tight, all right?"

"Don't worry, I'm not going anywhere." I wince as I pull up my shirt to assess the damage. Blackberry bruises color one side of my ribcage. The waist of my skirt is torn where several large scrapes now decorate my hip and upper leg. I see minimal blood, so I think I'll survive, but the wounds still sting something awful. At least my vision is clear again, and I feel the warmth from the fire seeping into my bones.

Nathaniel returns with a brown bottle and a handful of bandages. "I don't get why there isn't a proper first aid kit in this house, but this should do the trick." He gives me a wicked smile. "A slightly more ancient remedy."

The brown bottle is most definitely whisky, not hydrogen peroxide.

"I'm warning you, if you pour alcohol on my open wounds, I *will* fight back."

Nathaniel pulls the cap off the bottle with his teeth. "Come on, Taylor, it'll burn, but it'll also keep those scrapes from getting infected. Let's just hope Giles doesn't walk in and see we've got his last bottle of small batch Special Reserve."

I brace myself against the back of the couch as Nathaniel pours the whisky onto a washcloth and presses it to my side.

And now I know how branded cattle feel.

Fortunately, the ever-methodical Nathaniel has my cuts cleaned in no time. It's only after the stinging subsides that I become intensely aware of the fact that he's kneeling, oh, about two inches from my bare stomach. For once, I'm glad for Nathaniel's forced professionalism.

"All better." He rises to his feet, shifting to his heels before extending a hand to help me up. "You should probably get out of these soaked clothes."

As I stand, trying not to read into those words, my head throbs anew and the room spins. I'm so dizzy, I stumble right into his firm rower's chest. The scent of sandalwood soap on Nathaniel's skin does nothing to settle my vertigo.

"Easy there." He grins as he catches me. Without warning, I find myself flashing him my best damsel-in-distress smile.

Seriously, Taylor?

I must have hit my head *hard*. It's bad enough the guy had to drag me out of a freezing river like this is a lame Victorian novel. Dad taught me to change a flat tire when I was thirteen, and I've done a decent job taking care of myself (and Mom) since he's been gone. No way am I about to backtrack because of an alluring foreign accent.

"Thanks. I've got it from here." I brush off Nathaniel's hands as I regain my footing, but I can still feel the pressure of his fingertips lingering on my hips. Okay, time to change the subject. "Uh, so that cemetery across the river. Why do I feel like I've seen those willow trees before?"

The ghost of an image, familiar yet not, flits through my mind. Without waiting for an answer, I find myself wobbling down the hall, fighting how lightheaded I feel as I search for the picture. Next to the Knight family portrait there's another photograph, this one of a young woman, between two willow trees, her flowy dress and fair hair blowing in the wind.

A shiver works its way up my legs, but not because I'm cold.

Wool grazes my skin as Nathaniel wraps a blanket around my shoulders. "That's Mae. She was seventeen or eighteen in that photo, I think."

The captured image of Lady Knight standing in a spot where I distinctly felt a woman's presence, plus the warm tickle of Nathaniel's breath along the back of my neck, makes me feel weak. My legs buckle.

I catch myself against the wall, annoyed that I've completed the transformation to swooning Gothic heroine. The lame girl who screams and faints every five minutes.

Nathaniel's arm wraps carefully around my waist. "Come on, Tay, I've got you."

Tay.

His deep voice guides me upstairs. The support of his arm feels foreign, but it warms me faster than a roaring fire ever could. Even if I don't *need-need* his help, I've got to admit.

Every now and then, it's nice to be rescued.

After I change out of my wet clothes, Nathaniel helps me down to the kitchen where he whips up a simple but delicious dinner of egg drop soup—"An old recipe my mom was famous for back in Beijing," he said proudly as he spooned the rustic soup into fancy porcelain bowls. As he slurped his soup in a manner that's somehow endearing, he regaled me with the story of how his Scottish dad and Chinese mom first met while studying at Oxford. I don't volunteer information about my own family, but he doesn't seem to mind.

After dinner, we move to the library, where Nathaniel unearths a selection of board games from the fifties. Following a round of two-person Clue—called Cluedo in the UK, which is weird—Giles drops by to let us know the storm has taken out the phone lines. This means no calling Oxford to let my program know I'm alive, and no reaching out to Mom to prevent a serious anxiety-spiral in case said program has already informed her that I'm missing in action.

Very reassuring.

The storm rages on, but it's strange—despite how desperate I was to get out of here earlier, it ends up being a regular, even cozy, evening. No more tingly presences. No disembodied voices. Just conversation with Nathaniel about normal, non-creepy stuff.

Only now, it's nighttime.

Lightning flashes across the window as I pull back the down-feather comforter and climb into a nest of Egyptian cotton sheets. Compared to the budget brand Mom always buys—the kind purchased in bulk by prisons—this is heaven.

The silence in my lonely wing makes it feel like I have Meadowbrook all to myself. Nathaniel said dozens of servants lived here way back in the day, but now he, Giles, and Mrs. Porter pretty much run the show, and they're staying in rooms on the other end of the hall. According to Nathaniel, most of the bedrooms right around mine belonged to long-deceased relatives and haven't been used in decades.

Nope, not disturbing *at all*.

The stiffness of this room makes me suspect it hasn't hosted a guest for some time. An enormous canopy bed takes up most of the sleeping area, but there's also a small sitting room with a velvet sofa the color of cranberries and a fireplace bordered with light pink tiles that matches the carpeting. Across from the bed sits a large chest of drawers, over which hangs an ornate mirror. I can easily picture an Edwardian woman standing there in a flowy white nightgown while a lady's maid brushes her waist-length hair.

Despite the old-fashioned elegance, something about the room leaves me cold, driving away the warmth of an evening by the fireplace in Nathaniel's company. It feels like I'll never fully get rid of this chill that's burrowed into my bones ever since hearing of Mae Knight's demise.

Her demise... No matter her age, the suddenness of Lady Knight's death still seems suspicious. At least I feel more confident about trusting Nathaniel now, since he probably wouldn't have risked hypothermia if he had sinister intentions. That leaves Giles the butler. The fact that he was the only staff member in the house the night before Lady Knight died doesn't help his case, but I have no proof besides a nagging feeling that something about him isn't quite right.

A gust of wind rattles the bedroom windows, awakening the warning I haven't been able to forget no matter how many times I've tried to stifle it.

Some say the spirits that die in that house never leave.

Bill the bartender's words make me shiver like I've stepped into the icy river all over again. I don't expect to fall asleep any time soon—not with the wind howling like an angry cat—but maybe that's a good thing. It's time to figure out why Lady Knight left me this book. Our connection has to be more than unfaithful fathers.

As soon as I'm cozy under the covers, I flip through the pages of the red book, searching for where I left off. A light tap on the bedroom door makes me startle so fiercely, I nearly fall out of the bed. With a groan, I throw back the inviting comforter to answer it.

Nathaniel is standing in the dimly lit hallway, holding a silver tray. On it sits a bone-china teapot, a plate of chocolate biscuits, and a single pink rose. It's so cute that any remaining chill in my core transforms into a burst of heat that rushes all the way to my bare feet.

"Thought you might like some herbal tea to help you sleep." Nathaniel avoids my gaze by looking past me into the bedroom. "Everything comfortable?"

I hug the door frame like I'm hiding a scandalous nightgown, when in reality, I'm wearing the baggy boy gym clothes Nathaniel loaned me. "How'd you know I'm an insomniac?"

"You seemed the type." A shy smile on his lips, one of a few to crack his proper exterior this evening, Nathaniel hands over the tray. "How's the head?"

"Better, I took a few—"

He presses his hand to my forehead before I can finish that thought. If he's feeling for a fever, I don't think I had one… until now.

"A bit warm, but not too bad." He drops his hand. "Right. I should let you rest."

"No, wait." I focus on steadying the tray, so I don't spill hot water all over Nathaniel's slippers. Because that is such a *me* move. "I meant to thank you earlier."

"There's no need. Really." Nathaniel studies me with a curious expression, almost like we're meeting for the first time. After a small eternity, he clears his throat. "Well, goodnight then. Let me know if you need anything else."

"Sleep tight," I reply, shutting the door.

Okay, sleep is *really* out of the question now. A late-night tea delivery might seem like a simple gesture, but I tend to attract the non-sentimental, non-gesturing type. My last boyfriend's idea of a love letter was a text message that didn't include a single reference to the Pittsburgh Steelers.

Get a grip. I can't let one semi-romantic gesture go to my head. Not when I need to figure out how Lady Knight knew my dad and what he was doing in England in the first place.

I try drowning the butterflies in my stomach with tea, though not before taking a cautious whiff of its steam. Mint and chamomile. Nothing weird. Nothing like what I smelled in the tea that had spilled in Mae's room.

As I crawl back into bed, the manor creaks like a ship in a storm, even though stones this old can't possibly sway. Or can they? I doubt humans will ever build something so solid that it can withstand the chaotic forces of nature for long.

Titanic blew that theory apart a hundred years ago.

14

$\mathcal{A}$VA

I refused to sit still a moment longer after witnessing Father's betrayal. It took circling the ship ten times, but I came up with a plan. I'd had my reservations about handing Mrs. Lakovic's letter over to Plavsic, but it was clear the woman was far from innocent. And while the soldier was threatening, the psychic was a threat manifest. He had been right to warn me away from having pity for her.

When the lieutenant found me tonight, I would tell him all I knew.

Until then, I had no choice but to continue my act as the dutiful yet clueless daughter. The only way to uncover the details I required to help my mother was to get as close to Mrs. Lakovic as possible, which meant she must remain unaware of my suspicions… and my wrath. Lieutenant Plavsic might be eager to stir up a war that would consume nations, but the only conflict I had the power to affect was the one about to take place between me and my father's mistress.

And so, I prepared for our final evening on the *Titanic*. I dressed for battle.

This was no small feat since I'd refused to bring a lady's maid. I wanted our most trusted servants to stay behind with Mother while we were away. Besides, the endless doting of servants was going out of fashion anyway. Father thought traveling without a few at least was terribly middle class, but I preferred the liberation from their constant fussing. This newfound independence also meant my evening gowns could lack a corset, as there was no one around to lace up the dreaded torture device.

Fortunately, the dress I'd saved for tonight didn't require one to make its wearer formidable.

The floor-length evening gown of dark blue satin was covered by an overlay of black lace with detailed beadwork. Its gown's empire waistline was high, but the square neckline was lower than any other dress I owned, and it made me feel five years older as soon as I slipped it over my head. Accentuating the décolletage was a cameo necklace I'd picked up in London. To make it more fashionable, I'd added a large black pearl and a few Austrian crystals.

As I stood in front of the mirror securing my sapphire earrings, I was struck by the reality that I *did* look older. Much older—more woman than girl, even if my pampered life often left me feeling as useless as a lamb. Mother often criticized my poor posture, but tonight I intended to walk into this den of wolves with my shoulders back and my head held high.

I was a child no longer. My future was my own.

Out on deck, the evening promised to be clear, but the temperature dropped steadily as nightfall settled in and the horizon disappeared. I brought along my fur wrap in case we took a stroll after dinner, though that wasn't likely due to the brutal chill.

My chin raised and eyes resolute, I strode into the Palm Court, where dozens of first- class passengers sized each other up while waiting for the dining room to open. I ignored the male stares and female scowls that followed me. Aloofness could be intriguing… or so I had heard. All the first-class ladies were wearing their finest gowns, yet they wasted their charms by standing in exclusive circles, clucking in clusters like a bunch of silly hens.

To my left, a group of men in tuxedos debated the treaties the Balkan League had established a few weeks ago. Father had been following these political developments, but given that he and the Serbian Mrs. Lakovic were more than acquaintances, I wondered if there was another reason for Father's interest in this region of the world. Hoping I might listen in and learn something about the foreign affairs that had motivated Mrs. Lakovic to cross the Atlantic when she clearly feared sailing on open water, I approached a potted plant near the men. Once my position was secured, I did my best impression of an empty-headed female, fanning my face while smiling vacantly at the fashionable crowd.

A stout man in an archaic top hat led the charge in a bellowing voice. "With all due respect, this alliance among the Balkan states is a necessary evil. Tell me, how else are we to keep the Ottomans in check?"

"I must disagree, Mr. Maxwell," replied his companion, swirling his dirty martini. "The league will only lead to war with Austria-Hungary. And that's exactly what the Russians want!"

"Then perhaps the Habsburgs should keep their Slav populations under control—"

The conversation quickly deteriorated into a debate as muddled and confusing as the web of alliances itself, but these forceful opinions faded to the background as Galena Lakovic stepped into the Palm Court. The woman spoke with a tall gentleman on the opposite side of the room, her face as animated as always. Madeleine Astor's story about Mrs. Lakovic's ability to tap into the spiritual realm was ludicrous, but I had to admit she looked the part. She wore a dress of crimson velvet and had threaded a string of rubies through her ebony hair, which she wore in a piled updo. Her presence exuded an otherworldliness that both lured and repulsed. I watched the other passengers watching her, their faces consumed by a potent mixture of curiosity and fear. But I wouldn't let Galena Lakovic intimidate me with her imaginary powers. She was a mortal woman, nothing more.

And you are no longer a child, I reminded myself with every step. Though this seemed the perfect opportunity to approach her, I had to remember to keep my temper and resist lashing out at this jezebel who'd contaminated my life with scandal.

We locked eyes across the room and in that moment, I felt a bottomless unease that I can only describe as drowning in a hopeless ocean on a starless night. Galena appeared to find me equally threatening, for as soon as she saw me approach, she bid farewell to the man and hurried into the dining room, now opened for seating.

"Ava, there you are. No longer need your old man to escort you to dinner, is that it?" More chipper than usual—dear me, I wonder why?—Father came up alongside me, extending his arm. I took it out of habit, though I felt sullied by the touch. My heart towards him had hardened, and I couldn't imagine the ice ever thawing.

Glancing up, I forced a smile. Father had always looked handsome in his dinner tux. Flecks of grey peppered his auburn hair and the skin around his blue eyes crinkled when he smiled. He was one of those fortunate men who wore age well, so I could see how Mrs. Lakovic had come to fancy him. No doubt his wealth and aristocratic title did not hurt either, but I was not about to let some upstart gold digger destroy a family that had endured for generations. The Knights of Meadowbrook Manor had made kings... and we'd dethroned them. We would not let one unhappy marriage be our downfall. Mother may have been a shadow of her former self, but she was still Jonathan Knight's wife.

She was not dead yet.

I could not help *some* bitterness, however. "I would have waited for you, but I was under the impression you were escorting another woman to dinner. And all over this ship, it seems," I said as Father led me to the dining room.

Father sighed, as if readying himself for a lengthy explanation. As if anything could explain away what I'd seen. Yet before he could begin, Bruce Ismay—the managing director of the White Star Line and quite possibly the most pompous man who ever lived—stepped up behind us. He gave my father a friendly but firm slap on the back, which nearly sent the Scotch snifter soaring from Father's hand.

"Good evening, Jonathan." Mr. Ismay swirled his own glass, the smile on his face permanently smug. "Your daughter is looking lovely, as usual. Tell me, are you prepared to enjoy the finest meal ever indulged in at sea? Tonight's shall be a special grand finale."

Helen Crawford stood next to the ship manager, also sipping Scotch—a bold drink for a lady, but one that matched her unconventional persona. I wondered if she was aware that I'd been attempting to include her in my photograph this morning. She smiled warmly at my father, a sentiment she did not share for Mr. Ismay, who she leaned away from as he continued to bluster. "Based on the menu, we ought to pray this ship will keep us afloat. Ten courses! Why, it's ridiculous."

Bruce Ismay's reptilian smile persisted beneath his oiled moustache, yet the twitch of his lips suggested he resented any criticism of his glorious ship, no matter how slight. "Come now, Mrs. Crawford, you've spent far too much time with those yogis in India, living on nothing but rice and Darjeeling tea. If we can *afford* a ten-course meal, why shouldn't we enjoy it? This ship is capable of supporting several additional tons, to say nothing of a few gluttonous passengers."

Father and I shared in an obligatory chuckle, but Mrs. Crawford's lips pressed into a thin line.

"Look here, Jonathan. I've received something quite extraordinary." Mr. Ismay pulled a slip of paper from his lapel pocket and handed it to Father, who was securing his glasses.

"We're set to arrive in New York early?" He glanced up over the rims at Mr. Ismay.

"Are we really?" Mrs. Crawford rested a hand on Father's arm, leaning over him to get a glimpse of the wire.

My, the familiarizing affect my father had on middle-aged women.

"Yes, *quite* early, by the looks of it," he replied, apparently unaware of Mrs. Crawford's looming proximity.

"Marvelous, isn't it? The papers will be all over us." Ismay struggled to contain a giddiness that made him seem more like a schoolboy than a multi-millionaire. "Mark my words, Jonathan. *Titanic*'s crossing shall go down in history."

Mrs. Crawford shivered and pulled away from Father to drape a shawl over her sleeveless dress—an elegant but dreadfully thin gown made of ivory silk. With an arched eyebrow, she gave me a knowing look. "Men. Really, must everything be a competition?"

Ismay snorted. "Competition is what drives this world forward, Mrs. Crawford."

"Yes, but where exactly are we driving it *to*?"

Mr. Ismay glared at me, visibly shocked that a girl my age had dared to question his wisdom. Mrs. Crawford's nod of approval made me go on.

I spoke cautiously at first, but my voice grew bolder with every syllable. "I hear nothing these days but *progress, progress, progress*, but I have yet to hear anyone describe the destination we have in mind. For all our mechanical advancements, human beings don't strike me as any less arrogant or self-interested, nor is the high society pretense that we can control the hand of destiny any less tedious."

At first, the response to my outburst was a stunned silence, but Mr. Ismay surprised us all by laughing so hard his entire body shook. He gave Father a second slap on the back. "For heaven's sake, Knight! What a cynical child you've raised. Tell me, do you feed the girl a spoon full of bitters before bed every night?"

Mortified, my father tightened his grip on my arm, but Helen Crawford clasped her hands in delight.

"I have to agree with you, Lady Ava." She gestured to the chandeliers, the paneled walls, the sparkling china and polished silver. "What does all this extravagance matter in the end? So what if it's *the best*? Eventually it will crack and decay, just like everything else."

Bruce Ismay cleared his throat. "The answer is simple, ladies. In fact, it is science: the best *wins*. You've heard of Charles Darwin, I'm sure. Men are no different from animals, you see. Only those who adapt to the times and strive for a better tomorrow will perpetuate our race. And in this world of constant strife, I intend to be among the few who survive."

The new mating call of the industrious man, I thought, resisting the urge to roll my eyes. It was obvious Mrs. Crawford did the same. If Bruce Ismay hoped to impress women by claiming humans were no different than sea slugs trapped in a great chain of ruthless competition, he'd better come up with a better strategy, lest his own genetic line die out.

Father, who was more reserved and not one prone to controversy, entered the conversation with reluctance, and only to change the topic. "There's a second message here, Mr. Ismay. It appears to be an iceberg warning. In fact, this wire contains several iceberg warnings."

Something was hardening behind Father's cool blue eyes, and it took me a moment to identify it as fear. Surely Galena had shared her ill feelings about the voyage with him, but my father had not respected his mistress's opinions enough to listen.

I looked to the ship manager for reassurance, but the mention of ice only seemed to excite Mr. Ismay even more. "It's nothing to worry about. A formal precaution, I'm sure. Even if there is an ice field ahead, we shall speed right through it, mark my words. This ship will not only establish a new record, she will do so with utmost class."

Somewhere behind us a door opened, letting in a gust of air that pierced my gown with its arctic daggers. For the first time since boarding, I felt seasick.

Mr. Ismay stiffened in the brisk breeze, resting his eyes on me. "Fear not, friends. Lesser vessels may anchor for the night, but it will take more than a little ice to stop *Titanic*."

A frown on his face, Father dragged me from Ismay like he was protecting me from the propositions of a lecherous pimp. "Come now, Ava. Let's find our seats."

"Would you mind escorting a poor divorcee as well, Lord Knight? We're seated at the same table." Mrs. Crawford grabbed hold of my father's other arm, lest she be forced to enter the dining room with Bruce Ismay by her side.

"Of course, Helen," Father replied with a familiarity that suggested he knew this intriguing woman quite well. But from where?

I watched with some amusement as Mrs. Crawford batted her eyelashes at my father, though my stomach quickly soured. She was clearly drawn to him, but it seemed Lord Knight was immune. Apparently when it came to extramarital dalliances, Jonathan Knight preferred unstable neediness to refinement and intelligence.

The cliché made me despise Galena Lakovic even more.

As we entered the dining room, a gentle sway caused the chandeliers to tinkle, a reminder that past a few walls was the uncaring sea. I hated entertaining the thought, but what if Mrs.

Lakovic's premonition was right and our ship was in danger? We were in the middle of the Atlantic, hundreds of miles from shore, and Mr. Ismay was clearly arrogant enough to tempt fate.

I found myself glancing around the room before I consciously acknowledged for whom I searched. For all his threats, the Serbian soldier was the only person I knew on this ship who seemed confidently capable of handling whatever might happen. But of course, he'd never show his face at an occasion like this—not unless he wanted Mrs. Lakovic to know he was still a hound in pursuit.

Not to worry, Lady Knight. I'll find you.

Though Mr. Ismay was part of our dinner party, it was a relief to see Mr. Stead and Miss Rosenbaum already seated at our table when we arrived. William Thomas Stead was a journalist and social reformer, as well as the editor of *Borderland* magazine, the publication that fueled the Spiritualism movement that enchanted many of England's elite. Edith Rosenbaum was an American fashion reporter, and I hoped that between the two journalists and Mrs. Crawford, the travel writer, our dinner conversation would focus more on current events and less on stoking Mr. Ismay's ego. A few tables away, Galena Lakovic watched us from beneath her coal black lashes.

Our previous dinners on *Titanic* were largely forgettable, but tonight felt different. Despite Father's betrayal, I longed to enjoy the glow of the moment. Every sensation of the evening begged to be experienced, so I forgot about the storms of my past and the hazy horizon of the future, giving myself over to the tidal pull of the present.

The first course of oysters Rockefeller was accompanied by the lively storytelling of Miss Rosenbaum, the energetic woman's nasally voice holding our attention with a dramatic account of her visit to Madame de Thebes, the most famous fortune teller in Paris.

"Mind you, as a journalist I tend to be skeptical about anything that isn't backed up by solid evidence," Edith claimed—a statement that left me wondering about the "hard facts" that existed in the world of fashion magazines. "Yet Madame de Thebes was most convincing. She claimed I was about to endure an experience that would put me to the ultimate test, resulting in the loss of personal possessions and friends. How she knew I was sailing home to deal with my ungrateful siblings and the division of our inheritance, I'll never understand."

His face turning bright red, Bruce Ismay looked as though he might burst if he did not interject. "Pardon me, Miss Rosenbaum, but as a self-made man who believes the future is what he *makes* of it, I'm curious to hear Mr. Stead's thoughts on this notion of direct communication with the spirit world. Surely such efforts go against all the methods of science?"

Mr. Stead sat directly across from me, buttering his bread roll in silence. He wore a gold pin on his lapel identical to Father's—two interlinked rings, the emblem of the Psychical Research Society. Mr. Stead's unassuming smile suggested he'd been waiting to share his thoughts but was in no hurry to speak. When he did, the deep voice that emerged from his white beard reminded me of jolly St. Nick.

"Well, Mr. Ismay, a phenomenon which can neither be handled nor weighed, analyzed nor dissected, is naturally regarded as troublesome. Yet the Inquisitor who forbade inquiry into religion was the natural precursor of the modern scientist who forbids the use of reason when it comes to investigating the subject of the afterlife. For centuries and across cultures, there have been men and women who claimed they could connect with a world beyond our own. Why shouldn't we treat this universal human experience as a subject worthy of rational inquiry? As a journalist, I feel I have a duty to do so."

"Why Mr. Stead! Surely you don't deny that dabbling in the occult is blasphemy," retorted an indignant woman seated next to Father. "It will only lead to disaster."

"If by *occult* you mean a misguided curiosity regarding the diabolical, then I agree with you wholeheartedly, Mrs. Norris. Still, I do not believe we need to look much further than man's lust for power to find real evil in our midst. On the other hand, if you mean to say *any* interest in unexplained spiritual phenomenon is contrary to religious piety, then it is fortunate the women who met that angel at an empty tomb in Jerusalem did not hold to such a theory."

We all chortled at that, even the reverent Mrs. Norris. William Stead's calm and deliberate manner of speaking captured us all, for here was a man who found every aspect of life worthy of wonder.

As the next course of filet mignon was served, I glanced over my shoulder to where Galena Lakovic's stare pulled on me like an undertow. Whatever existed between her and my father, my instincts claimed their relationship went deeper than mere adultery. Plavsic followed this woman to America for a reason, and I needed to discover why tonight. No matter the nature of the information she carried, I must pry it from her icy fingers.

"The whole question that lies at the bottom," Mr. Stead continued, bringing my attention back to my own table, "is whether the forces behind this world are divine or diabolic. Those who believe they are ultimately divine must regard each spiritual phenomenon as a window through which we may gain fresh glimpses of the Infinite. In this area of inquiry, as in most others, faith and fear go ill together."

"But what if both exist in this world?" I'd had no intention of contributing to the discussion, but it seemed I could not help myself. "What if our world contains the divine *and* diabolic, depending on where one looks?"

Take the woman at the table behind me—a deceitful blend of mesmerizing darkness and splendid light.

Mr. Stead smiled warmly. "I suspect one finds what one seeks. Then again, we need not look beyond our own souls to witness the unfolding battle between good and evil, gallantry and greed. That is why all our utopian schemes will ultimately fail, for to truly change society, we must first find a way to soften the human heart. At least that is what I've witnessed during my many years on this fascinating planet."

"And you've seen much worth noting," said Helen Crawford in a clear, confident voice. Her shawl, now draped over the back of her chair, bore the gold pin of the Psychical Research Society. That must be how she knew my father, and it was apparent that she and Mr. Stead were old friends as well. "Come now, William, won't you tell us one of your famous yarns?"

This request incited a chorus of agreement from the rest of the table.

"If you insist." Mr. Stead leaned back in his chair, as if he were a grandfather passing a winter evening before the hearth.

He then proceeded to tell us a series of bizarre stories he'd gathered during his years as a journalist. My favorite was his tale of a cursed Egyptian mummy housed in the British Museum, whose handlers all met tragic and untimely deaths. I listened with childlike fascination—that is until a deep, skin-prickling voice tore me from the fantasy.

"Pardon me, Lady Ava."

Glancing up from my dessert, I met a clever, all-knowing eye that missed nothing. My soldier had found me, just as he promised. Despite his unnerving gaze, in his full uniform he looked devastatingly handsome beneath the muted glow of the electric lamps.

But what was he doing *here*? I glanced back to where Mrs. Lakovic's chair now sat empty. Naturally, she'd run off again precisely when I was prepared to trail her.

"Would you care to dance?" Plavsic extended his hand.

My face grew warm. I knew *how* to waltz, but I'd never actually been asked by a man who was not a relative. The soldier's hard smile made me hesitate, though it also told me that declining his dance was not an option.

My superior officer had come to collect. And while I had some information—Galena Lakovic believed our ship was doomed, was rumored to possess psychic abilities, and, oh yes, had succeeded in seducing my father—it would not be enough to satisfy him. I would need to stall.

"Good evening, sir," Father said in an overprotective tone, interrupting my thoughts.

"It most certainly is, Lord Knight." The lieutenant gave a deep bow. "Allow me to introduce myself. I am Ivan Markovic of the Serbian Army. I wondered if I might have a waltz with your lovely daughter."

"Markovic, you say?" Father chewed on the name. "Why, I'm sure Ava—"

"—would love to dance with you, Lieutenant!" I glared at my father. Surely I could decide on the simple matter of a dancing partner. These two men would not talk as if I did not exist. The soldier's use of an alias hadn't escaped my notice either.

"Good evening, Lieutenant *Markovic*," I whispered as we walked away.

He ignored my hard tone, keeping an equally firm grip on my arm. "It appears your father is even closer to Galena than we initially suspected."

Plavsic's lips pursed with pleasure as he took my hand, guiding me to the open floor where the band played. Resting a hand on my waist, he stood at the appropriate distance, leading with surprising grace as we glided across the floor. I'd not expected a solider from the Balkans to be familiar with our style of dance, yet his timing was as consistent as his fixed eye, which never left my face. My cheeks tingled, but I couldn't say if that was from excitement or fear. Perhaps there isn't much difference in the end.

"Tell me, Lady Ava. What have you learned thus far?" the soldier asked as the band played "On the Beautiful Blue Danube."

Twirling beneath his arm, I gave him my most radiant smile. "Well, to start, I've learned that this woman you've taken such a keen interest in is remarkably difficult to follow. She rarely leaves her stateroom unless—"

"Unless she's with your father."

I hid my shame by staring beyond Plavsic's shoulder. It appeared everyone on this ship had already seen what I was only now admitting. Mother said the worst thing we can do is lie—to ourselves. Perhaps it was a blessing she was no longer capable of such deceptions. As of late, her troubled mind failed to grasp the difference between fact and fiction.

Plavsic still stared at me, expecting a response. I lifted my chin. "Their acquaintance is a detail that will only make my task even easier. Tell me, sir, how did you come to know this unusual woman in the first place?"

The lieutenant stiffened, an indication he was not used to being so directly questioned by his inferiors. "Her husband was a dear friend, as well as a brother in arms."

Ah, so she had a husband. Splendid, that meant Mrs. Lakovic had destroyed *two* marriages instead of only one. "Well, then I can understand your concern—"

"He's dead because of her," Plavsic continued. "And thousands more Serbians will die if she persists in her obstinacy."

The solider pulled me in close, all charisma vanishing from his face as he hissed into my ear. "*Documents*, Lady Ava. I want documents. Not gossip, not hearsay, but hard *proof* of her treason. This isn't a game, girl. Galena Lakovic carries secret intelligence that has the power to destroy the Serbian cause if it falls into the wrong hands."

I tried to pull away, yet Plavsic held fast, increasing the pace of our twirls until I felt like I was drowning in the Danube itself.

"You've heard about the turmoil in my country, I'm sure. The rumors of a brewing war? Believe me, Lady Ava, the last thing you want is a black widow like Galena drawing your family into her web. Find what she intends to deliver to the American press and perhaps *yours* will be one of the few aristocratic households spared once the dust of our revolution has settled."

Revolution? What was this man prattling on about, and what did it have to do with healing my mother? "But Dr. Jung—"

"Don't you see this is bigger than you and your mad mother?" Plavsic cut in, whirling me around. "Get me the evidence I need to condemn Galena and I'll arrange your precious meeting with Dr. Jung. But if you *fail*, Lady Ava, I cannot protect you from the coming clash that is sure to dismantle Europe's class system once and for all."

He cannot protect me, or he will not protect me?

I took a deep breath, determined not to reveal my growing fear. Lieutenant Plavsic was not the first nationalist revolutionary of our new century, nor did I suspect he would be the last. My father seemed intent on destroying the Knight name with or without a class revolt, so only Mother mattered now—she was the only family I had left.

Documents.

"There is one thing, lieutenant." I hesitated, for once I spoke the words, I could not take them back. "I managed to intercept one of Mrs. Lakovic's letters. I did not mention it earlier because the contents seemed so insignificant, but perhaps a man with your skills would be able ascertain more—"

"Where is the letter?"

"In my stateroom. I'll deliver it to you first thing in the morning."

"You will deliver it to me tonight. And if it doesn't contain the information I need, you will find Galena and press her for more until she caves. You *don't* want to disappoint me more than you already have."

Terror constricted my throat, so I attempted a lighthearted laugh. "Of course, lieutenant. I simply need a bit more time. No female shares her secrets with a stranger right away. We women must be wooed."

"Indeed. Galena's wooing needs have certainly increased since the last time I saw her." A long-held resentment consumed the soldier's good eye. "Sitting there in her expensive gown, growing fat on a dozen courses while her own countrymen starve. She was once a formidable part of our movement! The woman joined us in the trenches, for God's sake. Yet here she sits on the *Titanic*, deluded into thinking she's one of you." Plavsic expelled the words like a bad taste.

One of you.

"Forgive me, lieutenant, but do you not also carry a first-class ticket?" I kept my tone playful and light, but I was increasingly vexed by this man who hurled insults while ignoring the huge plank that poked from his one good eye.

Plavsic's smile took on a reptilian quality. "You are correct, but there's an important distinction. I infiltrate your social class not because I desire to become one of you, but because I long to *destroy* you. The future course for a more egalitarian world is set, Lady Ava, and our destination will be a day of reckoning. If you hope to spare your parents the judgment they deserve, you will give me what I require. Yet if you fail, your family, your estate, your inheritance… they will go down in flames when our world war begins."

Was there any place on earth where Mother and I might hide from such a conflict? There were certainly injustices in our world, though I was ashamed to admit I'd never lost much sleep over them. Was Plavsic's path the only way to set things right? Through senseless violence, the overthrow of every tradition, and the destruction of all that was beautiful and good?

I was not knowledgeable in the ways of the world, despite the airs I put on, but life as a woman, even a young one, had taught me that power was what ruled society, and that power nearly always resided in the hands of men. A total revolution would do nothing but transfer power from one group to another, turning Plavsic into what he proclaimed to hate—a new ruling elite, just as addicted to staying on top as those who reigned before them.

"I'll get you the information you require," I said once my head stopped spinning. "But tell me, lieutenant, why are you so confident this war will engulf the entire world?"

The soldier studied my face as if he had witnessed all the troubled thoughts sifting through my mind. For weeks, the papers claimed a European war was on the horizon, yet a conflict so colossal had never seemed plausible, never felt quite *real*. Not until I'd glimpsed the fires of it kindling in Plavsic's gaze.

Though perhaps that was the way of all disasters—they descended out of nowhere, and by the time the dust settled, not a soul could remember the original cause.

"Oh, I intend to make sure our revolution reaches every corner of the globe," Plavsic replied. "And the world is ready for it. Just look around this ship, Lady Ava, if your eyesight is truly better than mine. We bask in unearned luxury while the poor beneath these shimmering decks, just like the poor on every continent, cry out for justice."

Though I sensed a forced passion in his words—justice for the least of these was the last thing on Lieutenant Plavsic's mind—I was not required to trust the limited vision of his fanaticism. I did have to continue cooperating with him, however. How else could I secure both aid and protection for my mother when Father had abandoned her already? Besides, I could not deny the severity of Plavsic's warnings. If he demanded that I hand over a single adulteress to spare the annihilation of both my mother's mental health and the Knight family legacy, then I would happily take my place beside Pilate and wash my hands.

"The clock is ticking, Lady Ava," Plavsic said as our dance finally came to an end. "By the time we reach America, the battle lines will have been clearly drawn."

I tried to swallow the fear that tightened my throat. "I'll find a way into Mrs. Lakovic's stateroom. I'm sure the information you seek will be there. Now if you'll excuse me, lieutenant, I had better sit down. It's grown quite warm, and I'm feeling rather lightheaded."

"Yes, they're blasting those electric heaters, aren't they?" The soldier's grin reminded me of Lewis Carroll's Cheshire Cat. "It's been a pleasure, Lady Ava."

I returned to my seat on shaky legs, where I found Father's wary eyes fixed on Lieutenant Plavsic's back. I suspect he'd watched the entire dance.

"That man," he said as I guzzled an entire glass of water. "Where did you meet him?"

"Oh, who knows? You cross paths with everyone in first class at some point." I waved away Father's concerns with my dessert spoon, but after one bite of Waldorf pudding, I felt so sickened by the decadence that I had to push the plate away.

"Perhaps, but I sense your meeting him may not have been chance. You stay away from that man, Ava. Understand? Nothing but trouble comes out of Serbia."

Yes, well, you would know, wouldn't you?

"Jonathan, listen here, what do you think about…"

As Father turned to Mr. Ismay, I glanced at Mrs. Lakovic's table, but she hadn't returned. My stomach churned. Edith Rosenbaum's relentless voice, a high-pitched whine not even the string quartet could drown out, was making my head throb.

"May I return to the room?" I whispered to Father, liberating him from Mr. Ismay's dull descriptions of *Titanic*'s original deck design. "I feel positively dreadful."

"As do I," Father replied with a sigh of relief. "Come on, I'll walk you back."

We excused ourselves, leaving the orchestra, the clanking crystal, and the deceptive warmth of the dining room behind. On deck, an ink spill sea bled into a starry sky. There was no wind, only cold, static air that cut like a pair of sewing shears.

It was the kind of bitterness that hurt to breathe.

"Be sure to turn up the heaters in your stateroom, Lord Knight," called a distant figure walking toward us. "It's extra frigid this evening, and it's only bound to get worse."

My throat tightened.

"Thank you, seaman," my father replied as the Irishman came closer.

Caleb Donohue met my eyes as he passed, his gaze as frosty as the night. "I would run ahead and do it *for* you, but I'm on watch in the crow's nest in a few minutes, and we need all the eyes we can get on a night like this."

I see. Apparently, Mr. Donohue hadn't forgiven my earlier insult. Instead of retorting with a jibe of my own, the heat of shame spread through me. Though the seaman was almost nothing like the soldier I had just left, both were part of a class of title-less men who were making it clear they would no longer tolerate such slights. I believed envy was as much a sin as greed, but I could not deny that my careless treatment of those below my status had likely contributed to the silent hatred so many harbored against us.

And if the Serbian soldier had his way, their animosity would soon grow murderously loud.

"Thank you, Seaman Donohue. We appreciate your dedication to our safety," I said in the most genuine tone I could muster.

The sailor's face softened for a moment, but he still tipped his hat in exaggerated deference—a sign he would not play my girlish games. Before long, the darkness on deck swallowed him back up.

Both the soldier and the sailor who had so ardently sought my attention the day we boarded *Titanic* now treated me like a pampered brat who was hardly worthy of a second glance.

"He seems a decent young man," Father remarked. I glanced at him, surprised to find he had paid attention to the brief exchange. "Hard to find a Fenian these days with actual manners."

I stared in the direction the sailor had gone. "No, Mr. Donohue is much too honest for etiquette."

Father chuckled, though I had not meant to be funny. "Come now, darling, it's almost midnight. According to Mr. Ismay, tomorrow will be a most memorable day."

15

TAYLOR

S cratch, scratch.
I look up from the book.
Scratch, scratch.

Strange noises have echoed through the halls of Meadow-brook all night, but this one is new. And close. I shut the book, straining to hear something other than my pounding heart.

Scratch, scratch.

A scratching sound coming from inside the walls of your room is worse than any other bump in the night, hands down.

Maybe it's a tree branch scraping the window. I climb out of bed, knowing even as I pad to the one window that the sound is not branch to glass but claw to plaster. Outside, as I expected, none of the swaying trees come close to touching the house.

Scratch, scratch.

My gaze shifts toward the sound, and I see the antique chest of drawers with its large mirror. I hate mirrors. Especially in bedrooms. And at night. You never know when you might look in one and see something you wish you hadn't.

Old Bill's warning pushes its way into my mind. *Curse, curse, curse.* With every scratch, I wish I was back in Maine, back with Mom, back in my own bed.

Deep breaths, deep breaths...

But my pulse quickens as the walls close in. My body disobeys every direct order as fear takes hold, fighting my brain for control. The scratching seems to fill my head, and I crouch down, breathing fast, clutching the red book tightly in both hands. Before I totally lose it, I remember something Mom told me during one of my panic attacks the year Dad died: "No matter what your body claims, *you are safe*. This feeling, as awful as it is, will pass. All you've got to do is ride the wave."

Ride the wave.

So that's what I do. I let the panic wash over me, allowing it to do its worst. It takes all my concentration, all my focus, but I survive. And what I'm left with when the water rolls away from the shore is a logical explanation.

This noise, while horrible, isn't a set of bloody fingernails scraping down wood. Besides, I don't believe in ghosts. Once you've seen death's shadow overtake the face of someone you love, you've already experienced the scariest scene this world has to offer, and all those stories about goblins and ghouls lose their hold.

I swallow hard, stand, and approach the dresser, determined to end this Tell-Tale Heart situation right now. As I get closer, the scratching stops. I notice a crack in the floral wallpaper behind the mirror, almost like the outline of a door.

I push the chest of drawers away from the wall, hoping I'm not damaging the wooden planked floor. But I don't have much time to worry about it, because behind the dresser *is* a door. A small, creepy door.

Scratch, scratch, scratch.

The creature on the other side wants out, so before my imagination can run wild again, I silently count to three and pull the handle, ready to face whatever long-nailed phantom has disrupted my absorbing read.

The beast springs from the darkness in a flutter of wings, releasing a falsetto cry as it flaps toward my face.

A bat!

I figured the culprit was a critter of some kind, but why does it have to be a filthy, bloodsucking bat with a puny rodent face and tiny talon claws?

I duck to the floor, issuing a screech of my own.

Okay, maybe it's more of a scream. A full-on, blood-curling, Gothic-novel scream.

The bedroom door flies open. A shirtless Nathaniel bursts into the room, his eyes wild from their launch out of a dead sleep. "What's the matter? What is it?"

"*That!*" I don't have time for a debrief because the flying rat is headed straight for his head. Nathaniel grabs a pillow off the bed, swinging it around like this is Wimbledon.

"Over here! Direct it this way." I force open the window, but Nathaniel's extra encouragement isn't necessary. As soon as the bat senses an escape hatch, it sails through, disappearing into the damp night.

I drop to the floor, gulping in air along with relief. When Nathaniel's eyes meet mine, we're both laughing so hard, hot tears stream down my cheeks.

"What an angry bugger! You all right? You screamed like you saw a ghost."

"A ghost I could have handled." My entire body shudders with revulsion. "I bloody *hate* bloody bats."

Nathaniel chuckles at my overly British emphasis. "You know, we don't say that word half as often as you Americans think. You're just lucky Giles snores like the bulldog he resembles. If he'd woken up, we'd really be in a bloody mess." Nathaniel's smile fades when he sees the small doorway behind the dresser. "What do we have here?"

"You tell me, Bruce Wayne. Is this the secret entrance to your bat cave?"

"I wish. Sadly, Giles is no Alfred." Nathaniel steps into the small space and pulls on a cord hanging from the ceiling. When the light bulb flickers on, a world painted in shades of grey replaces the murky darkness. The closet is filled with dozens of photographs, hidden away like stolen secrets.

Snapshots of children.

Each portrait is a black-and-white close-up of a sweet child's face. Some of them smile slightly, but all have a hardness behind their eyes. It isn't sadness necessarily. It's… resilience. These are the faces of souls much older than they look.

"Someone must have taken these during the war. Both world wars, apparently," Nathaniel says excitedly, gesturing for me to join him deeper in the closet. He points to the dates scribbled in pencil on the backs of the photos. "See? 1916, 1918, 1939, 1943."

"Two generations who grew up with their entire world at war." My eyes land on one image that's different from the other portraits, and I pick it up. Two girls and a boy sit on their suitcases in the middle of the train station. They must be about four or five years old, dressed in little peacoats and knee socks and wool caps. The smiling girl in the middle has her arms wrapped around the other two. If it wasn't for the evacuee tags hanging around their necks, you'd think they were off to summer camp.

"Ava took this," I realize, putting it back. "Ava took all of these."

"How can you tell?"

"I just can." These images not only reveal the spirit of the children, they somehow reveal Ava's spirit as well. Her eye for the candid truth. It's hard to explain, but something about them fits with her memoir's description of the two girls lying on *Titanic*'s deck.

She captures both their innocence and freedom—a freedom that isn't based on external circumstances but that comes from the soul, somewhere deep within.

"This must have been Ava's room then," Nathaniel says. "I wonder why Giles put you in here of all places. Does that freak you out?"

"Yeah, a little. But it also feels… right." After all, I've been immersed in Ava's mind for hours while reading her account.

I've often wondered if a person's personality can be felt through the objects they once used. Even when they're long gone, a part of them lingers, clinging to the fibers of a scarf or hairbrush like cigarette smoke. Right now, I wouldn't be surprised if Ava *did* walk through the door to reclaim her memories—that's how real, how *present*, she feels when I read her memoir or study her photographs.

Maybe that's why Mom couldn't handle it. Maybe that's why she rid herself of everything that brought Dad to mind.

My eyes fall to the book in my hand, my direct line of communication with Ava. It's incredible when you stop and think about it. Decades, even centuries, after she's gone, her words, her thoughts, will live on. That alone makes the memoir worth the read, but there's something very personal about her story. Something that deeply resonates with me. I can't shake the sense that there's got to be a connection to my dad. Some explanation that will reveal why he visited England just before he died.

Could the seemingly incriminating photo he left behind have been an intentional clue?

After all, if Ava can still speak through her photographs a hundred years later, then why can't Dad?

"Earth to Taylor! Did you hear anything I just said?" Nathaniel clangs his crystal orange juice glass with a fork. "I asked about your dream. You said you had a strange one. Right after the bat incident?"

I stare at the bedraggled roses glistening beyond our breakfast table in the atrium, survivors of last night's storm. The birds are chirping with a level of enthusiasm I'll never possess at eight in the morning. "I don't remember the details; I just remember feeling cold. Really, really cold."

After stirring a bunch of cream and three lumps of sugar into my coffee, I throw it back like a shot. Then I pour myself another, seeing how the tea-drinking Giles only made this pot of "American mud" upon my request. Based on his exaggerated sigh, you'd have thought I'd asked for a rare brand of unicorn milk found only in the deepest regions of the Scottish Highlands.

"This old house can have strange effects on people," Nathaniel observes.

"Yeah, well, so can a concussion."

"Don't be surprised if your subconscious starts lashing out. It happens to the best of us, thanks to the way this manor creaks and groans."

"Are you sure you didn't hear anything weird last night?"

"You mean besides your operatic solo?" Nathaniel smirks as he spreads a layer of orange marmalade over his buttered toast. "Actually, I'm surprised you woke me. Most of the time, I sleep like the dead."

Unless the dead don't sleep.

I push the thought away, touching the tender bruise near my temple.

A throat clears behind us.

"Pardon the interruption." Giles steps into the atrium.

Speaking of the dead returning… I haven't seen or heard a peep from Giles since he told us the phone lines were down. What's he been up to all this time?

"Miss Romano, I'm pleased to inform you that the road crew is repairing the bridge as we speak. It should be ready for crossing in just a few hours. In the meantime, might I request your assistance with a rather urgent matter?"

"Sure, Giles," I reply, my mouth full of dry toast. "What's up?"

The butler frowns, then clears his throat again. "Nothing is *up*, I'm afraid. In fact, things are most decidedly down in the gutter." His wary eyes study me, as if deciding whether I can be trusted or not, though his sigh indicates he doesn't have much of a choice. "It appears Lady Knight has misplaced her will. We went over it several weeks ago, and I was certain she had returned it to the safe in her downstairs office. But I've checked and it isn't there. I have no idea where else it could be."

"Did you try her bedroom?" Nathaniel asks.

Giles's face turns as purple as an eggplant. "Of course I checked her bloody bedroom! However, I was not the *first* to search Lady Knight's private chambers following her departure from this world."

The butler narrows his bushy eyebrows, casting a cold stare in my direction. It doesn't take long for Nathaniel to join him. "What's he talking about, Taylor?"

"Like I already told you, when we first arrived at the manor, I tried finding someone who could explain what had happened to Lady Knight. And I kind of ended up in her bedroom. On accident."

"On accident, she says," Giles grumbles.

I cross my arms stubbornly. "Something about the room didn't feel right… the broken cup, the way the nightstand drawer was almost pulled out of its track. So yeah, I decided to have a look around. But this is the first time I've heard anything about a will, I swear."

Giles seems unconvinced. "Yet you show up from across the pond, all of a sudden dear friends with Lady Knight, ready to have tea together."

"She was the one who invited *me*." It takes every bit of self-control I possess to stay calm. "Why does everyone seem to forget that? Tell him, Nathaniel."

But the butler isn't finished. "Our troubles began when *you* appeared out of nowhere, and I highly doubt that's a coincidence."

"Then maybe you should look into what caused Mae's death," I retort. "Because it seems an awful coincidence that a legal document *you* helped her revise went missing right around the time she died."

Nathaniel's torn glance bounces between us, like he isn't sure who to believe. "She's telling the truth, Giles. I was a bit suspicious at first, but Mae did invite Taylor here, though I agree it's a strange set of circumstances."

The butler frowns at his coworker. "In any case, we still need to locate the will as soon as possible, which means I have no choice but to request your assistance."

I'm still processing that Nathaniel took my side, but I try to keep my face as serious as Giles's grimace. "No problem. I'm sure it will turn up soon if we're all searching for it."

"If only the matter were that *laissez-faire*, Miss Romano," Giles replies. "Unfortunately, if we fail to locate the revised will soon, the lawyers claim they will need to refer to an earlier copy, drafted by Lady Knight's father many years ago."

"And what's wrong with that?" Nathaniel asks.

"What's wrong..." The butler scoffs. "Why, the earlier version states that if neither Knight daughter gave birth to a son, Meadowbrook was to be sold at auction. *At auction*! Can you imagine? Sadly, Lord Knight did not have the foresight to amend this longstanding custom. When Mae was named Meadowbrook's guardian, she had the power to change the clause regarding male heirs. And so, she did."

"Are there other relatives around to contest the change?" I don't get the sense that Mae Knight has had many visitors lately.

"Oh, there's a scattering of distant cousins lurking about. None with Lady Knight's aristocratic status, of course, but rest assured—they'll venture out from the backwoods of England for a few pounds as soon as they hear the news of her death. Still, keeping Meadowbrook in the family would be better than handing it off to some shortsighted businessman who'll only turn the place into another gaudy hotel or spa. Or worse—one of those convalescent homes for the elderly that Mae so despised."

Something about this scenario doesn't add up. Lady Knight, who was completely lucid as far as I know, updates her will and knows that if it goes missing, her father's outdated version takes its place, something she really didn't want to happen. And then she oh-so-conveniently dies right when the will disappears? I'm beginning to agree with Giles—not that *I* took the will, but that someone else may have.

"All right then, finish your breakfast and clean up. Time to get at it. I'll continue my search on the ground level and you two can take the floors upstairs." Giles sets down a tray for clearing the table, the loud clank of its impact still ringing as he marches from the room. Abrupt exits and entrances are definitely his specialty.

I help Nathaniel stack the dirty dishes. "Based on the way Giles requests help, you'd think he was doing *us* a favor."

"Poor old chap. Try not to be too hard on him. I know he doesn't look it, but Giles is grieving for Mae… in his own way. He's worked in this house his entire life, see. Who knows what will become of him now. I imagine the prospect of reentering the job market at his age is making him extra irritable."

I guess that makes me a little more sympathetic to Giles's frequent outbursts.

"That reminds me. Ava's memoir says her father became a shrink following what sounds like a major midlife crisis. But if he was an English lord, he wasn't expected to have a profession like that, right?"

"Definitely not. The aristocracy traditionally lived off their land, though that began to change in the early twentieth century. Lord Knight began studying psychology right before the First World War, when the discipline was fairly new and still intertwined with other intellectual movements like Spiritualism. But once the conflict began, Mae said Lord Knight's interests shifted from all the esoteric stuff to a more earthy, practical focus. He intended to treat returning soldiers suffering from shell shock—what we now call PTSD—but sadly, Lord Knight was killed in action himself before he had the chance." Nathaniel glances around the atrium, looking glum. "It's hard to imagine, isn't it? All this history being auctioned off to strangers?"

"But isn't that what's happened to most of England's old manors? They become fancy hotels. Or, like Giles said, old folks' homes." I had seen a sign for just such a nursing home on the bus ride from Heathrow.

"Maybe, but to do that to Meadowbrook would be like spitting on Mae's grave. All those distant relatives Giles mentioned? I'm sure at least one of them was pressuring Mae to move into a retirement home. Remember those letters I told you about that left Mae quite upset? There were constant phone calls, too, where the caller refused to give us their name. What I don't get is why anyone would think that Mae would willingly leave the house where she'd lived her entire life just to spend her final days among strangers." Visibly irritated, Nathaniel brushes back his hair with both hands. "Anyway, enough Knight family drama. We should start searching for the will."

"Maybe on the second floor?"

That's the location of Lady Knight's bedroom and thus the potential crime scene, after all. A crime that has all the necessary components, including an increasingly clear motive. Greedy relatives who try to push a wealthy old spinster out of her own home. A sudden death. And a missing will that has the potential to change the fate of this estate.

"That's a good idea," Nathaniel replies, picking up the tray stacked with dirty dishes. "And I know just the place to start searching—Lord Knight's study. Let me go run and ask Giles for the study's key."

My visit to Meadowbrook is starting to resemble the game of Clue we played last night. I just hope I'm wrong and the envelope that contains Lady Knight's will, if we ever find it, doesn't reveal the identity of a murderer, too.

When the sound of clanking china fades with Nathaniel's exit, my eyes fall to the red book resting on the table. What if the story Mae Knight left me has less to do with my own dad and more to do with the troubled family history that put her in such a dangerous position?

What if Lady Knight's abrupt invitation to tea was really a final cry for help?

16

$\mathcal{A}$VA

Father and I did not talk as we walked back to our stateroom, in part because I feigned exhaustion. As soon as Father was snoring away in his bed—as he always did after a few drams of Scotch—I would sneak from our room and confront Galena Lakovic in hers.

Unfortunately, when we reached the Grand Staircase, Benjamin Guggenheim and Ira Strauss, two prominent American businessmen I recognized immediately from their photographs in the paper, trapped Father in another dull conversation about the stock exchange. While the three men conversed, I leaned against the railing, nibbling at my nails. That was when it hit me. If I was unable to uncover the information Mrs. Lakovic carried tonight while Father slept, there'd only be one tool left at my disposal.

Blackmail.

If necessary, I would tell Father I knew all about his illicit affair. Then I would cry, and wail, and demand that he allow me to speak with his mistress alone, otherwise I'd head to the papers with this juicy scandal the second we reached New York, and then stay with Mother's cousin until I could arrange passage back to England… alone.

Of course, I'd never *actually* go to the papers, but Father did not need to know that. Like many men of his status, his blood ran blue with vanity. A respectable reputation was what kept it flowing. I knew he'd choose to preserve the Knight family name. Extorting my own father seemed heartless, but it would be my last resort if I was to save him from a worse fate. Hopefully, it would not come to that.

As I listened to the men drone on, my muscles tightened and my breath grew shallow—time was running out. The relentless ticking of the clock at the top of the staircase made this feeling even more pronounced.

"Lady Ava?"

I lifted my chin and met Seaman Donohue's cool scrutiny. His eyes glowed an even brighter shade of green beneath the magic of electricity.

"Are you all right? You look… ill."

I swallowed the nausea rising in my throat. "I'm fine."

"No. You're not." Caleb gently grabbed my wrist, pulling me down to a seated position on the step. Crouching in front of me, he removed a small paper bag from his back pocket. "Here, take deep breaths in this. There you go."

"Ugh." I pulled the bag from my mouth. "What was in here? It's retched."

Caleb blushed. "Sorry about that. Captain Smith likes his cigars. I'm responsible for making sure he receives his nightly delivery."

The leftover tobacco smell wasn't so bad once I got used to it. In fact, the more I inhaled, the calmer I became. The bag's sweet, peppery taste brought me back to a time when Father had been my hero and I his little darling, balanced on his knee while he read the evening paper and smoked his pipe.

"There now. All better?" Caleb asked as I lowered the paper bag. "I've got a condition where my lungs become so inflamed that I can hardly breathe, so I've been there myself."

The tightness in my chest had faded, but the sight of this sailor yet again left me flustered. "You said you were in the crow's nest tonight."

He nodded. "Thought I was covering for Fleet. Chap's been ill the past few days, but he's feeling better and needed the wages, so he wanted to take over his shift." A smirk rose in the corner of the sailor's mouth. "Good riddance, I say. It was bloody freezing up there. It's hard to see anything on account of the ship's binoculars going missing. Didn't fancy a night of squinting into the dark."

"Then I'm glad you escaped such a fate." I forced a smile, though I felt unsure of how to proceed. This whole misunderstanding between us was ridiculous. Besides, why was I so distraught over the poor impression I'd made when I'd never see this young man again in just a few hours' time?

"Well, good evening." Caleb helped me to my feet, then tipped his hat and continued up the stairs. No doubt he was off to rescue another pampered princess whose corset was laced too tight. Pathetic though I was, I did not even have *that* as an excuse, which made the swell of self-loathing in my chest push its way up my throat.

"Seaman Donohue, wait. If I may have a word?"

The sailor turned slowly. "How else might I serve you, Lady Ava?"

There was no sarcasm in his voice, but the words sliced deep nonetheless. Serving was what this seaman did from sunup to sunset, and I'd never given Caleb's existence or the millions like him a second thought. Until meeting him. Somehow, every time we crossed paths, this sailor managed to shove me in front of a mirror bathed in the harshest light.

The reflection was not flattering.

I joined Caleb at the top of the stairs. Yet I could not bring myself to apologize for my treatment of him earlier. Feeling ridiculous, I pointed to the carved panels before blurting out the first words that came to my mind. "This most unusual clock. Do you have any idea what it's meant to symbolize?"

Caleb studied me, unsure if I was being sincere. "It's called 'Honour and Glory Crowning Time.' See, the angel with the palm leaf symbolizes Glory, and the one with the tablet is Honour."

"And what is Honour copying ever so diligently?"

With his index finger, Caleb traced the angel draped around the clock face. "I like to think she's recording man's victories over time. See that globe beneath her foot? It's a sign man has conquered the world. Thanks to inventions like the railroad and the steamer, the vast distances that used to divide us are no longer an impediment. Before long, we'll have defeated time itself. *Titanic* is the ultimate icon of man's triumph over nature."

"That's a bit presumptuous, isn't it?" Apparently, I was incapable of speaking to this young man without shoving my foot into my mouth, and I hastily clarified. "What I mean to say, Seaman Donohue, is you must be a well-read sailor indeed to see all that symbolism in two little angels."

"I'm no expert, Lady Ava." Caleb's eyes fell to the floor. I feared I'd made yet another belligerent remark, but when he lifted his chin, I saw that he was flustered as well. Nervous, not offended. "I suppose most of us tend to see what we want to see."

I was making him anxious—that I could see. The most alarming aspect of this insight was that the feeling was mutual.

"I'm impressed by your astute analysis regardless." I hesitated, unsure what to say next. So, I did what Father always did: cleared my throat and cut to the chase. "Mr. Donohue, I would like to apologize for my rude behavior earlier this morning. You see, I—"

"No need to explain, Lady Ava. You meant no harm by it, and I was foolish to think you'd want to walk with me as a, as a… well, friend." The sailor's ruddy complexion became even ruddier. "Though I've been meaning to ask—have you ever actually been to Ireland? To Derry, where you said your mother was born?"

"Not since I was too young to remember." The fact that he recalled the details of our first conversation lit something inside me. Something earnest that begged to be stoked. "I hear it is a lovely country."

Caleb nodded. "That it is, but it has its own troubles. Like most places, I suppose."

I smoothed my gown. "Yes, my father often speaks of the ongoing conflict with the Irish rebels."

"Or revolutionaries, depending on where you're standing."

The mention of revolution had me tense up as I recalled Lieutenant Plavsic's sneer, but Caleb's casual tone and easy-going nature made it difficult for me to picture him as the fanatical type.

"I've never been one for politics, to be honest," he continued. "All I mean to say is people often make a big ruckus out of the minor differences. Yet what good does that do? We're all going the same way, trying to figure things out according to whatever fragment of the story we've inherited."

"I'm not sure I follow."

"All right, well, take my family. My mother is a Catholic and my father's a Protestant, which can cause problems in Ireland, mind you. But to us kids, all we knew was that they loved the Almighty, they loved each other, and they loved us."

"How did they come together in the first place?" I asked, unable to hide my shock. Caleb spoke as if such a union was no great matter, but I knew from my own Anglo-Irish mother that such a thing simply wasn't done. Her mostly Anglican, aristocratic family in mostly Catholic Ireland had sought a more suitable marriage for her in mostly Protestant England. Mother did inherit some of the Roman flourishes of her maternal grandmother, however, such as a miraculous medal depicting a stamp of the Virgin Mary in a cobalt resin, which she'd passed on to me on my thirteenth birthday—"Only don't let your father see you wearing it," Mother had said with a wink.

I felt the meaningless cameo charm at my throat, wishing I had worn Mother's protective medal instead.

"Oh, it was nothing so dramatic as Romeo and Juliet," Caleb continued. "They met in the Harland and Wolff shipyards, where Ma sold corned beef sandwiches to the workers at lunchtime. Da was one of them—one of the men who built the ship you're standing on."

Yet another reminder that we came from different worlds.

"How unusual. Your parents' marriage, I mean. Not your father's profession, which of course is a most respectable one." Good grief, now I was rambling! And every word that left my mouth felt capable of giving insult. "And did your family experience much hardship as a result of your parents' unconventional decision to marry?"

Caleb shrugged. "It isn't that the differences between them don't matter. The Donohue family would just rather be known for what we're *for*—and there's a lot of common ground—than for what we're against. Besides, there will always be talk, not to mention people who like to make trouble where none should exist." The sailor placed a bold hand on my arm, casting a cautious eye in Father's direction. "You shouldn't let such things bother you."

My stomach fluttered. It seemed even this humble crewmember knew about my father's infidelity. "I, well, I'm not quite sure what—"

"Forgive me, Lady Ava. I've spoken out of turn." Yet Caleb's grip held steady as his eyes clung to mine. "It's just that I've heard the rumors and—"

"Thank you for your concern." Tears blurred my vision, so I turned to the elegant clock face in an effort to blink them away. The hands struck eleven-thirty. "But there's no need to apologize. We live in insincere times. Your honesty is most refreshing."

Caleb released my arm, but before I could walk away, he gently clasped my chin, pulling my startled eyes back to his. That this sailor could be so forward was shocking enough, yet all I could see in his candid face was a determined conviction.

"Don't listen to them, Ava. Some people are so blinded by pride, they have no idea what to make of what they *think* they see." As if suddenly aware that he'd crossed all lines of propriety, Caleb dropped his hand. "They certainly don't see what I see."

And what *did* he see? Not when looking at my father and Mrs. Lakovic, but when looking at me?

"Come now, Ava. Let's be off," Father called from below. I took a hasty step away from Mr. Donohue and looked down at my father, who had a deep line creasing his brow as he looked at the two of us. "It's getting late."

Caleb continued up the staircase, glancing over his shoulder with a look so brutally frank in its affection, I had to grip the railing behind me. "Sweet dreams, Lady Ava. May they be sincere ones, too."

TAYLOR

I close the book and use it to fan my face. Forget class divisions and denominational strife, this Caleb is a keeper. If Ava is too blind to see that, the girl will live to regret it.

Maybe she did.

Nathaniel returns to the atrium, holding up a plain key in triumph. "Okay, let's get started. Giles is skeptical, though—Mae always kept her father's study locked, so no one has been in there in quite some time."

"You mean it's still considered Jonathan Knight's study? Even though he died nearly a century ago?"

"Ah, yes, this quirk is one of Meadowbrook's most endearing features… or one of its creepiest, depending on how you look at it."

"I'm going to go out on a limb and say creepiest. Please elaborate."

"Seeing as how the house is so massive, whenever a family member passed away, Mae just left their favorite room intact. Almost like a shrine. In short, her father's study is *exactly* the way it was the day he died. And that room you slept in last night…" Nathaniel grins. "Let's just hope Mrs. Porter washed the sheets."

"That's disgusting!" I elbow him in the side as we head toward the staircase in the foyer. "You'd better be kidding."

"Of course I'm kidding, though Ava's bedroom is definitely furnished the way it was when she died."

"And when was that?"

Nathaniel shrugs. "Not sure. The 1980s maybe?"

"What I don't understand is why Ava's gorgeous photographs were hidden in that closet. I'd much rather hang them on the walls than look at *those* two grumps all day." I nod at the intimidating portraits of the first Lord and Lady Knight above the staircase.

"Don't ask me. By this point, you probably know more about Ava than I do. Mae didn't really talk about her family much. It seemed like a sore subject, so I never pried."

We head upstairs. "Speaking of which, why didn't Lady Knight—Mae, I mean—ever marry or have children?"

Nathaniel nods. "I always got the sense Mae wanted a family, but I don't think she was lucky in the romance department. Again, she never talked about it, but based on a few offhanded comments by Mrs. Porter, my hunch is Mae lost someone during the war. The Second World War, that is."

"So she swore off love for good? That was probably wise." After all, my mom had done the exact opposite—diving headfirst into another marriage because she couldn't bear being alone. Except she wasn't alone. She had me. But that wasn't enough. "I don't understand how people can keep trying to find love after experiencing such a devastating loss. Isn't that just inviting more heartache into your life?"

I never understood how Mom fell for someone else after being married to my dad. My stepfather, Derek—comic book connoisseur and real estate agent extraordinaire—is a nice enough guy, but he can't hold a candle to Dad.

"I couldn't disagree more," Nathaniel says. "I think it's when you lose someone that you begin to realize how bottomless love is... how much you actually have to give. I'm guessing that's how Giles captured Mae's heart."

I wrinkle my nose. "Gross. Wasn't she a little old for him?"

"Oh no, it was nothing like that." Nathaniel laughs. "Giles was among the thousands of children evacuated from London during the Blitz. He spent several years of the war here at Meadowbrook with Ava and Mae. When his parents were killed, they invited him to stay."

"As their butler? How generous."

"Actually, it was, given that the arrangement was Giles's idea. He insisted he be given proper employment. Turning fourteen in 1945 was a lot different than being fourteen now, and he was hardly considered a child. He wanted a job to help support the younger siblings who were split up among relatives, so he started his service in the kitchen, then became a footman, and eventually worked his way up to butler. Even after the service-industry apocalypse that put an end to such roles, Giles stuck around." Nathaniel gives me a sly wink. "Like a cockroach."

That makes me laugh more than it probably should. I've had this weird, fishy feeling about Giles ever since our first interaction in Lady Knight's bedroom, but it's hard to imagine him harming the woman who spared him a war orphan's life on the streets.

"Here we are." Nathaniel brings the key to the door's lock, but the knob turns effortlessly. "Strange. It's already unlocked."

The door swings open with a low creak, and I stifle a gasp. Nathaniel was right about the creepy time capsule thing.

Jonathan Knight's study looks exactly as he must have left it on his final day in the manor, right down to the ceramic tray of ash from a pipe or cigar. A glass tumbler of amber liquor, hardened into thick syrup, sits on the coffee table, along with a yellowed newspaper from 1915. I read the eye-catching headline on the front page:

GERMANS GAIN GROUND NEAR YPRES BY USING ASPHYXIATING GAS

"Wow, this really *is* a shrine. How does a clean-freak like Giles stand it?" I drag my finger across one of the bookcase shelves. Not a speck of dust.

"Fortunately, he doesn't have to. Mrs. Porter occasionally cleans the rooms, but according to Mae's strict guidelines. She's probably the one who left the door unlocked." Nathaniel points to the Edwardian still-life on the coffee table. "See, after she dusts, she returns everything to its original location."

"Talk about neurotic."

"I'm not sure if that was it. Mae claimed she wanted to capture a moment in time. Like I said, the Knights were all rather eccentric. Even Mae had her quirks."

This time capsule is a lot more than a quirk, but it really isn't a point worth debating when we've got work to do. I step further into the room, looking about for a likely place to stash a will, and my eyes widen.

Mrs. Porter missed a spot.

In an alcove not visible from the doorway sits Jonathan Knight's antique writing desk and an oak filing cabinet. Stacks of paper cover every square inch of the desk's surface, and all the drawers of the filing cabinet are open, their contents strewn across the floor.

"What a slob. Is this really how Lord Knight left it?"

The color drains from Nathaniel's face. "I doubt it. Mae always said her father was a most fastidious man. Looks to me like someone's been in here snooping around."

"But who?"

Nathaniel shakes his head. "That's what I can't figure out. The will hasn't been missing for that long, and Mrs. Porter was home sick the day before Mae died. Giles was the only one here that night."

Giles, Giles... all roads lead to Giles.

"Do you think he could be lying?" I ask. "About the will, I mean."

"I don't know why he would," Nathaniel replies. "Giles has been nothing but loyal to Mae his entire life."

A weird feeling slowly creeps up my back. That déjà vu sense that you've been here before. Not *here* as in this study—it's more like the feeling I always got when Dad sent me on one of his treasure hunts. Like all the pieces of the puzzle are in front of me and I just have to find the correct combination.

I pick up a cracked picture frame from the mess on the floor. The stern, mustached face of Jonathan Knight, dressed in his World War I uniform, stares back at me.

Not long after Dad's funeral, I found an album of old military photos just like this. It didn't take long for Mom to pack it away in a box with the rest of Dad's belongings, but not before I memorized what was scrawled on the back of the photographs of my great-grandfather, grandfather, and Dad.

William Romano, Petty Officer, US Navy, killed in action
December 7, 1941

Lou Romano, Corporal, US Marines, killed in action
August 23, 1968

Thomas Romano, Sergeant, US Army, killed in action
April 15, 2008

That's all I really know about the men who lost their lives at Pearl Harbor and in Vietnam—their names, ranks, and the dates of their deaths. Both sons had been too young when their own fathers passed away to recall much else.

My dad, on the other hand, was killed when I was old enough to store up every excruciating detail. I *remember* the man, which means if I ever have children of my own, they'll hear all about how their grandfather died for something he believed in. Usually I'm proud of that, but every now and then, I wish I could ask Dad if his ideals were worth the cost.

Worth the shattering of his family.

Nathaniel stops shuffling through the mess. "Are you okay, Taylor?"

"I'm fine," I say as I riffle through a folder of old tax documents. Nathaniel's probing eyes say *you can tell me*, but I never talk about Dad and I'm not about to start now. "Do you think Mae misplaced the will on accident, or could she have had a reason to hide it?"

Nathaniel chews his bottom lip. "I suspect it has something to do with those distressing letters and phone calls. My guess is someone was pressuring Mae to sell the manor. Maybe she hid her will because she was worried they would find a way to tamper with it? I doubt it's in here, though. Based on the dates of these documents, these files haven't been opened in years."

"I think you're right. So far all I've found is evidence that Jonathan Knight had some serious hoarding issues." I pick up an especially crinkled piece of paper shoved into a manilla folder—then stand so fast the room spins as the blood struggles to reach my head.

Nathaniel places a hand on my back to steady me. "You must have found something more interesting than old cigar receipts."

I nod, sitting back down before my legs give out. "This symbol. I've seen it somewhere before."

Two linked rings, two perfect circles that create an almond shape where they overlap. Beneath the drawing, in the center of the page, there's a poetic line in fresh ink that matches the handwriting of Mae's last letter.

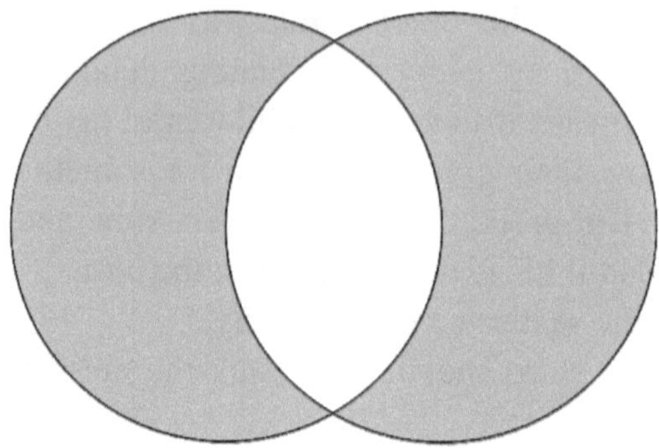

Only through time is time conquered, at the still point of the turning world.

Nathaniel peers over my shoulder. The tickle of his breath on the back of my neck makes it difficult to register his words. "How odd. That's a *vesica pisces*."

"A *vesica* what?" I let the paper fall to my lap, so Nathaniel won't see it trembling in my hands.

"A *vesica pisces*," he repeats. "It's a symbol found in many ancient cultures. See how the teardrop in the center of the two circles almost resembles a fish?"

I nod. Mom's zodiac sign is Pisces and she's as obsessed with astrology almost as much as she is with tarot-card-wielding psychics. "But what does it mean? And how do you know all this?"

"It's sacred geometry. There are certain shapes and patterns that appear repeatedly in nature. Some psychologists believe they point to subconscious truths, a mystical wisdom we're born knowing, but that we forget as we age. Jung's archetypes and all that." Nathaniel smiles shyly. "The focus of my history degree is the rise of psychology in Edwardian England, so I get a bit nerdy about this stuff."

Nerdy… and kind of adorable. My ears register the name of Carl Jung—the psychologist Ava mentioned in her memoir—but at the word *mystical*, my BS detector switches on. "What kind of subconscious truths?"

"Well, think of it like this: most of us tend to conceptualize reality in terms of contrasting opposites. A.k.a., dualities." Nathaniel points to one circle, then the other. "Male and female, good and evil, time and eternity, life and death."

I nod. "Darth Vader vs. Luke Skywalker. Got it."

Nathaniel smirks. "Not so fast. That's a perfect example of why dualistic thinking doesn't always work out. As father and son, Vader and Luke shared genetic material. So really, they're connected. Two apparent opposites who, on another level, are united in a realm that exists outside of time and space. That's what the *still point* is all about." He points at Mae's line.

"Are you being serious right now?" Because no matter how Nathaniel tries to dress it up as academic, this sounds like esoteric mumbo jumbo. The kind of New Age theories Mom buys into when she's looking for cheap answers to things that are simply unanswerable.

Nathaniel's smile widens—to the point that I'm almost willing to buy whatever nonsense he's selling. "Okay, maybe *Star Wars* isn't the best analogy. Still, the *vesica pisces* does pop up in all kinds of world religions, from Jewish mystics to Celtic pagans to medieval Catholics to modern day Buddhists. You've got to admit that's a strange coincidence. The shared belief is that while we do live in a dualistic dimension called *time*, there's another reality where these apparent opposites fall away to reveal a deeper wholeness—a realm called *eternity*, which exists outside of time and space. But even here in our world, there are moments where we get a taste of the eternal. Instances where the extremes of time and eternity meet." Nathaniel traces the center of the two circles. "That's what this teardrop, the almond-fish thing, represents. It's the place where time and eternity touch."

Nathaniel's explanation makes me feel tingly all over, like I'm remembering something I've always known but just forgot about. "You really got all this bizarre stuff out of an English History 101 class?"

Nathaniel rocks back and forth on his sneakers. "Uh, well, I initially learned about it in a video game, to be honest. But after that I did more research on my own."

"A video game, huh?" I chuckle, relieved to know this Oxford genius can be a normal eighteen-year-old guy at times. "But I'm not buying the 'evidence' of the symbol appearing in a few religious practices. Every religion is full of symbols. It's no surprise some of them match up. It just sounds like a nice story."

"But for nearly *all* of them to share this specific symbol? At different points in history and on different continents? That seems highly unlikely. What are the chances of finding the same symbol across cultures and centuries unless it's evidence of some universal truth?" Nathaniel shakes his head. "It has to mean something. Besides, stories are often the truest things of all."

I wave a hand. "Okay, sure, say I buy the shared symbol. You said the symbol is all about eternity, but I don't even get what that means." I fold up the paper with the *vesica pisces* drawing and slip it into my back pocket. "Just look around. There isn't much evidence that anything is eternal. Nothing lasts forever. Healthy bodies get sick. Empires fall. Leaves decompose."

People die.

"I agree it *seems* that way," Nathaniel replies. "Just think about how much life has changed since Mae was a child. It's only been a century, and yet we live in a completely different world. Mae rode in one of the very first automobiles, and already we've put men on the moon. Her parents sent messages by telegram, and we shoot texts across space in seconds. On the surface nothing seems stable or consistent, but there's a question I can't shake."

The soft blanket of Nathaniel's conviction draws me in. Despite my initial skepticism, I admire how he can sound assured and yet express doubts at the same time. There aren't many people willing to hang out in such a risky space.

"Oh? What's that?"

He looks away. "It sounds absurd, and a little lame, when I try to explain it…"

"Try anyway."

"All right." Nathaniel exhales but refuses to meet my gaze. "What about… love? No one *forces* us to love, and yet it's what we long for more than anything else. But one day we'll lose what we love, which means pain is a part of the deal. So why do we keep putting ourselves through the torture if love is as temporary as everything else?"

His question reminds me of the massive argument I had with Mom right after she told me she was getting married to Derek.

I know you think I'm being foolish, Taylor, or that I'm betraying your dad. One day, I hope you'll see that opening yourself up to love is always an act of courage.

My frown deepens. "I don't know. Why do we?"

"Perhaps because love—I'm talking *real* love, difficult love that sticks with it, not the sappy stuff you see at the cinema—is our one shot at something permanent. If it's so obvious that nothing lasts forever in this world, then why have so many different people across the ages believed love might be the *one* thing that endures, even after death?"

Nathaniel makes decent points, but hope carries its own set of obligations, and I can't handle that kind of pressure right now. It's impossible to imagine still points in a chaotic world where the people you love most could be snatched away at any second. But there's no reason to drag Nathaniel into my jaded whirlwind. He can be a bit of a know-it-all, but that doesn't make his idealism any less magnetic.

Too bad it won't be rubbing off. Death has already taught me that there are only two ways to respond to this baffling life:

keep swimming no matter what it throws at you or stop and sink to the bottom.

Which means I've got to keep moving.

Mae tried to honor the deceased by turning their rooms into something static, but my frightened, controlling mother is what happens when you get stuck in a single moment. Once that memory owns you, it defines the rest of your life.

I'm ready to get out of this stifling shrine. "This is pointless. If Lady Knight's will was even in here, somebody else already found it."

The cryptic symbol is interesting, but it isn't going to lead us to a legal document, or explain my father's connection to the Knights, let alone redeem his memory.

I glance at Nathaniel, who's preoccupied by something behind me. His eyes widen as if the ghost of Jonathan Knight is standing over me, but his gaze leads me to a large bulletin board behind the desk that I hadn't noticed. Black-and-white newspaper clippings from the First World War cover every bit of cork, along with disturbing images of dead bodies in trenches and entire cities reduced to rubble.

Scrawled across the clippings in blood red ink are the interlocking circles of the *vesica pisces*, along with multiple references to Deut. 5:8-9. The collage looks like the ravings of a madman, but I guess war can have that effect on people.

Life can have that effect.

"What do you think Deut. 5 means?" I ask.

"It's a Bible verse, I'm guessing, from the book of Deuteronomy." Nathaniel begins searching a nearby bookshelf, finally removing a gigantic, leather-bound tome. He flips through its thin pages until he finds what he's looking for.

"You shall not make for yourself a graven image—any likeness of anything that is in heaven above, or that is in the earth beneath, or that is in the water under the earth; you shall not bow down to them nor serve them. For I, the Lord your

God, am a jealous God, visiting the sins of the fathers upon the children to the third and fourth generations."

"Third and fourth generations? Sounds like a family curse to me," I say, recalling what Bill said about the Knight men meeting tragic ends.

I study Jonathan Knight's chaotic war collage again. Maybe the dead can communicate with the living, after all.

18

$\mathcal{A}$VA

"What were you and that young sailor going on about?" Father asked as we left the Grand Staircase. "You looked rather entranced."

Caleb Donohue's attention clearly bothered him, but I knew as well as Father that a poor, title-less Irishman could never present himself as a potential suitor, let alone inherit Meadowbrook Manor. Then again, even *I* could not inherit my family home—not without securing an aristocratic husband first.

"Mr. Donohue was simply explaining some of *Titanic*'s artwork. It seems his father had a hand in the construction of the ship and—"

"One moment." Father stopped abruptly as we approached our stateroom. The door was ajar. "Don't take another step. It appears someone has been inside our suite."

I didn't see any immediate reason for alarm. "I'm sure the steward just failed to shut it all the way. They've been turning up the heaters, so the rooms are nice and toasty when we return."

Father shook his head, his face draining of color. "That's not it. You wait here. If I call out to you, run for the Master of Arms at once."

Father slipped into the room and released a startled gasp. Peering back at me through the crack in the door, his liquid blue eyes glimmered like ice.

"What is it, Father? What's the matter? Is anyone inside?"

"Not anymore." Father held the door open wide. "Our room has been ransacked."

I pushed past him into the suite. There could be no doubt it had been raided, but what the thief took was far from obvious. The small writing desk was overturned, a washing pitcher and basin were shattered, and the sofa cushions had been slashed to shreds.

I rushed to my bedroom in search of my camera and dark room supplies. Thank God everything was intact. The ignorant thief clearly knew nothing of photography if he hadn't thought the equipment worth anything. Then again, he hadn't thought my jewels or designer gowns worth stealing either; they were merely torn from their hangers and flung around the room.

This was no ordinary robbery. This thief searched for something specific.

Based on my father's lack of surprise, I suspected he was hiding a secret even more disastrous than his extramarital affair. Now was the time for directness. "What are you keeping from me, Father? Other than your mistress, that is."

"Ava, sit down." He met my eye calmly, then brushed aside the goose feathers strewn across my torn mattress, not at all shocked by my knowledge of his infidelity. "I need to alert the authorities, but first, there is something I must tell you."

I took a seat while Father paced the room, his eyes in search of a stiff drink. "Should have brought more bloody Scotch," he murmured.

"Well? Out with it!" I did not intend to make this confession easy on him.

Father twisted his moustache. "Tell me, dear, do you know what the word *psychology* means?"

"For heaven's sake, we've been robbed! This is no time to quiz me on my knowledge of Latin roots."

"It's Greek, actually. And it means the study of the soul, which is what I am trying to do: study souls in their many forms."

"Wonderful!" I held up the detached sleeve of a favorite gown. "But what does that have to do with the destruction of our property?"

"I am about to tell you. For the past year, I've attended many gatherings of psychologists all over Europe in order to gain new insights into—"

"I know, I know, into discovering a cure for Mother's illness. So she might be happy again. Well, a lot of good it's done." The tears Caleb Donohue roused seared my eyes again, but my fury forced them back. "And here we are in the middle of the Atlantic while Mother is home alone, soon to receive word that her husband is carrying on with some crystal-ball-reading charlatan!"

Father stared out the porthole in silence, his face deflated with a sadness I could not understand. Why should *he* be disappointed? Mother and I were the ones wronged by his selfishness and lust.

"No. Dear God, no!" Father turned from the porthole, terror forming rigid lines in the corners of his mouth. He looked as though he'd seen a phantom ship riding upon the waves. "She was right. Galena foresaw it all. I must reach her before—"

The world stopped turning.

Father lurched forward the moment of the shudder—a low rumble that rose from the sea, shaking every object in our cabin, from the light fixtures to the teacup on my nightstand. The vibrations sent Father flying, his foot catching the leg of a table as he tumbled to the floor.

A low groan rattled in my ears as the lights flickered out. Darkness pressed in from every side. When the shuddering stopped, the only sound I could hear was Father moaning. Blindly feeling in front of me, I crawled toward him, holding my breath as an eerie stillness swept over the ship.

The engines had stopped.

When the lights flickered back on, I found Father in a crumpled heap. "Are you all right? Don't move! We must find help and get you to the infirmary."

"No, Ava. Wait." Father pushed himself upright, straining to speak. "Walk over to that porthole. Tell me what you see. I… I want to be certain."

I tried to do as he asked, but I could hardly comprehend what I saw, let alone describe it. Beyond the porthole, a wall of ice rose into a sky that had all but vanished. The sea had vanished. Perhaps our entire world had vanished.

Craning my neck, I strained to catch sight of a single star beyond this frozen mountain. A sigh of relief escaped my lips when I saw that the heavens still twinkled, the stars a scattering of silent witnesses to the end of our gilded dream.

"An iceberg," I whispered.

"Galena foresaw it, but I wouldn't listen." Father moaned. "I thought she was overworked and exhausted. On the verge of collapse. Yet all this time… she knew."

I understood he was in pain, but his vagueness had become unbearable. "Father, what on earth is going on? Explain your mistress. Who *is* this Lakovic woman?" Even now, I maintained hope that he would say I was mistaken—that Galena was merely a client or colleague.

Leaning back, Father rested his head against the wall. "She's a special case. A very special case. Ours is a long and winding story, and there isn't time to get into it now. What you need to know is Galena was once married to a member of the Black Hand—a secret intelligence organization with connections to the Serbian military. After her husband was killed carrying out a secret operation, Galena fled to friends in England. I met her at a Society for Psychical Research gathering in London a few years ago, and we've been working on a research project ever since. This effort has given us access to extremely sensitive information that we *must* deliver to powerful influencers in America. Now please, help me stand. I must find Galena at once."

Psychic research? As in chasers of ghosts?

"Listen to yourself! This is no time to worry about Mrs. Lakovic's dubious past. We must get you to a doctor."

"No, *you* listen to me," Father said, breathing rapidly. "If this ship sinks—"

"Don't be ridiculous. *Titanic* can't sink. Whatever this setback entails, I'm sure the crew will have it repaired in no time and we'll be on our way."

Father pulled himself to his feet. "Enough, Ava!" I had never heard him speak to me so forcefully. "I've tried to be patient with you, but I'll no longer indulge your delusions. Why, you're nearly as exasperating as your mother—" Father winced at his harsh words, but his low blow had achieved its desired effect.

I fell silent.

"Now," Father continued, glancing around the ransacked room, "we clearly have enemies on this ship—people who must never get their hands on the information we carry. If Galena and I are unable to make it to New York for any reason, you must find our friend and colleague William Stead and relay the message I am about to tell you."

"Why Mr. Stead?" I asked.

"He'll know what to do with our secret. He's trustworthy and is traveling to the same gathering."

I recalled something William Stead had mentioned at our last dinner. "You mean the international peace conference at Carnegie Hall?"

"Precisely." Father slammed his fist against the wall. "*One of us must make it off this bloody ship alive!*"

I couldn't understand why Father believed we'd been issued such a death blow. *Titanic* was made of the world's strongest steel and even if the worst came to pass, we still had the lifeboats. Yet I'd never seen the collected man consumed by such panic, and it left me untethered. It was all I could do to keep from shaking where I stood.

"What message could possibly be so urgent, Father?"

Father searched his pockets for his watch, as if it were imperative that he note the time. "I am about to tell you, my dear, but you must never repeat my words to anyone but William Stead. *No one* else, Ava. Do you understand?"

A realization washed over me before Father could say more. The secret message he referred to was undoubtedly the same information Lieutenant Plavsic desired. All this time I'd believed I was merely thwarting the plans of a madwoman when I was also sabotaging the schemes of my own father.

Perhaps it was fortunate that his betrayals had shattered any remaining loyalty I might have felt toward him. We had never been close, as I'd long sensed his apathy in response to the fact that I was not the son and heir he'd hoped for, and he'd largely left me to my mother's care, until even that had become untenable.

The fact that he requested my help now after so many years of indifference caused a tidal wave of rage to build inside me, so overwhelming that my next words did not even feel like a lie. "I won't say a word, Father."

Unless you give me no choice.

Father pointed to the linked rings of his lapel pin. "Mr. Stead is also a member of the Society for Psychical Research, and President Taft has personally requested his presence at the conference, so he'll likely hear the man out at least. But if Stead doesn't survive the sinking either, then you must deliver the message yourself."

"*Me?*"

"Yes, *you,* Ava. I hate to leave you this burden, but I suspect we are about to endure quite an ordeal. An ordeal whose outcome even Galena cannot foresee, despite her many gifts." Father looked me straight in the eye. "But you are strong, and young…"

And a first-class female. The first to be loaded in a lifeboat.

"What about Helen Crawford? She's a member of your little club as well, is she not?"

Father frowned. "Yes, but that woman rubs me the wrong way—"

"I know, I know, a woman with a brain is such a bore," I said with an exaggerated sigh.

"Ava." Father's eyes flashed at my mockery. "It isn't that. There isn't time to explain more but suffice it to say that your prudence and common sense are exactly why this task must fall to you. Out of all of us, you stand the best chance of survival."

Father's ominous words hung in the air. The stateroom grew colder by the second.

I stared at my father. After going to such great lengths to get him to notice me ever since mother miscarried the son who would have inherited Father's land and title, it was odd to no longer care what he thought of me. Before *Titanic*, I would have done whatever he asked to make him proud. But if we were all facing the possibility of death, why should I waste my remaining time on earth doing the bidding of soldiers and lords?

I was sick of being acknowledged only when I served some purpose or could be of use in an ambitious man's schemes, even if that man were my own father. Tonight, I would pursue the only thing I had left.

My survival. My freedom.

But Father did not need to know that. Two could play at this game of treachery.

"All right. What must I do?"

The man's eyes softened. "Galena Lakovic possesses a prophetic gift, a sight that has enabled her to see a coming war."

I shrugged, unimpressed. "That isn't such a stretch of the imagination. Wars happen every day."

"Perhaps, but this one will change the course of Western civilization as we know it, and certainly not for the better. Thanks to our latest technological advances, there are new weapons on the horizon that will only increase the brutality of warfare, new ways of fighting that will lead to the deaths of millions, Ava. *Millions.* That is the warning we must deliver to the world leaders in New York. The United States is a young power, but she is not yet tangled in Europe's web of alliances, which makes President Taft the ideal mediator. We must guarantee that our proof of Galena's prophecy finds its way into a lifeboat."

But how can one *prove* a prophecy, I wonder, shaking my head. "This is absurd, Father. President Taft knows about the troubles in the Baltic. Everyone does. We all assume there will be another war in the region. Why would a so-called prophecy make any difference?"

"Perhaps it won't," Father said quietly, his voice trembling. "But we must try. The rest is out of our hands. All I know is this war will be unlike anything we've ever seen, and there will be no turning back the clock once the darkness of modern weaponry is unleashed. It will engulf the entire world, resulting in a conflict so complete in its destruction, it is sure to be a war to end *all* wars."

The fear and trembling I experienced at these words was defeated by one thing—the renewed sense of loyalty I felt for Mother, a blameless victim of the domestic conflict Father had invited into our household.

If what Father claimed was true and war was imminent, then we were already on opposing sides—he and Galena Lakovic stood on one bank, and Mother and I on the other.

19

TAYLOR

"But *Titanic* sank on April 15, 1912. Two *years* before World War I. How could they have known?"

"It doesn't make any sense," Nathaniel replies. He listened to me read aloud with great interest, but now he looks more alarmed than intrigued.

"And yet they *did* know." I glance around Lord Knight's study. We're alone still, but it doesn't feel that way. How can the Knights I've been reading about be dead when they seem so alive? This family's presence is like a layer of dust that clings to everything, refusing to be swept under the rug.

"Hard at work from a seated position, I see." Giles enters the study wearing his usual scowl. "And what a mess you've made! It looks like a bloody bomb went off."

"Listen Giles, there's something strange going on," Nathaniel says. "Lord Knight's office was like this when we got here. Someone's been searching his desk and filing cabinets. You're sure you haven't looked in here already?"

The butler swallows hard. "Of course not. I haven't been inside this room in… I can't even remember how long. In any case, you'll be relieved to know we no longer require your assistance."

I spring to my feet. "You mean you found the will?"

"Afraid not, Miss Romano. But there's no need for *you* to look any further. The bridge has been repaired. You are free to return to Oxford whenever it is most convenient."

And by *convenient*, I'm pretty sure Giles means *now*.

If he's trying to get rid of me, I might as well bring up the only question I can think of that would link my father to Mae. "You've lived at Meadowbrook a long time, Giles. Does the name Thomas Romano mean anything to you?"

The butler narrows his busy eyebrows, his face about as revealing as concrete. "Can't say that it does. Now you'll have to excuse me. Lady Knight's lawyer will be arriving soon, and I need to go put on the tea."

Giles shuts the study door with a bang.

I shake my head. "I really don't know about him…"

"Who's Thomas Romano?" Nathaniel asks. The blank look on his face tells me he truly hasn't heard the name before.

"He was my dad."

"Was?"

"He died a few years ago. He was a soldier in Afghanistan."

"Taylor, I'm so sorry." Nathaniel's eyes fall to the floor. "And you think Mae knew him?"

"That's what the letter she left me suggested, but I've spent the last twenty-four hours trying to figure out *how* and I've got nothing. I mean, why invite me here just to share the story of her sister surviving the *Titanic*? There's got to be another connection."

Nathaniel starts to pace. "You're right, and that connection must be what put you on Mae's radar in the first place. All right, let's think this through. Your father died in a war, and so did

Mae's. Do you think they were both part of some military frater-nity?"

"Maybe, though that would still be a pretty random way to meet. Besides, what about Giles? Don't you get the sense he knows more than he's letting on?"

Nathaniel rolls his eyes. "Giles believes a butler's duty is to overhear everything and say nothing. If he doesn't feel at liberty to tell you something, there's no point in badgering him. He's old school like that."

"Still, something about him rubs me the wrong way." I'm not sure how to phrase my next question. "Do you think Giles would have a reason to… hurt Lady Knight?"

Nathaniel stares at me like I've slapped him. "How can you even *think* something like that?"

"Well, he was the only person here the night of her death. Relax, it was just a question. A good journalist always considers every angle."

"Giles would never hurt Mae. He adored her… in his own prickly way. Besides, I don't see why you find it so suspicious that a woman as old as Mae passed away in her sleep."

"Then let me give you a recap," I say with more attitude than intended. "Lady Knight brought me here because she knew my father, but no one else seems to know how she knew him. Then she dies *right before* she's about to tell me. We suspect someone was rifling through this study the night of her death, and her will has turned up missing. Maybe we don't have enough evidence to convince the police, but I'd say we have reasons to be suspicious. And so far, Giles is the only suspect that makes any sense."

"You're mental, you know that?" Nathaniel is staring at me like he doesn't know me. "I don't know who you think you are, but you can't just show up and start accusing people of *murder*. I understand that Giles may not be the most sentimental type, but he isn't some cold-blooded killer."

The forceful reaction leaves me speechless. I take a few breaths and start to close the gap between us. "Look, I was only trying—"

"Come on. I'd better get you back to Oxford." Nathaniel's frigid voice makes me feel like I have both the stature and slime-factor of a snail.

So, I grab Ava's memoir, the only ally I have left, and follow the driver downstairs.

20

AVA

While Father searched for Galena, I went to look for someone who might assist with our disaster of a stateroom. The tangible crime of theft still felt more urgent than unfounded predictions of coming wars and sinking ships.

My willful blindness proved how much faith we moderns put in Progress, the god of our generation. The thought that the comfortable world we'd built for ourselves could ever be disturbed in the slightest seemed impossible.

I was not alone in my delusions. As I hurried down the corridor, dozens of nightcaps peeked out from their rooms—passengers innocently inquiring about the silent engines. When I reached the end of this pajama parade, a crewmember rushed out from the lift at the end of the hall, his hands bogged down by a stack of lifejackets.

"Beg your pardon, Lady Ava," the sailor said after nearly plowing me over. "Here, put this on please."

I pushed the white vest aside. "Seaman Donohue, I need to report a break-in."

"Are you all right?" Caleb's eyes hardened like he was the one who'd been violated. "Has anything been stolen? Are your photographs secure?"

My heart jumped at his concern for my art. "Well, no. I mean they're fine, but that's not the point—"

"Then you'd better listen to the lad and put that hideous thing on." From behind me, Mrs. Brown thrusted a sturdy arm forward to hold open the lift door. "They're not likely to drag us out in the middle of the night for nothing, now are they? Come on, Ava. Get in."

Mrs. Brown marched into the lift with Helen Crawford on her heels. The women looked more sleepy than anxious. Layered in furs, the stout Mrs. Brown must have donned every item of clothing she owned beneath her bulky lifejacket, whereas the willowy Mrs. Crawford wore only her silk evening gown and a man's overcoat.

"That's right, Lady Ava," Caleb said with a serious nod. "The captain has ordered all passengers to put on lifejackets and head to the upper decks at once. Merely a precaution, I'm sure. Not to worry—I'll report the break-in to the first officer and have Lord Knight meet you on the starboard side."

Mrs. Brown nodded. "Sounds like a sensible plan."

"Yes, do come with us," Mrs. Crawford urged. "Don't you want to see what the fuss is about?"

"I suppose I should... You'll be sure to help Lord Knight upstairs?" I asked Caleb. Despite everything that now divided us, I did not wish Father any harm. Once we reached New York I'd be fatherless by choice, but until then, I would do my best to guarantee his safety. "He's a nervous wreck, so don't be alarmed if he's acting rather strange. I'm afraid he suffered a bad fall when the engines stopped so abruptly."

"You have my word." Caleb gave me an encouraging smile, but his eyes betrayed his true feelings. The distress he was trying hard to hide frightened me more than the iceberg, more than the crash, more than this frantic distribution of lifejackets. I'd expected passengers to be anxious about the disturbance, but not him. Yet if the calm and composed Caleb Donohue could not conceal his fear, then perhaps this midnight exercise was not so precautionary after all.

"Once I locate your father, we'll meet you up on deck. But if they start loading the lifeboats, you be sure to find a seat. Don't wait on us, understand?" Caleb grabbed my hand and squeezed it tight. "*Please*, Lady Knight."

The sailor's forward gesture did not shock me in the least. It felt entirely natural—a friend concerned for a friend. "My name is Ava."

"All right then, Ava." Caleb smiled again. The heat of it traveled to my fingertips, which were still in his grasp. "You take care of yourself, and don't worry about your father. I'll find him. I promise."

Never had a promise felt so secure. Father's poor example of fidelity had certainly tainted my ability to trust, but I felt safe in Caleb's presence. How I longed to put my faith in *someone* before I stepped into this dark night alone. At least Caleb had been more honest with me than anyone else on this ship.

"I know," I said, squeezing his hand back.

Caleb smiled as shyly as he had the time we first met and then released me.

When I turned to enter the lift, I found a pair of perplexed but grinning faces. Not surprisingly, Mrs. Brown was the first to comment as the lift door's closed. She gave a low whistle. "And I thought it'd take a sledgehammer to get that boy to release your hand."

A smile danced on my lips, but I could not forget the fear in Caleb's eyes. His wary, sea-green eyes, watchful for a coming storm. His trepidation was as palpable as Father's, though they were afraid for different reasons. Caleb feared for this ship and her passengers, whereas my father feared for the entire world.

I hoped the fate of one would not impact the destiny of the other.

Out on deck, a chaotic scene stretched before us like a midnight circus. Crewmembers uncovered lifeboats while passengers huddled in clusters. Those who came from after-dinner cocktails or the smoking lounge were unsuitably dressed for the weather, whereas those awoken in their staterooms were even more ridiculous, garbed in nightgowns and slippers beneath heavy overcoats.

The white lifejackets were our great unifier. Mr. Ismay's talk of the strongest surviving was irrelevant against a leveling foe like the Atlantic, for even the best swimmer could not endure the freezing water for long. Yet I still refused to believe this ship would sink... *could* sink. It carried too many important people. Invincible people. How on earth would the world function without us? The casual conversations and exasperated, rather than fearful, expressions around me indicated many passengers felt the same.

Pride is the most blind of all vices. Its sole mission is to prevent us from seeing ourselves as we truly are.

Was *Titanic* about to hold up a mirror?

"Why, this is like a fancy-dress ball in Dante's hell." Mrs. Crawford stared at her own thin shift and frowned. "The medieval poet's hell was made of ice, you see, not fire."

Mrs. Brown pointed to a nearby lifeboat where women and children waited in an orderly line. "Looks like we're not cut off from salvation just yet. Let's see if we can get ourselves some seats while the sea is calm. Even if it's only a safety drill, I've been aching for a change of scenery, not to mention a little excitement."

The two women began weaving through the throng, but I could not move. It was all so absurd. The *Titanic* band played behind me—another assurance this was nothing more than a drill. As their ordered notes rose to a clear night sky, the thought of chaos leaking in beneath our feet seemed unfathomable. Feeling utterly alone even in the midst of a crowd, I scanned the horde of humanity for a familiar face.

She stood motionless as dozens of white lifejackets moved about her, like worker bees laboring for their queen. The woman's eyes gleamed in the moonlight when they met mine, beckoning me closer.

Galena Lakovic.

My legs obeyed without my consent. As soon as I reached her, she clasped my wrist and pulled me out of sight behind a collapsible lifeboat.

"Did I not warn you? Did I not tell you there'd be trouble at sea?" she hissed. "It appears you are as stubborn as your father. Where is that man anyway?"

"Looking for you!" I cried, wrenching my arm from her talons. "Besides, whatever made you think he'd listen to me? He believed *your* predictions about a world war, after all."

"Ah, so he's told you. It's for the best. We will likely require your assistance." Galena peered around the collapsible to make sure we were alone. "You must understand Lord Knight believed me about the war because I have proof. Powerful men only ever believe a woman like me when there's proof."

My heart thudded with excitement. The witch was about to tell me everything—no blackmail required.

"Your father is a good man with a curious mind, but he interprets matters of the spirit from the perspective of a psychologist, a scientist. He trusts only what he can measure and verify. And automatic writing is not a process that is easily falsified."

"Automatic writing?" I'd heard of it, a parlor trick popular among Spiritualists, but I couldn't believe Father would take part in such a thing. He was not an especially devout man, but he'd never behaved like an outright heretic either.

The woman crossed herself, kissing the gold medallion around her neck. "It was a mistake, one I will repent of for the rest of my life. By attempting to peer into the future, we've only caused more fear and misfortune. I am a *seer*, you see, not a medium, though I was tempted to use my gifts in ways I never should have agreed to. It is one thing to be *granted* a prophecy or *sent* a vision from beyond… it is quite another to go looking for one, for you open yourself up to all manners of evil. Yet there is no going back now. We possess critical information and must do all that we can to prevent what I have seen from coming to pass."

Her words spilled from her mouth like a waterfall, and it was hard for me to grasp the picture they painted. "How is changing the course of fate even possible?"

"Because the future is never fixed, not while men possess free will." Galena tore at the fringe of her shawl, pinned with the familiar brooch of interlinked circles. "Back in Serbia, I was no one, you see. Not even my husband took my gifts seriously. Yet once I joined the Society for Psychical Research in London, important people—people such as your father—began to respect my intuitive talents." Dark eyes shining, Galena stood a little straighter. "When Dr. Bond and Lord Knight asked me to take part in their research project, I joined an inner circle for the first time in my life, a society of inquisitive intellects who sought to understand the greatest mysteries of our universe."

Head shaking, she seemed to deflate. "Yet the temptation for knowledge became too great. We reached beyond our grasp. We grew as prideful as the men who declared this ship unsinkable, and now we shall *all* pay the price."

My cold resolve for revenge threatened to thaw as I recalled the intensity of Galena's fear the day we boarded *Titanic*. "Your children…"

The woman's eyes filled with tears. "I should have had them depart the ship when we docked in Ireland, but I'd hoped my feelings about the voyage were merely the result of overwork and exhaustion like your father insisted. It is not an easy thing to part from the little souls you have carried with you for so long, even in the face of danger—such a separation goes against every instinct."

I can almost smell Mother's perfume as an early memory flashes before me. Father had hired a governess to tutor me, but Mother insisted she would be the one to teach me to read. They'd argued intensely about it, and Father had tried to pry me from my mother's embrace.

The memory grew hazy after that, but Mother must have resisted, for I can still feel the firm resolve of her will wrapped around my tiny body. Though I hadn't been in any grave danger—most girls of my station had survived a governess—Mother would not hand over my mind to a stranger, denying a responsibility she instinctively understood as hers.

"Besides," Galena continued, "my task is larger than preserving my own family. If we do not prevent this war, it will make orphans of thousands."

Because she'd lured away my father, I'd hated this woman more than I'd ever hated anyone, and yet I found myself believing all she said. She'd truly foreseen that there'd be trouble on *Titanic*. I also knew what it was like to long to use your gifts for some greater purpose when no one took you seriously. And while I'd never condone Father's betrayal or accept this woman as his mistress, she was visibly, at her core, a mother who feared for her children, which made it difficult to silence all sympathy for her.

"Have you had additional visions since we set sail?"

"Yes," Galena replied with a shudder, closing her eyes. "That's why I left dinner early. I saw a dreadful image of *Titanic*'s stern sticking out of black water as still as a pond, surrounded by a sea of ice before it sank to the ocean floor. The vision was so clear, like a photograph in a newspaper."

Pinpricks of fear traveled up my spine as her eyes shot open and her hand grasped mine. "If it happens—*when* it happens—the evidence we carry must make it into a lifeboat. Will you help us?"

My legs turned to lead. Lieutenant Plavsic and his threats sought to force me in one direction, while Galena and my father wished me to do the opposite. Yet helping Father's cause would mean assisting his mistress, and how could I betray my own mother like that?

Galena must have glimpsed my inner turmoil. "Ava, please. This is far greater than any disagreement between us. It even goes beyond *Titanic*. If a world war comes to pass, millions will die. *Millions*."

I remembered Father's similar warning as I peered around the lifeboat, watching this collection of souls scurrying around the ship like ants. Why must I sacrifice my mother—the person who'd sacrificed so much for me—on behalf of strangers? *Hers* was the only face I could see right now, not a sea of anonymous millions. And yet I was being asked to help the very woman who was trying to take her place in my father's heart.

"I already know Vaso Plavsic has come to you," Galena's voice cut in. "That he asked you to follow me."

I met her direct gaze with a gasp. "How?"

Galena laughed. "What do you take me for, some fortune teller in a roadside caravan? The man is no stranger to me. He's been trailing me for months, but he's not nearly as clever as he thinks. Don't feel bad about trusting him. You would not be the first. Vaso is a master at taking what people want most, and then using those desires—and them—for his own ends."

And I'd fallen for it. Plavsic had made it seem like our meeting the day we'd boarded *Titanic* was random, but perhaps he'd known my family situation and targeted me from the very beginning.

I avoided the woman's probing eyes. It was pointless to lie when she possessed the ability to peer past every false story I told myself. "Plavsic wanted to know the details of the information you carried to New York. He promised me—"

"The moon, I'm sure. The architects of utopias always do." Galena pointed to the golden orb high in the sky, so serene despite the panicked shouts that had begun to echo across the ship. "Vaso Plavsic was a comrade of my late husband, Dejan. Both men were officers in the Serbian military, as well as brothers of the *Crna Ruka*, the Black Hand—a secret organization intent on establishing a Greater Serbia liberated from Austro-Hungarian rule. On the night before Dejan and Vaso departed on a covert mission, I had a horrible dream of the mission ending in disaster. I tried to warn them, but they refused to listen."

She grimaced and covered her eyes with her hand for a moment. "Events unfolded exactly as I foresaw, and my beloved Dejan was killed. When Vaso returned, he demanded to know how I'd made such a prediction. He desired to use my gifts as a weapon in his revolution, but by then I'd come to see that the Black Hand would commit many evils on behalf of their cause. Even if their final goal was just, they intended to kill unarmed civilians, assassinate heads of state—whatever it took to achieve their desired ends. I refused to take part in Vaso's reign of terror, and so he labeled me a traitor. If I hadn't left for England immediately, Vaso would have had me killed."

"But why follow you halfway across the world?"

"My predictions about the outcome of their mission were very specific, and when they came to pass, Vaso knew my prophetic powers were real. When he learned about my involvement in the Society for Psychical Research, he confronted me at a society meeting in Vienna. That's where I made another grave error—I demanded that he disband the Black Hand, and in doing so revealed that we'd made a discovery that could affect his precious war." Galena struggled to steady her trembling hands. "This is why the evidence we carry must end up in the hands of those who will not use it for their own shortsighted ends. We possess knowledge we were never meant to have. It is a Pandora's Box—that is the correct expression, no? Once the mere idea of a world war is released, it won't take much for it to spread like a fever, for there are always those who *desire* violence."

I frowned, thinking on her words. "I'm sure you're right, but I don't see how delivering this information to some peace conference is going to change any of that."

"And yet we must try. Once war is presented as an option, it quickly becomes the only option. And this war, I fear, will begin with a single shot."

I nearly leapt out of my lifejacket as a flare gun went off on the other side of the lifeboat we hid behind. "What do you mean? And what is this evidence you speak of? What exactly did you see and why would those at this conference even care?"

The questions poured from my mouth as though the flare gun had started a race to an unclear finish line. If Galena wanted me to assist in their mission, it was time I learned the specifics of what this secret information she carried was all about.

Galena gripped her forehead with both hands, her body rocking back and forth. "It is too dangerous to speak of in great detail… but I saw one man dead… a very important man… and suddenly the world is at war." When the woman lifted her chin, it was as if she'd returned from another realm. Somewhere far away. "Many influential leaders will attend the conference at Carnegie Hall, including Booker T. Washington and Andrew Carnegie himself. If we are able to present our evidence at the peace conference, perhaps we can enlist more American allies who will help us issue the leaders of Europe a warning. If Plavsic gets his hand on our evidence first, he will use it as the match to light his blaze. It will become his battle cry, a way to rally people to his cause and plant even more seeds of mistrust. The tension exists already among Europe's powers, like a rubber band pulled to the brink. Plavsic needs only to tug a bit more to make it snap."

Helen Crawford appeared around the side of the lifeboat, eyes anxious until they landed on me. She gave Galena a disdainful glance, but she did not address her. "Ava, thank heavens! Maggie and I have been worried sick. Hurry, we've found a lifeboat with open seats."

I turned to Galena to say goodbye and found the woman's face flooded with sorrow. "Find your father, Ava. No matter what you may think at this moment, he is a good man. He may yet escape this great judgment and deliver our warning. I must find my children and the box with the," she paused, eyeing Mrs. Crawford, then cryptically added, "the match."

A match that could eventually ignite a world war.

But who should I trust right *now*? Who should I help? I felt too many conflicting emotions to give the woman a decisive response. As I turned to follow Mrs. Crawford into the torrent, my body felt numb, a dead weight pulling me under.

"Ava?" Galena called after me. The woman's pale face normally had a ghostly quality, but now she seemed to fade to a spirit before my eyes. "If I do not make it into a lifeboat, can I trust you with one more task? Will you help my children to safety?"

I wanted to utterly despise this woman who served as the final tear in the fragile fabric of my parents' marriage, even if my mother's addiction to laudanum had unraveled many of the threads. Yet Galena's children hadn't asked for this disaster any more than I had. We were the true casualties. The young and innocent always are when it comes to conflict, whether that clash is between two women, two households, or two nations.

"They are the key, you understand. The key to our future."

No doubt every mother felt this way about her children, but the sentiment was strong enough to soften my heart. With a single nod, I agreed to aid my enemy.

And then I turned my back on her and walked away.

21

$\mathcal{A}$VA

"That woman has eyes like the devil." Helen Crawford shuddered as she pulled me away from Galena's reach. "What on earth was she prattling on about?"

"Mrs. Lakovic was simply reminding me that pride goes before the fall," I recited, dazed as I left the relative calm behind the lifeboat. The swirling chaos had become more frantic, but it still didn't feel quite real. Not on this opulent ship with its whitewashed railing and gleaming deck.

A ship that, according to Galena, would soon kiss the ocean floor.

I now felt confident the woman's vision would come to pass, yet the realization left me more numb than afraid. It was only a matter of time—an hour or a few minutes—before the frigid sea rocked us all to sleep.

Mrs. Brown stood by a group of passengers waiting to load a lifeboat that looked half full. She beckoned us to join her in line. Ahead of us, John Astor was helping his young bride into her seat. The man turned to the sailor in charge. "Might I accompany my wife? She's in a delicate condition, you see."

The sailor's name badge read Second Officer Lightoller. He was a formidable man with a commanding voice, which he used most effectively. "Afraid not, Mr. Astor. At this time, we are boarding women and children only."

"No matter one's class?" Madeleine asked sweetly, batting her eyes. "Surely that violates the White Star Line's policies."

The officer clenched his teeth. "Perhaps it does, Mrs. Astor, but thanks to the recent discoveries of Dr. Albert Einstein, I'm afraid the only rules that cannot be broken by men belong to the realm of physics. Now, if you'd like to remain on *Titanic* and observe the law of gravity in action, I'm happy to offer your seat to another passenger."

Madeleine gave the officer a pouty scowl as she reached for her husband. "John, please don't leave me. I can't possibly go without you."

"You can, my dear. And you must. The sea is calm." Astor patted Madeleine's hand, making him seem more like a doting father than a husband. "You'll be all right. I'll meet you in the morning."

"But John—"

"Officer Lightoller. Ladies." With a curt nod, John Jacob Astor turned from the lifeboats, his expression void of hope. He disappeared into the crowd, tall and dignified, the cash lining his pockets useless. I never saw him again. Neither did Madeleine—a widow just weeks after she'd wed. Poor thing. I wasn't fond of the girl, but she didn't deserve a story with such a tragic end.

Her eyes glistening with tears at her husband's abrupt good-bye, Madeleine glanced at us and forced a smile. She patted the empty seats beside her, the last open on the vessel, as if inviting us on an afternoon pleasure cruise. I couldn't decide if I pitied her naivety regarding the ship's situation or envied it. Either way, my condescension must have shown.

"Oh, don't think so poorly of me, Ava." Madeleine rested her hands on the barely visible swell of her belly. "Not all of us are brave enough to strike out on our own. Besides, I've got a life to save… in my own way."

Was that truly how she saw me? As someone brave who forged her own path? I certainly didn't *feel* brave. Before I could apologize for my harsh judgment of her, a shrill wail tore through the crowd.

"What in heaven's name?" Mrs. Brown gasped as we turned toward the sound. "Look at that. They're starting to force women onto the boats whether they're ready or not."

A few lifeboats away, a young crewmember struggled to hold down a flailing woman. That woman was Galena Lakovic, her fingers twisting into claws as she fought with harpy screams that created a scene not unlike her meltdown the day we boarded.

"No! I won't go without them. My babies! Please. I must find my babies!"

A seasoned sailor rushed over to assist his colleague, but it did not matter. Galena refused to enter the lifeboat. The single-minded determination of a mother whose children were in danger was a sight to behold, I must say. Galena's fury never dwindled, not for an instant. I found my heart swelling with a newfound respect.

"To hell with her then. Give the lady's bloody seat to someone who actually *wants* to live!" One sailor released his grip on Galena's wrists and the second quickly followed suit, lest he face the woman's talons alone. Liberated but no less enraged, Galena fled into the crowd, a whirlwind of crimson silk and jet-black curls.

"Allow me to assist you into the boat, miss," said an Irish voice behind me.

I turned to embrace the lyrical accent but found a much older sailor—not the omnipresent Caleb Donohue. The man seemed confused by my hesitation, as my legs refused to leave the deck.

Find your father. He may yet escape this final judgment.

Freedom was within my grasp, in the form of an empty seat. One small leap and my dreams of a new start in America were in reach. I would survive this night, and the blank film strip of New York would be waiting for me.

Millions will die, Ava. Millions.

"Thank you, sir, but I'm waiting for someone." The words left my mouth before I could consider their consequences. "He's meeting me on the other side, you see."

"They'll only be loading women and children there as well." The seaman shrugged, unwilling to argue with another obstinate woman after what he just witnessed. "All right then, who's next?"

Mrs. Brown and Mrs. Crawford deferred, following me out of line. A third-class passenger shoved her little boy up to the front, accepting the sailor's offer. Once the child was seated beside Madeleine Astor, the lifeboat lowered, filled with mournful faces.

I turned to make my way starboard where Father had said he would meet me, only to find the entire walkway full of frantic passengers.

"People are starting to lose their wits," Mrs. Brown said as a fist fight broke out between two enraged men not far from us. "Not to worry, ladies. We'll find a spot soon. Ava, are you truly set on waiting for your father? The boats are filling fast. Surely he'll secure a place on his own."

"Perhaps, but I'd like to wait." And my resolute tone made it clear that I *would* wait, no matter how they tried to convince me otherwise.

"Yes, let's assess our options first," Mrs. Crawford added. "If we're abandoning this ship, then I need to return to my stateroom and collect the research for my book. It would be a pity to lose all the material that made me cross this ocean in the first place."

My camera. My photographs.

I wished I'd had the foresight to bring my own tools, but my priority had to be finding Father and making sure the evidence Galena spoke of made it onto a lifeboat. The urgency with which she spoke thrummed through me, driving me away from the lifeboats.

Mrs. Crawford squeezed my hand. "Be careful, dear. Find a boat before they're too crowded. At least they're quite large. I suspect there will be enough room for everyone in the end."

"Yes, I'm sure. You ladies do the same."

If only I could go back to being ignorant of what this night had in store.

Knowledge may be power, but it could be a burden, too.

A burden Helen Crawford had been spared of. For there was *not* enough room in the lifeboats for everyone on board. Not even close. In less than an hour, most of these poor souls would find themselves adrift in icy waters.

Most of us would die.

And for the sake of Galena's millions, I did not intend to be one of them.

TAYLOR

"All set?"

I'm vaguely aware that Nathaniel is asking me a question, but my mind can't string together the syllables. I've been reading in the parlor while he pulled the car around, but now I'm stuck in 1912 and I don't want to leave. When did Ava sit down to write this book? Even if it was only a few weeks after the sinking, her memory is uncanny. I flip back to the title page, double checking that there's no publisher, and notice a small stamp at the bottom, almost like a publisher's logo.

Two stone towers of a crumbling ruin that mirror each other perfectly. The logo sparks a kind of recognition—like when you visit a place for the first time but feel like you've been there before, or read a story you know you've never read that resonates deeply with the story of your life.

Ava's story is kind of like that. Her tale has nothing to do with me or my dad, but that doesn't lessen the feeling of familiarity. The feeling that every last word is *true*.

"Uh, hello?" Nathaniel tries again. "We should really get going."

The sharp edge in his voice pulls my eyes from the book. If Nathaniel is still upset with me for accusing Giles—they're best buds, apparently, despite their constant bickering—then it's going to be a long, awkward drive back to Oxford.

I shrug. "Ready if you are."

Raised voices meet us as we enter the foyer. Mrs. Porter, still in her coat, has a face as red as her hair from arguing with Giles. They both clam up when they see us.

Nathaniel refits his driving cap. "Everything all right?"

Mrs. Porter is a lot more composed than she was yesterday—a full night's sleep must have done her good—but she still looks harried. "Yes, dear. Mr. Bosko was just mentioning the state of Lord Knight's study, so I was telling him about an odd phone call and occurrence that took place the other day."

"What kind of occurrence?" I ask.

"Well, you see…" Mrs. Porter hesitates, shooting an uncertain look at Giles, who seems extra perturbed. She continues at his tight nod. "It's possible Mr. Bosko wasn't the only person in the manor right before Lady Knight passed. On my nights off, a nurse's aide from a home healthcare service always stopped by to help her ladyship take her medications before bed. Given her age, there were quite a few, and it was important the doses were accurate so as not to mix—"

"But what about the phone call?" Nathaniel asks impatiently. "What made it so suspicious?"

"Oh, I don't know if I'd go so far as to call it suspicious. Just odd. The nurse's aide called to request the key code to the servants' entrance downstairs. Claimed she was already in the car and on her way but had forgotten to jot it down. Mae never had an Aussie aide before, but I thought she was just new. The woman sounded very professional. I gave her the code without a second thought." Mrs. Porter wrings her hands. "Then the next morning, the healthcare company called to see how long we wanted to put a hold on their services. I had no idea what they were talking about, so I went upstairs to ask Lady Mae if she had cancelled… and that's when I discovered she had passed during the night."

Nathaniel's eyes dart to me. "That means the person who showed up was likely the one snooping around Lord Knight's study."

"That's preposterous." Giles snorts. "I've got the only key to the study."

Apparently, Giles has never searched "How to pick a lock" on YouTube.

"Even if someone had managed to sneak into this house under my nose," he continues, "I doubt they found anything relevant to the twenty-first century. Lord Knight's files haven't been opened in years. Why bother with them?"

"Perfect," I say, voice shaking with excitement. "This is just perfect."

The three Meadowbrook staff members turn to stare at me.

"Don't you see? If this so-called nurse's aide was searching for something but didn't find it, she'll likely try again, given the sheer number of rooms. What's to stop her from returning if she still believes Mae needs her medications and she can use that as her cover?"

"My goodness, you're right." Mrs. Porter gasps. "And I am scheduled to have tonight off."

"Fine investigative work…" Giles murmurs.

It almost sounds like a compliment.

"…but I believe we can take it from here, Miss Romano. Have a safe drive back to Oxford."

Ah, that's more like it.

Nathaniel opens the front door, but something stops him from leading me back to the car. Something startling, given the look of sheer awe on his face.

"Hello," says a smooth female voice.

I peer into the open doorway and my jaw drops. "Dalia!"

At the sight of me, Dalia beams, relief radiating from her face. "Taylor! Oh, thank goodness you're not dead." She reaches in her pocket and pulls out my phone as she steps inside. "Thought you might want this."

"Wait… h-how?" I stutter, taking my phone. "I mean, what are you doing here?"

"Found this on our floor." She holds up the cream card stamped with Meadowbrook's address, the one Mae included with her letter. "And it wouldn't stop ringing. Your phone, that is." In a state of utter calm, Dalia circles the foyer, her dark eyes piercing the old portraits like a detective investigating a crime scene.

I check the phone. Sixty-seven missed called. All from the same number.

"I'm sorry, Taylor, but I was going to go mad. Eventually, I just had to answer it."

Great…

"Your poor mother is beside herself." The hardness in Dalia's voice tells me she doesn't get how I could be so cruel. Or selfish.

I guess putting your mom through twenty-four hours of mental anguish because she can't get ahold of you in a foreign country *is* a pretty low thing to do. I feel even worse that I had hardly thought of her.

My shoulders slump forward. "What did you tell her? And what made you come all the way out here?"

"You'd been in the country less than a day. I figured the address on that card had to have something to do with your disappearance, so during free time this afternoon, I called a taxi." For the first time ever, Dalia looks worried. "The study abroad staff is losing their mind, Taylor. It took a while due to the inherent chaos of orientation, but your absence has definitely been noted."

"Not to worry, I was just getting ready to drive her back to Oxford." Nathaniel is still staring at my gorgeous roommate like he can't believe she's real. "I'll save you the return taxi fare and give you a lift too."

"That may not be necessary," Dalia replies coolly, peering down the hall like she's ready to move in for good. She meets my gaze with some hesitation, though it quickly hardens into conviction. "Taylor, the second time I talked to your mom, she was at an airport."

My knees wobble as dread rears its ugly head. *Oh no...*

Dalia lifts her chin, confident that telling my mom I'd gone missing was the right thing to do. "She's on her way here."

23

Ava

Things were unraveling fast. Everywhere I looked, the hordes were pressing against lifeboats that crewmembers could hardly load, let alone defend. "Women and children!" became their battle cry, one most of the passengers were willing to accept.

But not for much longer.

I searched a sea of panicked faces as I wove through the crowds filling the starboard side, but there was no sign of Father. Or Caleb for that matter. *He promised...*

If Father went down with the ship, Mother would lose all will to live. *Titanic* would take both my parents in one night. Paralyzed, I searched for a quiet corner where I might curl into a ball and wait for it all to end.

Stop it, Ava. You are no longer a child, remember?

And that meant I could no longer wait for someone else to come to my rescue. *I* had to find Father. *I* had to do everything I could to make sure Galena's warning reached President Taft. If I could not summon the courage to at least *try*, there were others on this ship who deserved to survive far more than I did.

"Please, let me through!" I shouted, moving against the current of the crowd until I reached the stairs that led to the lower decks. As soon as I descended, a sheet of ice-cold water soaked the hem of my dress. Frantic passengers sprinted down the hallway, lugging whatever belongings they could carry. Two crewmen weaved through the swarm as well, so lost in conversation they didn't notice that I was headed in the wrong direction.

"McCourt says the hold, the luggage, and the mail have all gone," the shorter steward reported, his face as bleached as his White Star Line uniform.

"Sweet Mother Mary in heaven," replied his colleague. "There's no way the ship can sustain such flooding. She'll be kissin' the seafloor in less than an hour, mark my word."

I tried to ignore the ominous words, forcing down the fear that crept along my spine as I walked. These men were not engineers—we had more time than that, surely. Still, their pronouncement felt like the overturning of an hourglass. I needed to find my father *now*.

I pushed open the unlocked door to our suite. "Hello? Father? Are you here?"

The cabin was silent. Empty. I could not understand it. If Father wasn't here, and he wasn't with Galena Lakovic, and he wasn't on the starboard side, where else could he be?

Lieutenant Plavsic.

The rest of my body went as numb as my soaked feet. What if the Serbian soldier had determined that the quickest way to Galena Lakovic was not me, but Lord Knight himself? If Plavsic believed this ship was doomed, he'd become desperate, like an animal backed into a corner. What was to stop him from confronting my father directly, or even threatening violence in order to get the information he wanted?

I stared at my smeared mascara and frizzy hair in the floor-length mirror, at the drenched hem of my evening gown, now the color of navy ink.

You are more, my reflection demanded. *So* be *more.*

This strange girl who chastised me was right. No matter what it cost, I wanted my life to be more than a blur of self-indulgent color that bled when splashed with a little water.

Before me stood Lady Ava Knight of Meadowbrook Manor—a privilege I'd been born to, like it or not. As I stared her down, every false promise of freedom slowly released its grip. After learning of Father's affair, I'd felt justified in breaking every chain that held me back—my family, my country, my past. In the process, I'd crafted a new restraint that coiled around my neck and squeezed. This blind ambition threatened to cut me off from everything that had made me who I was. But what if I used the gifts and privileges that had been given to me for good instead of rejecting them?

If I survived this sinking and wished to face myself in a mirror again, then I had to save more than my own skin.

Still, the dream of liberation from every responsibility does not die quietly. Before leaving the stateroom, I rifled through my photographs and grabbed two images—my shot of the girls on the day we boarded, and Father Browne's unusual photo of Galena and the looming shadow. My camera equipment was too heavy to carry, but I shoved several film rolls and vials of developing solution into the pockets of the overcoat I'd thrown on after Father injured himself.

Goodbye, old friend. Leaving my Brownie behind made my chest ache, but the camera was too bulky and if it became a scramble to get into a lifeboat, I would need my hands free. Though a part of me feared witnessing the horrors of the sinking without the shelter of my camera lens, I also couldn't imagine documenting so many helpless souls as they faced their end.

After giving my Brownie a farewell pat, I raced into the corridor. The silence of the hallway slammed against me like a wave. Frigid water, past my ankles now, shot shivers up my legs. Except for a scattering of clothing and a few broken suitcases, the corridor was empty. As the icy current picked up speed around my shins, a horrible image came to mind: my father sinking below the ocean's surface, his pocket watch dangling from his doublet.

Both defeated by time in the end.

A high-pitched cry—a child's, I was sure of it—pierced the silence. It came from the other end of the hallway, in the opposite direction of the stairs that would lead me back to a chance at life. I searched frantically for someone who might answer this terrified wail, but there was no one else.

No one else but me.

I splashed toward the shriek, not bothering to knock on the stateroom's door before barging in. A sharp metallic odor made me halt. Then gag. I glanced around for its source. Apart from the water trickling in beneath the door, everything in the suite appeared normal. The electric heater hummed in the corner of the sitting area that connected the two bedrooms.

The one thing clearly *out* of order was the sound of an abandoned child screaming. I followed the stream of advancing seawater toward the left bedroom but stopped when the water darkened to a cloudy red. Bile rose in my throat. A gradual roar filled my ears, as if the ocean drowned me already.

Trembling, I pushed the door inward. A heavy iron lay in the middle of the floor, and beyond it, a heap of crimson velvet and ebony hair.

Galena Lakovic. Lying in a puddle of her own blood.

As if suspended above my body, I saw myself crouching down to check her pulse. The woman was already cooling. The blood from her head wound made rivers down her cheeks, and her vacant eyes stared back at me, lifeless. I did not really need this confirmation, seeing how the enchantment that followed the woman everywhere had vanished. The forceful spirit that made her Galena was long gone. My stomach heaved as I turned from the husk left behind. After purging all ten courses of *Titanic*'s final meal into a rubbish bin, I raced to the other bedroom, expecting to find Galena's twins crying their poor little hearts out.

There was only one.

The girl's strawberry-blond curls stuck to her forehead as tears streamed down her blazing cheeks. She screamed so hard, her tiny chest shook as she gasped for air.

"There, there. I have you," I cooed, gathering the girl into my arms. She was heavier than anticipated, but then again, I'd only held a few children and not for a moment longer than necessary.

"Where is your brother? Did he find a good hiding place?" I asked in that phony voice adults always used when trying to convince children that all was well in the world.

The little girl must have been about two, so perhaps her brother had had the wherewith all to hide. I searched for the boy inside the wardrobe and beneath the bed, but there was no sign of him—or the intricate jewelry box that held Galena's evidence. But I could only focus on so much at once, and at in this moment, the crying child in my arms consumed everything. Her brother must be with Galena's Irish maid—two toddlers would be too much for the small woman to carry. Perhaps they'd each taken a twin and Galena had lagged behind.

Her delay was her doom.

Yet what kind of beast would murder a mother within earshot of her own child?

There was no need to ask. My skin prickled as I pictured Vaso Plavsic's deceptively polished face. An image of evil incarnate.

Wrapping the girl in a warm quilt, we fled the stench of death.

When we reached the Grand Staircase, the tremors of shock racing through my system slowed. I realized what I'd done: taken responsibility for Galena's orphaned child. Had the poor woman received another premonition when she asked me to help her children to safety if necessary? I had no experience with children, I had never even cared for a younger sibling, and so I found myself searching the faces that passed for an older, kind woman who might help the girl into a lifeboat. Yet all I saw were tuxes and top hats—a gathering of penguins waiting for the tide that would take them out to sea.

The group of first-class men congregated beneath the staircase's dome, as if the illusion of elegance and prosperity might protect them. I recognized Benjamin Guggenheim lounging in a deck chair beside his valet. Master and servant a mere hour ago, the two men now sipped brandy on equal footing.

Guggenheim removed his top hat as I passed. "Young lady, if you survive, please tell my wife I played the game out to the end. No woman or child will be left on this ship because Ben Guggenheim was a coward. Now go find a lifeboat before it's too late."

A nod was all I could manage. My body ran on liquid terror, and soon there would be nothing left but fumes. It was all too much. I'd made too many promises to too many people. I needed to find Father, find the box with Galena's warning, and get her child to safety. How was I to accomplish everything and still have enough wit left over to make it off this ship alive?

Frantically, I searched for a friendly face, yet these dour men—already dressed for a funeral—seemed resigned to their fates.

And the dead cannot help the living.

But then… *Mr. Stead.*

The mere sight of him produced a much-needed warmth. William Stead sat in a plush chair beside a potted palm tree, stroking his white beard while reading a book, as if this were a normal Sunday evening. Father had urged me to confide in him if anything should go wrong, and something certainly had. *Everything*.

"Mr. Stead?" I called out, shifting the child to my other hip.

He looked at me with gentle eyes. Steady eyes. Eyes at peace with their destiny.

"Why hello, Lady Ava." The man spoke cheerfully, as if there was nothing unusual about our encounter. "Shouldn't you be in a lifeboat by now?"

"My father…" I strained to form coherent words as my entire body shivered. "I can't find him anywhere. He told me to tell you something."

At this moment, William Stead so resembled St. Nick that all I wanted to do was sit at his feet and beg him to make this nightmare go away. Yet the weight of the girl in my arms reminded me that *she* was the child here, and she needed protection—not only from the sinking, but from a ruthless murderer and a war that would worsen our world.

Leaning forward, I whispered everything Galena and Father had told me into Mr. Stead's ear, half expecting him to say I'd lost my mind. Instead, he nodded sympathetically. "Well, Lady Ava, it appears it is up to you then."

"What? No, you don't understand. You're a friend of Andrew Carnegie. Father said you would deliver the news to him and perhaps even to President Taft. Surely these men will listen to you!" At the sound of my panicked cries, critical gazes drifted toward us, as if I'd shouted in the middle of a church service. I lowered my voice to a whisper. "Mr. Stead, will you really give up without so much as a fight? Just sit here and read your book instead of doing something to prevent a *world war*?"

"Surrender is not the same thing as resignation, my dear. Years ago, I had a dream I'd meet my end on open water. As you can see, it never kept me from sailing." Mr. Stead smiled before tapping his book and quoting, "'For now we see but through a glass darkly.' None of us are given a clear glimpse of the future, Lady Ava, though the more intuitive among us may perceive the possibilities better than others. Still, we are all capable of redeeming the time with our courage. That is why you must decide if you are willing to be an *actor* in history, or merely one of its many spectators."

"But why would anyone listen to me? You speak of *war*, not an afternoon house call!"

William Stead had a reputation as a valiant crusader on behalf of women; a man who'd used his reach as a journalist to rail against the "purchase" of thirteen-year-old girls in London who were forced into prostitution by their greedy male relatives. Yet I doubted most men of his generation would see the potential Mr. Stead apparently saw in me. If *I* tried to present a prediction of war to the president of the United States—assuming I could even secure an audience—I'd be laughed right out of the Oval Office.

Chuckling, Mr. Stead opened his arms to the millionaires nearby, a dozen tycoons about to face a crisis no amount of capital could fix. "Our reign is coming to an end, my dear. Soon we men of business won't be the only ones with the power to shape our world. Yet there are some truths that remain timeless. Take the human lust for license—a drive too often mislabeled *freedom* in our democratic age. For freedom, my dear, *true* freedom, is not the permission to do whatever one wants. It is the ability to become a player in the story rather than a prop. It is the chance to do what one *ought*. That is why freedom is such a heavy burden. Those who lack the character it demands won't be able to bear the weight for long, and that is when the real darkness will descend—an oppression of the spirit."

Based on what I'd observed of human nature so far and if what Mr. Stead claimed was true, I wasn't confident that most of us would use the coming freedoms for the common good. "But if there's no hope, then what am I to do?"

"Oh, there's always hope, Lady Ava." Reaching beneath his chair, Mr. Stead handed me a lifejacket for the girl in my arms, along with a thick envelope. "And the flame of hope is fanned by memory. This is why you must try to store in your heart everything you witness tonight—everything your father and Mrs. Lakovic told you, along with everything that is about to unfold, for tonight shall be a night to remember. I pray the world leaders who gather at Carnegie Hall heed your warning, yet if this war takes place regardless, then you must use the gifts enclosed here, a final legacy of the men you see before you—successful and mighty in this world, though how we shall fair in the one beyond remains to be seen. Please, use this to aid the innocent. Protect the little ones like that child in your arms. Now be a dear and ease an old man's heart by getting that sweet babe into a lifeboat. And yourself as well."

My eyes filled with tears as I accepted Mr. Stead's parting gift. I couldn't understand how he could just sit there like a solid oak, convinced the seeds he'd planted in me would somehow prosper in different soil.

"You must promise me one thing, Lady Ava."

No more promises. I had nothing left to give. And yet, I could not refuse this wise and gentle soul in his final hour. "Anything, Mr. Stead."

"Promise me you will live a good life. A life of purpose. A life of love." Mr. Stead smiled sadly like he was remembering all *he* loved, and therefore all he was about to lose. Or perhaps gain. "In the end, that's all any of us can do. And it is enough. For the meaning is in the trying. The rest is not up to us."

My eyes burned, but before I could reply, a sharp cry shattered our stillness.

"Ava! What are you doing?"

I whirled around to see Caleb Donohue standing at the top of the staircase, his sailor's cap gone and the striped collar around his neck untied. Visibly shaken, he raced down the stairs, wrapping his arm around my shoulder as if shielding me from a stiff breeze.

My rigid body relaxed for a moment. Caleb's presence lifted a few ounces of responsibility from my shoulders, despite Mr. Stead's assurance that the weight was here to stay in the new world about to be born.

But some burdens would not be forgotten. I gripped the sailor's forearm. "Where's my father? Please tell me you found him."

"Lord Knight is waiting for a lifeboat, just as I promised." Sweat trickled from Caleb's temples. He eyed the child in my arms. "You should be in a boat yourself. Come on, there may still be a few left portside, but we must hurry."

"Wait. I found a… a body. A woman." I pushed away the blank stare of Galena's coal black eyes. The coppery tang of her blood. "She's dead. And it wasn't an accident."

Caleb grabbed my shoulders, bringing his face close to mine. His voice was low but firm. "Ava, listen to me. Tonight, there will be *many* deaths. I don't say that to frighten you, but I've been down to the lower decks, and they're filled with water up to my chest. *Titanic will* sink. I heard it from the captain's own lips. Do you understand?"

I knew all this of course, but I could tell that Caleb needed to say the words out loud. Needed to make them real. Glancing around, he added, "Now don't go repeating this, but we're short on lifeboats, meaning we need to get you in one *right now*."

I nodded, turning to bid William Stead farewell. His chair was already empty. My heart sank, for I doubted I'd see him again. In this world, at least.

But I would not let him down.

Fleeing the ship now meant Galena's hidden evidence would likely sink with it, unless Plavsic had found what he was searching for. And he very well may have, seeing how the box was not in Galena's room. But if my father and I both knew a world war was on the horizon and at least one of us survived to spread this warning, wasn't that enough?

Galena hadn't seemed to think so, insisting that *proof* of her prophecy mattered. Yet there was no more time to uncover the nature of that evidence—there was no more time for anything.

I began to follow Caleb's insistent pull when a familiar voice turned me around.

"Ah, my friend the budding photographer."

"Why, Mr. Laroche. It's good to see you again."

"I only wish we were meeting under better circumstances." The Haitian engineer held his youngest daughter, dressed in a frilly white nightgown. He looked far more frightened than his child, who hummed a little song as she played with his cravat. "You are headed to the lifeboats, I imagine?"

"Indeed, we are."

"Might we accompany you? Perhaps my Simonne can join you in the lifeboat, seeing how these two girls are acquaintances already."

A lump rose in my throat. "But… where is your wife?"

"God willing, she and little Louise have found seats. My wife is pregnant, you see. Simonne has a rare health condition, so she and I ran back to our cabin for her medicine. When we returned to the deck, Juliette and Louise were gone."

"You mean you didn't have a chance to say goodbye?" It was a stupid thing to say, something Mr. Laroche's trembling lip confirmed.

He nodded at his dark-haired daughter, who studied the blond girl in my arms, her old playmate from the deck floor. "The crew will not allow me to accompany her on a lifeboat. I doubt they will even when men are permitted to board..."

He did not need to explain any further. My hands shook at the unfairness of it all. Swallowing hard, I nodded. "Of course Simonne can sit with us. Let's all head to the lifeboats together."

With that, Mr. Laroche, Caleb, and I rushed to the portside deck, where the crowds had grown even rowdier. We hurried to the nearest lifeboat, nearly ready to be lowered. The holdup was an elderly couple. The husband—a balding man named Isidor Straus, co-owner of Macy's Department store—was attempting to coax his wife into taking the last seat, but she refused to leave him behind.

"We've been together for many years. Where you go, I go," insisted Ida Straus.

"I'll take her seat!" cried another voice from the crowd.

Mr. Straus's eyes glistened behind his round spectacles as he accepted his defeat with a sigh. Grabbing hold of his wife's hand, he led her from her final chance at survival. Instead, they'd chosen to face whatever came next the same way they'd faced all of life—side by side.

"Let's keep trying," Caleb whispered as he pushed us through to the next boat. There we met a wall of men covered in black dust. Their red-rimmed eyes burned as intensely as the heat they'd endured while feeding coal into *Titanic*'s furnaces below. One of the men pressed a mangled stump of an arm, wrapped in a filthy cloth, to his abdomen.

"Stokers," Caleb murmured into my ear. "Stay close. These men know the fate of the ship better than anyone."

Mr. Laroche hugged his daughter tightly. "Then they're bound to be desperate."

"Aren't we all?" I replied. "But what will happen to them? To my father? To the two of *you*?"

"Lord Knight will be fine," Caleb said. "A trusted friend assured me he'd get a place as soon as they began loading men."

I noticed that neither Caleb nor Mr. Laroche answered my question regarding their own plan of escape. Although there were no assurances for any of us, the prospects couldn't be good for an Irish sailor and a male passenger whose skin color was an additional strike against him.

"Look, there's the chap now. If anyone can get you into a boat, it's him." Caleb brought two fingers to his lips and whistled. "Officer Lightoller, over here!"

I recognized the Second Officer as the serious sailor who'd dealt so firmly with Madeleine Astor. The man stood along the railing next to a boat with a few remaining seats. Raising his hand like a shield, he beckoned us forward with the other. "Make way! We have a woman with children here. Step aside, lads!"

"Is that so? Tell us, Officer, why should another spoiled duchess and her brats live while the rest of us drink seawater?" shouted one of the stokers.

"That's right," another man joined in. "*We're* the ones who kept this ship going so the likes of her could keep pissin' in porcelain. Their bloody dogs ate better than we did!"

A few women in the lifeboat gasped at such vulgarity, but the rest of the crowd muttered in agreement. I could feel the mob's unabashed hatred, sharp pinpricks along my skin, and yet I had to wonder: Why *should* I live while they died? Why should I survive when my companions—a doting father and a sailor trained to save others—had so much more to live for? Was I not as useless as these stokers claimed?

Mr. Stead hadn't seemed to think so, and his words suggested our value never lay in our *use* to begin with. Besides, I'd made him a promise.

A promise to live a much harder life, but a far better one.

"You heard the officer!" Caleb caught an oar tossed by Lightoller and used it to push against the throng. "Now clear a path, or I'll make one through you!"

The stokers obeyed begrudgingly, muttering curses among themselves in a variety of brogues.

Mr. Laroche offered me his arm. "I'll take the lead." His assured smile and soft eyes did not deceive me—what he was offering to take were the first blows issued by a group of brawny men who were making no effort to hide their envious scorn.

Hoisting Galena's child higher on my hip, I grabbed hold of Mr. Laroche, my eyes fastened on Caleb as we all headed toward the boat. A shrill cry broke my concentration, and I looked down to see a palm slicked with coal dust latched onto the leg of the girl in my arms, who was watching the chaos unfold with wide blue eyes. The shock of this sudden assault caused me to release Mr. Laroche's arm, and in the space of a shallow breath, he and Simonne were swallowed up by the crowd.

"Let go, you animal!" I pulled back from the stoker as Galena's little girl screamed again. "Are you really such a coward that you'd take the place of a helpless child?"

"Just your place, sweetheart. The little one can come if she wants."

A few men chuckled at that, but the stoker's narrowed eyebrows assured me he meant every word. He'd already given one hand to *Titanic*—he did not intend to grant her anything else. Mother used to say there was nothing more dangerous than a person who lacked hope, and here was a man with nothing left to lose.

"Stop! You're hurting her!" I screamed as the child's cries grew louder.

Caleb pushed his way back to us, his neck strained and his jaw clenched. "Let go of the girl. *Now*."

"And what you gonna do if I don't, Paddy?" the stoker spat, pulling us closer. The man was twice Caleb's size, and it was clear the authority of a sailor's uniform meant nothing to him now.

Without a word, Caleb darted forward, pummeling the man in the face with two quick jabs. His nose gushing blood, the brute fell into the throng of stokers, now livid at this attack on one of their own. As the mob surged around us, I screamed as I had never screamed before. Yet not even that was enough to suppress this anarchy released upon the world.

Two gunshots, however, did just the trick.

"Perhaps you gentlemen failed to hear me the first time!" Officer Lightoller roared, the pistol high above his head. "It's been a long night, so do *not* tempt me. We must maintain law and order. Without order, *all* of us will drown. Now let the girls through."

The second a path emerged, we rushed down it without hesitation. I handed Galena's child off to the officer, who passed her to the outstretched arms of Mrs. Brown, a familiar face I was relieved to see in the boat. For a few seconds, Galena's babe dangled over the Atlantic—enough time for her to glimpse the long drop below, reducing her wails to whimpers.

Now it was Simonne's turn. Caleb took the child from her father's arms, and the instant she realized what was happening, her sweet face broke into sobs.

Despite his stoic bearing, Mr. Laroche could not stop the tears from streaming down his cheeks. I could see he wanted to be strong for his child, but he struggled to find composure as he turned his back to us and surrendered to the truth.

His time was nearly up.

"There, there, Simonne," I said, my voice cracking as I patted her back and watched her father's heart break before my eyes. "It will be all right. We're going to find your mummy and baby sister when all of this is over."

Mr. Laroche's broad shoulders shook as he took a deep breath. Smiling through his sorrow, he turned to behold his daughter, likely for the last time. Ever so gently, he kissed Simonne's tear-stained cheek. "Goodbye, my sweet. Be brave for Papa. He loves you dearly."

Raising his mournful brown eyes to mine, Mr. Laroche added, "I hope your photograph of these two angels turns out, Lady

Ava. I suspect they'll be lifelong friends after their adventures tonight." With a final brush of his daughter's cheek, he turned to face a mob that had been muttering insults this entire time, so jealous were they that a child with the tawny brown skin of her father had taken a seat they felt entitled to.

"Mr. Laroche, wait!" I riffled through the folder I'd grabbed from my suite until I located the photograph he spoke of. "I believe I promised you a copy."

A spark lit in the man's eyes as he studied the black-and-white image. This was his daughter as she'd remain to him forever. Full of wonder. Free. "You shouldn't, Lady Ava. It may be worth more than you think—"

"And it is yours." I pushed the photo towards him. "I insist."

No matter how much this image was worth, there was no one it would matter more to than Mr. Laroche, and I would not rob a father of this small joy in what were likely his final minutes on earth. For whenever he gazed at his little Simonne, I glimpsed a look of loving pride, a look my own father had never once given me.

Now Mr. Laroche could take that adoration with him into eternity.

Before I could say another word, the elegant Haitian nodded, slipped the photo into his breast pocket, and disappeared into the crowd, which had grown so disorderly that Officer Lightoller raised his pistol again and released another warning shot.

My heart racing, I turned to Caleb, who lifted his hand to help me aboard. "Please take care of yourself… Caleb."

It pained me to use his first name now, for I'd only become brave enough to strip away the formal barrier when this ship was about to make it permanent.

The sailor smiled with his usual shyness, the bold aggression he'd displayed minutes before vanishing. "If *I* don't take care, who will?"

He was right. There was nothing I could do to help him or any man trapped aboard this ship. A hot tear slid down my cheek, but Caleb's eyes shone with a determined hope. A survivor's hope. This small flame—a promise he'd make a go of it, that he would *try*—would soon be the only source of warmth to sustain me through hours of bone-numbing darkness.

Caleb grabbed me by the waist, pulling me toward him. I gasped as he lifted me up past his lips and into Lightoller's arms, a cry escaping my throat as the Second Officer threw me like a sack of grain over the railing and into the lifeboat.

A sharp pain followed the ethereal moment of weightlessness. It felt like my tailbone had been shattered with a sledgehammer. I moaned, seeing nothing but swirling stars in a black sky.

Helen Crawford helped me up from the hull. "There you are, dear. Have a seat. That officer is far from gentle, but he's accurate." She smiled weakly, though the rest of her face grimaced in pain. "I'm afraid my descent was even less graceful than yours."

I looked down at Mrs. Crawford's ankle, swollen three times its normal size. Before I could ask if it was broken, the ropes holding us over the ocean creaked and our vessel made its slow decent into darkness.

"Wait! Stop the boat!" shouted an elderly woman wrapped in mink. As she stood, the boat swayed in the air. "I forgot a pair of pearl earrings back in my stateroom, and I'd greatly appreciate it if a crewmember would run and fetch them for me."

"Fetch my husband and son and I'll buy you more jewels," snapped a steerage woman seated across from her. "Along with Buckingham Palace while we're at it."

The older lady grumbled but sat back down. Soon we all fell silent. A few women began to weep. Some shivered. Others prayed. No matter what one did during those cruel moments suspended above the sea, each jerky drop served as a reminder that our survival depended on another's sacrifice.

If we lived, it was because someone else who didn't have a seat was about to die.

Seconds before the decks disappeared for good, I searched the glowering faces for one final glimpse of Caleb. He'd made me a promise—not a verbal one, but a promise all the same—and I needed to behold it one last time. I needed to *see* his will to fight.

To survive.

Yet Caleb's was not the final face I saw. A much sterner man leaned against the railing, staring down at me, a boy in one arm and a wooden box beneath the other—a box I recognized.

Galena's jewelry chest.

The little boy's eyes were so wide with fear that although he and the man had the same dark hair and pale skin, any fool could see he was not in the arms of his father.

He was in the grip of Lieutenant Plavsic.

And so was Pandora's Box.

24

TAYLOR

I lower the book and look at Nathaniel and Dalia sitting on the edge of the library's overstuffed armchairs, faces showing their rapt attention. "Galena's jewelry box. The locked compartment. That must have been where the secret information, the proof of her prophecy, was hidden all along."

"It had to have gone down with the ship then," Dalia observes.

"And a world war came to pass just as they feared, which means Ava either didn't make it to Carnegie Hall or no one listened to her if she did." Nathaniel rises from his seat, running a hand through his hair like he often does before he announces a big idea. "But in that case, why not try to influence Parliament here? Didn't you say Galena tried to send a letter to someone back in London, another member of their research team?"

"That's right. Oh, what was his name?" I flip through the memoir's earlier chapters. "There it is. Bond. Dr. Frederick Bligh Bond."

Nathaniel stares at me like I've punched him in the gut. "You're kidding."

"Nope. See? Ava mentions him right here."

"But, but… I know him," Nathaniel stammers. "Not *know* him, know him, I've just been researching his work for a summer paper. Mae was the one who turned me onto Bligh Bond when I told her about my interest in Edwardian perspectives on psychology. She said he was an old friend of her father's."

Nathaniel walks over to a bookcase near one of the library's stained-glass windows and searches its shelves. "Here it is. The book Mae recommended I read." He holds up a slim volume so we can see its cover.

The Hill of Vision: A Forecast of the Great War, by Frederick Bligh Bond.

"So who was this guy?" I ask.

"Quite a character, it turns out. Dr. Bond was an archaeologist, best known for his excavations of Glastonbury Abbey in the early 1900s, which he completed using some rather unorthodox methods."

"Like what?" Dalia asks, eyebrow raised.

Nathaniel's chest seems to puff a little at Dalia's attention. "Bond used clairvoyant mediums who were members of the Society of Psychical Research to help him determine the locations where he should dig. He mainly employed a process called automatic writing, which is where the medium taps into information from another dimension or spiritual plane by writing. Usually he or she isn't even consciously aware of what they're recording, and the writing will be in a different voice and style from the medium's own. Bond claimed this practice helped him discover the location of two chapels historians hadn't even known existed, but it also got him into big trouble with the Church of England, the employer who'd funded the abbey excavation. Before long, he was considered a quack. A disgrace."

All the tiny hairs on my arm stand up. "Automatic writing. I'm pretty sure that's the process Galena used to uncover the war prophecy. The method she later regretted."

Dalia wrinkles her nose, as if such claims are an affront to academic scholarship. "You mean to say these eccentrics were communicating with *ghosts*?"

"Not exactly," Nathaniel explains. "Frederick Bligh Bond proposed an interesting theory, one that blended science with spiritualism. He believed in another plane or dimension that he called 'The Great Memorium,' a kind of universal memory that all conscious beings shared and could tap into, almost like a realm suspended between time and eternity."

"How Jungian." Dalia rolls her eyes, clearly not impressed. *And now they've lost me.* "Go on."

"Bond believed there were certain moments in history that were so powerful, so potent, that they attached themselves to significant locations in a kind of residual energy. Often these events were tragic, which is why the living tended to interpret them as a haunting. In reality, the disturbances were memories imprinted on matter—almost like a film strip or recording that keeps playing on a loop. The stronger the emotions surrounding the event, the stronger the presence of the collective memory."

"Then how did Galena uncover information about a *future* event like World War I if this dimension holds memories?" I ask.

"I'm still working on that part." Nathaniel furrows his brow. "Do you have that *vesica pisces* drawing from Lord Knight's study?"

"Yep." I'd used the folded paper as a bookmark for the memoir. "Here you go."

Nathaniel studies the drawing. "Think of it like this. The circle on the left is the past, and the circle on the right is the future. That means this almond shape in the middle is a space *outside* of time, a realm where events no longer take place in a linear order—they simply exist. Maybe that's what this Great Memorium,

Collective Unconscious thing is all about. If it is, then Galena was actually tapping into a source where there is no past and future because it exists outside of time."

"A place where time and eternity meet," I say. "A timeless moment."

"Okay, enough of this esoteric theorizing," Dalia announces. "Let's hear what this war prophecy is all about."

"And how are we going to do that?" I say. "As far as I can tell, Ava never mentions the exact words of the prophecy in her memoir."

Nathaniel holds up *The Hill of Vision*. "Maybe not, but Frederick Bligh Bond published many of the automatic writing sessions he and his team recorded while excavating Glastonbury Abbey right here in this book."

Dalia plucks the thin volume from Nathaniel's hand, flips through several pages, and starts to read in a dramatic voice.

"THE PROPHECIES OF WAR

Question: *What is impending?*

Answer: *War—horrid war. The weak must suffer. The strong must die. Chaos—darkness—and a new dawn in crimson skies. Red world! Red poppies of forgetfulness in the graveyard of the past.*

They dance to a music of madness, which is not of their piping. They swell and sweep the earth and say: "Behold! We have changed the face of the Universe!"

But out of the ocean of the Infinite the ripples come. Deaf ears hear not their murmur. Hearing, they will not hear, and seeing, they will not believe, and who can change the course of Destiny?

Learn the great secret. Let others strive for the shadows. To the earth the earth, and to the stars the souls of the free."

Dalia sets the book down on the coffee table, pushing it away like a party appetizer that doesn't inspire seconds. "I don't buy a word. It's too vague. If this text is supposed to predict World War I, it's a stretch to say the least. This could describe almost any violent conflict."

"Maybe that's why Galena insisted the proof she carried was so crucial," I add.

"But the mention of red poppies can't be a coincidence…" Nathaniel jumps to his feet, pacing the library excitedly. "Poppies were *the* symbol of the Great War."

"Yes, and according to its publication date, this book was released *after* the war ended in 1919, so Bond would know that by then, now wouldn't he?" Dalia crosses her arms. "Smells like a scam to me. Or at the very least, like someone's subconscious mind writing exactly what it wanted to hear. What do you think, Taylor?"

I pause, letting both of their claims sink in. "It is strange, isn't it? That Dr. Bond had his own copy of the prophecy, but he didn't share it with anyone after whatever was in Galena's jewelry box went down with the *Titanic*."

"*If* it went down," Nathaniel replies, ever optimistic.

"Regardless, if this Bond guy warned people here in Britain, I doubt it made a difference, no matter when he published his book," I muse. "Given his poor reputation, he would have needed evidence a lot more substantial than flowery predictions of war to convince world leaders to change course. But what kind of proof would have the power to actually convince people—so much so that Plavsic would be willing to cross the world to track it down and then murder a woman to get his hands on it?"

We sit in silence, considering.

"We've got to keep reading," Nathaniel concludes. "I don't think we'll understand anything until we figure out what happened to Lieutenant Plavsic."

"And the little boy," Dalia adds.

Nathaniel is right. The Serbian soldier is the final piece in this mosaic, and we won't know what the complete picture looks like until we know if he made it off the ship alive.

I glance out the library window at a white jet stream streaking across the robin egg sky. That's when it hits me—my mom is crossing the same frigid ocean that caused the death of so many.

With a shiver of foreboding, I open Ava's memoir to pick up where we left off.

AVA

Once our lifeboat touched water, the child bundled in Mrs. Brown's heavy furs refused to stop squirming. Simonne sat quietly, but Galena's daughter fought every restraint. Mrs. Crawford tried cuddling her on her lap, but the girl screamed and clawed, her bottom lip quivering as her plump little arms reached out for… me.

"Looks like she's taken to you." Mrs. Brown smiled weakly.

With the girl finally settled in my arms, I sang her an old lullaby that Mother used to sing me. The words were Gaelic, so I didn't understand them, but that had never mattered, and it didn't seem to bother this child either. Smoothing her fair curls, my fingers grazed something cold. A chain. At the end of it hung a small brass key, it's handle forming two interlinked rings that matched the design of Father's lapel pin.

My chest tightened.

They are the key to our future.

Wasn't that what Galena had said?

Only what if she'd meant it literally? What if this was the key to the jewelry box's locked compartment? If that was the case, it was a good thing this girl was with me and not Lieutenant Plavsic.

But the boy...

I pushed the thought away, breathing in the sweetness of the child's hair. Even her name was a mystery, but I already felt an unfathomable connection to the girl. Perhaps the bond between survivors was like that, just like the key's two inseparable rings.

And what of those who didn't survive? I imagined all the innocent children trapped in the belly of *Titanic*. Children who might never see a lifeboat, never see another dawn.

Cold tears stung my cheeks. "It isn't fair."

"No, it's not," Mrs. Crawford agreed, staring at the ship's flickering lights as the weeping comet of a rescue flare streamed across the night sky. Her glowing face seemed radically altered. She'd always exuded a quiet strength, but now her confidence had hardened into ice.

The burst of light above provided little comfort. We were alone in the middle of the ocean. No rescue ship was on its way. Deep down, I already knew the abandoned faces we'd left onboard would haunt me for the rest of my life.

Why you and not us? they asked with lips tinted blue.

There was one other face I'd never forget—Bruce Ismay's smug expression as he jumped into the lifeboat next to ours just before it was lowered, abandoning the very ship his ego had built. A ship his thirst for ruthless competition would sink.

Apparently, the face of the fittest looked a lot like the face of a coward.

Even if natural selection had not deemed Mr. Ismay worthy of a spine, on one level he'd spoken the truth. He would be among the few who survived.

I peered through the mist of our collective breath, turning to the stars that gave the false impression of a peaceful evening at sea. Officer Lightoller had ordered the sailors manning our vessel to row as far from the sinking ship as possible, which meant we had the best seats in the house.

A morbid thought, and yet none of us could look away.

"When the ship goes down, the suction will be so tremendous that any lifeboats nearby will capsize," the Second Officer had warned. "Don't come back for those in the water. They'll only swamp the boat and drag you down with them. You must get out while you can."

We'd followed his advice and did not linger as *Titanic* released a few more labored breaths—the ship's great death rattle. This gave time for the harsh reality of our situation to become clear as we examined it from a distance. When our crewmen stopped rowing, the bow of *Titanic* had all but disappeared. With each passing second, her massive stern rose higher and higher into the tar-black sky.

No one spoke, for all words had been sucked into a void that stretched into eternity. We were but a tiny speck in a vast ocean, a single star in an infinite galaxy. For those on deck, it was every man for himself. For those shivering in a lifeboat, the mere thought of the isolation ahead once the ship vanished was stifling. Each of us sat alone in our tortured imaginations.

Until the music, that is. A harmony that surfaced like a battle cry.

The mournful melody touched the places words could not, shattering our loneliness as it heightened our loss. With each bittersweet note played by the *Titanic* band, the musicians reminded us of who we were—that we had souls not even this cruel ocean could submerge. Like the final fire of an ancient oak before its leaves fell and winter descended, the band's melodies proved that even in death there could be beauty.

Or perhaps I was hypothermic.

Maybe these ramblings are merely vain insights gained from a privileged vantage. Yet I knew of no other way to explain the actions of these musicians—brave men who voiced their farewell to the world not with blame or blubbering, but with the balanced duet of a cello and violin.

Their song was a promise, one I clung to it as tightly as the child pressed against my breast. In this moment of stillness, I finally understood that every choice we made—no matter how insignificant it seemed on the surface—was pressed into the plaster of eternity. Mr. Ismay had clung to survival and would live, but any worthwhile memory of him would perish. *Titanic*'s musicians had grabbed hold of beauty and would die, but their memory would endure in every person who heard their story.

We are the color splashed across the canvas.
We are the melody while the music lasts.

A forgotten verse from another song Mother liked. How strange that I should remember it now.

"Listen, they're playing *Nearer My God to Thee*," Mrs. Crawford said. "A final plea for mercy." Her voice trembled with fear, as if she believed those of us in the lifeboats needed as much mercy as those stuck on the ship.

"Mercy?" scoffed the sailor—Frederick Fleet, according to his name badge. I remembered the name—Caleb had been going to take his place at the crow's nest when I ran into him before dinner. "Judgment would be more fitting, for that's what man gets when he extends his reach too far, putting luxury above peoples' lives."

Mrs. Crawford met the sailor's critique with a blank stare. He shook his head. "You old broads don't get it, do you? There aren't enough lifeboats because your precious decks needed plenty of space for strolling. Greed has a price, ladies. It sure does."

Fleet's words stung like a slap across the cheek. None of us were responsible for the ship's faulty design, yet that design was made on *our* behalf and we all felt the pressing guilt. I pitied

Fleet, realizing he must have been the one to spot the iceberg. Would events have unfolded the same way if Caleb had been the lookout instead? Yet Fate had claimed Fleet's story, and in his bitterness, he sought someone else to blame. But finger pointing was pointless.

Sometimes icebergs showed up out of nowhere.

Soft sobs rose from the lifeboat. Those who didn't weep sat in a silent stupor like Mrs. Crawford, as if they were frozen corpses already. The only person who kept her head was Maggie Brown. Driven by purpose even in the middle of the freezing Atlantic, she hiked up her skirts, stripping layers of stockings from her sturdy legs.

"Here you go, girls. Put these on. If they don't fit, you can always stuff 'em in your ears to block that boy's bellyaching. That's right, there's plenty to go around."

"My goodness, how many pairs did you put on?" I almost laughed as I passed a set to Mrs. Crawford, whose lips were purple. "Forgive me. There's nothing funny about this."

"Nonsense," Mrs. Brown said, her amber eyes glowing in the dark. "When it comes to tragedy, there are only two options: laugh or cry. Something your boy Shakespeare nailed. As for the stockings, I put on every pair I had. When you survive as many winters in the Rocky Mountains as I have, you learn to come prepared."

How I admired her. Even in a crisis, Mrs. Brown took decisive action. She refused to give in to fear or self-pity. As a result, her generous spirit lit up our night. The sea had laid our souls bare, filling the cracks with salt water. We each stood naked before the world, our deepest weaknesses revealed. Most of us could not stop shivering at the sudden exposure, but not Mrs. Brown. Her true spirit had been visible all along, and now it warmed her from the inside out.

Who am I? I wondered as I tucked the fur coat around the child in my lap. Her pink face peeked out from the velvety pelt, transforming the girl into one of the Eskimo children whose photographs I'd studied in Father's *National Geographic* magazines.

Despite my recent obsession with becoming such a world-famous photographer, *that* was the child I'd been: a curious girl in a ridiculously large library, safe in the home of her ancestors, certain of her place in a family that had endured wars and survived schisms.

But now *Titanic* stripped away everything until all that remained was the best and worst we each had to offer. The musicians who spent their final breaths in the rapture of song had done more good in a few minutes than I had in my seventeen years. Instead of fighting their neighbors for a seat, the final act of their drama had been spent sharing the gift of hope. Hope in something that might just survive the long darkness of this night.

Who am I?

By the time the music faded, drowned out by the cries of men, women, and children who were plunged into a cold, indifferent sea, I knew I wanted my second chance at life to be a symphony, not a stampede.

26

*A*VA

The sound of people drowning was the most dreadful noise I'd ever heard. Or so I thought. It turned out the suffocating silence that followed was even worse.

When the ship went down, it felt like standing beneath a railroad bridge while a train passed overhead. The scream of compressing steel punctured the night as boilers exploded and funnels toppled forward, the shattering of china and cries of desperation piercing our hearts. Before long, those cries faded to a deafening calm.

It was an absence that could be felt.

A nothingness that was real.

For its grand finale, *Titanic*'s stern climbed into the starry heavens like a lone Manhattan skyscraper, transforming the miracle of electric lighting into a horror—a great and terrible beauty. The ship loomed above the water for what felt like an eternity, then descended with an unearthly roar. A deep growl rose from the ocean floor as though from the belly of a sea monster that had swallowed its latest meal.

After the ship vanished beneath the waves, the true torture began. Patience had never been my virtue, but I soon learned what inner resources could be forged in the fires of fortitude. *Waiting* cracked open even hearts as hard as a walnut shell, and only an open heart can be filled.

Yet my heart was neither open nor closed, for it lay in a thousand pieces at my feet.

"We should go back," Mrs. Brown insisted. "We should at least *try*."

"Didn't you hear what the Second Officer said?" snapped Fleet. "If we go back, they'll pull us right under with 'em. *You* can go swimming if you have a death wish, but I won't be getting in that frigid water."

"Easy there, lad," said Robert Hitchens, the other, less aggressive sailor in command. "Rowing would at least keep 'em warm."

"Exactly. And we should take turns, so we don't freeze to death!" A spark in Mrs. Brown's eyes kindled. "Hell's bells! Give those here."

The unmovable woman shoved Frederick Fleet aside, taking up the reins herself. "Give me some help, Ava. You're a strong gal." She raised her oar defensively, glaring at Hitchens and Fleet like a mother lioness defending her young. "Don't try me. For all you know, I've got a pistol hidden under all these furs. And if I do, you can bet I know how to use it. I'm just an upstart from the hills, remember?"

Mrs. Brown was a member of Denver's high society, no longer some rough frontierswoman with a gun on her hip. Yet the far-reaching imagery of Buffalo Bill was enough to make these sailors buy her bluff.

Simonne slept slumped against me and Galena's child had taken up my entire lap, so Mrs. Crawford took over the role of pillow for the two children so I could grab an oar. The other women in the boat stared like we'd lost our minds, but Mrs. Brown was right—we had to do something.

We had to try.

"Now sit down and relax, boys," she barked. "We just need a little exercise, that's all."

For a time, the repetitive rhythm of our oars dipping into the sea shielded us from the wails across the water, but soon those cries faded as heartbeats slowed. I could tell from her grimace that Mrs. Brown intended to row as close to those in the water as possible, without getting *so* close that Hitchens and Fleet sensed our true motive and overtook us. Perhaps a few strong swimmers would be able to reach the boat.

If only we'd acted sooner.

Hundreds of human faces—people whose eyes had radiated life mere moments ago—bobbed past us like buoys, their mouths hanging open and their lips kissed by frost. Vomit rose in my throat when my oar accidently struck a dead man. Her lower lip trembling, Mrs. Brown muttered that it felt like hitting a frozen pumpkin with a garden hoe. I bit the inside of my cheek until I tasted copper, but my face was so cold, I couldn't release the tears. The transformation from warm, pulsing life to still, icy death had happened so fast.

In less than an hour, over a thousand souls had left the familiar terrain of time for an eternal land whose geography none of us knew with any certainty.

After trading places with Mrs. Crawford so she could work up some warmth, I tried to sleep—my spirit exhausted by emotions that words will never fully capture. I remember staring at Orion's Belt, straining to piece together all that had happened, even though it was impossible to rationalize this night. Before long, every inch of my body was numb, but I never stopped clutching the child to my chest. It's possible that my burning desire to preserve her little life with whatever heat I could muster ended up saving my own in the end.

I must have dozed for time. When I opened my eyes, the sharp pain of a swelling headache railed against my skull, blinding me with confusion. Across the way, Frederick Fleet sat on the floor hunched in a ball—both arms wrapped tightly around his legs, his hollow cheeks the color of stripped chicken bones. He coughed, but his expression remained blank as he stared at me.

"Ever gone to bed cold and hungry before, miss? No, course not. This night must mark your first taste of such discomforts, am I right?"

He was right. So right I could not respond. I'd been given everything, and look how I'd squandered it, using my status for nothing but my own selfish gain. Worst of all, I knew, deep down, that there was nothing I could do to make things right. And still, I was sorry. So very sorry.

Remember the music.

What music? The final notes of hope produced by the *Titanic* players, or the music that moved everything, from the stars to the sea tides?

They are one and the same.

Wherever this quiet voice inside me had come from, it emboldened me to return the sailor's hard gaze. He would not bully me for surviving, for living, even if I did not deserve to any more than the steerage child in the water who lay frozen against his mother's breast had deserved to perish.

Not when I intended to live the song I was meant to from now on.

"Things will change. You'll see. You'll *all* see," the bitter sailor continued. "Soon it'll be the rich who get thrown into the sea by the thousands. Sometimes sacrifices must be made for a greater good. Sometimes all you need to start a revolution is a spark."

If only he realized that the match was held by a most sinister hand—the Black Hand. Whatever information Plavsic had captured in taking Galena's box, I prayed its influence was merely symbolic.

Yet the cold, hard ball in my stomach claimed otherwise. For symbols only have power when they embody realities that can take on flesh, inciting either good or ill in this realm where soul connects with bone.

There was a period as a little girl when I was intensely frightened of the dark, thanks to a scratching noise I often heard inside the tiny closet behind my chest of drawers. When Mother tucked me into bed, she would recite, "By bell, book, and candle, I cast out all evil spirits," along with the prayer of St. Michael the Archangel, taught to her by her Irish Catholic grandmother.

But what holy objects and sacred declarations could be used to cast out an evil as tremendous as a world war?

Sensing he could not goad me into an argument, Fleet pulled the collar of his jacket up around his ears and closed his eyes. The girl in my arms coughed so violently, I worried what damage the cold was doing to her lungs. My eyes fell to Mrs. Crawford's open handbag, which sat next to me as she rowed. I reached for the silk scarf at the top of her purse, intending to wrap it around the child's head.

My hand stilled. Beneath the scarf sat a pair of binoculars. Binoculars stamped with the logo of The White Star Line.

Something Caleb had mentioned earlier worked its way into my foggy mind—he hadn't been looking forward to squinting all night on lookout because the ship's binoculars had gone missing.

So why did Helen Crawford have them?

I was too drained to give it much thought. Between the gentle rocking of the lifeboat and the alluring tug of darkness, I couldn't keep my eyes open much longer. This time, I must have slept for hours. When I next looked out across the water, the blush sky did not seem real. Neither did the icebergs shooting up from the sea like mountains, as stunning as they were deadly. Their bright blue crystals shimmered in the pink dawn, transforming this ocean from a freezing purgatory to a purple paradise.

The only signs *Titanic* had existed were a few fragments of wood and a scant scattering of straw. There would be no survivors. No intact ones, at least. By the time *Carpathia* appeared on the horizon a few hours later, a part of each of us had died. Whether that part was gone forever or simply waiting to be reborn, only time would tell.

The meaning is in the trying.

William Stead's words of wisdom stirred yet another promise within me.

I vowed then and there to *remember* everything I'd seen, and to one day write it down. Reaching into my coat pocket, I felt for the envelope Mr. Stead had given me. In the chaos of trying to find a lifeboat, I'd forgotten all about it.

My hands trembled as I removed the wad of sterling notes and hundred-dollar bills stuffed inside. The paper money was worth thousands, maybe more—every bit of pocket cash from the tycoons awaiting their end in the shadow of the Grand Staircase. Knowing Mr. Stead had gathered it to do some final good generated a tear that froze to my cheek.

Only then did William Stead's parting words make any sense. He'd asked me to use this gift to aid the innocent—the blameless victims of a war that hadn't even begun.

I was ready to give him my answer.

I will try.

27

Ava

By the time the sun spread its liquid gold across the sea, we'd boarded *Carpathia* alive, but forever changed. Once more, there was nothing to do but wait. Yet thanks to generous souls like Maggie Brown and William Stead, my understanding of *how* to wait had altered radically.

We were not helpless victims. If it were possible for some small good to come out of this tragedy, I would pour my heart into making it happen. I would *try*.

The decks of *Carpathia* were nearly as chaotic as *Titanic*'s during the sinking. Every survivor now searched for a missing friend or loved one, and most of us were bound to be disappointed. I watched vigilantly for Father and Caleb, knowing the chances of their survival was slim. Yet instead of letting this probability cripple me with grief, I got to work.

My life had not been spared for nothing.

"Fleet was right, you know," Mrs. Brown said as the crew wrapped us in wool blankets after feeding us steaming broth. "There's nothing moral about greed. Then again, there's nothing admirable about envy either. To whom much has been given, much is expected—that's my motto. I've been on both extremes of the rags and riches seesaw, and let me tell you—a gal can do a lot more good with money in her pockets than she can with sawdust."

And so, good was what the two of us set out to do. We began by recording the names of steerage survivors immigrating to the United States. Most spoke little English and many had become widows and orphans overnight. Seeing how they carried nothing with them but the memories of their men, Mrs. Brown came up with a brilliant idea. We would launch a first-class fundraiser in order to house these women and children in Manhattan's finest hotels, at least until relatives or friends in America could be located.

Once we declared our mission, we hounded every first-class passenger we came across like a pair of door-to-door Bible salesmen. Most were happy to contribute, but Mrs. Brown had a clever solution for those feeling stingy. At dinner that evening, she posted two lists outside the dining room door. One read FIRST-CLASS PASSENGERS WHO HAVE DONATED TO THE *TITANIC* DISTASTER FUND, while the other boldly declared FIRST-CLASS PASSENGERS WHO HAVE <u>FAILED</u> TO DONATE TO THE *TITANIC* DISASTER FUND.

"If they won't give out of gratitude to the Almighty for being alive, then we'll shame them into feeling charitable." Mrs. Brown grinned, a wicked glimmer in her eye.

During our campaign, I thought about adding Mr. Stead's contribution to the pot. Yet he had asked me explicitly to use the money to aid *war* orphans, and it didn't feel right to go against the man's final wish. I just hoped his war fund would not be needed.

Besides, Mrs. Brown's strategy worked well. We raised $10,000 in no time.

By the end of that first day on *Carpathia*, I'd seen no sign of Lieutenant Plavsic, but that was not enough to set my mind at ease. Given the number of extra passengers on the ship, it would be easy for a man with his surveillance skills to get lost in the crowd—especially if he wanted to. As I kept watch for the one-eyed soldier, my heart skipped a beat whenever I glimpsed a sandy-haired sailor.

Stop, Ava. It isn't him.

One thing was certain: no survivor, whether rich or poor, had been left unscathed. We all searched for a sign that *our* love had not perished with all the rest. In fact, before setting her sights on Lady Liberty, *Carpathia* returned to the sight of the sinking. I joined a row of somber widows along the ship's railing, two dozen women who gazed out on fresh graves that had left no mark in the dirt. That the grandest ocean liner in the world had floated here a few hours ago seemed unfathomable, yet the burning sensation that lingered in my frostbitten toes assured me none of this had been a dream.

We'd been granted one small miracle. Simonne was reunited with her mother and baby sister as soon as we boarded the rescue ship. Tears filled Mrs. Laroche's weary eyes as I spoke of her husband's dignified courage, but the woman was unable to utter a word. The fresh cut of loss had sliced too deep.

As I stared into the lethal ocean, Galena's daughter sat content in my arms, her fingers twirling the strands of my salt-mangled hair. A few women wailed uncontrollably at the waves, at the monster that had shattered families and swallowed whole lives. The same doubts and delusions ran through each of our minds.

Did he drown?

Did he freeze to death?

Or maybe, just maybe, did he manage to survive?

Carpathia's crew pulled several corpses from the sea—Madeleine Astor's beloved J.J. was one of them—but that was all the confirmation we received. Everyone else had vanished beneath the surface, leaving those behind with nothing to do but wonder.

"He must have been picked up by another boat!" cried a steerage woman beside me.

"My Patrick was a most excellent swimmer," a millionaire's wife moaned. "He couldn't have drowned! It isn't possible."

I told myself no such fairytales, for the pit inside me did not lie. I'd accepted that my father, Caleb Donohue, and every other man on *Titanic* whom I'd admired was likely dead, yet I was too calloused to cry, too bitter at the Atlantic to add the salt of my tears to its murderous waves. My body trembled at the injustice until a strong wind drowned my silent sobs, pulling my eyes from the underwater graves. Slowly, I turned toward it.

And there he was.

Father.

My living, breathing father, rushing toward me with open arms.

"Oh, Ava. Thank God!"

A cry escaped me as I threw myself into his embrace, pressing the child between us. Tears streamed down Father's face, soaking the bandage that covered his left cheek. His eyes were as red as a stoker's and he wore the moth-eaten coat of a steerage man, but he'd survived. He was still here.

"You're safe. Both my girls are safe!"

Such simple words, but enough to drown my newfound joy.

I stepped back. "What do you mean *both*?"

Father took the toddler and buried his face in her feathery hair. His tears were no longer streams of relief, but rivers of shame. "I can't do this, Ava. I can't lie to you... not after all that's happened. This is my daughter. Her name is Maebeline—we call her Mae."

Another truth I'd refused to accept.

I'd come to love the girl as a sister by convincing myself she wasn't one, that she was Galena's child by her Serbian husband. My hands grasped the ship's railing as the revelation crashed against me. Father had another child. *Two* other children.

I saw now what had always been there. Mae had his blue eyes.

Father's icy *liar's* eyes.

"Ava, please." He knelt beside me, but I recoiled at his touch. "I'm sorry you had to hear it like this. I intended to tell you everything once we reached New York, I swear it. But your mother…you must understand, dear, your mother was unwell for so long."

As if that's an excuse! I wanted to scream. But my chapped lips would not form the words unless a sob escaped with them, and this man was not worthy of my tears.

"Sweetheart, please. Look at me," Father pleaded as he fidgeted with the thin silver chain around Mae's neck. "Your mother is a shadow hanging over you, but you must accept the way things are."

"It's *all* a shadow now," I spat back, rising to my feet.

I could accept that Mother's mind had left her years ago, that she was no longer herself, but that didn't mean she deserved such treachery. Neither of us did. Everything I thought I believed in was exactly what Father said—a shadow.

A lie.

The familiar warmth of rage kindled deep inside my core, but the sparks would not catch fire in such a cold vessel. Besides, there wasn't much I could say that would break my father's heart any further. He turned to the ocean that had stripped him of everything. "I don't believe Galena made it. Nor William… my son."

My lips parted to tell him that no, indeed she hadn't because she'd been murdered, but the words that rose to the surface were too blunt, too harsh… even for me. The wretched man had lost his only son, after all.

Had he believed the illegitimate boy would one day be heir to his fortune? It was odd, the things men did when their virility stalled. King Henry VIII had transformed from golden prince to ranting tyrant when he could not produce the son who'd give him legitimacy, though of course it was his wives who suffered for it. Oh, I knew our family history—Father's ancestor had served that same unhinged king, murdering priests and pillaging sacred property on his behalf. Perhaps we were cursed like Galena had warned—and her poor son, with diluted Knight blood flowing through his veins, had paid the ultimate price.

Why must the innocent always pay the price?

"Goodbye, Father."

I hoped he could tell from my tone that this was a forever farewell. *Jane Eyre* was a captivating story, but Father was not some brooding Mr. Rochester with a mad wife he could simply lock away on the third floor! I could understand that his loneliness had made him susceptible to Galena's charms and I might forgive him for that, but the fact that he'd started a new family and kept them a secret for so long…

No, *that* deceit, like grief, cut too deep.

And I was done making promises to people who did not uphold theirs. This coming war was his burden to bear, not mine.

Mae cried out as I walked away, but I refused to turn back and face the undertow of their identical gaze. In a daze, I walked the ship's corridors and decks. All I wanted was solitude, a private place to mourn for my fractured family, yet there were people in every crevice. Filthy people. Grieving people. Survivors who stalked about like the living dead.

I needed a haven, a place where I could sit and think. Yet there were no still points in this world turned upside down, a world where even the mightiest could be dragged to the bottom of the sea.

Perhaps the bottom was where I needed to go. I searched for a staircase that led to the belly of the ship, discovering a door beyond the steerage kitchen that was labeled CREW. It looked like a storage closet, the ideal place for a bit of silence. When no one was looking, I slipped inside. A blast of frigid air rustled my skirts, but I no longer cared about the cold—it had become a friend and I welcomed the numbness.

As I rounded a pile of wooden crates storing bottles of amber liquor, I nearly knocked an entire stack to the ground. A low moan made me stop. It seemed I'd intruded upon another seeker of silence. Anyone else would have made my fuming head explode, but now my heart swelled to the point of bursting.

Caleb Donohue sat on the hard floor, his head resting against the steel wall, his hair drawn like a curtain over his eyes. A half-empty bottle sat on the crate beside him. Both the spirit's strong smell and the sorrow it was meant to drown reached me where I stood.

A small cry parted my lips. Caleb's eyes shot open, his grief transforming into a grin no camera could have captured. The dam I'd built behind my eyes began to crumble, my hardened composure slipping between the cracks.

All our masks fell away as I collided with Caleb, both of us sinking to the floor in a tearful embrace. Because of the ship's thunderous engine, we could hardly hear each other speak, but that didn't matter for there were no words that could hold everything we felt.

So we held each other instead.

Caleb kissed the hot tears streaming down my cheeks, a damp trail guiding him to my lips. His piano hands became tangled in the strands of my wind-battered hair, but I no longer cared that this sailor could not afford a piano.

I'd never liked playing it anyway.

28

TAYLOR

"Why'd you stop?" Nathaniel demands when I put the book down.

"Really, Taylor. This is the juiciest part so far!" Dalia walks over to my seat on the stone hearth, reaching out like she's going to feel my temperature. "Are you all right?"

"I'm…" I want to say *fine*, but that's a lie.

It's cute that Ava and Caleb finally got together, but I was never in this for the love story. We've almost reached the end of the memoir, and there hasn't been a single clue that explains how my dad is connected to Mae, let alone information that might clear his name. If Mom will be here soon to drag me home, then I'm nearly out of time.

My one small solace is these chapters have verified my suspicions that the little girl Ava rescued from the ship was Mae, her half sister. Maybe that's what all of this was about—every year, a lonely old lady invites one of her scholarship recipients to visit her grand estate to share the story of how she and her sister survived the *Titanic*. I've visited enough elderly homes to know that some people like to tell the same story over and over. All they want is someone who will listen.

I guess Mae saw me as a fresh pair of ears.

Through the Gothic window and beyond Meadowbrook, the sky is both light and dark, lavender with blackberry swirls. There's no storm tonight, but an eerie gloom settles over the estate as the sun sets and shadows stretch across the lawn, a mounting fog on their heels. I look toward the cemetery across the river. Sometimes when I'm reading the memoir, Ava's presence is so strong, I wouldn't be surprised if she came strolling down this gravel drive, dressed in her midnight blue evening gown. It isn't hard to imagine Mae running up behind her, reaching for her older sister's hand.

Pinpricks tickle the ends of my fingers at the thought, so I shove my hands deep into my cardigan pockets.

Dad's photograph.

I pull it out and study Dad and the redhaired woman standing along the cliff and wonder why I ever bothered to hope that Mae's odd invitation had anything to do with this image. It'd be one thing if the pair had been standing in front of her house, but Meadowbrook is about as far from the ocean as you can get in England.

Tragedy has a way of revealing the truth of things. *Titanic* exposed the lie Ava's father lived, just as Dad's untimely death divulged his own secrets. No matter how I try to come up with a logical explanation for this photograph, Mom was right about one thing—Dad took a trip to England without telling us anything about it. He kept the truth from his own family, which is almost as bad as a straight-up lie.

A renegade tear slides down my cheek. I brush it away, but once the first falls, a thousand followers I've been storing up for days demand release. Now I understand why Mom was so anxious about me coming here. Searching for answers and finding nothing but more reasons to doubt is the worst kind of torture.

We weren't enough for him.

At the end of the day, maybe that's the truth Dad did his best to hide.

Nathaniel comes up behind me and gives my shoulders a light squeeze. "It's okay. We've all heard about *Titanic*, but Ava's account made it feel much more real. There's nothing to be embarrassed—"

"That's not why I'm crying," I snap, wiping my tears with one hand while I hand him the photograph with the other.

He's silent for a long thirty seconds. "Is this your… dad?"

"Yes. And that's *not* my mom."

"Oh." Nathaniel doesn't say anything for another long stretch, but I can practically hear his mind putting the pieces together. I continue staring down the gravel driveway, willing an American soldier to appear in his spiffy dress blue uniform, wishing it was possible for the dead to come back and walk among us—only in a non-creepy way.

"Taylor, I don't know who this woman in the photo is, but let's not draw any conclusions until we get to the end of Ava's story, okay? Let's keep reading."

With a deep breath, I nod. As I open the book, bright headlights cut through the fog that is swirling down the manor's long drive, illuminating the tear-stained page.

AVA

"Tell me how you did it. Please." Resting my head on Caleb's shoulder, I relished the warmth of the sun. We'd moved from our cold storage closet to an upper deck where wandering passengers eyed our blatant affection with mild disapproval. Yet no one was about to openly chastise a young couple who'd been through hell and now sought a little heaven in a warm embrace.

"What do you mean?" Caleb asked.

I watch his pulse beneath the soft skin of his throat. How could something so mundane suddenly feel so miraculous? *Life* circulated through him, through all of us, without any conscious effort on our part. And to think that all it took was a little ice water for this faithful rhythm to cease.

"How did you manage to survive the sinking?"

"Well, no one who made it off *Titanic* did so alone, that's for sure."

"You helped my father, didn't you?"

You kept your promise.

"Neither of us would have made it if it hadn't been for Officer Lightoller," Caleb said, turning toward the foreign ring of laughter coming from the other end of the deck.

A child wearing knickers and a newsboy cap bounced a rubber ball along the stretch of wooden slats. I recognized the boy from one of the lifeboats. He was a survivor like the rest of us, but he played as though nothing particularly significant had happened.

"Tell me about your escape, Caleb. I want to know everything."

The urge to share our stories was strong. During the midday meal, several Irish survivors from steerage had described their experiences in vivid detail, even the most tragic parts. In the Knight family, all the most unsavory aspects of our history were kept hidden behind a veil of invulnerability. No one talked about shameful things. Yet here on *Carpathia*, the simple act of sharing our memories became our ode to the dead. It was as if their lives somehow endured in the retelling. In the remembering.

"After your lifeboat departed, I joined forces with a few other sailors. We came across Captain Smith, looking very grave." Caleb laced his fingers through mine. "'Men,' Smith said to the crew, 'you've done your full duty. You can do no more. Now it's every man for himself. I release you.' And with that, the captain walked away, leaving the rest of us in a stupor. A sailor can't simply abandon his duty without a second thought, see? It doesn't work like that."

I traced the faint lines in Caleb's palm, searching for one that promised a long life. "What did you do then?"

"Once the ship began climbing out of the sea, most of the passengers went with her, racing toward the rising stern." Caleb shook his head, sighing deeply. "Poor fools. It was a natural response—they wanted to stay out of the water for as long as possible, yet by staying on the ship to the end, most were sucked under by the sheer force of *Titanic* as she sank."

"But you and Father found another way?"

"It was all Lightoller's doing. His plan sounded insane at first, but I trusted him. It's a good thing, too—I wouldn't be here if I hadn't. When *Titanic* started going down, Lightoller ordered us to dive into the water and swim as far from the ship as possible. Seconds after he gave the order, the Second Officer disappeared. Dove into the sea like he was going for a moonlight swim."

"And you just followed him?" It was hard to believe any sane person would dive into water in sub-zero temperatures on command.

"That's right, which speaks to the man's leadership, I suppose. Lightoller inspires trust, even when there's no logic in it. But I won't lie, that water hurt something awful." Caleb's body tensed against mine, as if he experienced the stab of a million tiny needles all over again. "We managed to swim to where Lightoller had climbed onto a collapsible lifeboat that had flipped over. The only way to stay out of the water was to stand on top of the blasted thing for hours. There were about thirty of us, and we had to keep our balance, even when we began shaking with hypothermia. If *one* man had slipped, we'd all have gone right back into the water. Somehow, we managed to stand strong. They were the longest hours of my life."

"That's incredible." I lifted my head from Caleb's chest, so I could glimpse his sea-foam eyes. "Weren't your legs frozen?"

"My legs and everything else. But I suppose the will to live either takes hold or doesn't. It helps when you know you have something to live for."

My face burned a bit at that, but there was nowhere to hide. Caleb's lips were inches from mine. "Caleb, I'm so sorry I ever—"

"Shhh. There'll be none of that." He pressed a finger to my mouth.

And his mouth followed.

The kiss felt like sinking all over again, only these waves were as warm as bath water, speeding up our hearts instead of slowing them.

Time stopped. The present was everything.

That is, until a flying rubber ball brought the eternal moment to an abrupt end. I pulled away from Caleb with a start, catching the flash of an impish grin as the giggling boy disappeared around a corner.

Caleb's eyes met mine as laughter erupted from both of us, the welcomed release of a pressure valve. This child had endured the same nightmare, yet he still managed to make mischief. Neither of us could scold him for that.

"Children are resilient creatures." My smile faded as I pictured another little boy—one who would never laugh, never play silly games, never torture his twin sister while she kissed a young man. I hadn't known him like I'd come to know Mae, but he was still my half brother. An innocent.

And now he was buried beneath the waves.

"I don't mind being the source of the lad's amusement." Caleb chuckled, tossing back the ball in the boy's direction. "Besides, there will be time for kissing later on, I hope." He frowned when he saw the tears in my eyes. "Ah, what did I say now?"

I pushed aside the haunting image of Galena's small son struggling in the dark water alone. "How will life ever to go back to normal? Nothing will be the same. Not after this."

"You're right, it won't. But *life* will go on. Just as it always has." Caleb held me in his quiet strength, and I snuggled into the silence. Minutes passed.

"There was another little boy," I said finally, fearful of leaving this safe harbor but unable to bear the unknowing alone. "I'm worried he didn't make it to safety. Perhaps you saw him? He had black hair… the darkest eyes."

"I'm sorry, Ava, but many steerage passengers could meet that description."

"He wasn't traveling in steerage, though."

"Then why wasn't he in a lifeboat? All the children from the first and second classes were loaded from the beginning."

"Because he was kidnapped, taken by a most vile man. A soldier carrying a mahogany jewelry box..."

Caleb tensed. "Did the man have a false eye?"

"That's right."

"Then I did see him. The boy, too. It was before the sinking, though. Your soldier was trying to use the child as his ticket into a lifeboat. Not sure if that ploy worked—plenty of desperate men tried it—but he refused to let the boy go otherwise. And he refused to let go of that box."

Despicable coward. "When was this? About what time?"

"Oh, it must have been around half past midnight—right after I gave you, Mrs. Brown, and Mrs. Crawford your lifejackets."

But that made no sense. It was far too early. I'd spoken with Galena behind the collapsible only moments later, so how could Plavsic have already been attempting to escape with Galena's son and the jewelry chest if he'd obtained both by murdering her?

The words of Galena's letter to Dr. Bond bubbled up in my mind.

This voyage will end in disaster. There is someone on this ship who seeks to do us harm—do me *harm—only the presence I experienced this time was unmistakably feminine.*

"Unmistakably feminine," I whispered. Despite what I'd thought when I read the letter, Galena had not feared *me*, even if I was spying on her. In fact, she'd trusted me with her greatest secret.

The ship began to spin as the sky overhead grew dark with clouds.

Dark.

I fumbled through my pockets in search of the tiny bottles that held my magic potion—developing solution. "Hurry, Caleb! I need to find a lavatory."

"Well, all right." His cheeks turned crimson. "Though if you need one that badly, I don't see why you didn't say so earlier."

"No, it's not that! I need a place to develop film. A place where the sunlight can't get in, understand?"

Usually it was light that exposed the truth, but today it would be the dark.

Inside the washroom, I created a series of stop baths with the vials of developing solution I'd take from the sinking ship. When everything was ready, I removed Father Browne's photograph from the folder I'd also salvaged and placed it into chemicals that would strip it of shadows.

Strip it of lies.

The dark shape looming on the deck above Galena's head lightened gradually. Father Browne had been wrong in his assessment—this image wasn't double exposed; it just hadn't been exposed enough.

Before long, the shadow wasn't just a dark blob. It was a woman. A woman wearing a large boater hat. I peered closer, growing dizzy from deep inhales of the chemical solution. The woman held a pair of binoculars, fixed on Galena below. I couldn't see the shadow lady's face, but I knew her identity, for I'd photographed her in the same outfit made for strolling.

"He didn't do it," I whispered. "It wasn't Plavsic."

"Didn't do what?" asked Caleb in the cramped space behind me, his warm breath tickling my neck even as a chill clawed up my spine. "Who's that in the background?"

"That, I suspect, is Galena Lakovic's murderer."

We found her at *Carpathia*'s stern, prepared to make the ultimate leap.

"Don't do it, Mrs. Crawford!" I shouted over the steamer's roar. "It'd be a slap in the face of every person *forced* into that water."

"Such a tragedy...."

I'd expected her to be defiant or even angry; instead, she seemed resigned. Remorseful, even. I almost wondered if I'd made a mistake in accusing Helen Crawford of such a grievous crime.

Yet if it had been a mistake, she wouldn't be perched on the ship's railing, ready to jump five stories.

"You stole the ship's binoculars," Caleb growled beside me. He'd made a similar noise when I told him I'd seen those same binoculars in Mrs. Crawford's bag.

It was one of the details of our ill-fated voyage that would haunt the White Star Line for years to come. Why had there only been one pair of binoculars on board a ship so large?

"The iceberg... we couldn't see it in time. Do you have any idea what you've done?"

Mrs. Crawford glanced at Caleb over her shoulder with red-rimmed eyes. "I'm perfectly aware."

"But *why*?" I asked, inching closer, the photographic evidence against her clutched in my hand.

"Because Galena did not love him!" Mrs. Crawford cried, her loose hair tossed every which way by the wind. "She was *using* him as her escape from that the soldier who hunted her for her past crimes."

Hands clenched, a wave of anger rose inside me at yet another reminder that instead of protecting me and Mother, my father had been a fool. "And what concern is that of yours?"

Mrs. Crawford's face wasn't visible as she looked out across the sea, but I could hear the trembling of her voice. "I never meant to contribute to the sinking. I was only trying to protect him. To help Jonathan find happiness again. Though I suppose you know better than anyone how Lord Knight repays those who show him nothing but loyalty and devotion."

Given her current state, it didn't seem wise to pepper the woman with too many questions, but I could now fill in the picture on my own. The many glances of longing Mrs. Crawford had cast in my father's direction came to mind—though at the time, I hadn't recognized them as such. Helen Crawford was in love with him. It seemed Father would win Most Eligible Bachelor if only he'd *been* one. Still, that hardly explained why she'd murdered his current mistress in cold blood.

"Your father and I met through the PRS several years ago," Mrs. Crawford called out over the engines. "I was working with Jonathan and Frederick Bligh Bond on the Glastonbury excavation long before that woman came along. We grew close, Jonathan and I. Quite close, especially when your mother's health declined, and he needed comforting. Yet as soon as Galena appeared with her hocus pocus tricks, I was cast aside. Forgotten. It seems the allure of mystery is stronger than logic, even for the modern man."

I took a hesitant step closer as Mrs. Crawford's voice turned scornful.

"Well, I'll not be forgotten now."

"No, I should think not," I muttered callously. And here I'd believed Galena Lakovic was the madwoman on *Titanic*. In reality, she'd seen more clearly than all of us, with or without binoculars.

"I'm not insane, you know," Mrs. Crawford insisted, still facing the water. She sounded as if she worked to convince herself instead of us. "Everything I did, I did for love, and love often demands great sacrifice."

"Of a thousand innocent people?" Caleb was shaking with such rage, I feared if Mrs. Crawford did not jump in soon, he'd finish the job. "You call that *love*?"

The woman's voice reached a hysterical pitch. "I never meant for that to happen! Besides, there were surely many other factors that led to *Titanic*'s sinking—Bruce Ismay's enormous ego, for one."

I held up the photo of Mrs. Crawford watching Galena through the ship's binoculars. "I understand you were jealous of my father's new flame. But why did you think stalking her would change anything?"

Mrs. Crawford released a low chuckle. "The same reason you did, my dear. Lieutenant Plavsic assured me that if I helped him uncover the information Galena carried, he'd make sure the woman was out of my way when we reached New York. Then I could console Jonathan once more. Only when I confronted Galena in her stateroom, the desperate soldier had already taken her little boy from her maid and was holding him hostage, along with the box harboring her secret. The woman was so distraught, she told me everything—the truth about her children's parentage and the full extent of her relationship with your father." Mrs. Crawford's white knuckles as she climbed to clutch the ship's flagpole did little to hold back her trembling, but whether it was from rage or remorse, I could not tell. "I never meant to strike her so hard. I certainly did not intend to kill her—I just wanted her to *shut up*. To stop speaking *lies*... each word an icy dagger of Jonathan's betrayal plunged into my heart."

"All right then, we believe you. You didn't mean to kill Mrs. Lakovic. It was an accident." Caleb's wrath had been replaced by his usual calmness and some pity as he inched closer to Mrs.

Crawford. "Now come on down so we can clear up this misunderstanding once and for all."

"What's the point?" The woman's slender body shook as she sobbed. "None of it matters now! Galena is gone, but Nature is the harshest judge. The sea still claimed my love."

Oh God. She doesn't know Father survived.

"It's all right." Mrs. Crawford glanced back at us with the strangest smile. "While we're over open water, I still have a chance to join him."

"No, wait! My father, he—"

Caleb lunged for the woman's arm, but time was not his ally.

Helen Crawford released her grip on this world and leapt into a merciless sea.

30

TAYLOR

"**M**rs. Crawford!" Nathaniel jumps up from his seat by the fire. "How is that possible? She had such class."

"I guess intelligence and charm aren't safeguards against a jealous lover's rage," I say as Giles bursts into the room, looking undone. His frantic state is heightened by the fact that he isn't wearing a tux for once. The sight of the butler in a polo shirt and khakis is honestly more unnerving than his urgent tone.

"Thank heavens. Now we can put this bloody business behind us."

I slip Ava's book behind my back. "What are you talking about?"

"Come with me to the dining room, please. Yes, yes, right this way." Giles straightens his shirt. "It's a miracle I've kept the bloodshed at bay for this long."

I turn to Nathaniel, but he just shrugs, as confused as I am. The three of us follow Giles into the dining room, where my heart nearly falls from my chest. After all, it isn't every day you see your worst nightmare at a table long enough to seat half the lords and ladies of England.

The woman from Dad's photograph is at one end, and my mother is at the other.

Potential mistress and wife perfectly positioned for a duel to the death. Or in this case, a glaring contest over two glasses of cabernet.

"Mom?"

My mother's face floods with relief as she jumps up from her chair. "Taylor, thank goodness! Do you have any idea how worried I've been?"

She gathers me in a hug that brims with her signature scent—potting soil and coconut shampoo. The fragrances of the carefree mother I still remember but haven't seen in a long time.

"Why did you come all the way here?" I say, pulling back. "As you can see, I'm fine."

"And I'm relieved, considering that I couldn't get ahold of you for *two days*, Taylor. Your phone just kept ringing, and when I called Magdalen College, no one could find you. The staff have been searching everywhere! Thankfully, your friend Dalia here saved me from a total nervous breakdown."

I wince. For once I can't really blame Mom for freaking out. "I'm sorry. I should have tried harder to call and explain what was going on."

Mom's fury fades a little. "Yes, you should have."

"When did you get here?"

"Just a few minutes ago." Mom nods down the dark mahogany table, so glossy it looks like a sheet of black ice. "Right before *she* showed up."

The woman seems unaffected by Mom's glare. She sits with a satisfied smile on her wine-stained lips. Or maybe that's purple lipstick. Her long, red hair has been transformed into a short pixie cut that gives her facial expressions a severe, unfamiliar edge. Despite these differences, she's definitely the woman from Dad's photograph. Thanks to all the time I've spent studying it, I'd know that green, cat-eyed gaze anywhere.

"Who are you?" I ask bluntly before turning to Giles. "Will someone please explain what's going on?"

"We're here to settle this matter once and for all," the stranger replies before the butler has a chance. She speaks with an accent that isn't quite British, though I'm having trouble placing it. "My name is Camila Blake. I'm Mae Knight's niece and rightful heir. Now, please tell us Miss Romano, where did Aunt Mae have you hide her will?"

I cross my arms. This again? "Well, let's see. I knew Mae for about twenty minutes. And in that extensive period of time, she never once spoke of a will. So sorry to disappoint you."

The woman frowns at my sarcasm but continues her cross-examination. "That's funny, because Giles tells me you were one of the last people to speak with Lady Knight before her death. I understand she mentioned her intentions to share some significant information with you. Isn't that right, Mr. Price?"

"It is." Nathaniel scowls in Giles's direction, though I can't say I'm surprised the butler has turned traitor on us. "Mae wanted to tell Taylor her story. Her family history. Last time I checked, that's not a crime."

Camila sighs impatiently. "Perhaps not, but tampering with a woman's last will and testament most certainly is. But if you tell us where it is now, all will be forgiven. There's no need to involve the authorities if it can be avoided."

My temper is at a rolling boil. "I already told you, I don't know anything about Lady Knight's will."

"And before you badger my daughter or make more accusations without any evidence, why don't you tell us how you came to know my late husband, Ms. Blake?" Mom cuts in, her voice surprisingly firm.

A tense silence settles over the room. Mom sounds confident, but her shaking hand on my arm tells me she doesn't really want to hear the answer to her question. She's asked for my sake and my sake alone. Now that the moment is here, I'm not so sure I want to know the truth either. Just like the photograph Ava exposed in the dark to learn who killed Galena, this doesn't feel like a revelation that will be made by the solace of light.

Camila's eyes widen for a moment before resuming her signature glare. "Oh, don't play dumb with me. I already know Mae gave you the other key."

A lump falls from my throat to my gut. "What are you talking about?"

"This." Camila removes a chain from beneath her blouse. A small brass skeleton key dangles from the end.

Suddenly, I'm back in a muggy forest, reaching my hand into an old oak tree.

Dad's last treasure, hidden right before his final deployment. The key disappeared during our move to Maine. I figured it either got lost or Mom packed it away with the rest of Dad's belongings.

"Where did you get that?" I demand.

"It belonged to my grandfather, William Knight."

I open Ava's book to the desperate scrawl on the first page:

FIND WILL. As in the document… or the person?

They are the key.

Wills, keys, prophecies. There are too many threads. And they're all tangled in my head, leaving me with nothing but a giant knot.

"I don't understand. Mae's twin brother, William, died on the *Titanic*."

Camila gives me an arrogant grin, nodding at the book in my hands. "Apparently that account hasn't told you everything then. Grandpa Will survived the sinking, but he was raised in America. William was also Thomas Romano's grandfather, which is why your father visited Meadowbrook a few years back."

"Wait, his *grandfather*? No way. That isn't possible."

Mom nods at me. "Taylor's right. That's ridiculous. Tom's side of the family was from Italy originally, not England. I never knew a group of people so proud of their heritage," Mom explains as I try to focus on something steady in this spinning room. "*His* Grandpa Will—William *Romano*—grew up in central California. The man died at Pearl Harbor in his mid-twenties. Tom never even knew him."

Camila is still smirking. "All that is true, but Romano was the name of Grandpa Will's adoptive parents, not his biological ones." She gestures to the many chairs surrounding the dining room table. "Please. It's a long and rather complicated story."

I do need to sit down. I also need to see a doctor about my head, which is pulsing so hard I'm about to faint. Again.

"I didn't realize I had English ancestry either. Not until I started investigating my family history," Camila continues. "You see, in late April of 1912, Will was dropped off at a Brooklyn orphanage run by the Sisters of Charity. The sisters knew nothing about the boy's identity other than that his Christian name was William and his parents were poor immigrants in steerage who'd perished on the *Titanic*. He wore this key around his neck. Eventually, the boy was adopted by Jim and Hazel Romano. The young couple moved to California, where Will grew up, married, and joined the US Navy. He had two children of his own before he was killed in the bombing of Pearl Harbor—Pamela, my mother, and Louis, *your* grandfather."

Weird, even *if* it was true. I hadn't known my grandfather either—just like Dad hadn't—but his name *was* Louis. "Grandpa Lou was killed when my dad was pretty young. In Vietnam."

"Are you noticing a trend?" Camila asks. "Forgive me for putting it so candidly, but the Knight men had a knack for dying in war. I never met Uncle Lou either. My mother, Pamela, ran off with an Australian when she was nineteen, so I never knew my family in the States. She didn't talk about them much, due to the falling out she had with her mother over the man she eventually eloped with. Let's just say my father made the criminals first exiled to Australia look like public servants."

"Then how did you learn about William Knight's true identity?" Dalia asks, scribbling furiously in a purple notebook covered in Shakespeare quotes. "Presumably, he was adopted too young to know his real last name, correct? Or that he'd survived the *Titanic*?"

"Correct—and I'll get to that. You see, when my mother was diagnosed with congestive heart failure, all the old family stories started coming out. She gave me this key, the only token she had that once belonged to her father. Mother also told me her brother Lou in America had died in the Vietnam War, not long after the birth of his only son…" Camila turns back to me. "That child's name was Thomas. Your father."

I release a breath it feels like I've been holding for years. "You were cousins."

Not lovers, not liars, maybe not even friends.

The photograph of Camila hugging Dad showed the embrace of long-lost relatives miraculously reunited. That was it. That was all.

And yet, the hungry look in the eyes of the woman across from me suggests she now views this shared DNA as an inconvenience rather than a welcomed revelation.

Your father was not the man you thought he was.

No, he wasn't. But at least he wasn't a traitor and a cheat.

"Take a look at this." Dalia hands me her notebook. In impeccably petite handwriting, she's put together a family tree that makes sense of all the connections. Seeing my own name below the list of Jonathan and Galena's children and grandchildren is way too bizarre.

I glance at the ornate dining room, its crimson walls lined with more paintings of long-dead ancestors—*my* ancestors. Could I really be from this ancient place, part of this long and illustrious lineage?

Or a cursed one.

That's right. I knew it sounded too good to be true.

I face Camila. "How did you and my dad meet in the first place?"

"After my mother told me about her relatives in California, I hired a genealogist to search through public records, hoping to learn more about this branch of the family. This inquiry eventually led me to Tom, but then the genealogist discovered something even more intriguing: Grandpa Will's adoption records, which dated back to 1912. Mother said her father had become a sailor during the Second World War because his earliest memories were of the ocean, of sailing on a giant ship. Given this anecdote, plus the year of Will's adoption and the fact that he was in a New York orphanage, I followed what I can only describe as a hunch, an inkling, and began researching *Titanic* passengers named William who were about two years old at the time of the sinking. At that point, it wasn't difficult to determine that William Romano and William Knight, son of an English lord, were likely the same person."

But how did William survive? I wonder. Did Vaso Plavsic make it off the ship alive too? With Galena's mahogany box?

Despite this flood of revelation, there are still so many questions we might never have answers to. What was it that Mr. Stead had said as he awaited his death—something about seeing through a darkened glass?

Camila pauses to take a sip of wine. "When I began researching the Knight family, I learned that Lord Jonathan Knight, along with his two daughters, had been among the *Titanic*'s survivors. Once I traced the Knights back to Meadowbrook, I discovered that one of Jonathan's children—our Great Aunt Mae—was still alive. After I shared this information with Tom, we decided to meet her here. Our visit was brief, but it was an exciting reunion nonetheless."

"Wait. Something doesn't add up," Nathaniel interjects. "Why would Mae even believe you? An Australian and an American show up out of nowhere, claiming to be her long-lost relatives, and she just buys it?"

Camila nods. "Aunt Mae was skeptical at first, and it was difficult for her to face the possibility that her twin brother had survived without her knowing it in time. I'm sure she assumed Tom and I were scam artists trying to steal her inheritance, which was why, when we first reached out to her to make our travel arrangements, she made us swear to keep our visit to Meadowbrook a secret, even from our families, until she verified our identities. She didn't want so-called relatives from around the globe to begin pestering her to no end."

A piece of the puzzle falls into place. "But you had your grandfather's key as proof. And once Mae decided she believed your story, she gave my dad *her* key in return."

The same key Dad gave to me at our cabin by the lake.

"Yes. That's right," Camila replies, somewhat impressed.

This revelation should leave me ecstatic, but it doesn't. At the very least I should feel relieved, but instead, a heavy weight presses down on my chest. Something about Camila Blake is rubbing me the wrong way, distant cousin or not.

Her accent. *Mae never had an Aussie aide before* is what Mrs. Porter said about the phone call she received the night before Mae's death.

Camila is wearing normal clothes, a white medical badge with her photo pinned to her blouse. I don't think I've ever seen a fake ID, but even I can tell this "badge" was made on a home printer and laminated.

"You're the nurse's aide!" I leap up from my chair with such force, it topples over. "That's why you came here tonight, so you could sneak into the house again."

"Caught her red-handed at the servant's entrance," Giles declares proudly.

Camila says nothing, but her deepening frown confirms my accusations.

"But why wouldn't Mae just meet with you if you're family?" I continue.

A long-suppressed resentment overtakes the woman's face. "And this is where the problem of patriarchy begins. Not long after your father's visit, Aunt Mae and I had a bit of a falling out. I'll spare you the details, but the truth is Mae Knight was an ungrateful woman who never trusted me, never really trusted anyone—hence her long life of isolation—even though *I* did all the hard work of bringing our family back together. Tom, on the other hand, managed to worm his way into her affections without trying. He didn't even have a key, but she took one look at him and *knew* he was her nephew. Said he was the spitting image of her mother, whom she seemed to remember."

There's another thought that makes the room spin: Galena Lakovic was my great-great-grandmother.

Which means there is now a genetic explanation for why I'm so weird.

"I gave up everything and moved to England to save the Knight family legacy," Camila continues, her voice pulsing with bitterness. "I sacrificed my last few weeks with my dying mother, my law practice back in Sydney, even my marriage… though to be fair, that was always a lost cause. And *still* Aunt Mae believed I was only after her money."

I raise my eyebrows at her. "Well. Were you?"

This shifty-eyed woman doesn't exactly inspire trust, especially given her recent track record of sneaking around and breaking in to locked rooms. She's clearly ambitious, plus she has a knack for making everyone around her feel like a pawn in her master plan.

"Of course not! All I wanted was to start a new life in a new place. Now, would inheriting Meadowbrook have given me a fresh start? Without a doubt. Yet after Tom was killed—such a tragedy—Mae wouldn't even talk to me. Said she wanted nothing to do with her family's tainted past."

"I apologize, but I must interrupt." Clearing his throat, Giles turns on Camila with a low growl just like the bulldog he resembles. "*You*, Ms. Blake, are the one who brought Lady Knight's distrust upon yourself. Mae tried to mend fences by asking for your legal advice in the revision of her will, but you pressured her to make the most ludicrous changes. Perhaps if you hadn't been so intent on destroying everything her ancestors built, she'd have thought better of you. There are many things you might say of Lady Mae Knight, but she never forgot who she was or where she belonged."

"And that was all *I* wanted… to belong!" Camila shouts. "Belong the way Tom seemed to belong without any effort. Can't you see how clinging to these silly, antiquated traditions will only lead this house to ruin? Why, with a little effort, Meadowbrook might be made fit for the modern era. We could transform the house into a world-class hotel, but instead, Aunt Mae prefers to let the Knight family legacy sit here and rot."

"So is that why you snuck into the manor the night before she died?" The butler's voice explodes like a bomb. "Admit it, Ms. Blake—you came here that evening to find the will and then threaten Lady Knight. To *force* her to add you to her inheritance!"

Whoa, Giles.

I take back every misgiving I had about the butler's loyalty to Mae. He's about to go berserk on her niece.

"I beg your pardon? Aunt Mae is *dead*?" Camila's face pales as her dubious eyes travel to the only exit, which Giles is blocking with his solid stance. "My, that's a sad and sudden development. But your accusations are still ludicrous, Mr. Bosko."

Her shock seems so genuine, it's hard to know what to think. My long-lost cousin may be abrasive and most likely a little greedy, but I can almost understand what made her that way. She gave up a lot to bring the Knight family back together. What if Mae really did slight her in favor of my dad just because that's how these old families have done things for generations? The guys get all the goods, and the gals get to grow old in frilly nightgowns and wander mournfully through the halls of a giant house they'll never actually own.

With a wave of her hand, Camila releases an exaggerated sigh. "I admit that sneaking into the manor was a mistake, but I only went to such extremes after Mae ignored my letters and phone calls for months. After all, can't you see how dire the situation had become? Mae was an entire century old and still she refused to name an heir! Time was running out. I had to reason with her before it was too late."

"And by 'reason with her,' you mean convince her to name *you* as her sole heir," Nathaniel accuses just as Mrs. Porter pokes her head into the room.

"Pardon the intrusion, Mr. Bosko," the housekeeper announces, looking at each of us. She clearly wants everyone to hear what she's about to say. "There's a phone call for you in the other room. I believe it's one you'll want to take."

Giles shifts back and forth, unwilling to abandon his post in front of the doorway. Without any hesitation, Nathaniel jumps up to fill in.

"Pardon me." Even though he's in his off-duty attire, old habits die hard and the butler bows before leaving the room.

For two minutes, no one speaks. I'm still processing all the information when Dalia breaks the tense silence. "So. *Did* you try to have Mae name you as her heir or not?"

"Of course I did. And why shouldn't I?" Camila releases a nervous, hyena-like laugh. "After all my labor and research, who better to inherit the Knight family fortune? I deserve Meadowbrook. I *earned* it."

"Then it's most regrettable for you that there *is* no fortune, Ms. Blake," Giles says in his leaden tone as he reenters the dining room. "As least not one with the substantial number of digits you likely expect."

"That's preposterous. Of course, there's a fortune..." Camila keeps up her outraged monologue, but I'm distracted by Giles as he whispers into Nathaniel's ear.

Nathaniel walks over to me. "Get ready to follow my lead," he whispers as he tugs me to my feet. "When I grab her left arm, you get a good grip on the right. I'll explain later. Just trust me."

Before I can commit, Nathaniel gives me a nod that says *go!*

"What are you doing?" Camila cries as we move toward her like a pair of defensive linemen rushing the quarterback, each grabbing ahold of a wrist. "Let go of me!"

The woman thrashes like a wild animal, but I hold firm, imitating Nathaniel as he pins Camila's bony hand to the arm of her chair. Giles steps up behind us with four zip-tie restraints, which he uses to secure the woman's arms and legs.

"What is this, a bloody citizen's arrest? You've all lost your minds! And you can bet I'll be calling the police to press charges of assault!"

"Not to worry, Ms. Blake, the police have been called already," Giles replies.

Camila's sneer suggests she's thinking about spitting in the butler's face. "Oh, is that right? Then tell me, you little worm of a man—whatever for?"

"For the murder of Mae Knight," I blurt out, even surprising myself.

Everyone turns to stare at me. I feel the pinpricks of the ethereal presence again, though I can't say for sure if the muse who has inspired me to speak is Mae or her sister, Ava.

Tell them, says the silent whisper tugging at my heart.

I study Camila, who's given up struggling in favor of glaring at me. The awful smell of the stain next to Mae's bed has never left me, and now I'm convinced my gut reaction was right. "What did you put in Mae's tea that night?"

The woman opens her mouth, then closes it, her eyes bulging. "I, I… it was nothing. A homeopathic tincture. All-natural ingredients, I swear. Something to calm Mae's nerves so she'd actually listen to what I had to say."

"Is that so? I wasn't aware that *opium* was considered a safe, natural remedy," Giles spits back. "Miss Romano's suspicions are right. After I learned someone had weaseled their way into Meadowbrook, my mind wouldn't rest, so I took Taylor's initial advice and spoke with the coroner. They ran some tests, and that phone call was a report of the results. It appears there were significant traces of opium in Lady Knight's system. A tincture called *laudanum* to be specific, which was once quite popular among the Victorians and Edwardians, though it isn't prescribed today due to its highly addictive nature. Not to mention it's illegal."

"Oh, don't be so overdramatic. Laudanum has been used to calm people's anxieties for centuries," Camila insists. "The small amount I added to Mae's tea was nowhere near enough to cause an overdose."

"And yet you felt entitled to give an elderly woman this dangerous substance in the first place!" Giles bellows, his face turning the full spectrum of purple. "For goodness' sake, Ms. Blake, be honest with yourself. There's no point in denying it— you were trying to *force* Lady Knight into a malleable state. That way you could manipulate her into altering her will, naming you sole heir of Meadowbrook."

Camila's eyes harden into glass. "And so what if I did? None of it matters now. The old ox was just as stubborn as ever, even *with* the opium. She wouldn't even show me the will, let alone change it." She lifts her chin. "Look, I understand that I frightened Aunt Mae by showing up here unannounced, but there's no way the laudanum killed her. She was an old, obstinate creature as immune to drugs as she was to common sense!"

"Yes, well, sadly, she wasn't invincible." Giles lowers his voice, his gaze falling to the floor. "The medical examiner concluded that while there wasn't enough opium in Mae's bloodstream to kill her on its own, when mixed with the other prescription drugs she took that night, the extra depressant likely slowed Lady Knight's heart to a stop."

"I don't believe this." Camila releases another ill-timed laugh. "What are you saying? That I *murdered* a one-hundred-year-old woman already on death's doorstep?"

"Her age makes no difference. None of us have the power to decide who lives and who dies. But yes, that's precisely what I'm saying." Giles turns to the dining room window, where red and blue lights are flashing at the end of Meadowbrook's long drive. "Though, of course, we'll leave the final verdict up to a jury of your peers."

31

*A*VA

August 12, 1914

Caleb held my hand firmly, the black pearl of my ring rubbing against his wedding band. We did not speak, for there was no need. The rustling leaves and crunching gravel beneath our feet were enough of a warning—a sign we were headed down a path of memories I'd rather not face. Yet knowing Caleb walked beside me made all the difference.

Meadowbrook felt foreign to me now, an empty shell filled with shadows who wandered its lonely halls.

It had been two years since *Titanic*. Two years since I'd spoken to either of my parents. If I was being honest, it wasn't just my anger about Father's affair that kept me away.

It was fear.

Those of us who had survived the Atlantic learned to look ahead, never behind.

Father had clearly sent Mother to some dreadful institution as he'd often threatened—that was the most logical explanation for why she never responded to my letters. When I didn't receive a response to our wedding invitation, it was the final confirmation to me that Father had locked her away.

I'm ashamed to admit it, but I could not bear to see her in person. I wanted her to forever be the lively, whimsical Mother she'd been *before*—not the catatonic invalid she surely resembled once the lobotomist was through with her.

But perhaps I was finally ready. Ready to face the truth.

"It'll be all right, luv," Caleb promised, wrapping his arm around my shoulder. "At least hear him out. If your father goes off to war and, God forbid, he doesn't return, you'll never forgive yourself."

He had spoken similar sentiments as we prepared for and undertook this journey, and he was right. The guilt of abandoning one parent was already too much to bear. Even if I couldn't forgive Father, I could at least see him. But he wasn't the real reason I had returned.

Fortunately, Caleb's parents and four sisters had accepted me as one of their own. I'd grown accustomed to their more modest lifestyle in Belfast, discovering the freedom found in simplicity. I also learned that I enjoyed being part of a large, noisy family. A *normal* family—if such a thing existed.

Meadowbrook's ivy cloaked walls loomed ahead, and I wondered how I'd lived in such a stifling place for so long. A house filled with many beautiful things but devoid of all laughter. A place that was opulent but empty. Meadowbrook's oppressive stones stood silent in my memories, but I knew this house harbored voices. Voices I did not wish to hear.

"We've come for Mae and that's all," I declared, reaching for the door's brass knocker. "I'll do my best to be civil, but the man's actions can never be condoned."

"Maybe so, but none of that is the girl's fault," Caleb replied in his sensible way.

I studied my husband's steady face—still young but already weary from shipwrecks and storms. He wanted children of his own more than anything, yet I worried this was not to be our destiny. We'd been married over a year, and I'd felt no fluttering of tiny feet. Deep down, perhaps we both hoped little Mae would fill this void with her laughter.

I never anticipated such a sense of responsibility for a half sister born of my father's dead mistress. Yet if Father was off to fight the Germans, I would not leave the child to be raised by strangers, especially when Caleb and every other young man in Britain would join him on the battlefield before long.

Together, Mae and I had survived an eternal night once. We could do so again.

"Lady Ava!" cried the blushing servant who took our hats. "Beg your pardon, I meant *Mrs.* Donohue."

"Hello, Rebecca. It's good to see you again."

The servant nodded like she wasn't sure she felt the same. Regardless, she guided us graciously to the parlor where Mother's grand piano sat in silence. As usual, the room smelled of fresh cut roses.

"We'd prefer to wait in the library, Rebecca. If you don't mind."

"Certainly, my lady," the servant replied, leading the way.

While we awaited the appearance of the lord of the manor, my foot tapped nervously with the ticking clock on the mantelpiece. I couldn't understand it—why did my childhood home suddenly make my skin crawl?

"Mrs. Donohue!"

A girl the spitting image of my father burst into the room. With a shy smile, Mae extended a bouquet of wilting flowers. "Here you are, Mrs. Donohue. These are for you."

"Thank you, dear, but you may call me Ava. We are sisters, after all." I crouched down to the four-year-old's level. Her sundress matched the white and yellow roses in her grip, though the fabric of her skirt was covered in grass stains.

So *this* was what happened when Father raised a daughter on his own. Smiling despite myself, I removed a dried leaf from the child's gilded hair, recalling my lost photograph from the day *Titanic* set sail. It almost felt like a prophecy of her wildness.

"These are lovely, Mae. Thank you," I replied, though something kept me from accepting the bouquet. "Why don't you go ask the maids for a vase to put them in?"

With a nod, Mae raced down the hall, hair and petals flying, right as my father entered the library. Caleb rose to shake his hand, but I could hardly utter a greeting. Arms crossed over my chest, I remained in my seat.

"Hello, Ava." Father sat down across from me. He seemed anxious, uncomfortable—as well he should. "Mae has certainly grown, hasn't she?"

"Children usually do," I replied flatly.

Father's smile vanished as it became clear I was not going to make this easy for him. Rumors claimed that Jonathan Knight had become quite the hermit, consumed by the writings of his beloved psychologists and their unsubstantiated theories. His shadowed eyes bore the rings of many sleepless nights, but I doubted he'd spent the time confessing his sins.

"Thank you both for coming. It seems Galena's war is finally upon us. I'm glad my letter found you, for all the rest were returned—"

Not an accident, I assure you.

"Yes, the war," I cut in, my skin prickling at the mere mention of *her* name in *my* house. In Mother's house. "Alas, we were unable to bend Fate to our will, which isn't to say we didn't try."

For we *had* tried. Once *Carpathia* arrived in New York, Caleb and I traveled to Carnegie Hall on the day of the scheduled peace conference, only to learn the event had been canceled due to the loss of the conference's main speaker, Mr. William Stead.

What else could we do?

Plavsic had taken the box with Galena's evidence, and both appeared to have gone down with the ship. We would never know what secret information had been sealed inside, or if it might have altered the fate of the war.

Regardless, Caleb and I had spent months in New York campaigning for a peaceful solution to the growing tensions in Europe, but Galena had been right about more than *Titanic*. As she'd claimed, once war was presented as an option, it soon became the only option. Perhaps that was what Lieutenant Plavsic had hoped for all along, and why he worked so hard to keep Galena's mysterious warning out of the limelight.

Now, thanks to the recent assassination of the Archduke Franz Ferdinand, Britain would enter the fray with the rest of Europe, and there was nothing we could do to stop yet another ship from sinking.

"My efforts were also futile," Father said, smoothing his mustache. "I gained an audience with President Taft's staff, but as you might imagine, they hardly humored me. Galena and I had hoped the peace conference would provide a forum for unveiling her warning to open-minded influencers on the world stage, especially when we had the support of a renowned journalist like William Stead. Yet sadly, it was not to be. I'm sure Taft's people thought me a raving lunatic."

"No doubt," I agreed.

Caleb cleared his throat, eager to change the subject before I emasculated my father any further. "And the archeologist? Dr. Bond, is it? Did he have any success in warning Parliament?"

Father shook his head. "Bond's relationship with the Church of England was too strained for anyone to take him seriously, and I doubt he'll be publishing research with a whiff of Spiritualism any time soon. To be honest, I'm grateful for it. The last thing I need before joining the Officer Corps is for my name to be dragged through the mud."

"So, you doubt your mistress's supernatural talents then?" I asked.

Father frowned. "Not at all, though Galena deeply regretted how we used them. My views on the supernatural are stronger than ever, yet I now recognize that the spirit world isn't neutral, and it certainly won't bend to the will of men. Efforts by ambitious intellectuals like Dr. Bond are inherently dangerous because when we seek to communicate with the realms beyond this one, we can never know for certain whether the forces we toy with work on behalf of evil or good. Perhaps that is why we were never meant to know the future, lest we become slaves to our limited interpretations of it."

Caleb nodded. "It often seems that the more men know about the things that give us power, the more harm we end up doing with them."

"I suspect those who've stared down a machine gun or choked on mustard gas would agree." Father shook his head as he poured himself a brandy in the corner. "If not, they will soon. It's just too bad that my awareness of my own family's past failings hasn't prevented the cycle from repeating itself."

Enough.

I couldn't hear any more. This man had the audacity to blame Mother's illness and their poor excuse for a marriage on folklore spread by the villagers—some longstanding rumor about a Knight family curse. It was true Mother was addicted to a substance concocted by the devil himself, but perhaps the reason laudanum had spread across England like a plague was because it kept aristocratic wives as docile as house cats.

I clenched both fists. "If anyone is to blame for our family's troubles, it's *you.*"

He turned to face me, eyes downcast, and nodded. "I couldn't agree with you more, Ava. *The sins of the father shall be visited upon the sons...* isn't that how the verse goes?" His voice grew weary with sorrow. "Perhaps the silver lining in all this is I have only daughters now."

"Then you truly believe your family name is cursed?" Caleb seemed surprised, though this diagnosis would suffice as a perfectly reasonable explanation among his kin. The Donohue clan loved a good curse.

"I believe the actions of one generation directly impact the lives of the next, yes. Whether that's a curse or merely a law of nature, I cannot say. All I know is the Knight family has reaped as much misery as it has sown. I only wish I knew how to make it stop." His blue eyes looked past us into the unknown. "Galena's evidence might have prevented this tragedy from coming to pass, but I suppose we'll never know."

"And what *was* Galena's evidence? Surely describing it to President Taft would have had the same effect."

"Some truths are so bold they must be shown or given flesh. Telling does little good." Father's stare turned bitter as he looked out the window at his estate. All this inherited wealth had little influence when it came to this new world order men sought to build by marring the face of Europe with miles of muddy trenches. "But none of that matters now. Events have come to pass exactly as we feared."

He would not weasel out of an explanation so easily. "But what was it that Vaso Plavsic hunted so desperately?" I insisted. "After everything that has happened, I think you owe me *that* explanation at the very least."

Father turned to me, his face brightening with a connection he'd only just made. "It was right up your alley, actually. Our evidence was a photograph."

My look of confusion was enough that he continued his explanation. "The evidence in the jewelry box. It was a photograph we uncovered during our excavation of Glastonbury Abbey with Dr. Bond." His eyes went distant again. "Bond is the oddest gentleman you'll ever meet. One conversation with him and you'll cover both Eastern and Western spirituality, the role of sacred geometry in the science of archaeology, the fourth dimension, and the mathematical relation of form to color."

"You were saying something about a photograph," I pressed.

"Yes, of course. You see, during our early excavations of Glastonbury, Bond and Galena conducted nightly automatic writing sessions. They encountered spirits who claimed to be former monks of the abbey, a group that called themselves The Watchers. These sessions revealed the locations of several of the abbey's main towers with uncanny accuracy, so even I began to acknowledge their validity."

Father stroke his chin, lost in the memory. "But then one of the ghostly transcripts revealed the strangest claim yet. A supposedly dead monk named Patraic told us in writing, 'There be a message in ye stones. In ye foundations be a mystery. Search the well and ye will find a well that goes deeper still—a cosmic reservoir where there be no barrier between past and future.'"

"A well?" Caleb asked. "What did he mean?"

"The Chalice Well, it turns out, just outside the town of Glastonbury," Father explained. "Also known as the Red Spring for the color of the water, which has led many to believe it was where Joseph of Arimathea buried the sacred chalice of the Last Supper, the Holy Grail. It was near this well, in a small cave at the foot of the Glastonbury Tor, that we discovered not a chalice but a tin cigar box. Inside was a preserved photograph that must be seen to be believed."

I listened intently, recalling the haunting image Father Browne had taken on *Titanic* that revealed Galena's murderer. Perhaps it was not so incredible to think a photo could capture the truth of things or even predict the future.

"It was a photograph of the Archduke Franz Ferdinand's assassination in Sarajevo. An image that captured the face of his young killer, Gavrilo Princip—a member of the Black Hand and a likely protégé of our friend Lieutenant Plavsic."

"But the archduke was assassinated by Princip less than two months ago!" I cried. The gunshot was the spark that had ignited this war, and images of the royal couple riding in their open automobile must have been printed in every paper from here to Hong Kong. "You're saying you dug up this photograph over two *years* ago?"

Father nodded. "I don't know how to explain it, Ava. But I saw Princip's face in that photograph *before* we set sail on *Titanic,* though of course we did not know his name at the time. Still, I saw the impossible with my own eyes. The message Galena had channeled from beyond the veil claimed we'd find a reservoir near the Chalice Well, a place where time and eternity intersected, where the past and the future were suspended and all that existed was the present moment."

"So the idea is if someone buried the photograph far in the future, it would exist at that location always, even in 1912, because the cave is a kind of eternal reservoir outside the bounds of time," Caleb mused, which had me gaping at him, utterly bewildered. But Caleb had always surprised me with his depth of understanding, which led him to see the truth long before I would admit it to myself.

I shook my head, which only made it spin more. "Well, you're right about one thing, Father. Such a ludicrous claim must be seen to be believed. Even then, I can't understand how delivering a photograph that's supposedly from the future would have convinced President Taft or any other leader that you were anything but a raving lunatic."

Father cracked a sad smile. "Our mission was always a long shot, my dear, perhaps even a lost cause, since the most we can hope for when it comes to preventing war among men is a temporary victory. Still, we hoped that in warning the world's powers of a plot against the archduke, and especially by revealing the face of his assassin, we might have planted seeds that could have changed the course of events."

The knowledge of such a future with little chance of altering it was indeed a heavy burden. An impossible one. No wonder Galena regretted their unorthodox means of inquiry—and repented of them bitterly in the end. How arrogant we humans were. To think we could use the spirit realm to change the course of history was as blasphemous as claiming that the *Titanic* was unsinkable.

And who had ultimately suffered as a result of their tampering, their consultations with poltergeists who were more likely deceitful devils than actual monks?

My baby brother. An innocent.

I wished I could see the photograph that had caused his demise. No one had ever heard from Plavsic again, so he was assumed to have perished as well, along with his otherworldly image. What other explanation could there be?

"Perhaps your evidence was meant to go down with the ship," I said finally. "Perhaps there is some knowledge we are simply not meant to have."

"I have agonized over similar thoughts these past two years, believe me," Father replied with a grimace. "And while I have mourned many, the loss of William will haunt me forever. I should have been more watchful. I should have heeded Galena's warnings. I never dreamed *Titanic* could be so… fallible. So like the rest of us."

Beyond the Gothic arches of the library's windows, dark storm clouds descended upon our estate, but they were nothing compared to the tempest stirring within me at the mention of a little boy who'd likely died because of my father's prideful dealings with the occult.

Any remaining restraint bled from the wounds Father had reopened. "Well, at least Mother won't have to learn that your mistress gave you *two* bastards when she was unable to bear other children. I trust you've kept Mae away from whatever dreadful institution you've imprisoned her in. Mother could never handle such an appalling revelation in her fragile state."

A knowing glance passed between Caleb and my father, as if they were in some secret alliance. Caleb reached for my hand.

"Ava, you must listen carefully. I know this has been difficult for you to accept, but Galena Lakovic was *not* my mistress," Father said, his blue eyes firm. "She was my wife. That's why I booked our trip to America. We hoped the fresh scenery of New York would enable you to acknowledge the new arrangement. Give you a chance to spend some time in a place with no memories. Somewhere… not *here*. Anywhere but here."

Caleb's grip tightened as the tall stacks of books closed in around me. I shook my head, blocking out the voices that bounced off the walls. "That's not possible. Mother is—"

"Stop it, Ava! I know it isn't easy, but it's high time you accepted the truth." Father's face shone with a longstanding grief that I only now recognized—because I'd been too busy drowning in my own.

"Ava, your mother is dead. She's been dead for years."

Rose petals.

My mind managed to bury the moment, but I'd never forgotten my distaste for that pungent aroma. When the subconscious tries to kill a memory, nothing revives it quite like the sense of smell.

On the day it happened, Father was away at one of his PRS gatherings. I was upstairs in my room, pressing flowers in the floral dictionary Mother had given me for my birthday, a treasure that belonged to her as a girl. The crash of shattering glass below was followed by the maid's shrill scream.

The old woman was the one who found her—draped across the chaise lounge like a wilted lily, her silk gown wrapped around her willowy body as if a shroud. The white hand that knocked over the vase had fallen limp at her side. The other clutched the opium pipe.

The murder weapon.

It was the next step up from laudanum. Mother said it stopped the pain. The pain of her latest miscarriage and all the accusations that came with it—the voices that assailed her, claiming she was worthless. Powerless. Unable to give Meadow-brook the heir it so desperately needed.

Only this time, the painkiller squeezed from the poppy flow-er had stopped her heart.

I stood in the parlor doorway, inhaling the sickening scent of roses while maids and footmen scurried about. My mother lay motionless on the floor before me. Dying. Yet instead of *doing* something, I just stood there. Staring at a pile of scattered petals.

I'd been stuck in that position ever since, despite Father's dive into psychological study. For four years, the traumatic memory had been hidden away in a secret compartment of my mind, so that the guilt of having done nothing would not force my head below water.

The girl in that doorway hadn't been *still*. She hadn't been constant or true.

She'd been scared. Stagnant.

Until *Titanic* forced her to move.

The rain railed against me as I ran from the manor, ran from the memories that cried out from every portrait and every heirloom. I could hear Caleb shouting my name, but I also heard Father telling him to let me go.

"She needs to do this. She needs to *see* for herself."

The storm swirled above me, the final barrier between my future and my past. I raced toward the churning river, crossing the bridge that led to the old cemetery. Two willow trees guarded its entrance. Beyond these silent gatekeepers lay a sanctuary of the dead, buried in rows like knights on a chessboard. Generations of Knights who'd served their king and fought for their country. Knights who had died for a reason.

Except for *Rosalind McKinley Knight*.

My mother—who had died for nothing.

I later learned that Father's hypnosis methods were his last-ditch effort to heal my trauma—the reoccurring nightmares of a girl who'd watched her beloved mother die of a self-inflicted illness that had overtaken her in the end. In fact, it was possible Father's experimental attempts at hypnosis had pushed the memory down even further.

Despite our modern advances, there was still so much we could not control.

Titanic had made that clear, which was how I knew I'd never be able to heal myself, no matter what newfangled methods Father employed. No, what I needed was to *remember*—to *be* remembered and thus made whole—for it was only through remembering that I could see how far I'd fallen and glimpse the path that led from the abyss.

And so, I let the harsh truth wash over me, one revelation at a time.

The spirited mother I'd adored had become mentally ill thanks to an addiction to a deadly substance, one that took her life in the end. My father had not had an affair—not an adulterous one, at least. He'd kept his relationship with Galena Lakovic hidden not only from me, but from everyone—for my sake, fearing that in my fragile state, I'd break as surely as my mother had if he forced me to face the truth before I was ready. Galena and the children must have had a flat in London that Father visited, though he intended to make their marriage public once we were in New York, where he'd hoped the echoing halls of Meadowbrook could not reach me.

Tears mingled with the raindrops streaking my cheeks as I stood before my mother's grave, shivering like I hadn't shivered since the lifeboat. A faint sound made me turn. It was not the cold whisper of a ghost or a buried memory, but a voice that was warm and real.

A child's voice.

Mae emerged from the two willows behind me—another motherless girl in a world that would eventually make orphans of us all. Her eyes pleaded with mine, just as they had on the long night we'd endured already.

Keep rowing, they begged. *Keep moving so we can stay warm.*

I'll try, Mae. I promise.

My own mother had left me because the weight of this world had pushed her under, but I would not do the same to this girl— my legitimate sister, no longer disgraced. No matter how cold the water, I'd keep kicking until my head broke past its lethal waves. If fighting against the current was what it took to keep Mae safe, then I would never stop swimming.

And together, we would survive.

TAYLOR

When I lower the book, there isn't a dry eye in the library. Except for Giles, of course, though even he struggles to keep that upper lip stiff. Nathaniel has been staring out the window since the police cruiser took Camila to the closest station for questioning, but he keeps up the act so no one will see him sniffling. A few silent tears stream down Mom's and Dalia's cheeks, and Mrs. Porter is full-on sobbing in the corner.

I have to admit—this isn't how I expected Ava's story to end. The revelation of her mother's death came out of nowhere, and yet the clues were there all along.

"I have my own confession to make," announces Giles in that gruff voice guys often get when they're trying to downplay their emotions. The butler walks over to where I'm seated on the stone hearth and removes a thick envelope from his breast pocket.

"What's this?"

"Lady Mae's will."

I stare at him, slack jawed. "You mean you had it this entire time?"

"Afraid so. Camila made it seem like her correspondence with Lady Knight was cordial, when in fact her frequent letters and calls took on an increasingly threatening tone. Mae worried her niece might try something drastic, so she asked me to keep the will safe and out of sight."

"That explains why Camila never found it during her search," I reply, raising my eyebrows. "But it doesn't explain why you sent us hunting for it all over this house."

Giles sighs and some of his stiffness is replaced with something more... caring. "Yes, well, sometimes you must permit a bit of suffering to fulfill a greater promise. You see, Miss Romano, when Mae and I first met your father, you were all Thomas could talk about. He said you were the most imaginative child, and he told us about a special game he'd created for you when you were quite young..."

Now tears are scratching at my throat. When I meet Mom's glistening eyes, I know she feels it too—the good hurt. The ache that's inevitable when someone you love is gone. The longing that seeps into even your happiest memories like a stain.

"Thomas couldn't wait to bring you here and play Treasure Hunt in this huge house. When he passed away before that dream could be brought to fruition, Mae decided to tell you about the Knights, and she insisted on carrying on the game your father had created. That's why she intended to give you her sister's memoir. She hoped it would help you put the pieces together yourself. When I saw that you'd discovered it in her bedroom, I thought it best to let the game play out to the end—in memory of both Mae and your father. Mentioning Mae's will when we had so much downtime after the storm seemed a way to spur things on."

That's when the butler does something he's never done. He smiles. "And I must say, Miss Romano, Mae was right. Your knack for investigative journalism did not disappoint."

My stare at him is part wonder, part annoyance. That second part of me wants to throttle the guy, but he's right that Dad would have preferred it this way. "Thank you, Giles." I walk over to the grouchy butler and give him a hug.

"Good heavens. That really isn't necessary," Giles sputters, tapping my back like he's swatting at horseflies. Despite his protests, when I release him, his hesitant smile has traveled to his eyes. "Now that *that's* out of the way, would you like to know the details of Lady Knight's will?"

The implications of tonight's revelations suddenly slam against me like a freight train. If Mae refused to name Camila Blake as her heir, who else does that leave?

Giles searches his pockets for his reading glasses with all the speed of a three-toed sloth. As he unfolds the document, he says, "First, let me assure you, Miss Romano, that despite Camila's resentful claims, Mae had no problem passing on the Knight estate to a woman, and as guardian, it was within her powers to do so." Giles casts me a conspiratorial smirk. "However, she intended to make sure it was left to the *right* woman."

But as the butler scans the will, his fleeting grin sags. "Oh dear. Oh no. It's much worse than I thought."

"What is? What's wrong?" Mom places both hands on my shoulders.

"You must understand that after the disaster of World War I, very few households like Meadowbrook survived," Giles explains. "Jonathan Knight's income as a psychotherapist provided some extra padding, as did a mysterious source of funding Ava came into after *Titanic*. She used the money to house dozens of London children at Meadowbrook during both world wars, but the manor continued accruing debt. Naturally, this wasn't a burden Mae wanted *you* to inherit, Miss Romano—what with the ridiculous death tax—so it appears she's already sold the estate."

"*What?*" the rest of us cry in unison.

"Yes, I'm afraid so." Giles shakes his head in disbelief. "The transfer of property won't take place until next month, but it says here that Lady Knight sold Meadowbrook to a nonprofit organization that will transform the estate into a treatment facility for those suffering from post-war trauma. Listen to what she wrote here: 'The Knights have lost enough men to war. Let us use our remaining resources for the healing of wounds rather than the making of them. My hope is this gift will go a distance in atoning for the offences of my ancestors, replacing any strife the Knights proliferated with a lasting peace.'"

It's a moving dedication, but my hopes sink. Although Mae gave up Meadowbrook for a cause I can support wholeheartedly, I can't help feeling disappointed that I came *this close* to having a real home.

I stand abruptly. "I'll be right back. I need a few minutes to… p-process things," I stutter, already moving toward the exit. With Ava's book in one coat pocket and a flashlight from the foyer in the other, I exit the house and head into the darkness. Before I can leave Meadowbrook Manor behind, before my family's past can serve as a compass instead of an anchor, there's one more conversation I need to have.

And it's with the dead.

I used to love old cemeteries. Our lake house in North Carolina was across the street from an overgrown graveyard with tombstones dating back to the Civil War. It never freaked me out. Life gets lonely without any siblings, but inside that cemetery, I never felt alone. It wasn't that I saw ghosts; it was more that I saw lives. People who had lived, and loved, and done something worth remembering. At least the flowers on their tombstones suggested that there were others who cared to remember. Somehow, all those floral bursts of color made the past tense not so past.

I remember wandering down aisles of headstones lined with weeds, reading faint inscriptions in the evening twilight. Even then, I understood that epitaphs mattered—a few lines that made the impossible effort to sum up a person, a life. The dead may be gone, but in the silence of a cemetery where time stands still, they continued to speak.

I shine my light over the lichen-kissed slab in front of me.

> *And what the dead had no speech for, when living,*
> *They can tell you, being dead: the communication*
> *Of the dead is tongued with fire beyond*
> *the language of the living.*
> *Here, the intersection of the timeless moment*
> *Is England and nowhere. Never and always.*

I trace my finger across these poetic words, etched into the side of a large mausoleum. The massive monument has a domed roof supported by four Roman columns. It sits in the farthest corner of the cemetery, shielded by an overgrown yew tree, the vines of a wild climbing rose bush, and an armor of thick green moss. The name *Knight* stands guard over the doorway, barely visible because of how the stone has blackened over time. My flashlight illuminates a list of names.

Thomas Knight is the freshest among them.

His father, Louis, is there too. And so is his grandfather, William. Then there's Jonathan Knight. At the end of this list, I come across another inscription:

*In honor of our family's fallen: Knights who sought to
redeem their time.
We who survive will remember.*

The relief of knowing I have something *good* to remember is
overwhelming. My dad was who he said he was, who I always
believed him to be. In fact, he was *more*, thanks to the long chain
of people who have entered his story, revealing the truth that
none of us is a blank slate. We're born with the fingerprints of a
thousand souls that came before us, their actions, for good or ill,
somehow written into our DNA. I don't know if I'd go as far as
to call that a curse, but it certainly is a mystery.

For a long time, I stand there staring at this list of names,
each marked by a date in time that will never come around again.

"We are survivors, you know." Mom's voice is followed by
her warm hands on my shoulders. "And survivors keep going,
even if they can never forget."

My eyes refuse to leave the stone. "All this time, I thought
that's what you wanted—to forget. To pretend Dad never existed."

"Sometimes that was what I wanted. There's a fine line between honoring a memory and idolizing it, between remembering
and obsessing. I've never been good at finding the right balance."
Mom strokes my hair like she used to when I was young. "After
your father died, a part of me just wanted to detach. For life to
stop then and there. But one morning you walked into my bedroom and said, 'Come on, Mom. It's time to get up.' And that's
what saved me, Taylor. *You* gave me a reason to survive. I
thought starting a new life in a new place would be the best thing
for us, but now I see that I was running from the past instead of
facing the difficult questions that came with it."

While I'm glad Mom didn't turn out like Ava's mother, her
confession isn't enough to diffuse my resentment. I turn out of
her grasp to face her. "Do you have any idea what it's been like?

Living with a shadow? Some days it's like you're not even there. And when you are there, you're freaking out over all the things that could possibly go wrong. All the things you can't control. It's suffocating, Mom."

"I know." She sighs. "And I'm sorry. I worried we'd end up confronting your dad's history here somehow, so when you left for Oxford, I lost myself all over again. Not being able to get in touch with you scared me like nothing else, Taylor, but it also made me *move*. You woke me up. Just like you did before."

Mom approaches the memorial and rests her hand on the grooves that spell out Dad's name. For a moment, her face brightens like she's reliving something good. I haven't seen an expression like that in a long time, but it makes her look young again. "I can't believe how much you and your dad loved that silly game."

My lips curl into a smile. "Treasure Hunt."

"Your dad would save all the brown paper bags from the grocery store, just so he could make you those treasure maps." Mom laughs. "Not to mention all those silly antiques he collected over the years. For a soldier who moved around a lot, he could be such a packrat. The exact opposite of me."

I'm elated to reminisce, something we've never done before. "Yeah, your idea of 'moving' was donating everything we owned to the thrift store."

I'm only teasing, but it makes Mom's smile evaporate.

"Not everything, Taylor. I understand that there are some things worth holding onto." Mom reaches into the pocket of her raincoat and removes a long chain.

On the end of the silver strand is a little brass key. A key whose lock is buried beneath the sea. It matches Camila's perfectly.

"Now I know why your father wanted you to have this. Mae must have given it to him during his visit to Meadowbrook. I'm sorry that I packed it up after he—"

"It's okay, Mom. I get it now."

And I do. Some objects hold a corpus of memories, and some of those memories speak too loudly, long before we're ready to hear them.

"There's something else. Giles finished reading the will after you left."

Mom hands me the document and takes the flashlight to let me read it, but as my eyes flash across my name and the mention of a cabin, everything starts spinning again.

Mom grabs my arms to steady me. "It's a lake house, Taylor. *Our* lake house."

"But how?"

"After Mae paid her debts from the sale of Meadowbrook, she didn't have much left over, but she had enough for this. Your dad must have told her about the property and how special it was to us."

I search for the right words, but they don't exist. Aunt Mae knew the home I needed all along—a home worth more than ten stately manors, a home where history was still being written.

"Sorry to interrupt," announces a voice behind us. Nathaniel's lanky outline and the glow of his flashlight appear beneath the willow trees. He raises an umbrella and smiles shyly. "I brought a brolly."

"And *I* was just getting ready to head inside." Mom gives me a wink that makes me roll my eyes. Nathaniel might be here for a hundred reasons, but none of them are worthy of an eye wink. Especially not with Dalia, his gorgeous intellectual equal, back in the manor to keep him company.

"Hot tea must be your remedy for everything," I say as Nathaniel hands me a thermos. He takes a seat next to me on a toppled headstone. "I hate to tell you this, but that's kind of a cliché," I add.

"It's hot chocolate, actually. So see? I've broken the British mold and proven we can embrace progress," Nathaniel replies with a wry grin. "Besides, if you just had one of those mother-daughter heart-to-hearts I've heard so much about, I figured you needed something a bit sweeter."

Warm Cadbury chocolate dances on my tongue. "You're right, though that was probably one of the best conversations I've had with my mom in years."

"Glad to hear it." Nathaniel pauses. "Though I can't say I'm glad you'll be leaving so soon. It's hard to imagine your Oxford program will let you stay after all this."

"You're probably right." My next sip is extra long. "But Dalia is sticking around. She'll be studying at Oxford full-time before too long."

Nathaniel shrugs. "I guess."

Huh. Maybe he isn't as captivated by her as I thought.

Nathaniel reaches for my hand as I take another swallow, causing me to down far more hot chocolate than I intended. After singing my tongue, I lower the thermos, and for nearly a minute, we sit in a semi-awkward silence.

"Is it also a terribly British cliché to ask permission for a kiss?"

A nervous laugh escapes my lips. "Maybe you should just make a habit of asking yourself, 'What would Mr. Darcy do?'"

"See, now you've exposed your ignorance." Nathaniel chuckles. "All true Austen fans know her characters never kiss on the page."

"Then that explains why I prefer the Brontë sisters."

"Ah, well, in that case: 'If you were to leave, I'm afraid that cord of communion would snap. And I have a notion that I'd take to bleeding inwardly. As for you, you'd forget me.'"

Is this one-in-a-million guy seriously quoting Jane Eyre *at me right now?*

Before I can register what's happening, Nathaniel's lips are melting into mine.

And I'm on Team Rochester for keeps.

A cemetery may be a morbid setting for a first kiss, but I don't mind. When Nathaniel wraps his arms around my waist and draws me closer, everything goes still.

Everything is *now*, somewhere between time and whatever lies beyond.

33

Ava

April 25, 1941

This is the last thing I shall write. Surviving two world wars is quite enough; there's no reason to relive them in ink, too. Perhaps I had the stamina when I was younger, but not anymore. It is time to hand off these memories to the next generation, for that is who I wrote this memoir for—not for fame or fortune, but for posterity's sake alone.

If you are reading this, dear descendants, I pray we have left you something worth preserving. Those who claimed to know better told us mankind had nearly progressed to perfection, that 1918 marked the end of warfare in the civilized world. Yet this cemetery of a city, the wasteland of a *second* war that has consumed the entire world, says otherwise.

The memories I've shared in these pages speak of how wars sometimes begin, so let me tell you how they *always* end. Violence never gives us a pleasant sendoff, but as with the sound of drowning men, the haunting silence that follows is far worse.

Rather than a ship, I write from a train. We're headed home to Meadowbrook following a visit to Coventry Cathedral. Or what is left of it, I should say. Caleb, Mae, and I traveled there to pay our respects to the thousands killed in the bombing, yet what we encountered was an utter desecration—the remnants of the worst air raid Britain has ever seen. It seemed like such an ordinary Sunday morning when we set out on our pilgrimage, but now we are beyond any prayers that can be put into words.

So, I shall attempt a recollection instead. A remembrance.

During the blitz, the cathedral's roof and arches were blown to bits, but as I stood in the shadow of what remained of its Gothic spire—a lone survivor—I wondered if a future could ever be found amidst the shipwrecks of our century. Every ending, after all, is a new beginning. The great saga is handed off and so it must continue.

After everything that has happened, I can no longer claim to know much, but the one truth I cling to is my hope that love will be the part of us that survives. Perhaps the only part. For love was what spurred me to care for my sister despite the loss of my mother, followed by the loss of our father, and then all the babies I carried who were never to be born. Love was what gave me the strength to stand by the young man I chose, even though our union had been strained by sorrow after sorrow.

"Is the church damaged badly? Describe it to me, luv." Caleb released my hand before taking a careful step toward the demolished altar of the roofless cathedral. "I can smell the charred wood."

"Words can't describe it, dear," I replied. "You wouldn't want me to try."

In truth, I was glad Caleb could not weep at the sight of this ruined city, even if he could still taste the bitter ash in the air. Make no mistake: I am one of the fortunate ones—thousands of husbands never made it home from the trenches of the First World War. And yet, Caleb did not return to me unmarred. A run-in with mustard gas left him blind, large portions of his body covered in burns. But he is still mine. My shy, courageous sailor. Our love has weathered many storms, but unlike anything else that men can build, it alone remains unsinkable.

Mae, too, has learned to withstand the rains of April—the cruelest month, one of our nation's poets said some years ago. As we walked through Coventry, Mae explored the blown-out buildings, climbing the mountains of rubble to capture the wreckage with her Kodak 35. She'd become the adventuring photographer I'd never been. As a photojournalist and war correspondent on the frontlines, she filled a role no woman my age could have envisioned. The most incredible part was I felt no bitterness about my lost ambition. It is one of life's strange gifts that when a dream dies in us but is resurrected in a person we love, the fulfillment of it is all the sweeter.

I've never grown accustomed to Mae's khakis, though. *Men's* trousers, which she insists on wearing whenever working in the field. Yet every day that Mae is with us in between her assignments at the front is a blessing. With our father's pale eyes and her long blond braid, my sister looks nothing like her otherworldly mother, though she's retained all of Galena's enchantment. She's also maintained a lifelong friendship with Simonne Laroche, who returned to France with her mother and sister after the sinking. Mae had visited their village when on assignment nearby, where she discovered that Simonne was a key figure in the French resistance against their Nazi occupiers. Simonne's proud father, whose body was never recovered from the sea, had recognized that bold spirit inside her long ago.

Sadly, no prediction or remnant of her mother's magic had spared Mae of heartache. For a season, she was engaged to the nephew of Charles Lightoller, the Second Officer who helped Caleb survive the *Titanic*, but the poor lad was killed at Dunkirk last year. A tragic waste, for he was so young. Too young.

But this is now our world. The world I'm afraid we have left to you.

Ever since *Titanic*, chaos has reigned, the only constant man's struggle for power. And yet, throughout the terror of the first world war and now a second, the words of William Stead—spoken when I was but a frightened, spoiled girl—have kept me going.

The meaning, my dear, is in the trying.

"Ava. Caleb. Stand together so I can take your photograph," Mae called out that day in the cathedral. She slid down a pile of bricks, her hair littered with bits of grass, as free-spirited as she was the day I returned to Meadowbrook. "We have so few of the two of you."

I felt uncomfortable with the idea of posing on this hallowed ground, but Mae's generation saw photography in a less formal light. And so, I grabbed Caleb's hand and pointed him in the direction of my sister's lens. Once she captured her timeless moment, we turned to depart. And that's when I saw it, growing in the center of the ruined cathedral.

A still point in an ever-expanding universe.

For out of the rubble climbed a blood red rose, its tenacious thorns pushing through the rock, its tender petals glistening with dew.

"What is it, luv?" Caleb asked when he heard my sharp inhale.

"Nothing, dear. It's nothing."

When really, it was everything.

For we become what we behold.

And as I beheld this beauty amidst chaos, I remembered my mother—too tender to survive this world. Then I remembered my father—too tenacious to be drowned by it.

I remembered, and so I hoped.

$\mathcal{E}$PILOGUE

As I close the book, I clutch the linked rings of the old key pressed against my chest, a key to a box that was never meant to be unlocked, and so it sank beyond the reach of memory.

It's almost as if Ava wrote the final words of her memoir for me. *To* me. How is that possible? My fingers graze the photograph of Ava and Caleb, hidden between the memoir's last few pages. The middle-aged couple stands among the rubble of war, their faces weather-beaten and weary, looking much older than their actual ages. I turn to the disintegrating walls of Tintagel Castle—a historic monument that declined more gradually than the bombed-out cathedral in Coventry, but that declined all the same.

After the night of revelation at Meadowbrook, we decided to journey to this edge of the world in remembrance of Mae. First, we stopped in Glastonbury to visit the Chalice Well, including its ornate cover designed in the shape of a *vesica pisces*, which Frederick Bligh Bond donated to the city in 1919 as a gift following the world war he predicted but couldn't prevent.

Now we've reached Tintagel along the coast of Cornwall, legendary birthplace of Arthur, Britain's once and future king. According to Giles, Ava and Caleb honeymooned in the area, and Mae brought my dad and Camila here during their visit—the site of his final photograph. It isn't hard to imagine him gazing out across this rugged sea.

Gazing toward home.

"You ready, Tay?" Nathaniel's face appears around a crumbling wall, his cheeks flushed from the brisk coastal breeze.

"Be right there." There's one more treasure I need to find first.

I search the grounds of the ruined castle for a rose like the one Ava mentioned at the end of her story. And when I turn a corner, a sea of tiny red faces peeking out from the fallen stones are there to greet me.

Only they aren't roses. They're poppies. A wilder, more dangerous beauty, but a beauty, nonetheless.

I pluck one and press it between two blank pages at the back of Ava's book. The flower seems like a proper note to end on, especially if death is really just a new beginning.

I join my traveling companions along the breezy cliff behind the castle, where Giles has his arm wrapped around a shivering Mrs. Porter. Mom stands beside them, clutching a small ornate urn. Most of Mae's remains will be housed in her family mausoleum, but she asked in her will that a small pinch of her ashes be thrown into the Atlantic, in order that she might join her mother at the bottom of the sea.

The white-tipped waves crashing against this shoreline make me wonder how long it will take the salt to refine these jagged rocks into polished stones. Then Nathaniel's grounded presence pulls me back to the current moment. I can sense it even before I feel the warmth of his hand grabbing hold of mine.

As the memorial begins, I turn my attention from the pulse in Nathaniel's palm to the row of faces lined along this cliff. We may be the only souls left to remember Lady Maebeline Knight and her unusual family, but I have hope we'll be enough to keep the memory alive.

"Ashes to ashes, dust to dust," Giles recites—ancient words that remind me of a poem I discovered in Meadowbrook's massive library right before we departed.

Dust in the air suspended
Marks the place where a story ended.

I take a pinch of dust from the urn and toss it over the cliff's edge, my heart flooded with a feeling so intense it hurts, but in the best possible way. The only word that comes close to describing it is *longing*. A deep, ravenous longing for dear ones beyond the pale and a home beyond the sea.

A longing for a love that endures because it remembers.

$\mathcal{A}$UTHOR'S $\mathcal{N}$OTE

Taylor Romano and Ava Knight are fictional characters, but many of the secondary characters in this story are based on historical people. Some of those people on the *Titanic* include William Stead, a journalist, activist, and leader of England's Spiritualist movement who was traveling to an international peace conference at Carnegie Hall at the request of President Taft; Margaret Brown, the "unsinkable" Denver socialite and philanthropist who sought to help her fellow passengers in some creative ways; Father Francis Browne, a Jesuit photographer who captured many of the images we still have of *Titanic* today and was unexpectedly ordered to get off the ship in Queenstown, Ireland; Joseph Philippe Lemercier Laroche, a Haitian engineer and one of the only passengers of African ancestry to sail on the *Titanic* (though in reality, the Laroche family boarded the ship in Cherbourg, not Southampton, and the story I crafted for Mr. Laroche's daughter, Simonne, is fictional); Bruce Ismay, probably as pompous as Ava describes; the Astors, truly that rich; and Officer Charles Lightoller, a heroic individual who saved many men by leading them to an overturned lifeboat, just as Caleb experiences.

Another fascinating historical character is Dr. Frederick Bligh Bond, the psychical researcher and archaeologist who excavated the ruins of Glastonbury Abbey from 1908–1921. Bond said he received strategic information about where to pursue his

Glastonbury excavation with the help of a medium who used "automatic writing" to communicate with spirits. Bond also published *The Hill of Vision* in 1919, in which he claimed to have uncovered a prophecy forecasting World War I. In this story I replaced Bond's actual medium, a man named John Alleyne, with Galena Lakovic—an entirely fictional character. However, the prophecy excerpts used in the novel are based on actual quotes from Bond's book, *The Hill of Vision*. Whether or not they are convincing as a war prophecy, I'll leave up to the reader to decide!

Although Lieutenant Vaso Plavsic is a fictional character, the *Crna Ruka*, or Black Hand, was a real and secret military society that sought a unified Serbia liberated from Austro-Hungarian rule. One of its members, nineteen-year-old Gavrilo Princip, was responsible for the assassination of the Archduke Franz Ferdinand and his wife—the events that ignited World War I. Of course, no historian has ever suggested that a prophetic photograph forecasting this event went down with the *Titanic*, but it made for an intriguing "what if?" scenario and a fantastical alternate history story. Many of the ideas, people, and events connected to this plot device are loosely based on historical coincidences—strange as they may be.

Finally, any reader familiar with T.S. Eliot's poem *Four Quartets* may notice his fingerprints throughout this story. For me, Eliot's poetry captures the atmosphere of Ava's soon-to-be war-torn twentieth century, and as I wrote this story, his words truly echoed in my mind.

Acknowledgements

The Poppy & The Rose isn't my first published novel, but it was one of the first I ever wrote, and the story revealed itself in many layers over time. After much research and enough drafts, beta readers, and rewrites to leave me "blind" editorially speaking, I knew it would take a talented editor to help me see the finishing touches the story still needed, and I was fortunate to find an entire *team* of fantastic editors at Owl Hollow Press. Thank you to Emma Nelson, Hannah Smith, and Olivia Swenson for your vision for this story and for your guidance in bringing it to life. Thanks also to Stephanie Paradis for the gorgeous cover design.

I am so grateful to my wonderful agent, Shannon Hassan, for believing in this story and for working tirelessly to find the right publishing home for it after much editorial input. You are such a delight to partner with; I could not ask for a better literary agent.

Thank you to the many friends and fellow writers who read this story in various stages, providing invaluable feedback and encouragement. Danielle Stinson, my number one reader, writing partner in crime, and dearest friend, I can't even keep track of how many times you've read this book, but I know it became a stronger story each time you did. I'm extremely grateful to Anita Romero, Adrianne Hanson, Anna Vanderwall, Andrea Kirk Assaf, Katherine Khorey, Heather Sappenfield, Evangeline Denmark, Mandy Houk, and Cindi Madsen—encouraging friends, critique partners, and beta readers of early drafts over the years. Thanks for the thoughtful insights and support!

Thank you also to Annette Kirk and the Russell Kirk Center for providing a physical writing place that certainly inspired my historical imagination. I'm immensely grateful to the Anselm Society and The Cultivating Project for providing communities that have formed me as a writer, as well as constant reminders that this work matters. *Soli Deo gloria.*

To my parents, Steve and Lea Anne Chowen, thank you for the ceaseless support, especially for the childcare help that makes it possible for me to continue pursuing this calling. I am so grateful for the love and support of many extended family members. Thanks to my in-laws, David and Anita Cowles, as well as the rest of the Cowles, Chowen, Sowell, Hayman, and Adams clans for your encouragement.

I am forever grateful to my generous husband, Jordan, for patiently enduring the many hours I spend typing away and for joining me on the adventures that have given me so much to write about. Your loving support as a partner and dedication as a father make this work possible. Finally, thank you to my children, Isla and Jack, for your love and for giving me one more reason to tell stories. I hope good books will shape your hearts as much as they shaped mine.

$\mathcal{A}$SHLEE $\mathcal{C}$OWLES is the author of *Beneath Wandering Stars*, winner of the Colorado Book Award. She wishes time travel was real, but until that happens, writing books is the next best thing.

Raised in a military family without roots, Ashlee spent her teen years in Europe and enjoys traveling the world almost as much as she loves telling stories.

Ashlee is represented by Shannon Hassan of Marsal Lyon Literary Agency.

Find Ashlee online and claim your *Titanic* bonus gift at AshleeCowles.com/titanic

www.ingramcontent.com/pod-product-compliance
Lightning Source LLC
Chambersburg PA
CBHW021233060726
47590CB00005B/1745